BEFORE THE GLORY ENDED

Ursula Zilinsky

BEFORE
THE GLORY
ENDED

J. B. LIPPINCOTT COMPANY

PHILADELPHIA AND NEW YORK

For Tom

✧ ONE ✧

In short, the essence of plebeianism, that which separates vulgarity from aristocracy, is perhaps less a defect than an excess, the constant need to animadvert upon matters which for the aristocratic temperament do not exist. To ignore, to disdain to consider, to overlook, are the essence of the 'gentleman.' Often most provokingly so; for the things ignored may be of the deepest moral consequence.

William James: Psychology

I

"Ça va?"

"Je me défends."

After four years in Indochina Jean Riebeck slipped gratefully back into the Parisian exchange that observed the courtesies and committed one to nothing, not even a break in one's stride. Away from home manners were more elaborate; even Parisians in Indochina would sometimes pause expectantly: "Well, how are you?" as if they really expected one to tell them.

It was good to have Paris cobbles under one's feet again, the Paris sun in one's eyes. It was the early fall of 1934; disaster hung small and willfully unrecognized, sharpening jaded appetites. It is a secret worldly cities know, that breath tastes sweetest to the condemned. When all pleasures grow dreary with repetition there remains still the embrace at the foot of the volcano, the feast in a town conquered by the plague.

Through this Paris, cherishing its disaster, Jean Riebeck moved with the assurance of a man at home. He had one arm in a sling; over the other he carried a trench coat, which concealed, on the

7

sleeve of his cavalry uniform, the five silver and gold stripes of a lieutenant-colonel. At twenty-seven this rank was too spectacular for him to carry comfortably.

Under the assurance of his rapid stride lay impatience and dissatisfaction. He was too wise in the ways of the army to quarrel with them for sending cavalry into Annam where horses could not be properly used; somewhere in his mind, under the surface code that one does not criticize one's superiors, lay the dissatisfaction that, like cavalry in the mountains, he had never been properly used. He was returning, as he had returned from St. Cyr and Saumur, at the top of the class, with another four years of his life wasted in boredom. His success had come to him through boredom; boredom had caused him to climb the mountain crag to put the Annamite gun out of order, boredom had sent him without qualifications into the unexplored interior of Indochina when the army had wanted maps, and what but boredom had inspired the feat which had brought him the *croix de guerre*. When the doctor had warned Riebeck that unless he allowed an operation at once he would be dead in fifteen minutes, had there not, behind the necessity of rallying his men and protecting the hospital, pricked the thought that those fifteen minutes at least would be full of interest? The fact that doctors may err had not occurred to him.

Neither life nor the army had as yet presented him with a problem that required mental effort, nor had there ever been asked of him a physical action that would demand all his courage. He was beginning to doubt that such a thing existed.

The military surgeon to whom he had been told to report untied the bandaged shoulder and examined it with the brusque carelessness of one who habitually deals with people who are paid for being brave.

"It's healing nicely," he said. "That was a fine thing you did, defending the hospital single-handed against all those savages."

Riebeck was uncomfortably aware that he would never be able to correct this assumption without sounding like a boaster.

"The Annamites aren't savages," he said.

"People who attack hospitals are savages," the doctor said firmly.

"There was hardly anybody in it. Only one man with measles."

"Two of your brothers are in Paris," said the doctor, changing the subject.

Two meant Pierre and Lucien, the twins. His other brothers, Paul and Robert, might be in Paris, but not together. The twins were as inseparable as only two people could be who, barring an accident, might quite as well have been one.

"The twins?"

"Yes. Lucien has a bullet in his leg and Pierre limps in sympathy. Or else it's Pierre who has the bullet and Lucien who limps. Can you tell them apart?"

"Pierre has an appendix scar."

"One can't always ask people to take their trousers off."

"No," Riebeck agreed. "That might be misunderstood."

"Be sure to keep your arm in the sling and come back next week, Colonel."

"Right," said Riebeck and took off the sling the moment he was in the street.

He found the twins at the Hôtel de Baro, his aunt's house in the Faubourg St. Germain. They were recovering from a monumental hangover. It was difficult to tell which had been shot, for both limped and leaned heavily on canes. They embraced their brother without consideration for his sore shoulder and denigrated his *croix de guerre*. Both twins had theirs from the Chemin des Dames, and in consequence thought but poorly of extraterritorial decorations.

The twins looked spectacularly like each other and not much like their youngest brother. They took after the de Baro side which was famous for its good looks, while Jean was pure Riebeck, a family noted for its charm and its long nose, affectionately known as the Riebeck Beak. François, the only one of the Riebeck boys to combine the de Baro looks with the Riebeck brains, had been killed at the Battle of Ypres.

The de Baros were fair-haired, freckled, blue-eyed and not overly intelligent. The Riebecks were dark and tall, with grey eyes and long, narrow faces that were often distinguished, but never handsome. Their intelligence was usually formidable, which is not necessarily an asset in the army and accounted for the fact that they numbered many colonels, one marshal of France, and no generals among them.

"*En bien, Bébé*," said Pierre affectionately.

Jean hooked his foot out from under him, so that Pierre lost his balance and rolled down the front steps. Too late Jean hoped that it was Lucien who had the wounded leg; his action had been too spontaneous to allow for reflection beforehand. Not since he was six had anyone called him Bébé unpunished. As the youngest of six brothers he had never found it wise to give too much ground.

Pierre picked himself up.

"I shall go and say hello to Aunt Albertine," said Jean.

"Assuredly, if you like to turn your back."

"You bought that one, Pierre," said his twin. "Anyway, Jean's got a sore shoulder."

"Oh all right. But I've a long memory, boy. Let's go."

Amiably, arm in arm, they went to find their aunt.

Albertine de Baro's husband had arrived in this world as the result of the most fervent prayers, endless novenas, donations to every church in Paris, and candles for every even remotely appropriate saint. Five daughters, the eldest of whom was Jean Riebeck's mother, had been born to the unhappy Marquis de Baro before the prayers for a son were answered. The mere fact that he was male, a continuer of the line of de Baros, had overshadowed the fact that he was an idiot. He grew up, surrounded by doctors, nurses, and servants, as pampered as if his existence were necessary to prevent a bloody civil war. Only one thing was demanded of him, that he marry suitably and beget a son.

From all this fuss one might be led to infer that the de Baro title went back to the Crusades and was too famous to be allowed to become extinct. That was not the case. The de Baros went back to Napoleon III. The Riebecks, who could take their family back to the Crusades without difficulty, tended to look down their beaks and sniff: "*Nouveaux riches!*" but in the happy days before the World War the *nouveaux riches* did at least have a lot of money, and Riebecks, always burdened with the double debts of landed gentry and cavalry officers, did not mind now and then marrying some of it.

After he had done his duty by the family, the Marquis de Baro was permitted to retire to his estates in the Dauphiné and live as he pleased. Albertine, who felt that she had earned it, was left in possession of the Hôtel de Baro and the de Baro fortune.

All the Riebeck boys had gone to school in Paris and had lived during this time with their Aunt Albertine. She was totally uninterested in what they did with themselves, never asked to see their marks or their homework, and when called to the Lycée Condorcet to hear their professors' complaints, she flirted so outrageously that nothing was accomplished. She was the favorite aunt of all the Riebeck boys except Jean, who cherished a deep affection for one Tante Régine, whom he had never met (she had married an American banker named Rosenstil before he was born) but who had, in her will, left her fortune to her brother François Riebeck's youngest son.

"It's all your fault that we're in such terrible shape," said Lucien as they went upstairs. "We've been celebrating your *croix de guerre*. Now that you're here you can help us. There is a new establishment rue—"

"I think I'll take Katalin out to dinner tonight."

"You can't. We called her. She's in Cairo."

"Cairo? What does anyone want in Cairo?"

"Who knows. We sent her a telegram, so she'll probably be here soon."

"I think I'll go to Fontaines," said Jean.

"Fontaines? Home, you mean? What for? There's nobody there but Papa and Elisabeth."

"Good," said Jean, who had plans of his own.

"Then can we have a go at Katalin while you're gone?"

"No."

"You let Istvan."

Jean grinned. "Did she tell you that? It was years ago. Anyway, no."

Hours later, after considerable celebrations, Pierre asked Lucien, "What do you suppose he wants to go to Fontaines for?"

"I think he's in love with Elisabeth."

Pierre gazed earnestly at the face that was so disconcertingly like his own. "Luc, *mon vieux,* you're drunk."

Lucien agreed. "Blind. But all the same I'm right."

"But I always thought that Katalin—"

"With our Jean one doesn't stop the other."

"I don't believe it."

"Then tell me this. Why is he going to Fontaines?"

"I don't know. But I sure as hell am going to find out."

The next morning the twins informed their brother that they had decided to come to Fontaines with him. After all, the bonds of home, filial duty . . .

"I thought you wanted to try your luck with Katalin."

"What's the use? All she ever wants to do is talk about you."

Pierre suddenly remembered something that would repay Jean for tumbling him down the stairs. "I think Robert is at Fontaines."

"Robert?" This was disconcerting news.

"Yes, Robert. Your brother, you know. Elisabeth's husband."

"How nice," said Jean.

Pierre wheedled until Albertine allowed him to borrow her new Ferrari. Triumphant at the wheel, he sped toward Nancy. There he cut South where the road ran along the Meurthe, the willow-edged river into which each young Riebeck had in turn been tossed to sink or learn to swim. The park of Fontaines was bordered by the Meurthe, and the Riebecks, with the strong proprietary feeling of the landed gentry, always called it "our river." Past St. Nicolas Pierre turned on two wheels into an avenue of poplars that really was theirs. It was the entrance to Fontaines.

Pierre tore up to the front of the house—he was not a good driver, only a very fast one—and leaned on the horn until the family came out; Colonel François Riebeck, his son Robert, and Robert's wife Elisabeth. Marthe, the housekeeper, followed them, sobbing loudly because Monsieur Jean was so thin, and no one had told her he was coming or she would have made ortolans. It was exactly like coming home from school, thought Jean. There had never been a time when he had been fat enough to please Marthe, and she had always made ortolans for him his first evening at home.

Later, sitting in the cool salon, turning the stem of a wineglass between his fingers and counting the star pattern of the parquet floor, he remembered again the paralyzing boredom that his father's presence invariably produced in a gathering.

François Riebeck had never been a father so much as a head of the family. His sons respected him; as children they had been afraid of him. He demanded neither love nor affection from them, only absolute obedience.

Robert and the twins made desultory conversation. Robert was a provincial garrison officer. He had been a major ever since 1918. Nothing of interest had ever happened to him. The twins, their skin burnt dark by the Moroccan sun, their eyes very light and wild in their tanned faces, restless and arrogant as soldiers are who have been fighting an enemy worthy of them, made Robert look like a fossil.

Lucien lit two cigarettes from force of habit, and seeing that Pierre was already smoking, threw one across to Jean, who caught it by the wrong end and suppressed a curse. How long Elisabeth was, putting her children to bed. She had stayed to say hello, and then had murmured an excuse and left.

"How is my old friend, Doctor Weber? He used to be the surgeon at the garrison in Nancy in my day," said Colonel Riebeck. "It was his hospital you saved, was it not, Jean?"

"Yes, Papa. Doctor Weber is fine. A little—I don't quite know how to put it, not crazy—out of touch, the way people get when they live a long time in the colonies and never come home."

"I am relieved to hear that. He wrote me a letter."

"Yes, Papa."

"Most gratifying. Most improbable."

"Yes, Papa."

"He said," Colonel Riebeck continued remorselessly, "that though fatally wounded, you successfully held off a regiment of heavily armed savages. Ridiculous."

13

"They weren't savages, they were Annamite rebels and there were only about twenty of them. And of course I wasn't fatally wounded."

"You had better tell us what really happened, I think."

Ever since they had pinned the *croix de guerre* on him at the hospital in Hué, Jean had realized that this story, any way it was told, would sound like a piece of intolerable showing off. He did not see how the situation could have been handled differently; there had been little time and no resources; but all the same it was embarrassing.

As simply as possible he told of the surprise attack on the tumbledown field hospital on Bastille Day, when most of the regiment had been on parade in Hué and he had been left, with a platoon of new recruits, to guard the hospital. A bullet in his shoulder had put him out of commission at once, and fright and surprise had done the same for the recruits.

"I wasn't in any shape to fight," he finished, "so I made a speech. I don't remember all I said, which judging by later reports is just as well; and when they were angry enough to tear me to pieces I yelled 'About face, charge,' and let them tear up the rebels instead. Then Doctor Weber told me he'd made a mistake, because if the bullet had been in my lung I would by then have been dead. Doctors!"

"You did well," said Colonel Riebeck who rarely praised his sons.

"Not really. Everyone made a lot of fuss about it afterwards, but I assure you, it wasn't a bit like the movies where you go around saying that it's a far far better thing. There wasn't time and anyway I'd lost a lot of blood very quickly, so probably I wasn't thinking straight."

Colonel Riebeck nodded. He did not say what he thought, that there is rarely time in battle to weigh the pros and cons of an action, and that courage that is almost a reflex is an invaluable asset in an officer. Praise came hard to his tongue, he had said as much as he was going to say.

Pierre spoke for him. "Congratulations, Bébé," he said. "If you live to grow up, you'll doubtless become a marshal of France."

But he would have done better to keep silence. Colonel Riebeck directed an intimidating glance at his twin son. "And how did you get shot?"

"Not me, Papa," said Pierre.

Lucien would have liked to blame the Riffs, but he never lied to his father. "A jealous husband, Papa," he said.

Elisabeth came to tell them that dinner was ready.

Jean contrived to enter the dining-room at her side. As he held her chair for her he smiled down into her eyes but was not aware that she blushed. The smile stated his intentions plainly enough, but his thoughts were years away. Nine years ago Robert had brought his bride to Fontaines, and Jean, who was at that time a very conceited and quite heart-whole cadet at St. Cyr, had instantly fallen in love with her. Too realistic to deceive himself with false hopes, he had been only too keenly aware that to Elisabeth he was nothing more than dear Robert's baby brother. But in nine years, four of them spent in adventure-filled absence, baby brothers may grow up and replace in romantic interest the husband who has remained at home. As he met and briefly held Elisabeth's eye, sharing with her a low-voiced conversation which on the surface was completely harmless and was in any case covered by the noise the twins were making, he was delighted to learn that Robert had become "dear old Robert" and once even "poor old Robert." Dear old Robert's leave, Elisabeth said, was over this evening. He was returning to the garrison in the morning.

The nine years, which had added an inch to Robert's forehead and several more to his middle, had barely touched Elisabeth. Her fair hair had darkened somewhat—it had never been a true blond— and four sons had given her a slight air of authority that was charming in one so shy. Her eyes were the exact color of star sapphires and, like the jewel, held in their depths the flash of a secret.

After dinner Colonel Riebeck muttered something about accounts and went off to the estate office. Robert said he was delighted to be able to spend his last evening at home with his brothers. Elisabeth, taking the hint, said she had letters to write and went upstairs.

Before long Robert's conversation brought upon Jean such a fit of yawns that for politeness' sake he had to excuse himself to go to bed. The twins, who dearly loved to tease the solemn Robert, undertook to tell him in horrifying detail just what they had done the night before and why Jean was so sleepy.

Jean found his room unchanged. It was the one to which he had returned ever since his schooldays in Paris: a large, whitewashed room, bare except for necessary furniture. It had originally been a nursery. The toy cupboards now held his riding things; in the large closet hung, carefully preserved by the pious Marthe, every uniform he had ever owned, from the fawn breeches and navy jacket with the emblem of the Balaton Junior Riding Team, which he had worn when he was eight, to the full dress uniforms of St. Cyr and Saumur.

The games of Halma and Racing Demon were gone from the shelves, but the books which had replaced them were still there; Dumas père, and *Roland*, Prinz Krafft and the technical volumes of military school and cavalry college, *Servitude et grandeur militaires*, *Les Liaisons dangéreuses*, Stendhal, Proust, and a complete shelf of Kipling given him, along with his language, by the English officer who had been Albertine's lover during the war.

The room's only ornament was the Gros portrait of Jean's favorite ancestor, Napoleon's young marshal who had died at Borodino.

He saluted him with a smile and reached for the most tattered of the Kipling volumes, which opened easily and familiarly in his hand to the story called *Only a Subaltern*. "He became an officer and a gentleman, which is an enviable thing." Yes indeed. Had he ever doubted it? Even now he rebelled to have to admit that this was not the whole of the truth.

He put the book away. It was for children.

Napoleon's marshal looked down from his white horse. It was unlikely that he had ever found the army less than perfect. But then, to have been Bonaparte's officer, to have been killed at Borodino, before the glory ended and the misery began, was enviable indeed.

A spurt of wind turned the leaves of the poplars and sent spray from the Pigalle fountain into the window. Jean took his cigarettes and went outside.

The park of Fontaines was designed with formal elegance. It stretched to the river and was divided by a laurel hedge from the land of Dr. St. Pierre who was the Riebecks' nearest neighbor.

The fountain was usually turned off at night. The gardener got drunk sometimes and forgot. On such nights the water turned silver in the lights from the house, and ran like silver cloth down the figures sculpted by Pigalle.

Jean Riebeck sat on the grass and tilted his head back against the rim of the fountain. Above him arched a civilized European sky. The stars were small, distant, and familiar. In Indochina they had been large, within the hand's reach, and foreign. For four years he had been accustomed to a sky filled with peacocks, toucans, sea serpents, and the keel of the boat Argo. Gemini was the first constellation he had been taught to recognize. "Ours," the twins said, as they said, "Our river." It was too early in the fall for Gemini; its stars were gone with Orion. But Cygnus stood in the sky, and Pegasus.

Jean dug in his pocket for a cigarette and his fingers touched, on the crumpled envelope, the ducal crest of Katalin de St. Leger. What stars were there in the sky over Cairo? Not that Katalin would be looking at them. At this hour Katalin would be either in a night club or in bed with somebody. It was one of the nice things about her that one could make certain assumptions with the absolute assurance of being right.

It did not strike Jean as odd that, having come to Fontaines to win his Elisabeth at last, he should now be thinking of Katalin instead. She had fed and chained his imagination too long for him ever to set himself entirely free.

Katalin had been his first mistress, and it was his hope that she would some day be his last. He did not love her. He loved Elisabeth. But no other woman had ever suited his moods the way Katalin did.

He had met her ten years ago at one of Aunt Albertine's teas. At seventeen he had enjoyed most parties, but even then he had made an exception of her teas and cocktails, which were usually a sickening combination of unlikely liqueurs. Albertine liked him to be present, however, feeling that any man, even if he is only a

17

nephew and still a boy, brightens a party. In self-defense he had evolved a routine consisting of a minimum of civilities, after which he would retire to the most secluded window of the room to turn his back on the party and to watch Paris at the time he loved it best, when the sky darkens and the town puts on her lights.

"I always think it's best from a hill so that one can see all of it." The girl had spoken from behind him, startling him. He turned and saw that he knew her, as one knows neighbors in the city, by name and sight. She was called Katalin de Pogany and lived in the rue de l'Université.

"We could walk up to Montmartre," he said.

"I'd like that. Let's climb out the window before my Maman notices."

He helped her out the window and they ran down to the river. Both were certain they had heard Madame de Pogany's outraged shriek behind them.

As they crossed the Pont Royale, Katalin took his arm and smiled at him. He decided he liked her.

She had the imperious face of a Tartar princess, black haired, black eyed, the eyes narrowed at the outer corners by the structure of the cheekbones. He remembered Albertine's gossip, now that he was interested.

"You are Hungarian."

"Yes. But we've lived here five years now. My father was shot by the Commune. An old aunt had left Maman the house here. It's about all we have, the house and Maman's jewels. She says I must restore the family fortunes by marrying a rich duke."

"That should be agreeable."

"Of course. But how many rich dukes are there that are not already married?"

"And if they are not, there are usually cogent reasons. My godfather, for example, is an unmarried rich duke. You may have heard of him. St. Leger."

"No," said Katalin, "I don't think so."

"His name isn't mentioned in good society very often."

"But he is your godfather?"

"Well, you know, it's the first rule in French families always to give pleasure to one's rich relatives."

Katalin laughed. They followed the man with the drum and the last straggle of children across the Tuileries.

"How old are you?" she asked him. "Are you still in school?"

"I'm at the Condorcet. I'll be going to St. Cyr next year."

"I like the uniform. You didn't say how old."

"Seventeen."

"That's rather young. I'm twenty." They stopped to look down to the Cimetière du Nord. "It's frightening at night. But I love it in the daytime. Have you ever been in love, Jean?"

"Only with a horse so far. Her name was Alexandra Grandioso. She was a white Lipizzaner mare and the most beautiful creature that ever lived."

"What happened to her?"

"She broke a leg, two years ago."

Katalin looked at him. There were two sharp lines between his brows and he did not look young at all. Then the moment and the memory passed and he smiled at her. "She had a son though, Xandi. He's three and a clown. He eats bottle tops and the buttons off people's riding jackets, and whenever he's supposed to be taught something he makes everybody laugh. I'm afraid the only thing he'll be fit for is a circus. He'll never make it as a show horse."

"You like horses, don't you?"

"Like?" His grey eyes narrowed in a glance that was to become very familiar to her; a polite effort to conceal derision. "There's nothing to like. It's part of my life, like breathing. You don't ask people whether they like to breathe."

"You talk like a Hungarian."

"Do I?" He seemed pleased. "Good."

Sudden curiosity prompted her to say, "Have you any money?"

"Some. Are you hungry? I could manage dinner."

"Now that is not Hungarian at all. A good Hungarian would immediately have known that I was thinking of hotel rooms. It's time you switched your affections to people, Jean."

"I'm quite ready. I can manage a hotel or dinner but not both."

"I would advise you to skip dinner," Katalin said seriously. "I think you will find it well worth while."

"Is that you, Jean?" The doors to the park opened and the twins came out. Pierre carried a towel, Lucien a bottle of brandy. "We finally got rid of Robert. We're going down for a swim. Come along."

Lucien pulled him to his feet. Pierre lit three cigarettes, put one between Lucien's lips and handed one to Jean. He never did this for his other brothers, and Jean never failed to feel absurdly flattered by it.

The river was very cold. While the twins stood on their heads and tried to drown each other, Jean swam to his favorite place on the opposite shore, where overhanging willows made a green chamber, cool and secret like an aquarium. At night it was always slightly unwelcoming for no very good reason. There was nothing haunted about the well-bred park of Fontaines. It was as if the river and park, so carefully designed to be enjoyed all day, felt the night to be their own and resented the intrusion.

Jean was up early enough the next morning to observe Robert's departure from the top of the stairs. Robert kissed Elisabeth's hand. *"Au revoir, Madame."*

Elisabeth said, "Take good care of yourself, Robert," and stood looking after him with the kind of smile people have for bores of whom they happen to be fond. She caught sight of Jean in his riding clothes at the top of the stairs. He ran down to greet her, kissing her hand in exuberant mockery of his brother. "Good morning, Madame."

"You mustn't make fun of poor Robert."

"He'll be shaving his head next and begin talking with a Prussian accent."

"It isn't Prussian. It's the *ancien régime* tone at the garrison at the moment. Some of the younger officers are so aristocratic they can hardly talk. They all call their wives Madame and wear an eyeglass. Have you had breakfast?"

"No. I don't want any, thank you. I want to go riding with you."

"With me?"

"Yes, with you."

"But Jean—"

His eyes laughed into hers and there was laughter in his voice, but he said composedly, "Go, get your riding things on. I'll get some coffee in the kitchen and meet you in the stable."

"But Jean—"

He was gone. The door to the kitchen passage swung shut behind him.

Pierre was in the stable. Jean had forgotten what an early riser he was. If one wanted to find only one twin the best time was six in the morning.

"You're up early, Jean. Is that coffee you've got?"

"Get your own." His eyes moved along the stalls. Colonel Riebeck's horses were all worth looking at. But for the moment Jean paid them no attention. His eyes came to rest on the white Lippizaner head awaiting—not a greeting—tribute.

"Ah, Xandi."

His full name was Vaik Alexandra. His head went up. This was not a tribute. This was an "I knew you when" voice.

"God, he's conceited," said his owner.

"If every visitor that comes to the stables exclaims that you're the most magnificent piece of horseflesh he's ever seen," said Pierre, "you'd be conceited too."

"He isn't a patch on Alexandra." Funny, thought Jean. After all those years, that still hurts. He turned aside to reach for a saddle. Pierre helpfully removed the coffee cup from his hand and drank the coffee.

"Thanks a lot, Pierre."

"Not at all. Shall we go riding?"

"Not this morning. I'm going riding with Elisabeth."

"Good God, then it's true."

Jean's silence was punitive. But silence was a disciplinary trick known to Pierre Riebeck as well; and did not intimidate him.

"She can't ride worth a damn, you know," he said, brazening it out. His impertinence succeeded where no apology would have. Jean laughed.

"Her riding is not a matter of overwhelming importance to me. Or hadn't you noticed?"

"Then why ride?"

"I don't know. I was on my way to the stable and there she was."

"Business and pleasure, *hein?*"

"I wonder," said Jean, "which you think is which."

"Hello, Elisabeth," said Pierre. "You look very nice in your riding things. I'll saddle your horse for you if you'll tell me which one."

Elisabeth pointed to the slowest and mildest matron in the stable, and Jean, who had been looking forward to what he called a brisk ride, which meant jumping every suitable and unsuitable fence, and racing all the cars on the Nancy road, regretted his invitation. He should have ridden with Pierre and seduced Elisabeth some other time.

Xandi was too well trained to balk at the sedate walk that took them down the poplar avenue, but there was impatience in his every step and his head lifted hopefully at the sight of a fence. Elisabeth, whose first concern was always the happiness of others, said, "Xandi hates walking. Why don't you give him a good run, Jean, and I'll meet you at the St. Pierre boat landing. I want to ask the doctor's gardener what he does about mildew. His roses are always so much nicer than ours. I suppose doctors have all kinds of things to put on their flowers. I'll see you there."

He found her interest in the Riebeck roses charming; he was constantly charmed by her domestic concerns and did not yet foresee how frenziedly such limitations would soon bore him.

With a tap of his heel he took Xandi over the nearest fence. Half an hour later, much happier, they leaped the St. Pierre laurel hedge, frightening the St. Pierre gardener half out of his wits. Followed by heartfelt curses, Jean rode laughing down to the river.

Elisabeth was there, looking kindly down at a very young man who stood holding her stirrup and mooning up at her. Elisabeth smiled at him tolerantly, and Jean was as annoyed with her smile as he was with the boy's possessive hold of her stirrup.

22

They had heard him and turned, Elisabeth still smiling, the young man with a look of curiosity and despair.

"Jean, this is Bertrand St. Pierre," Elisabeth said kindly. "The doctor's grandson."

Instead of showing sympathy with a fellow creature, Riebeck used the voice with which he had many times shriveled unsatisfactory recruits. "Indeed. And what does *he* do about mildew? Come along, Lisa, do."

They rode off without looking back. "You were very rude Jean."

"Silly young ass."

And Elisabeth laughed.

Bertrand St. Pierre threw himself on the grass, nearly weeping with despair. He decided to write a beautiful letter to Elisabeth and then kill himself. She would weep for him. Or would she show the letter to the man with the sunburnt, arrogant face, and would they laugh together?

He went into the house and climbed the stairs to the dovecote where his grandfather kept field glasses for bird-watching. It did not take him long to find Elisabeth and the man. They were dismounting by the clump of poplars at the river's edge, still laughing. The man flung himself on his back on the grass and lit a cigarette. Madame Riebeck (only rarely, in the darkest night, did Bertrand dare to call her Elisabeth, and never, never Lisa) sat by his side. Nothing happened. The man talked and Elisabeth listened. They laughed no longer. Bertrand had just remembered that the man must be Madame Riebeck's brother-in-law, just back from Indochina. There was no reason why they should not ride together, he thought, when he saw the man flick his cigarette into the river and reach up to take Elisabeth in his arms.

When Jean and Elisabeth returned to Fontaines they were met by the twins who asked awkward questions, and at dinner exchanged meaningful looks, while allowing awful silences to fall on the table. Their father went back to the estate office as soon as the meal was over, but the twins settled down to annoy their brother with endless patience. At ten o'clock Elisabeth wrapped up her knitting, wished everyone a pleasant good night, and went upstairs.

The twins involved Jean in a game of chemin de fer in which he won so much money that he could not in all decency rush off without giving them the chance to win some of it back. At last, long past midnight, Lucien yawned and said, "Time the Bébé went to bed."

"Whose bed?" Pierre was rather drunk.

"Oh, anybody's," said Lucien, who was always more tactful than his twin.

They exchanged one of those looks Jean had found so annoying at dinner. Knowing that they were only waiting for him to lose his temper, he controlled himself and went upstairs in silence.

The moment he closed the door of his room behind himself he discovered that he wanted no one's bed but his own.

The day he had first met Elisabeth he had been reading *La Princesse de Clèves*, and though the behavior of that lady and Monsieur de Nemours was completely foreign to his nature, there was something about Elisabeth that had imposed the pattern on their romance. He frankly thought Monsieur de Nemours a poor sort of man, and his brand of chivalry a game fit only for idiots or children; yet it was a game he had played with Elisabeth for nine years, and now that it was too late he knew that he could have kept on very happily for another nine.

However, after what had passed by the river it would be unpardonable rudeness to do nothing further. With a sigh Jean opened his door again and looked to make sure the hall was empty. The chivalry of the Don Juan has as strict a code of conduct as that of Monsieur de Nemours.

II

During the night Jean talked Elisabeth into coming to Paris with him. It was not his intention to stay in the country longer than was absolutely necessary.

After breakfast he went to take his leave of his father, who was still looking for an error in the accounts and was therefore rather vague. "I'm sorry you have to leave us so soon, Jean," he said.

"Me too, Papa. By the way, did Albertine write you?"

"If she did, I don't remember it. Why?"

"I think she wants Elisabeth to come for a visit."

"Then she probably wrote to Elisabeth."

"That wouldn't do any good. Elisabeth would never leave you with no one to look after you."

"Nonsense. Marthe looks after me. Tell Elisabeth to stop fussing and visit Albertine, if that's what she wants to do. Silly woman, Albertine. Always talking about her hats."

There was no way of getting the Ferrari without getting the twins as well. They were outraged at the mere suggestion. "You know Lucien has to see the doctor, Jean," said Pierre. "You're terribly inconsiderate. Besides, I don't want to miss this. Elisabeth was too delightful at breakfast."

Madame de Baro said she was delighted to see them all again. "And darling Elisabeth too. It must be years since Robert last brought you here. You should come to Paris more often."

Elisabeth said it was difficult with the children to get a holiday that was not by the seaside.

"Oh yes, of course, your darling children. How are they? All girls, isn't it?"

"Boys," said Elisabeth and proceeded to tell the marquise how they were, giving her ample time to repent her hospitality.

And so everyone settled down happily at the Hôtel de Baro. Jean, who had engineered it all so cleverly and should have been the happiest of all, felt exactly like the man in the fairy tale who had been granted his wish for sausages and finds them attached to his nose. For several weeks he refused to think about it, but eventually he had to admit that he had made a mistake. Elisabeth bored him. The sapphire blue of her eyes did not guard a secret but was merely a trick of light. While Albertine and her friends sparked conversation back and forth, Elisabeth smiled sweetly. The season had begun and Jean wanted to go to parties. Elisabeth's idea of a happy evening was one spent quietly with her lover by the fireside. They tried this once, and Jean, not usually at a loss for words, found that rack his brains as he might, he could not think of anything to say to his beloved. There was something about her air of earnest attention that killed every conversation at birth. She had no wit of her own and did not recognize it in others. Riebeck's nonsense merely bewildered her. They exchanged smiles full of embarrassed good will. It occurred to neither of them any more to spend the time in bed. Elisabeth was as sweet, kind, and boring in bed as she was out of it.

Riebeck fidgeted and finally said, "You know, this is what you have a husband for. I'm for fun. The Lansquenets are having a ball tonight. Let's go."

"I don't really like parties, Jean. And I haven't anything to wear."

"That's true. I don't understand it. You've been in Paris for four weeks and you haven't shopped once. Your clothes are all right at Fontaines, I suppose, but next to Albertine's they look as if you'd bought them at the Uniprix."

"Robert would think it horribly extravagant if I bought my clothes at the big houses, and anyway I should be afraid of the salesgirls there."

"What nonsense. If Robert is so stingy I'll give you the money. I'd love to see you in some decent frocks and a Mainbocher coat. Go with Albertine, and then the salesgirls won't bite you."

Elisabeth, who thought her dresses very suitable for the wife of a major in a provincial garrison, and who was still smarting under the remark about the Uniprix, said quite sharply, "Please be reasonable, Jean. I can't take money from you. I would feel like a kept woman."

Suppressing the remark that that was not a profession in which she would be successful, Riebeck said, "You are a prig. I'm going to the Lansquenets'. Good night."

"Good night, Jean dear," said Elisabeth. "Don't stay out too late."

It was Elisabeth's bad luck that Katalin de St. Leger had this day returned to Paris and had decided to accept Mimi de Lansquenet's invitation.

Riebeck had ready any number of glib stories to account for Elisabeth's presence in his aunt's house, but none of them, he feared, would convince Katalin. Not that she was jealous. She was too firm a believer in the sauce for the goose adage to be able to afford that emotion, but the circumstances were extraordinary. If driven into a corner he could always bring up the fact that when he had left for Indochina she had been Mlle de Pogany, while now she was the Duchesse de St. Leger and his aunt by marriage—an idiotic situation to say the least.

He saw her the moment he entered the room. She was dressed in black and wore all the St. Leger diamonds. Armored in formidably good manners, he nevertheless felt a certain amount of trepidation as he crossed the ballroom and bowed over her hand. Even a brave man may quail at meeting a mistress who, at his suggestion, has traveled all the way from Cairo, only to find him already established with his first love.

"*Enchanté, ma chère.*"

"Jean, how nice."

"If you don't spit in my eye they'll all die of disappointment."

"And you. Don't forget, I married St. Leger the moment your back was turned."

"Diamonds become you. Shall we forgive each other? Dance with me."

"Love to. Tell me about your *croix de guerre.*"

"Too dull. I'd much rather hear about your honeymoon with St. Leger. Is he here with you?"

"No, he's still in Cairo, living with the bearded lady of a traveling circus and two dwarfs."

"Male or female?"

"I don't know, and I don't think they do either."

"Please don't stop."

"I won't. I'll tell you about the man who swallowed swords."

Madame de Lansquenet, who had promised all her friends a first-class row, said crossly to her husband, "Really, if Katalin can't behave properly at parties, she doesn't deserve to be invited."

Elisabeth did not know Paris well, and Riebeck, who loved it, undertook to show it to her. With domestic concerns ever first in her mind, Elisabeth tended to look at the town as good or bad for

27

children to play in and thought the Parc Monceau adorable. But at least it gave them something to do and provided them with a good deal of ready-made conversation.

"Do look at the Flying Horses, Elisabeth."

"Darling, aren't all those children sweet, sailing their little boats. And that nice donkey."

"Would you like to visit the Louvre?"

"Let's just sit here and watch the children."

"You know," said Pierre to Albertine, "I never realized Jean had such a faithful nature. Every morning when he comes back from the Hôtel St. Leger he goes and has breakfast with Elisabeth."

"Oh, my dear, the whole thing is such a farce."

"What do you suppose Jacques Latour wants from him?"

"I haven't any idea. I did ask, but he wouldn't say. Since they gave Jacques that silly office in the Deuxième he has become very secretive. I met him in front of the Ministère de la Guerre last week and said, 'Isn't it a delightful day, Commandant Latour?' He looked at me as if I were a Riff spy and said, 'Officially, Madame la marquise, nothing has as yet been announced.' Jean does have silly friends."

Riebeck was still too new in his rank of lieutenant-colonel to resent being sent for by a mere major. If it amused Latour to pretend that seeing old friends could be conducted only under the cloak of profound secrecy, Riebeck was willing to play along.

He and Latour had first met at the *dépôt* at the beginning of the year that all French officer candidates must spend as privates of the line. It was a year to which Riebeck had frankly not looked forward. To waste twelve months at playing private, to be promoted to corporal at the end of it, seemed to him at eighteen a cruel waste of time.

Whether either officers or men would benefit from the association was a question he was not prepared to answer. But he had been certain that if familiarity did not breed contempt it would breed boredom. As it turned out, he had been mistaken. He never could discover whether there was any value in the masquerade, but he had found in it a great deal of amusement.

Three future St. Cyriens had run together like quicksilver: Jacques Latour, Comte Victor André Hercule Aristide Maria de Cavignac, and Jean Riebeck. Not one of them had ever made a bed, polished a boot, or peeled a potato. They had never even envisaged what it would be like to clean a latrine.

But they could bear the chicanery with equanimity, knowing that it was limited. Sergeants might tick them off fluently and address them habitually as "You there, you dirty lascar," but there was on both sides the knowledge that the names Cavignac and Riebeck had figured honorably in the great battles of France, and that the dirty lascars would in their turn grow into colonels, in charge of regiments and sergeants.

Cavignac, like Riebeck, was destined for the cavalry. Latour had a different ideal: an academic career in the army.

"No front line heroics for me."

"When I become a general," Riebeck had promised benignly, "I shall appoint you latrine inspector for the French army."

"A Riebeck a general. That would be the day."

"One was a marshal of France. How do you have an academic career in the army?"

"By using my head where it won't get shot at, in an office. All successful campaigns are fought behind desks."

Apparently Latour had realized his ambition. He sat behind a desk that almost entirely filled his tiny office. He looked immensely pleased with himself.

Once seated in the cramped space behind the desk, it was difficult for Latour to get up again. He managed it, however, together with an elaborate salute. "*Mon colonel.*"

"At ease, commandant," said Riebeck with the condescension of a major general.

"How are you, Jean?" They shook hands. Latour managed to put so much secrecy into this simple gesture that Riebeck was disappointed to find no mysterious piece of paper had been passed to him.

"Cigarette?"

"Can I smoke it or do I have to slice it open to search for the concealed message?"

"You may smoke it. How is Vic?"

"Still in Indochina. He sends you regards."

"Ah," said Latour, cleverly giving the impression that he was speaking in code.

"How long have you worked here?"

"A year or so. While you've been shot at by savages—"

"They weren't savages."

"—I've been putting my brains to use. Much the better way."

"Not so much promotion in it though."

"I have no ambitions. I only wish to serve my country."

Shocked, Riebeck said, "Come out quickly and have a drink with me. This place isn't good for you."

"First I must ask you a favor. If you agree, it will be best if we aren't seen together in public."

Riebeck burst out laughing. "You're doing it extremely well, you know. What sort of favor?"

"One you'll like. I want you to visit your relations in Vienna."

"Well, Jacques, so do I. But I've got myself into something of a muddle here."

"I know all about it. This will give you the chance to get out of the muddle."

"Now there is a temptation. What do you want me to do in Vienna?"

"Just what you'd do anyway. Go to parties and listen to people talk, more or less."

"It sounds silly. Couldn't you just read the Vienna papers?"

"I'm too intelligent to believe what they say."

"Everything people say at parties in Vienna is in the papers the next morning. I'm of no use to you, honestly."

"Look, you speak German like a native, you've got those cousins over there, you'll be just one of them. Everyone will talk to you."

"Especially when they find out what I do for a living."

"You'll go in civilian clothes, of course. I can't see the Nazis unburdening their innermost secrets to a French officer."

"I can't either. Not even in civilian clothes. Are there Nazis in Vienna?"

"You *have* been in the jungle. There are lots of Nazis in Vienna, my innocent. And the German Legation is nothing but a hangout for German spies. So will you go for me, please?"

"As long as you don't want to dress me up as a cook and smuggle me into the Legation," said Riebeck, more tempted by the trip to Vienna than by Latour's cloak-and-dagger nonsense, "I suppose I might. But just this once."

"Just this once," said Latour, hand on heart. "I solemnly swear it."

At dinner Riebeck told Aunt Albertine that he had had several letters from his Baranyi relatives in Vienna and that they wanted him to spend the rest of his leave with them. This was fortunately true, because he would have said it even if it hadn't been. Albertine waxed nostalgic over Vienna and Elisabeth looked hurt.

"Aunt Josephine was very kind to me after Maman died," Riebeck said to her.

Elisabeth cheered up and said of course Jean must go and see his aunt. "I've had a lovely holiday," she said to Albertine, "but I think I ought to go home now. I've neglected the children far too long."

The marquise confounded herself in exclamations of regret.

"Can I use your phone to call Budapest, Aunt Albertine? I'll pay you back."

"Don't be an idiot, Jean."

This protest was a formality. He would pay her and she would accept it.

He put through a call for Captain Istvan Halyi, Tisza Palace, Budapest. Though he knew it might take hours, he picked up a book and remained by the telephone. When it rang he put out his hand, let it ring twice more not to seem overeager, then picked it up. "*Servus* Istvan. *Comment ça va?*" His voice was so quiet it sounded subdued. "I'm coming to Vienna for a visit. Can you get leave? Day after tomorrow, on the Orient Express. Right. *Servus.*" He rang off well within the three-minute limit.

III

The Hungarian cousins, so known although most of them were Austrians and none were cousins, were Jean Riebeck's favorite relations. The connection between the families dated back to a Riebeck officer who had ridden to Hungary with the Duke of Lorraine in 1683 to fight the Turks, and had there married the Countess Maria Terezia Baranyi.

The present holder of the title, Count Istvan, lived, except during the hunting season, in Vienna with his wife Josephine, his cousin and life-long friend, Count Nicolas Tisza, and Josephine's sister Stefanie, who had married Count Nicolas because Josephine and Istvan had thought it would be nice.

Jean saw them first when he was six, at his mother's funeral.

If François Riebeck had been too stern to be much of a father to the boy, his wife Dominique was too social to be any kind of a mother. Jean's upbringing had been left to Marthe, the housekeeper, who looked after his clothes and cooked for him, and the sergeants at the Nancy garrison, who taught him to ride. They put him on a horse when he was still so small that his legs stuck straight out on either side, and they never failed to impress upon him, with blows if necessary, that a future officer of France, aged three, would be forgiven for being thrown off his pony, that it was permissible under such circumstances to swear, but that under no circumstances might a future officer of France cry.

His mother's death made no great impression on Jean, who had hardly ever seen her. But her funeral was unforgettable. He was taken by the twins to visit the Avenue of the Marshals of France and was shown the grave with battle scenes and FAMILLE RIEBECK carved in the stone. "This is where we'll go when we're dead, *Bébé.* Isn't it marvelous?" Jean thought that it was.

Dominique Riebeck had preferred burial in the de Baro family tomb, which had been designed, in the tasteless days of Napoleon III, by the same architects who had so distinguished themselves in the Parc Monceau. To this day Paris guidebooks describe the de Baro tomb as an architectural triumph, a tasteful blending of the grave of King Mausolus and the Taj Mahal.

Josephine Baranyi and her sister Stefanie attended the funeral not because they had been fond of Dominique; quite the contrary. But neither they nor their husbands ever passed up the chance of coming to Paris. Both countesses wore mourning so deep as to put all Dominique's near relations in the shade. Behind her handkerchief, bordered inch-wide in black, Stefanie peered at the fashions of the other mourners. As the obsequies grew longer and longer, Jean's eyes too began to wander, and in wandering caught the speculative gaze of the Countess Stefanie.

Stefanie, who had the sentimental liking of the childless for small boys, could hardly wait for the funeral to be over before she dashed up to Jean and introduced herself. Learning that he was the youngest Riebeck boy, she promptly showed him to her sister, explaining that he was poor Dominique's son. The Countesses had acquired from their husbands the habit of always referring to the dead as poor. Heaven was a bad bargain for the Dual Monarchy aristocracy.

One might have thought Josephine had been looking for Jean all her life. "The very thing for Istvan," she exclaimed, and at once invited him to come to them in Vienna. "We'll show you the horses at the Spaniards."

Jean liked his new aunt and said he would very much like to come to Vienna. Only years later did he realize that this prompt liking and trust must have been due to the fact that Aunt Josephine looked exactly like a horse.

Stefanie, who brooked no delays in the gratifying of her whims, took him by the hand and went to find Colonel Riebeck.

"François," she said, "what is to become of this poor motherless boy?"

"I don't know," said Colonel Riebeck. "Marthe will look after him, I imagine."

"Really, you're an appalling family, you Riebecks. Pepi and I have a suggestion. We would like to take little Schani to Vienna with us."

"His name is Jean, after St. Leger, not Schani."

"He can play with Istvan," said the Countess.

"I cannot imagine why Cousin Istvan needs a six-year-old boy to play with, my dear Steffi. He has surely many companions of a more suitable age."

"Try not to be so silly, François. Istvan Halyi, not Pepi's husband. He is a little boy, about Jean's age, one of Nikki's Esterhazy cousins. His mother died when he was a baby, so he lives with us. That's settled, isn't it?"

"Very well, Steffi," said Colonel Riebeck, knowing he had met his match. "But if there is another war you must send Jean back. It would not do at all to have my son living with the enemies of France."

"Really, François, you could hardly call us the enemies of France. Pepi and I adore Paris. Besides, there won't be a war. We are much too civilized."

The year was 1913 and many people still believed this.

After a week spent in Paris—the Countesses at the dressmaker's, their husbands quite elsewhere—mountains of luggage were piled at the door of the Hôtel de Baro, maids had hysterics, valets quarreled loudly in Hungarian, and they were off.

Jean had not seen much of his uncles until now. He thought them magnificent. They had loud, booming voices, told unsuitable jokes, and roared with laughter. They wore their moustaches twisted into fine points extending beyond each side of the face. Uncle Nicolas had a habit, when in thought, of pushing up the left point of his moustache with his thumb, so that it was always faintly askew. It gave him a rakish air that Jean very much admired.

But Baranyi Palace in Vienna disappointed him. It was not a palace at all, merely a town house in the Herrengasse, not far from the Hofburg.

"It was built by François Cuvilliers, a famous French architect," said Aunt Stefanie instructively. "1719–1786, Schani dear."

Her conversation was full of such information. She could not mention a famous person without the dates of his birth and death, or a city without the number of its inhabitants and its mean annual rainfall. In anyone else such a flow of information would have been maddening. Steffi was saved by the redeeming grace that most of her facts were wrong.

34

The moment they were inside, every door opened and spilled out relatives, for Baranyi hospitality was as generous as it was undiscriminating. Josephine and Stefanie welcomed with delight children whose mothers had died or run away with gypsy violinists; cherished to their dying day aunts with canaries and theosophist pamphlets; and harbored with equanimity uncles so eccentric that they should by rights have lived in padded cells. They gladly received nieces who were pregnant but not married, and were even pleased to have dashing cousins who had been expelled from their regiments, though the Austro-Hungarian army was tolerant of all things but three; impecunious marriage, homosexuality, and syphilis.

Among their friends, Baranyi Palace was known as the parrot house.

"Steffi! Pepi! Welcome back, we missed you. How was Paris, nice? What have you got there, is that poor Dominique's little boy, little Schani, isn't that nice."

Steffi's parrot shriek dominated the news of Uncle Koloman's most recent fit and Cousin Teresa's fortunate miscarriage.

"Istvan? Where are you, Istvan?"

Istvan Halyi was produced. ·

"I've brought you a little friend to play with," beamed Steffi.

Istvan, who had been expecting *marrons glacés*, looked at her without approval. He had green eyes slanted up at the outer corners by high, tartar cheekbones. He was an exceedingly ugly child.

"You'll be great friends," Steffi assured them. "Do shake hands, Istvan."

He obeyed, like a boxer about to go into the ring.

These nuances were lost on Jean, who was too tired to concentrate and completely confused by the number of people all talking at once about other people. He had never known well any children of his own age, and had no one to compare with Istvan Halyi. He liked his looks and his reserve, but was too sleepy to talk. Istvan felt at length compelled to say something.

"Can you ride?"

"Yes," said Jean politely. "Can you?"

Istvan gasped for breath. Before he could do anything more—could he ride indeed—Josephine pounced on them. "Friends already, isn't that nice. Off to bed with you now. Istvan, it's disgraceful that you are still up. I hope to goodness someone's remembered to put a hot-water bottle in the other bed in the nursery. Won't it be nice to have someone to talk to when you wake up in the morning?"

Josephine and Stefanie looked after the boys with a great sigh of sentimental satisfaction. Like Noah, they could not abide singles and had successfully matched up another pair.

No one had remembered the hot-water bottle, and the blue tile stove meant to heat the nursery had not worked since 1873 when the sweep (it was said) had put a live goose up the flue in an effort to clean it. But neither the damp sheets, the piercing cold, nor Istvan's icy silence could keep Jean awake another moment.

Sun streaming into the room awoke him. His breath made a cloud above his mouth. Blue and white checked featherbed, blue tile stove, his trunk, a shelf holding white porcelain horses and red-coated riders, a pair of green slanted eyes watching him, unblinking like a cat's; he remembered where he was.

"Bon jour," he said politely.

In the days when hospitality was a religious rather than a social duty, a host occasionally found himself in the position of having to entertain a mortal enemy, with only the consolation that the moment he stepped outside the door and ceased to be a guest the host could stop being polite and could skewer the departing on his sword. It was with a feeling akin to this that Istvan told Jean to put on his riding clothes; they would ride after breakfast.

Breakfast at Baranyi Palace was an extensive meal, and everyone pitched into it just as if they had not finished an eight-course dinner and probably a late supper the night before. Ham, eggs, sausages, brains, and sweetbreads were kept warm over spirit lamps on the sideboard. There were cakes and buns and bread, pitchers of cream and honey, butter in crinkly balls, bacon from Poland and oranges from Seville, so sour one had to roll them in sugar.

"Well, boys," said Uncle Nicolas, "getting on? What are you going to do after breakfast?"

"Ride," said Istvan, slightly less sure than before. Jean's riding breeches had given him pause. They were shabby, patched (inherited from older brothers in fact), and obviously hard used.

"Splendid. You ride, don't you, boy? Of course, with your father in the cavalry."

This did not shake Istvan. Most fathers, in his world, were in the cavalry. Cavalry fathers taught their sons to ride by the simple method of beating them black and blue when they were thrown. Several boys Istvan knew had not only never learned to ride but now burst into tears every time they saw a horse.

"Taking Janos?" asked Uncle Nicolas.

"Who is Janos?" Jean asked.

"My servant," said Istvan feudally, thereby silencing Jean, who had never before met a six-year-old boy with a servant of his own.

"Not today, Uncle Nikki," Istvan decided. He wanted to see the French brat make a fool of himself over the saddle. Perhaps he could offer to do it for him and leave the girth a bit loose. It was always a good joke to watch saddle and rider glide gently round to the horse's belly during a brisk gallop.

Count Istvan Baranyi's stables in Vienna were not large. He kept most of his horses on the estate in Hungary, where he owned a famous stud. In Vienna he kept horses for himself and his cousin, carriage horses for the countesses, and two ponies for Istvan.

Natasha was a superb jumper and Istvan, who was planning to do some showing-off, decided to ride her and leave Ziska for Jean. He did not think Ziska's ordeal would be long: Ziska's manner with inexperienced riders was, to say the least, abrupt.

Jean observed a polite preliminary by offering Ziska a lump of sugar, so earning her favor. "Greedy pig," muttered Istvan under his breath. Nor did Jean get into any difficulty with the saddle, and before mounting he slid his hand under the girth; a gesture so automatic that it had no doubt been taken over from a cavalry instructor without thought.

They rode at a walk to the Hofgarten. It was early still and they had it to themselves but for some riders exercising their jumpers. Istvan suggested a little gallop, and Jean, who was not fond of sedate walks, agreed. An unholy smile slanted up the corners of Istvan's eyes. "Like to jump?"

"Sure."

Istvan pointed out the path with the hurdles, but did not bother to mention that a sizable pool of water was concealed by one of them. "They'll clear out," he said with a derisive glance at the other riders. "They know me. Ready? Go!"

Over the course Istvan kept his pony deliberately a pace behind, more interested for once in observing another's form than in victory. He had forgotten at once Aunt Steffi's offensive remarks about little friends, forgotten too his iron determination not to be one. Ziska took the water jump neatly and Jean followed her lead, unperturbed. Istvan let out Natasha so that they could race down the path together and draw up, neither the winner.

"Hey," he said, breathless and laughing, "what's your name?"

"Jean Riebeck."

Istvan held out a grubby hand. "*Servus*, Schani."

Jean returned the grip, guessing it to be in the nature of a peace offering without quite knowing that there had been a war. For the last time he asserted his nationality. "It's Jean, not Schani."

He was Schani to all of them, over his protests. He was conscious, as a savage is, of the dignity of a name, but could not carry his argument in a house where people called each other by names he could not have given without embarrassment to a dog.

The Aunts were Pepi and Steffi, Count Nicolas was Nikki and Count Istvan was, all his life, regrettably, known as Pipi. Only Istvan Halyi was never Isti or Pista. When Jean indignantly asked why, Steffi said she didn't know. He was that kind of child.

"Well, boys," said Count Pipi at lunch, "did you have a good ride?"

"Yes, thank you, Uncle Pipi." If Istvan remembered his thoughts of the morning it was not with guilt, for they did not concern the boy who had taken the hurdles with such competence. It was in no way as an amend, but simply because nothing was too good for a rider like Schani Riebeck, that he offered the most precious gift he knew. "Uncle Pipi, do you think we could show Schani the Spaniards this afternoon?"

"Surely. It's going to rain. They'll ride inside."

This prompted Aunt Steffi to let loose a large number of facts about Fischer von Erlach, who had built the Spanish Riding School. "What are Spaniards," Jean asked. "Horses?"

"Lipizzaner," said Istvan, assuming this would explain all.

"Is it a breed?"

"It is a—Good God, Schani," thundered Uncle Nikki. Count Pipi, more tolerant, tried to make allowances. "After all, foreigners—"

Feeling as if he had taken his finger out of the dike, Jean listened to the flood of information about the Imperial Austrian Horses, named after their stud at Lipizza, and the Archduke Charles who in the sixteenth century had brought horses from Castile and Andalusia to found the stud, and the Spanish Riding Schools in Vienna and Budapest, which trained the Lipizzaner in the art of *haute école*. Steffi, thorough as always, dismissed the Archduke Charles, and for Jean's benefit traced the Lipizzaner breed back to a stud in Karst near Lipizza kept by the ancient Greeks.

Haute école riding is an art, not a sport. Like bull-fighting, it grew out of mortal necessity, and commands strong passions. But the Viennese, unlike the Spaniards, had made a graceful compromise. Once the need had passed they had retained only the beauty and not the blood. The art of mounted warfare gave *haute école* its shape, the Spanish Riding Schools preserve its form.

It is less spectacular than one expects, as precise, silent, and formal as a pavan. Many people can't see the point of it, and it bores them. There is no use trying to explain. Those who do appreciate it often find themselves watching through tears of admiration, as Jean that afternoon learned with surprise and dismay. But the uncles and Istvan only laughed, considering it no more than the *haute école's* due. Indeed his tears, the ultimate in disgrace at Fontaines, had earned his permanent membership in the family.

The Riebecks always maintained that all Baranyis were crazy. It was, Jean believed, possible. Certainly life with them was very different from that which he had known, but he loved it.

In the manner of children who know nothing else and accept the grown-up world without question, he had taken his solitary

39

childhood at Fontaines as the only possible one. Now his mother's death and Aunt Stefanie's whim had given him a family. He was too young to realize that the railway-station atmosphere of Baranyi Palace was no more like a normal family than were Marthe and the sergeants at Nancy. He accepted it with delight as his first real home.

Istvan had lived with the Baranyis since he was a baby, and because Count Xandi, Josephine's only son, lived much abroad at the request of his parents, who found it easier to love him at a distance, Istvan had taken a son's place in the house. They would have welcomed (and absorbed) Jean as warmly, but though he was deeply fond of them and they loved him, he knew he must remain a guest.

He put no distance between himself and Istvan Halyi. Istvan had the face of a gargoyle, the vocabulary of a trooper, and the scowl of an avenging angel. Jean loved him. There was never a time either boy had said to himself: "I would like to be his friend." Like all love it had come upon them seemingly from the outside, not after reflection but instantly, through a mutual recognition of things rooted too deeply for conscious awareness.

They had a year together. Then the Archduke Ferdinand was assassinated and the curtain rang down on the performance. Jean returned to France, taking with him, as parting gift and tribute to his horsemanship, Alexandra Grandioso, the white Lippizaner mare, and leaving behind, on the station platform, scowling and near tears, the person he loved most in the world.

IV

The Orient Express was not Riebeck's favorite mode of travel. He much preferred to fly. But so convincing had Latour's cloak-and-dagger atmosphere been that he chose the train almost without thinking.

Looking about him in the dining car, Riebeck decided that this would have been a poor day for the writers who people the Orient Express with spies and adventuresses. The passengers looked both respectable and dull. The men were neither mysterious nor dangerous looking and all talked incessantly about business and what food disagreed with their livers. The children yelled and spilled milk, and their mothers looked far too harassed to be in search of either sex or adventure.

Riebeck was just wondering why so many children should be traveling east (there were only five of them but it seemed that there were more) when someone stopped at his table and asked if he might sit down.

"Please do."

The stranger clicked his heels and bowed. "Von Fahrenkamp." Riebeck suppressed a sigh, half rose, and mumbled his name.

Herr von Fahrenkamp studied the menu, looked up and said, "What about the wine?"

"Don't drink it. The train shakes it up unmercifully."

"*Ach so,*" said Herr von Fahrenkamp and ordered coffee.

He was a man of about fifty, round without being fat. He had direct blue eyes and no back to his head. Riebeck guessed that like himself von Fahrenkamp belonged in uniform. Evidently both had been speculating on the same subject, for the German said. "Experience should have taught me by now that the Orient Express is far less exciting than the Métro, but I can never help hoping someone will be mysteriously murdered—"

A romantic Prussian, thought Riebeck. Is there such an animal? "—And Lady Diana Wyndham to come to your compartment in the middle of the night in search of love," Riebeck added.

Von Fahrenkamp, who had spoken French during their first civil exchanges, had now switched to German, and Riebeck, to whom it was almost the same, had answered in that language.

"Quite so. At any rate I have been playing Sherlock Holmes and I have tried to deduce from various pieces of evidence what your profession is."

"And?"

"I should say you are an officer."

"Quite right. And so are you."

"How did you know?"

"It's not difficult. Officers carry themselves differently. Straighter across the shoulders."

"I was much more Holmesian about you. You wear your handkerchief in your sleeve. You must be a soldier."

"Or an unfrocked priest."

"If you were a priest," said the German handsomely, "you would at least be a monsignor and certainly a Jesuit doing well in the church."

"How nice of you."

"That's all right, I'm a Protestant."

"That's what I thought."

"I couldn't guess your rank," said von Fahrenkamp. "I'm a major in the infantry."

"I'm a lieutenant-colonel in the cavalry."

"You seem young to be a colonel."

"The usual army fuck-up."

"Somehow I doubt that. Now, you can't be Prussian. You haven't the Potsdam air or the accent. Austrian?"

It was an understandable mistake, for Riebeck did not speak the German of his native Lorraine, but had long ago adopted the Baranyis' Viennese idiom. Like them he lengthened his vowels, softened his consonants and drawled through his nose. He grinned. "Sherlock Holmes appears to be a failure. I am French."

Major von Fahrenkamp turned purple and Riebeck politely suppressed his laughter.

"I'm damned. How do you come to speak my language so well?"

"I am from Lothringen," said Riebeck. He always called it Lorraine, but had this momentary inspiration. "And I spent part of my childhood in Vienna."

"But Lothringen—" von Fahrenkamp began and stopped. He had been about to say that had it not been for the unfair Treaty of Versailles, Lorraine would be German and its citizens properly Germans. He remembered in time that its French inhabitants did not relish this line of reasoning. "And after all," he said instead, "Sherlock Holmes is not to blame. I overlooked an important clue. You are too young to have been in the war, how could you possibly be a colonel in any army that has barely begun to exist."

Riebeck, beginning to be bored, said he didn't know. "I've just come back from Indochina and I'm afraid the French army trains one out of reading newspapers. Things seem to be changing for the better in Germany."

"It was high time they did."

"I am glad of it," said Riebeck insincerely.

"Quite a lot of French people are, as a matter of fact. Trade is only possible with a prosperous country and munitions-makers have discovered that one can sell armaments only to countries with armies. So they forgive us for breaking the treaty. But then, you are not an industrialist."

"As you said, I am too young to have fought in the last war. So I should like another one."

Von Fahrenkamp snorted. "You are an appallingly honest young man."

Since this was precisely the impression Riebeck had meant to give, he did not contradict. "Come to my compartment and have some brandy," he said.

"Is it better than the wine?"

"It's Château Cavignac," said Riebeck. Major von Fahrenkamp looked surprised and respectful. "Vic Cavignac and I were at St. Cyr and Saumur and then in Indochina together. He keeps me supplied."

"Friendship," said Herr von Fahrenkamp earnestly, "is a wonderful thing."

"Yes indeed."

Von Fahrenkamp had most of the brandy and did most of the talking.

"Are you traveling all the way?" he asked.

"Only to Vienna." Riebeck explained about visiting the Baranyis. There is something about a young man on his way to visit two elderly aunts that inspires confidence. Von Fahrenkamp, well into the brandy, said he had been in France to visit the Creusot works and was now on his way to Prague to see the Skoda people. He did not say whether he had been successful, but he seemed awfully pleased with himself.

"You surprise me," said Riebeck. "Or rather, Creusot surprises me."

"Money is money and time is the great healer. At Versailles you wanted to starve us to death and sow salt on our fields, but unless they have a Cato to remind them at the end of every speech that Carthage must be destroyed, people are apt to forget."

"We seem to behave badly in victory."

"That is human nature. And after all, we are very old enemies. But I do not think you will get your war, Riebeck. We are not arming for that. We merely don't like the feeling of being naked in a storm—should one come."

"Oh quite," said Riebeck, not believing a word.

Von Fahrenkamp finished the brandy and said Hitler would soon have served his purpose and that the Potsdam clique had no intention of allowing him to continue past that time.

Riebeck did not bother to point out that a man who had pushed himself into Herr Hitler's position of power would not be all that easy to dislodge. He had stopped paying attention some time back, being quite able to tell drunken indiscretion from drunken boasts. Von Fahrenkamp fell asleep in the middle of a sentence. Riebeck relinquished his berth and left his compartment to stand by an open window and smoke cigarettes till breakfast time.

He and Herr von Fahrenkamp met again at lunch. The German apologized for having usurped Riebeck's bed, and Riebeck was charming about it. He spent the afternoon in his compartment writing a long letter to Latour, a short one to Elisabeth, and another long one to Katalin. The one to Latour would go through the Legation, the other two he posted at the railway station in Vienna, chancing the censor. A man so embroiled with two ladies rarely has time to be a spy as well.

It rained in Vienna, but Riebeck did not mind. No one had come to meet him, which did not surprise him. The Aunts were terribly unpunctual; they might easily have mistaken not only the train but the day. Istvan was possibly still in Budapest.

He never arrived in Vienna without remembering his first broken-hearted departure, but the sorrow of it had been overlaid by many subsequent arrivals and departures. Except for the war this was the longest time he and Istvan had been separated. As boys they had spent all their summers together at Fontaines or Hommages, the Baranyi stud in Hungary. As young officers they had met for holidays and had set Venice and Vienna by the ears. And each meeting had taught them anew that time apart has no reality for friends, and that if there is a distance in space and time, there is no distance of the heart.

He whistled up a taxi, but when they passed by the rain-soaked Hofgarten he decided that the Aunts must wait a little longer. After being cooped up in the train he simply had to walk half an hour before going indoors again. He told the driver to deliver his luggage to Baranyi Palace and got out.

The Hofgarten was grey and misty in the rain; the trees, almost bare of their leaves, showed their plan of black bark. Riebeck felt at home at once. He always did in Vienna, even when he had been away for years. Turning up the collar of his coat, he walked off the stuffiness of the train. In the spring Vienna smelled of sewers and jasmine, in November it smelled only of sewers. But it was a familiar smell, part of a loved city.

Suddenly he heard footsteps behind him, quick and ineffective, as of a woman trying to run in heels too high for her, and a breathless gasp imploring him to stop. He turned with a shout of delighted laughter to see his aunt Josephine battling her skirts and umbrella and clutching desperately at her piled hair and preposterous hat.

"Dear Schani, you have such dreadfully long legs," she gasped. He caught her in his arms and swung her around. She shrieked. "Do put me down. My darling, how handsome you look, and so grown up. The taxi driver said he had a maniac for a fare who insisted on getting out by the Hofgarten and made him bring the luggage to Baranyi Palace. He said you were running around in the rain, mad but obviously harmless, and were you a relation. So I put on my coat and came to get you. Istvan meant to meet your train but he got held up with the Spaniards."

Riebeck, who did not think it at all strange that his best friend should forget him because of a horse, laughed and said, "My dear Aunt, it was sweet of you to come. You look magnificent. You

45

are ten times more beautiful than Albertine and you look fifty years younger."

"If I looked fifty years younger," Josephine lied, "I would not yet be born. Do something about this umbrella, Schani dear. It keeps turning inside out, but you're so clever, I'm sure you'll manage something."

Riebeck coped with the umbrella, leaving Josephine free to tame her hat—which was crowned with a dove, life size, holding a palm branch in its beak and surrounded by pineapples and other exotic fruits.

"I like that hat," said Riebeck. "Are you thrilled that I've come?"

"Don't be so conceited, you know quite well we've been in a dither about it. Did you bring me a present?"

"Of course I brought you a present."

She stood on tiptoe and he bent down while she whispered in his ear.

"You are a shameless creature, Pepi."

"For Steffi too?"

"Certainly. Trimmed with black lace."

"Lovely, lovely. Oh Schani, what fun you are."

They turned into the Herrengasse and walked up to the Palace. At the door Riebeck stopped, as he had so often done before, to look at the coat of arms above, and to read its inscription: " '*Mon coeur aux dames, ma vie au roi, à dieu mon âme, l'honneur pour moi.*' How nice. The Riebecks have some horrible Latin nonsense about onward and upward for King and Country."

They found the family in the smallest of the drawing rooms, where they were at once engulfed by a babel of voices clearly dominated by Steffi's parrot shriek. "Schani, so it was you. The idiot taxi driver said it was a harmless madman, did Pepi tell you?"

"What I think is so interesting is that he knew at once I was a relation of yours. *Servus* Istvan."

Istvan smiled. "*Servus* Schani. *Comment ça va?*"

"Still a captain? Did you know that I'm a colonel?"

"Lieutenant-colonel, you mean."

"What a ridiculous quibble."

There was in the Hungarian army always the danger that one

might be sent to some dreary provincial garrison and forgotten there amid pigs, mud, bad drink, and intolerable boredom only occasionally brightened by a scandal caused by the *faute de mieux* homosexuality of a brother officer. Istvan had escaped this fate. The Regent was a friend of the uncles; they met constantly at parties, and the peacock Horthy could not possibly overlook the young gargoyle who so honestly admired him. Then too, any riding team captained by Istvan Halyi could unfailingly count on at least one perfect score.

So Istvan remained in Budapest, riding for Hungary and holding down a number of choice appointments on Horthy's staff. The jobs involved little work and left ample time for hunting and parties and whoring and gambling. It was magnificent and if it was not war, a war was probably in the making and for the moment Istvan was content to wait.

In his Hungarian uniform he looked more than ever like an enraged Pan, with his high cheekbones and slanted Magyar eyes, two lines cutting deeply between the angled brows, turning his laughter into a scowl. His ugly face was redeemed by the green eyes, blazing with laughter, and the Esterhazy nose—a family property that filled all those who possessed it with unreasonable pride. His hands were remarkably fine: slender and very strong; a rider's hands. He was tall for a Hungarian, nearly six feet, and thin as a whip, with that same coiled energy that might suddenly lash out into ruthless destructiveness. As a child he had possessed an acrobat's physical ease; he never put a foot wrong. It was a quality he had not lost over the years, but his height and slenderness served to add to it a grace that made him in motion a figure from a boy's romance. He crossed a room as if he were going into battle, a sword buckled to his side, his cloak streaming behind him in the wind.

"I'll bet you're hungry, Schani," said Stefanie. "I never think the food on the Orient Express is worth eating."

"I agree with you."

Dinner at Baranyi Palace was always excessive. If the French believe that good taste lies in moderation, Hungarians are convinced that anything worth doing is worth overdoing. Watching them at it was one of Riebeck's private pleasures.

47

They were delighted to have him with them and said so, often, with enthusiasm. It meant nothing, he had heard them make the same fuss over Uncle Koloman, whom they all hated. It was all part of making life charming. At low ebb it was reminiscent of the bride and groom of an arranged marriage making the best of things, but when well done it unfailingly succeeded.

Riebeck sat back, relaxing in the noise they were making. He was tired after his sleepless night on the train, he had eaten too much dinner, and drunk too much wine. Horse shows, gambling debts, the love affairs of half of Vienna and all of Budapest made up the stuff of their after-dinner conversation. It required little attention and no contribution from him.

"And how did you get that heavenly tan in November?" asked Aunt Stefanie. "Have you been lounging about on the Riviera?"

"Riviera my eye. This is my Indochina tan. It doesn't seem to go away. I'm beginning to suspect that there is some native blood in the Riebeck family."

Istvan's ugly face was alive with interest. "How was the fighting in Indochina? Come on, tell."

"No, don't," Aunt Josephine interrupted. "Istvan, I've put you boys in the nursery. You can spend the whole night talking about hacking natives to pieces." Aunt Josephine had very antiquated ideas about imperialism.

"Mostly the other way round these days," Riebeck said. "All right, Pepi, we won't discuss it in front of you. I would rather like to go to bed, as a matter of fact. I didn't have any sleep last night, a Prussian officer passed out in my berth."

Stefanie cackled. "The strangest things always happen to you, darling Schani. Sleep well, my dear."

Istvan said, "I'll come up with you and you can tell me about Indochina," and then spent half the night talking about Admiral Horthy.

Riebeck did not work terribly hard for Jacques Latour. He was unable to take the thing seriously; it had too literary a flavor, and not of respectable literature at that. But Latour had given him a convenient way out of the impasse with Elisabeth, and in gratitude he faithfully sent a weekly letter through the French Legation to Paris.

Even without effort on his part information came to him. Confidence was offered him constantly, not in spite of the fact that he did not welcome it but precisely because he did not. People felt safe telling him things because he gave the impression that only good manners made him pretend to listen.

So much was told him that in one of his letters he felt it prudent to disclaim any special talent for the gathering of information. "Everyone gossips all day in Vienna," he wrote Latour. "A person who listens is like the straw in the river that collects all the rubbish afloat."

It was all so incidental, so secondary, compared with his real interest, which was to get back into the Baranyi routine; the Spanish Riding School with Istvan and the uncles, gossip over tea with the aunts, the elaborate dinners, the parties (often at embassies with plums for Latour) and finally, to end the day, the long talks with Istvan in the nursery.

The ends of their cigarettes glowing in the dark, a bottle of wine between them, Istvan told Riebeck of the years they had spent apart, of his regiment and Maria Terezia Barracks, of drunken parties and brawls and gambling for impossible stakes, of the horse shows—London and the King George V gold cup he had won, the apogee in the amateur rider's life, not to be surpassed except by winning the cup a second time—it was a glorious and rowdy picture, but seemed to Riebeck just a little askew, a hundred years behind the times. He hoped it would last Istvan's time, since he enjoyed it so much.

Sometimes when he was drunk Istvan was willing to talk of the years of their first separation, the war and the years after, when Bela Kun's rabble had ridden across Hungary and the Trianon Treaty had given the Tisza lands to Romania and General Halyi's estate to Czechoslovakia.

There could never be hostility between friends so mutually devoted, but there was at such times the unacknowledged strain between victor and vanquished, the boy who had lost nothing and the other who had seen his father shot, his house burnt, his land given

49

away. It often seemed to Riebeck that these unforgotten, unforgiven outrages were an earnest of trouble to come far more than Hitler's rise in Germany.

Istvan and his father had loved each other with an affection that had apparently needed neither words nor even physical presence. Never an outgoing man, General Halyi had squandered what little conversation he had on the lovely Kira Esterhazy who had so surprisingly fallen in love with him and consented to marry him. Finding himself after his wife's death with a new baby, he had no doubt been glad to have it taken off his hands by Josephine.

The summer of 1919 was the first that father and son had spent together. They enjoyed each other's company in silence, riding and eating together with speechless mutual approval.

Everyone who could manage it had fled to Vienna before Bela Kun. General Halyi refused to leave his house.

"It was a beautiful house," Istvan said. "I was twelve that year. Papa and Janos and I spent all our time with the horses. I don't think I had a bath for weeks. Then one day a group of hoodlums, riding horses they weren't fit to clean, came up to the estate to loot it. Papa met them at the door, wearing his general's uniform of a defeated army, holding a gun." Istvan had to stop to laugh. "Forgive me, but it was a funny sight, poor Papa standing like a ramrod, ready to defend his house against a group of bandits and murderers, all armed to the teeth. He told them he would kill the first one who came a step closer. I ran into the house and took down the first pistol I could see from the wall. I don't know why it was loaded, but it was. Then I went to join Papa. Janos and I had stolen apples the day before, so I was sure if I got killed I would go to hell. I think it was Papa's officer's voice that held them back for a moment, but they were drunk with pillaged wine and newly acquired power, and nothing could have stopped them long. They shot Papa; he never even had the time to kill one of them. I got the man who had shot him very neatly in the face and it made a most satisfactory mess. They paid no attention to me at all, they simply ran past me and began tearing the house to pieces. There was nothing I could do but watch. In the end they found their way to the wine cellar and stayed there for hours. While they were out of the way Janos and I quickly dug a grave for Papa under a plum tree behind the house. It was his tree, I mean grandpapa planted it the day Papa was born. I'm afraid it wasn't a very nice grave. I wasn't experienced at digging. Then we let all the horses out and chased them into the *puszta*. Janos and I had a rare job collecting them again later. We were gone when they burned the house. We could see the smoke from where we were hiding.

"Of course Janos said I must go straight to Hommages to stay with the uncles. He was quite right, there wasn't anywhere else to go. But I couldn't go without my horses. I wasn't a baby any more, and I couldn't ask for charity. Janos and I had a terrific fight about it. We were in Czechoslovakia, you see, and according to your bloody treaty my horses belonged to the Slovaks. I still had Papa's pistol, and I told Janos I'd shoot him if he didn't shut up. There must have been a good five years, you know, when no Hungarian could talk about anything but the Trianon Treaty. And a damned dirty deal it was too."

"I was twelve when it was drafted, Istvan. I gather Janos shut up," said Riebeck, knowing Istvan's threats were rarely idle.

"Well, not really. He kept on muttering, you know the way he does when he doesn't approve of something. But he helped me round up the horses. It took a long time. We couldn't get about during the day much. Fortunately the Slovaks couldn't tell a Lippizaner from a jackass most of the time, so we were pretty safe. It takes more than a treaty to make people fit to own land and horses, thank God."

"It didn't last five years. Hungarians still talk about nothing else," said Riebeck, laughing.

"How would you like a lot of foreigners splitting up your country and giving pieces to whoever wants them?"

"Well, you know, Germans have helped themselves to Lorraine on and off for a good many years. One always gets it back."

"We mean to."

"By ganging up with Hitler?"

"Can't make an omelet, as you Frogs keep saying in Indochina and Morocco."

"Go on about your horses," said Riebeck prudently.

"Oh. There wasn't much more. We made it to Hommages. We hadn't been under a roof in months, and certainly not near soap and water. We were in rags and half starved, and you know what Steffi said when she saw me? 'Istvan, your fingernails are simply disgusting.' "

Riebeck laughed. "Istvan, have you considered that if you're still with Horthy, and if we have a war, we'll be on opposite sides?"

"Goodness. Wouldn't it be embarrassing if we had to kill each other in the line of duty? Let's get up early and ride before breakfast."

"Fine. Don't Horthy officers ever do any work?"

"This Horthy officer does pretty much as he pleases."

"What an army," said Riebeck. "I hope you gang up with Hitler. It will be much better for our side."

V

After a great deal of arguing back and forth the family decided to spend Christmas in Budapest. The aunts preferred Vienna for the midnight mass in the Stefansdom, but the uncles wanted to hunt in Hungary. Besides, they said, there was no city on earth so beautiful as Budapest.

Budapest, said the uncles, had the prettiest women, the best food, the noisiest parties, the biggest bedbugs as well as—they said this to Riebeck, not to their wives—the most depraved brothels.

Vienna, said the Aunts, had *Kultur*. The Burgtheater, the Hofoper, the Musikevereinsaal—"

"And the Wurstelprater," Istvan finished wickedly.

The divided loyalties presented no problems. The Baranyis had their Cuvilliers Palace in Vienna, the Tiszas owned a jewel-box of a house on Disz Ter, the lovely baroque square on top of Buda Hill.

During the nineteenth century the rich had turned their backs on Buda and had built their monstrous houses in Pest, but the Tiszas had remained in the old town. Now everyone else was once again discovering the charm of Buda, thereby proving, in Count Nikki's opinion, that the Tiszas are always right.

They gave a dinner party and a ball on New Year's Eve. Riebeck, looking down the long table at the splendid uncles, Istvan, and his officer friends, asked himself once again why these people suited him so much better than his own kind. They were handsome and gay, but the lacquer of civilization covered them very thinly and often showed cracks. They played more wildly and fought more brutally than the people Riebeck knew. Like Istvan, many of them had seen their houses looted and burned, their fortunes lost, members of their families murdered. The fortunes had been restored. Those who had not been able to fight their way back to the top had quietly removed themselves into an impoverished obscurity where they were decently starving to death. Their rich relatives ignored them. It was a dog-eat-dog world, but it had style.

They were already half drunk, surfeited with the prodigal food, prepared for a night of dancing, gambling, drinking, making love; to get up again after two or three hours' sleep to go hunting all day, to feast again all night. This had been going on for weeks. They looked handsome, tough, and energetic. Their wives, by contrast, looked not only tired but plain. Riebeck wondered where the myth about beautiful Hungarian women had started. In an operetta, probably.

The aunts, being Viennese, had never approved of the Hungarian custom of seating all the men at one end of the table (with linen napkins the size of bedsheets tied around their necks and sticking up in rabbit's ears) and all the women at the other. The aunts alternated their ladies and gentlemen and supplied napkins the wrong size for tying.

Riebeck, with his usual good luck, found himself seated next to one of the few pretty Hungarian girls. He did not know who she was, only that she had recently come back from Paris, on which thin grounds Aunt Josephine had said, "But of course you two know each other."

She did appear to know him, and he felt that he had met her before. He was teased not only by the thought of knowing her but

53

also by a family resemblance—black eyes in a white face, black, black hair. He craned to see the name on the place card.

"I am Eva de Pogany," she said. "You know my sister Katalin."

"But yes," he agreed demurely. "Her husband is my uncle."

"Indeed," said Eva agreeably.

"I apologize for not recognizing you. You've been away at school or something, haven't you?"

"Not for years. You're the one who's been away."

"Too long, evidently."

She scarcely listened. "Do you think your cousin would remember me? I was ten when I saw him last, at the horse auction at Babolny."

Istvan was across the table from them, trapped between two dowdy officers' wives. His eyes had been wandering to Eva all through dinner. She really was very pretty, Riebeck thought, especially if you did not try to compare her to Katalin. There weren't many pretty girls at Stefanie's party. In Paris the Pogany sisters were known as "one so good and the other not." As a rule good little girls did not interest Riebeck; he preferred them bad. But Eva de Pogany might just be worth investigating.

"Never mind my cousin," he told her. "May I have all the dances to supper and lots afterwards? We can sit out if we get bored."

Realizing that in Count Xandi's absence Istvan was the son of the house and would therefore have many duty dances, and reasoning that a cousin was better than nothing, Eva said, "I'd like that. Katalin says you sit out very well."

After dinner Riebeck told her, "Come and see the fountains. Have you got a coat? It's cold out and I shan't give you mine."

Eva looked about her. Istvan was firmly in the grip of the German Ambassadress. "I'll get my wrap."

"Good. I'll find us some champagne."

Eva returned shortly wrapped in a cape of white silk lined with white mink. Riebeck recognized it easily as a hand-me-down from Katalin and grew nostalgic. They sat on the terrace steps. The fountains rose in delicate arcs in the frosty night.

"How is it they don't freeze?" asked Eva, accepting a glass of champagne.

"I think Uncle Nikki heats them or something," said Riebeck, already bored.

"I must have left Paris just when you came back from Indochina," said Eva. "I saw you the day before I left. You were getting into a Ferrari with my sister, and you looked terribly handsome. Why aren't you in uniform tonight?"

Riebeck, who knew that he never looked handsome, began to be curious about the purpose of such thick flattery. "I'm on leave," he said, "so I don't have to look handsome."

"Are you in love with my sister?"

"I adore her."

"And Captain Halyi, is he in love with anyone?"

"Aha!"

"Don't say aha like that. Is he?"

"I don't believe so."

"I'm so glad."

"Are you indeed. Well, better him than me."

"You are terribly rude."

"Have some more champagne."

"Thank you, I adore champagne. Why did you say that, better him than me?"

"Because I don't like being fallen in love with. Perhaps Istvan will."

"Will you help me?"

"Help you what? To get Istvan?"

"Yes, of course."

"Certainly not."

"But why not? I've been in love with him ever since I was ten years old."

"I don't believe it. Little girls don't stay in love with someone they haven't seen in years."

"But I did. That's why I made Mama come to Budapest. Why won't you help me? You're his best friend, he'd listen to you. Don't you think I could make him happy?"

"Happy! Dear God, what a word. A cat sleeping by the fire."

"You don't know anything about it."

"Probably not."

"Do you think I'm beautiful?" She turned her face to the light. St. Leger diamonds glittered in her hair and at her throat.

"No. You're very pretty. Why do you ask?"

"Because they said in Paris that you've never refused anything to a beautiful woman except marriage."

Riebeck laughed out loud. "I'd really promised to share this champagne with Istvan. I think there's just a glass left. Shall we take it to him?"

They found Istvan by the door of the ballroom. Behind them the orchestra was playing the *Merry Widow Waltz*. Stefanie's musical program was always conservative.

"Hullo, Istvan. I've saved you a glass of champagne."

Istvan looked at the label. It was a bottle of Uncle Nikki's best. "That was nice of you, considering I was supposed to have half. I need it, I can tell you. I've just been dancing with the Ambassadress."

"Captain Halyi, Mademoiselle de Pogany. She says she remembers you from the horse auction at Babolny."

Eva smiled at him and Istvan was struck speechless. Having served a long apprenticeship of first love, Riebeck was more familiar with the symptoms than Istvan, and realized at once what had happened. And as quickly as the space closes between question and answer everything turned upside down—the little Pogany became a person, a woman with whom Istvan was falling in love. And if Istvan wanted her, of course he must have her. "You'd better dance with Mademoiselle de Pogany," he said. Eva gave him a surprised and delighted look. "Make a nice change from the Ambassadress."

Istvan, who had talked himself in and out of many a bedroom in his day, stammered like a schoolboy. "Will you?" he managed to ask at last.

"Please," said Eva.

He gave her his arm and led her down the terrace steps to the park among the fountains. The white mink wrap had fallen from Eva's shoulders and the diamonds at her throat caught the light. Istvan was an exceptionally good dancer. They were very handsome together, the tall young officer in uniform and the girl with the dark hair and white furs. The orchestra was still indulging itself in the *Merry Widow*. Riebeck looked down at them and his shoulders shook with silent laughter until a diamond-covered claw was put on his sleeve and he looked down at his Aunt Stefanie.

"All alone and laughing? Why?"

"Look down in the park. Istvan and a girl whose name is Eva de Pogany. I believe they are in love."

"I knew her as a child, but of course they've been in France for years. Her mother is a dreadful woman. Why is Istvan in love with her?"

Riebeck grinned. "I do believe you are jealous. *On aime sur un sourire, sur un regard, sur une epaule. Cela suffit.* I cannot describe better than M. Proust what Eva is like and why Istvan is in love."

"I think you did it beautifully. I know just what you mean. It reminds me of when I was young. We did things like that then, dancing among the fountains and falling in love. Nikki proposed to me down there by the fountains."

"That stick of a girl Istvan is in love with looked at them and could think of nothing but to ask how it is they don't freeze."

"Your generation has murdered romance," said Steffi.

"How can you say that? Look at the Dual Monarchy romance Istvan has arranged for himself, Tisza fountains, *Merry Widow*, and all."

"I do wish you'd fall in love too, Schani."

He looked down at her with perfect gravity. "You know I've harbored a guilty and secret passion for you for years. Come inside and get drunk with me, Steffi."

"All right. Do you know I have never been really drunk in my whole life?"

It was five in the morning when Riebeck handed his uproarious aunt over to her maid and went to bed himself. Istvan did not come upstairs until it was time to dress for the trip to Hommages.

"Wear layers of everything, Schani. It's freezing."

"What did you do with Mademoiselle de Pogany?"

"Danced, drank champagne, talked a lot."

"Talked!" This was most unlike Istvan, who believed in prompt and unconsidered action.

"Talked, talked, talked. She's coming to Hommages, you know."

"So is her mother."

Istvan sat down on the bed and extended his boot. "Schani, when you fell in love with Elisabeth, what was it like?"

Riebeck pulled at the boot. "Just like this, probably."

Istvan extended his other leg. "But you made a mistake."

"They don't give guarantees, you know. Here, let me have my shower first. I promise to use up all the hot water. A cold bath will do you good."

"Don't you dare."

"Someday I'm going to charm the aunts into giving me a bathroom of my own."

"They won't. When we're ninety they'll still put us in the nursery together. I'd hate it if they didn't."

Riebeck, who had turned on the shower, shouted over the clanking of the old-fashioned pipes: "Surely you'll want a room of your own now."

"Schani, this isn't Eva's sister you're talking about," said Istvan, who owing to their deplorable habit of sharing all treats that came their way had one summer in Venice enjoyed, together with his cousin, the impartial favors of the beautiful Katalin and knew what he was talking about.

"Too true."

All through breakfast Istvan continued to sing the praises of his beloved, and, his subject far from exhausted, continued it in the car on the way to Hommages, while Riebeck caught up on his sleep.

That night Istvan again danced only with Eva. In the morning they went out shooting. Istvan shot a pheasant and gave her the long, golden tail feathers. Eva stuck them in her hat. She was lovely, really.

The uncles wore sheepskin coats and looked very feudal. Riebeck would dearly have loved a sheepskin coat of his own. The cold was terrible.

Istvan and Eva hunted together every day and danced together every night. If there were other people in the world or even in the house party, they were by now entirely unaware of it. After two weeks of this impassioned proximity Istvan confessed to Riebeck that he had not, as yet, even found the courage to kiss her.

"In Vienna," said Steffi, "nothing so enhances a woman's reputation as to have a few men killed for her."

"Wouldn't Budapest do as well?" asked Eva.

"Oh no, my dear. In Budapest the young men fight so many duels they no longer take them seriously. They shoot at each other, and if they miss they go away friends for life. No, Vienna is the place for a really scandalous duel."

The aunts adored Eva with their customary absent-minded lavishness. Had the earth suddenly opened up and swallowed her they would probably not have noticed it, but while she was there they admired her, told her improbable stories, and fed her sweets.

"It's time to go to Vienna anyway for the carnival," said Josephine. "That is something Vienna does better than Budapest."

The uncles would scarcely have agreed with her, but they had had their hunting holiday and were docile. Eva persuaded her mother to visit relatives in Vienna. She had no doubt that Istvan would follow her. And where Istvan went, apparently, Colonel Riebeck went too, which was good. She needed him.

Riebeck was glad to leave Hungary. His boredom had been extreme, and he was not a man who endured boredom with equanimity. Hungary was then still ruled by its aristocracy, so that the politicians could be met at Steffi's dinner parties. Riebeck felt he owed it to Latour to listen to what they had to say. Latour seemed to feel that their gossip was helpful, but they were the first politicians Riebeck had ever known personally and he was astounded at the magnitude of their stupidity.

They had been back in Vienna only a few days when Eva asked him to take her to the Ibsen revival at the Burgtheater. Riebeck thought an Ibsen revival a poor way to spend an evening, but politeness made him say he would. He added that he could not guarantee jealousy on Istvan's part, however. Eva said she had no idea what he was talking about.

After the play (*Peer Gynt* in modern dress) Eva asked if they could go to a night club, as she had never been to one.

"Certainly. Would you prefer a big fashionable place, or a dim hole-in-corner one?"

"Could I have both?"

"With pleasure."

They danced and drank champagne in indecently expensive night clubs and solemnly amused themselves in a cellar lit by candles where a bearded young man read at length from his unpublished works.

"When I think of the wisdom of all the publishers who wouldn't print his books I want to cry," said Eva and did.

"My dear, you are drunk. It's getting light. When you've been out all night in Vienna it is obligatory to take a cab with a sleepy driver and go to the top of the Kahlenberg to watch the sun rise."

"Will there be a sun? It looks like rain."

"It always looks like rain in Vienna."

The Kahlenberg was damp, cold, and not conducive to romance. Riebeck thought resentfully that if he had been with Katalin they could have pulled the moth-eaten carriage rug over their heads and everything would have been marvelous. This girl of Istvan's was a pest. Vienna lay below them in a thin fog; the blue Danube slid brown and dirty around the city. The sun was paltry, not worth watching.

"I wonder why it bothers to rise if that's the best it can do," said Riebeck crossly. "Not worth the effort, I should think."

The moment he finished complaining the bells from Vienna's churches rang out for early mass, the sun gave it up, and a cold drizzle began to fall.

"I must have some hot coffee and then I am going home to bed," said Riebeck.

"Do you think Istvan will be angry when he finds out that I spent the night with you?" asked Eva when they were on their way home.

"Hardly. We've been enormously respectable. You're the first girl I've ever watched the sunrise with that I didn't kiss."

"You may kiss me if you like."

"No, thank you."

"You are the rudest man. Why not?"

"I don't kiss Istvan's girls."

"Goodness, that's the first decent thing I've ever heard you say. What will I do if Istvan isn't angry?"

"Have an affair with a riding master at the Spanish Riding School."

"That wouldn't do a bit of good, Schani. You know nothing's too good for the Spaniards."

"That's true."

"Could you make him angry?"

"I don't know. I've never tried."

"Well, could you make him challenge you to a duel?"

Riebeck howled with laughter. "Oh, you're mad. How funny you are."

"Countess Steffi said—"

"I know. I'm better at fencing than Istvan and we shoot about the same. Are you sure you want to take the chance?"

"Schani, could I ask you a big favor?"

Riebeck, curious to see how far she would go, said, "Please."

"Promise me you won't hurt Istvan."

"All right. It puts me at a disadvantage, of course."

"Yes," said Eva cheerfully. "You might get killed, mightn't you?"

Riebeck agreed that under the circumstances he might.

"Oh, thank you," said Eva. "How kind you are."

It was still raining when they returned to the city: a chilly, penetrating rain which, together with his chastely spent night, made Riebeck cross. He climbed the stairs to the nursery and had a shower that began warm and turned cold long before he had rinsed the soap off. Istvan had as usual used all the towels and had left them wadded in a lump so that they had not dried. Wet and shivering, Riebeck went into the bedroom, which was arctic. Istvan opened one eye, looked at him, mumbled "Good morning," and closed his eye again.

"You've let the fire go out," said Riebeck in a voice that would have been appropriate to Oedipus Rex at his lowest moments. "I'm cold. Istvan, please—"

"No, Schani. I would do almost anything for you but you may not come into my nice warm bed. It took me hours to get it this way."

"Istvan."

"No, Schani."

Riebeck took the blanket from his own bed, found some matches to light the fire and pulled up an armchair. Wrapped in the blanket, which was now also wet, he sat down and looked encouragingly at the small flame.

"Where've you been all night, Schani?"

"Out with Eva. *Peer Gynt* and about ten night clubs and finally the sunrise from the Kahlenberg. The program."

"It sounds like rain."

"It is raining, but there was a very little sunrise earlier."

"Oh," said Istvan and went back to sleep.

"You're not doing this right," Riebeck said crossly. "You're supposed to suspect me of the customary things and be very angry and challenge me to a duel."

Istvan opened both eyes and looked suddenly very much awake. "Why?"

"Steffi's told her big lies about all the duels men used to fight over her and Pepi when they were young."

"Did you tell her you're better at fencing and could probably kill me if you tried?"

"You needn't worry about that. She made me promise not to hurt you and to let you kill me."

Istvan remained silent. Finally he said out of his deep reflections: "Women have no sense of proportion."

"No," said Riebeck. "They haven't."

Istvan became silent again while Riebeck cursed the fire, which would not burn.

"Are you still cold, Schani?"

"Yes."

"If you swear by all that's sacred to keep your cold feet to yourself you can come into my bed."

Admiring Istvan's splendid common sense—one cannot kill in a duel someone who has already perished of cold—Riebeck gratefully crawled into the warm bed and at once fell asleep.

When he awoke the fire was blazing, the room was warm, Istvan was gone, and he was late for lunch.

He spent the afternoon in Josephine's sitting room, close by the fire, reading Proust. The thought of the duel did not worry him. He had been shot at by too many jealous husbands to feel concern, and he could not make himself believe that Istvan, madly in love though he was, would actually require his lifeless corpse as a tribute to his beloved.

Josephine was muttering over a dressmaker's bill for which her husband had that morning demanded an explanation she had been entirely unable to supply.

"What are you reading, Schani?"

"*Sodome et Gomorrhe*, darling."

"Goodness. What's it about?"

He told her.

"How ghastly," said Josephine.

"Oh no. It's the perfect book for a rainy afternoon. I always read it when the weather is bad and I have a hangover."

Just before dinner Count Xandi came to his mother's room. He had lost more money in Monte Carlo than even his indulgent father would countenance, and was favoring his family with a visit.

"*Servus* Mama, Schani. The most amazing thing. Schani, guess whom I saw at the Spaniards?"

"Istvan and Eva. Considering that they spend most of their time there I don't quite see what's so amazing."

"They were on the stairs, on that dark turn, you know—"

"Yes."

"Guess what they were doing."

"Kissing."

"I thought you'd say that. They were not. Istvan had Eva up against the wall and he was yelling at her. He was simply furious. I haven't seen him like that since the time the stable boy didn't rub down Vaik after they'd been out riding all day."

63

"I wonder," thought Riebeck, "whether I was the favorite horse in this instance." To Xandi he said, "Don't worry. Love finds a way out of everything, they say."

Josephine groaned aloud and said love would never find a way out of her dressmaker's bill and Istvan had threatened to divorce her.

"He can't, Pepi. You were married by a cardinal."

"I do so hope you're right, my dear. I'd never find another husband at my age. You know, Steffi must be putting her things on my bill. I couldn't have spent that much."

Riebeck, who knew this to be a crisis occurring as regularly as the four seasons, made sympathetic noises. Pepi, noticing her son for the first time, said, "Please take your wet coat off my little table, Xandi. You know it stains."

"Sorry, Mama."

"Is it snowing?"

"Yes."

Riebeck pulled aside the curtain and looked down into the court. There was a thin covering of snow on the ground and the cupids on the fountain were getting white hats. They looked very cold. He shivered and drew the curtain closed again.

"Where have you been all day, Xandi?"

"The Spaniards," said Count Xandi, preferring not to detail some of his other occupations. "Istvan is behaving very badly to Eva, Mama."

"You must stop him, darling. What was he doing?"

"Shouting at her."

"Oh Xandi, your muddy riding boots right on my Aubusson."

Count Xandi, who had not yet removed his wet coat from the table, regarded his boots with dissatisfaction. "Where is Lazlo?"

"Who is Lazlo, dear?"

"Lazlo, Aunt Pepi, you know. The idiot that polishes our boots," explained Riebeck. "The one with the pop eyes and the teeth hanging out."

"Oh, Lazlo. Well, Xandi dear, where are the servants when they aren't working?" The Countess Josephine, with a wave of her hand,

64

indicated some vague lower depths where servants languish with the black-beetles during their free time.

"Eva was crying," said Xandi with the persistence of the stupid. "Why, dear?"

"Weren't you listening? I just told you—"

Pepi once more explained about the bills and her suspicions that Steffi had been adding to them.

"Yes," said Xandi, not interested. "It will be all right, you know. Eva was crying because Istvan was yelling at her."

"Oh, dear. I do wish Istvan had been brought up better," sighed Josephine, forgetting for the moment that she had brought him up. "And now I must go and dress for dinner."

At dinner Josephine once again mentioned her dressmaker's bill and suggested that Steffi was to blame. Steffi protested indignantly and within seconds the countesses had involved themselves in a quarrel that included every grievance they had harbored against each other since the age of three. Riebeck prudently removed himself to bed.

There, with the fire, a warm quilt, a very large glass of brandy, his cigarettes, and *Sodome et Gomorrhe* he felt safe. He was just falling asleep with a lit cigarette in his hand and the light on when Istvan Halyi stormed in. He threw himself across Riebeck's bed, scattering snow from his overcoat.

"Thank God, you're home, Schani. I've done it. We're going to get married as soon as her mother gets over the idea that Eva has to marry a rich duke. Could I have that brandy?"

"If you'll get your wet coat off my bed."

Istvan stood up, threw his overcoat into a corner, and drank down the whole glass of brandy in one breath. "Are you glad?"

"Of course, if you are. Sit down and tell me."

Istvan lit a cigarette and sat on the foot of Riebeck's bed. "After you fell asleep, hogging most of my blanket, by the way, I really got to thinking about things, and I got angrier and angrier. Schani, there isn't a woman in the world worth fighting with a friend over, not to mention killing. If you wanted Eva I wouldn't stop you. I wouldn't like it, but it would make no difference to us. I knew twenty years ago I'd never like anybody more than I like you, and no damned woman is going to interfere with that. Bloodthirsty little beast. She really meant it, you know. When you first told me about it I thought she was joking, but she wasn't."

"I know. She was charming about it, but she meant it."

"Well, anyhow, I got up and rushed off to the Spaniards. I knew she'd be there. We ate lunch at Sacher's and I told her I wouldn't fight a duel with you if you got her pregnant with triplets. I'd marry her and I'd be willing to bring them up as if they were my own—"

Riebeck, who hadn't even kissed the girl, protested.

"I know," said Istvan. "Of course you wouldn't. But I wouldn't mind if you did, not really. Then we went back to the Riding School and fought for hours. That girl has an abominable temper, you know. She said I didn't love her, and I said I did, and she said I didn't and I thought how lucky that Tibor always leaves the key to his flat with me when he goes to Budapest—"

"I have always told you," Riebeck interrupted, "that with women the shortest distance between two points is bed."

Istvan laughed, hunched at the foot of the bed like a gargoyle. "That's what I thought too, but Eva wouldn't hear of it. She says it's a sin, and she's quite right, of course it is, and that we aren't going to do anything until we get married." Istvan seemed rather proud of this eccentricity of his beloved. "It's going to be ghastly," he said with the horrible cheerfulness of one setting out to climb Everest for the first time.

Riebeck was horrified. "I've never heard of anything so unhealthy and foolish. Thank God I won't be here to see it."

"You won't? Why not?"

"I only have six months' leave and it happens to be up."

"Why don't you write and ask for an extension?"

"Who the hell do you think runs the French army, Admiral Horthy? I'll come back two years from now, when I get leave again, and see what you're like. You'll be as nervous as a desert father by then, no doubt."

"Two years from now," said Istvan firmly, "I expect to be married and the proud father of ten children."

VI

Colonel Riebeck returned to Paris one week before his leave was up. He telephoned Katalin from the station and then went directly to see Latour. He ignored with a rudeness unlike him Latour's greeting and asked, "Did you get those election results I sent you three weeks before the Saar plebiscite?"

"Yes, thank you. Very interesting. However did you manage to get hold of them?"

"Never mind that. Why weren't they made public before the election? You had plenty of time."

"I tried, you know. Nobody would touch them."

"Oh? Didn't they believe they were authentic?"

"Were they?"

"Of course. Couldn't you tell?"

"Yes. That's why they weren't published. We don't at this point in France do anything that might annoy Herr Hitler, and I think he would have been very annoyed."

"I dare say. So you give the Saar back without a fight. What goes next? Lorraine?"

"Even in an election supervised by a regiment of impartial angels we would have lost the Saar."

"Well, but Jacques, that was the entire point. That's why I sent you the faked-up German election results, so you could publish them ahead of time and discredit a perfectly honest election."

"What a professional you'd make with a nasty mind like that."

"What a profession when one goes through all that trouble for nothing."

"I know. Listen, if you had brought me an order signed by the entire German High Command to invade France next Thursday everybody would with the greatest firmness refuse to believe it. Thanks for your letter about the Dollfuss assassination, by the way. It was very interesting. How much of it was true?"

"What a question. Everybody in Vienna knows a little bit of what happened, nobody knows the same bit, and everybody has a different theory. Mine is that it was an accident. It was a wildly mismanaged affair."

"Yes, I wondered about that, that it should be done so badly. Surely the Nazis can do better than that."

"They weren't trying. They will next time."

"You think there will be a next time?"

"Assuredly. Before Habicht and Hitler put their backs up, many Austrians wanted an Anschluss, you know. Economically they need it desperately. Now von Papen is there with all those olive branches. If he's patient enough and tactful enough and if he can keep the Nazis on their good behavior for a few years—which I doubt—the Anschluss will happen quite amiably."

"Until it does happen I wish you'd stay in Vienna for me, Jean. I could manufacture a job at the Legation for you."

"No thanks."

"Why not?"

"Colonel Delambert would never allow it."

"A feeble excuse. He already has. You can have a leave of absence from your regiment for the asking."

"I won't ask. And I should be grateful in the future if you wouldn't try to arrange my life for me with Delambert and without me."

"Is that why you won't work for me, because you are annoyed?"

"No. Because I'm bored. It's dull, you know, sitting around and listening to people one doesn't like."

"It'll pick up. It will get rapidly more dangerous, more frightening, and therefore intensely fascinating. Jean, lots of people make good cavalry officers. But good intelligence officers are as rare as truffles. You have all the makings of one—an intelligence officer, I mean, not a truffle. You have brains, discipline, training, courage, no nerves, and something else, some other quality, I don't know what it's called. People talk to you, they like to tell you secrets. God only knows why. You're an unforthcoming bastard, really. I've watched you squirm when people insisted on unburdening their souls to you. But they do it."

"The pill tastes, Jacques. In spite of the jam."

"Jean, the time to sit on a horse and wave a saber has passed forever and ever. Perhaps you were born in the wrong century. You should have fought for Napoleon."

"I would have liked that."

"Only you weren't born then, you're alive now, and now the important thing is to keep an eye on the Nazis. You can do that by working for me. I won't tell you how badly I need you."

"You have."

"I know. I do."

The size of Latour's desk left no room for pacing. Riebeck was one of those who prefer to think on their feet.

"I'll go for a walk, Jacques."

"Do. I'll be here when you get back."

"Like the spider and the fly."

When Riebeck had returned his salute and closed the door behind him, Latour smiled. He knew what the result would be; he had known it from the moment he had sent Riebeck to Vienna.

Without an army background, without tradition, Latour was able to look at these things with a clearness that Riebeck would never achieve. Riebeck would have considered it an act of disloyalty to admit that the cavalry bored him. Latour, who owed it no loyalty, had long known that the only life in which Riebeck would ever successfully keep boredom away would be one lived unremittingly on a tightrope, where an instant's inattention, a false step, a clumsy move would be punished by a brutal death. He had offered the tightrope, done up nicely in a package of patriotism, and he had no doubt that it would be accepted.

Riebeck, walking impatiently across the Pont Royal, would have been glad of some of Latour's assurance. The suggestion that he remain with the Deuxième had not been unexpected, but he had never before considered it beyond a refusal.

Yet he had no real reason for refusing, no particular wish to return to Indochina. But an embassy job, even as a guise for more dangerous work, made no appeal to him either. In the stream of his life there was no strong current to compel him to go either way.

He stopped to look across the misty Tuileries, remembering the evenings of his childhood, when darkness had fallen like spiderwebs and it was time to go home, following the man with the drum, with a last look at the silenced Punch and Judy and the forgotten toy boats afloat like confetti; past one last hurdy-gurdy to the lights coming on across the river.

Above him Coysevox' Flying Horses reared in the rainy dusk. He had always loved them, bestriding the air with so much grace. He hoped they would never be plundered to replace the animals on Berlin's Siegestor. He lit a cigarette and looked with a faint smile toward the Arc du Carrousel, which had in Bonaparte's day been surmounted by the horses of St. Mark's. Sauce for the goose? Hardly. To be brought from Venice to Paris is a holiday, to be taken from Paris to Berlin is exile.

He reached out and touched the damp stone pedestal, then turned and walked quickly back to Latour's office.

"All right, Jacques."

"Good. Dinner at Lapérouse?"

"Sorry, not tonight. I'm taking Katalin to the Tour d'Argent. Come too."

"Try and stop me."

At five the next morning they—three proper Parisians—ate onion soup at Les Halles.

"Office at nine," groaned Latour.

"Not me," said Riebeck. "We'd only sit and yawn at each other. I'll stop by after lunch. Come along, Kat, time for bed."

After lunch Latour still looked slightly green. "I'm glad the fate of the republic doesn't depend on me. If I had to make a decision my head would burst. I've got you a job."

"I'll bet it's a stinker with a hangover like yours."

"Assistant to the military attaché at our legation in Vienna."

"I believe there's a society that helps people to stop drinking."

"What did you expect me to do, send you over with the Concours Hyppique?"

"Much better. Xandi and I'll get you lots of prizes."

"That is not the object of your trip. Anyway I don't like horses. Now I've thought this over a good deal and I think your father must be told what you are doing. The chief agrees with me. Your father is not the man to be satisfied with a feeble story of your taking a leave of absence from your regiment to grub around a legation. He'd ask questions and we don't want that."

"Is this necessary, Jacques?"

"Why, are you scared?"

"Have you ever met my father?"

"No, but my uncle was in his regiment during the war. I've heard stories. When you get back we'll get to work. Have you ever blown anything up?"

"A mortar once in Annam, with nitroglycerine."

Latour groaned. "Can you crack a safe?"

"No idea. Never tried it."

"You have much to learn."

"It sounds fascinating. I had no idea I was joining the criminal classes."

"You will find it amusing, I think."

Riebeck borrowed Albertine de Baro's Ferrari and drove to Fontaines. He had forgotten to tell anyone that he was coming.

His father, he learned to his relief, was not expected till the week end. He spoke soothing words to Marthe, who had burst into tears because he was so thin.

"Where is Madame Robert, Marthe?"

"In the garden."

"I'll go find her."

He went through the salon and stopped at the open french windows to watch Elisabeth picking daffodils. She was dressed in the kind of clothes he disliked most; a baggy flannel skirt, a gardening smock, and a red cardigan thrown over her shoulders. He smiled at his own long folly and called her name. She turned, dropping the flowers, and ran across the grass into his arms without a thought for the gardener, who was watching with interest.

"Jean, my dearest, I missed you so terribly," she said while he pulled her into the room out of the gardener's view. "My darling, I'm so glad you're back."

"I shall have to leave again in a few days. Don't cry."

71

"I'm not," she said against his shoulder.

"Shall I get you some wine? Have a cigarette."

"You know I don't smoke." She stopped crying and sat down on the sofa, pulling his hand until he sat down next to her. He gave her his handkerchief, and getting really his first good look at her realized with dismay that the smock was not only for the garden.

"Oh, my darling," said Elisabeth shocked, "who has been doing your laundry? All the edges are torn off the handkerchief."

This did not seem to Riebeck the time for domestic questions. "Do you think that perhaps we had better have a talk, Lisa?"

He had originally planned to tell her that much as he adored her he had behaved like a bounder where his brother was concerned, and that honor demanded that he break his heart and stop. He had been sure the romantic and moral aspects of this argument would appeal to Elisabeth. But now he said, "You first, I think."

"I do love you so, Jean."

"I know, darling."

"I'm going to have a baby."

"Yes, that's obvious. How nice. When?"

"In May."

"I was afraid of that. But fortunately Robert was here too last September, so that's all right."

Elisabeth was horrified. "But I don't want that, Jean. I want to tell Robert the truth and divorce him and marry you."

"My dear Elisabeth—" Even had he still loved her, this would not have appealed to him. He had never been fond of fuss, and Elisabeth divorcing one brother to marry another would occasion fuss of a considerable kind. He marveled at the ruthlessness of the gentler sex. "Listen, Lisa, it would never do. Poor Robert. Really, it's impossible."

"You should have thought of that before."

"Yes, perhaps. But in any case you aren't going to divorce my brother and upset everyone. There's nothing to say it isn't his baby, is there? If you try anything I'll deny the whole thing and you'll find yourself without a husband of any kind and five illegitimate children."

To his surprised relief, Elisabeth, who normally had not much sense of humor, burst out laughing at this. "I suppose you're right, Jean. It wouldn't do. I was only being silly. I've been missing you so and being pregnant and all I guess I didn't think very straight. We'd much better go on as we are. We'll always love each other, no matter what."

Riebeck did not find this solution much more attractive than divorce, but Vienna would be a haven of sorts, and there would be a war fairly soon. He hugged her and said, "Angel, do you think we could have dinner?"

He had to wait for two days for his father. The longer he waited the more squeamish he felt. It was not difficult to guess what Colonel Riebeck would feel about a son of his leaving his regiment to take a desk job. Riebeck did not remember ever having discussed the subject of espionage with his father, but it was not difficult to know his ideas. Levantines with brilliantined hair, Russian duchesses prowling through the Orient Express, inscrutable Orientals paying out greasy money; Colonel Riebeck would hardly countenance his youngest son moving into such an unwholesome crew.

Riebeck had to admit that while he had not as yet met any Russian duchesses or inscrutable Orientals, there was something about Latour's office and the mysterious chief that was straight out of the penny novelettes. It was all a great nuisance, and between the complications with Elisabeth and Latour he heartily wished he had stayed in Indochina.

Colonel Riebeck arrived on Saturday afternoon in a good mood. His son allowed him to re-enforce this with an excellent dinner and then asked to have a talk with him.

"Well, what is it?" asked the Colonel, rubbing his moustache askew with impatience. He did not enjoy talks with his sons. "Have a brandy. It's very good. Much too good for you. Young people will drink anything nowadays, I've often noticed it."

"Yes, Papa. I do appreciate your brandy, you know."

"Hm. Easy to say. I suppose you'll be going back to Indochina soon. High time. I never had a six-month leave. All a lot of nonsense. What can you have wanted in Vienna all the time? Women, I suppose."

"No, Papa. I was working for Major Latour."

"Well, you're grown up, you must do as you like. None of you ever listens to me. There's going to be another war, isn't there?"

"Yes, Papa."

It was very difficult to come to the point while Colonel Riebeck indulged himself in fighting the '14 war over again. When he paused to pour himself another brandy, his son took the opportunity of telling him what he was going to do. The Colonel heard him out in unbelieving silence.

"What do you mean, intelligence work? Spying?"

"Yes, I suppose so, Papa."

Colonel Riebeck looked longingly at his riding crop, then back at his grown-up son, and decided against it. "You've made up your mind to leave your regiment?"

"Definitely."

"Nothing can make you change it?"

"No."

"You're sure?"

"Yes, Papa, I'm sure."

"Then get out and stay out. I'm not having any spies in my house."

Fighting down a slight feeling of hilarity at his father's patriarchal behavior, Jean said, "I am sorry, Papa."

He went upstairs, packed his uniforms, and went to the stable for Albertine's car. At the gate Elisabeth caught up with him.

"Jean, what's the matter? You're not going?"

"I'm afraid I have to. I've been thrown out. You see, I was offered a job at the legation in Vienna which sounded amusing, so I took it. But it involves a leave of absence from the regiment and you can imagine how Papa reacted to that. He told me never to darken his doorstep again."

"Oh, darling, how dreadful. Why are you laughing?"

"The Riebecks. They are such a funny family. And Robert gets more like Papa every year. Poor you. It's sad about us, isn't it?"

He kissed her hand and let in the clutch. She called something after him, but he made a terrible noise with his gears and pretended he hadn't heard. There had been a look in Elisabeth's eyes that he hadn't liked at all. She had looked ready to offer to share his exile.

When Riebeck reported to Latour's office the next morning he saw that another stripe had been added to the four on Jacques' sleeve. He bowed. "*Mon colonel.*"

"I owe it all to you. I told the chief I couldn't possibly remain a major and bully you. The chief said I was chiseling, but he saw it my way eventually."

"I've never understood why they made you even a major. Who is this chief?"

"A gentleman who does not like his name bandied about. How was your father?"

"In fine form. We aren't even speaking at this point."

"Good. And now come along. I want you to meet some very dear friends of mine."

The "dear friends" proved to be three men in striped uniforms who answered to such entrancing names as Pépé le Cochon, Tantan le Louche and, simply and respectfully, the Safebreaker. They were excellent teachers and Riebeck found them the greatest fun.

He learned that locks respond to wires and hairpins as well as keys, that objects can be picked up and slipped in the pocket while a room full of people look on none the wiser, and from Tantan, who practiced this art on checks, he learned that there were few signatures that could not be copied. Riebeck was slightly depressed by the fact that his three instructors had all been caught, but did not like to point it out, feeling that it would be tactless. He learned of ways to enter houses never dreamed of by the respectable, and was treated to reminiscences that would have made Sherlock Holmes' hair curl. All three crooks assured him that he would do well. He had that certain something without which no criminal, no matter how wicked, could be a success. For criminals, like poets, they told him, are born, not made.

Latour himself instructed him in the use of piano wire for strangling people, a method, he assured Riebeck, that was silent and quick and made much less mess than a knife.

"Have you ever actually tried it on anyone?"

"No, but it's in the Intelligence Manual," said Latour trustingly.

They worked out a code and Latour made Riebeck acquainted with a wine merchant in Vienna who, thanks to his profession, came into contact with what appeared to be harmless commercial travelers. His attitude toward the Nazis would be undecided but with definite leanings. Many otherwise perfectly respectable people had a high regard for the Nazis as a bulwark against the Red Hordes, so this attitude would be most becoming in the legation.

If he got into trouble he would have to rely on his wits and the legation, not the Deuxième. "From now on," said Latour, "I don't know you. God help you."

Since Latour was an atheist, Riebeck gathered that the outlook was dim.

"Please sign for this," said Latour, handing him a capsule.

"What is it?"

"Your cyanide. Haven't you ever read spy novels? When they torture you and you get fed up you bite on it and pouf, you are gone, quickly and painlessly."

"I don't suppose you've ever really tried that either."

"No, but it says so in the manual."

"Look, Jacques, cyanide is going too far. First of all it is not quick and painless as you would know if you read detective stories, and secondly my Papa would never forgive me if I didn't return with my shield or on it. Here, take it back."

"In that case," said Latour, "do not let them take you alive." With which encouraging remark ringing in his ears, Riebeck returned to Vienna.

VII

"*The major industry* of this town," Riebeck wrote Latour a month after his return to Vienna, "is pouring coffee and drinks into newspapermen. You don't need me."

Latour wrote back: "Your news gets here two days before it's in the papers and at least three weeks before the confidential reports from the Legation. Keep off the drinks and stick to the coffee."

To this Riebeck replied with a word which the conscientious young man in the coding room refused to send.

Riebeck had felt extremely foolish to be returning after six weeks when he had made his farewells for years, but the uncles and aunts had received him with as much pleasure as if he had been made ambassador. To make life even more pleasant Katalin arrived shortly after on the pretext of visiting her mother. When she learned that Madame de Pogany was in Budapest with Eva she gave it up and settled down at Baranyi Palace. At thirty-two, she was at the height of her beauty. The uncles admired her extravagantly; the aunts less so.

Riebeck devoted rather more time to Katalin than to his reports for Latour, which seemed to him entirely unnecessary. Vienna is a town with few secrets. Everyone talks all the time about everything. It is true that there are usually many versions of the same story and that Riebeck had a slight advantage over the newspaper people in occasionally being able to discover which was the true one, but he also knew that it would have made no difference to anyone in France if he had sent one of the current versions or had invented an entirely new one of his own.

One of his most helpful sources proved to be Count Xandi, who had been a Nazi since the earliest days of the party in Austria. Why he had chosen such a bizarre allegiance no one quite knew. It was just one of the annoying things Xandi spent his life doing. He was an utter ass and of no use to a clandestine party. But since the party did not plan to remain underground forever, Captain Leopold, its leader, had orders from Germany to be kind to its aristocratic members. A name like Graf Sandor van Baranyi looks very effective on party lists when they are finally published.

The family bore with Xandi as something heaven had sent to try them. But they drew the line at his friends. Franz, the Baranyi doorman, had orders to throw certain visitors of Count Xandi's down the stairs without ceremony, and he did not hesitate to obey this order even when once it was Captain Leopold in person.

Riebeck shared the uncles' feelings about Xandi's gang. "I held my nose and jumped," he wrote Latour. "Fortunately it did not take me long to discover that I was ingratiating myself with the wrong people. They are completely controlled from Germany. Even von Papen can do nothing about them. It will be a sad day for Vienna when they come into power. If you have wondered what bad novelists mean when they talk about the dregs of society, here they are. I am sending you, for what good it may do, a list of their members and also a list they have made of people who are to be liquidated come the dawn. You will see that Baranyi and Tisza are on it. So, for that matter, is von Papen. When I told the uncles (please don't write to tell me that it was injudicious, I know it was, but they are after all my uncles) they laughed heartily and Uncle Nikki said, 'Hold my hand, Pipi, I'm scared.' I'm telling you this because it is a fairly common reaction here. Anyone that is tactless enough to mention the Nazis get a standard answer: 'Yo, yo, die Preissn'—Prussians to you—and a shrug of the shoulders."

Riebeck next turned his attention to the German Legation. They were polite people but they naturally didn't want a French officer minding their business and he was not making much headway until luck helped him. One night during the intermission at the opera someone tapped him on the shoulder and he turned to find himself looking into the smile of his companion of the Orient Express.

"Colonel von Fahrenkamp." He was really pleased to see him. "What are you doing in Vienna?"

"But I am the new Military Attaché."

"You are? That's wonderful."

"And you? I thought you would long be back in Indochina."

"I had bad luck. I was posted to the French Legation here, as assistant to the Military Attaché. I don't care at all for office work, but the fact that it is in Vienna softened the blow. All my favorite relatives live here."

"Aha. The lovely lady in the box with you is a relative."

"As a matter of fact she's my aunt."

"That is not very chivalrous. We used to call them cousins in my younger days."

"She really is my aunt. At least she is the wife of my uncle. Would you like to meet her?"

"With the greatest pleasure."

"Excuse me a moment." Riebeck went across to where Katalin was talking to some people and detached her. "You have a new admirer. The German military attaché. Come and meet him. He's rather a friend of mine. Colonel von Fahrenkamp, Katalin. The Duchesse de St. Leger."

Von Fahrenkamp looked impressed, not, as Riebeck later discovered, because Katalin was a duchess, but because he had heard of the duke. He was also introduced to the Countesses and at once remembered having danced with Steffi in Potsdam in 1898 when Count Nikki had been one of the Austrian officers sent to Berlin in exchange for a group of Prussian officers who were sent to Vienna. After this he was immediately and enthusiastically absorbed into the family, watched the rest of the opera from the Tisza box, and came back to Baranyi Palace for supper.

When he took his leave at four in the morning, drunk enough to become voluble, he said to Riebeck: "I sympathize with you because I too prefer regimental life to sitting in an office, but I can see why this family consoles you. They are the most delightful people I've ever met."

"You're not half bad yourself for a German," said Uncle Pipi and slapped him on the back.

Riebeck and Katalin took him to lunch at Sacher's the next day, then to the Spanish Riding School and back to the Palace for dinner. The Baranyis virtually adopted him, and took him everywhere with them. Riebeck was hard put to keep his friend a little to himself. Many eyebrows were raised in Vienna at this sudden friendship. That Steffi and Pepi, those ardent monarchists, and Nikki and Pipi, who not a week before had been plotting to make Prince von Starhemberg regent of Hungary, should suddenly be so thick with the German military attaché was something to make one goggle. Riebeck occasioned less surprise. He had been going Nazi for some time. It was regrettable but not uncommon. Many sons of Vienna's best families were doing the same.

Under von Papen the German Legation was still working for

an Anschluss, but an amiable one. In other words, they didn't want the Austrians to shoot back. Riebeck appeared very broadminded about these things and von Fahrenkamp often discussed them with him. Von Papen's patience appeared to be paying off. Mussolini, involved in Abyssinia, was no longer the strong protection for Austria he had been in '34. Chancellor Schuschnigg visited Paris and London and returned without reassurance. Officially France and England were pledged to defend Austrian independence; in fact they weren't going to lift a finger and Schuschnigg knew it. Economically the German boycott was killing him. He was trapped. And von Papen rode to the rescue.

He drew up an agreement between Austria and Germany in which Germany pledged itself to keep out of Austrian affairs if Schuschnigg would take the National Opposition, as the Nazis were officially called, into his government. This plan was supposed to be so top secret that apart from von Papen only two people in Germany (one of them Hitler) and only Schuschnigg in Austria knew about it. But in Vienna nothing is ever that secret. After having cultivated von Fahrenkamp for a year Riebeck might reasonably have expected the leak to come from the German Legation, but this being intelligence work the information naturally came by way of Aunt Steffi.

"Poor Otto is upset," she said one evening as they were walking together in the Hofgarten. Since she owned a fat and depressing spaniel by that name, Riebeck did not immediately grasp whom she meant.

"Have you wormed him?"

"Otto von Habsburg. Have you wormed him! Honestly, Schani!"

"Oh, him."

"You might at least sound as sympathetic as when you thought it was the dog."

Riebeck was always bored by Steffi's devotion for the Austrian crown prince. "What's he upset about this time?"

"I didn't quite understand it. Some sort of agreement von Papen wants Schuschnigg to sign. Honestly, Schani, have you ever in your life met anyone as dull as Schuschnigg?"

"No."

"When he first became chancellor they used to say that there was a man in the belltower of the Stefansdom whose job it was to ring the bell when the first joke about Schuschnigg went around."

"I never heard that."

"Because nobody's made the joke yet."

Riebeck had been concealing his impatience because he did not want Steffi to think he was interested. But now he said, "You never finished telling me about Prince Otto."

"Oh, yes. It's some kind of agreement Schuschnigg was supposed to keep secret but he sent a copy to Otto and Otto said whatever you do, don't sign it."

Steffi appeared to have come to the end of her annals of royal life.

"So what did Schuschnigg say?"

"He said he'd have to. Schani, you remember my cousin Resi?"

With an effort Riebeck kept himself from shaking his aunt. "Yes Steffi. How is she?"

"She's the Empress Zita's lady-in-waiting now, did I tell you?"

"Is that where you get all your court gossip from?"

"Yes. She's always writing me letters because there's so little to do in Belgium."

"Didn't she tell you what the agreement was about?" Riebeck remembered Cousin Resi as an impressive lady with a moustache and a strong interest in politics. ("I think like a man" was her favorite boast, to which it was reported her husband had once replied: "You look like one too.")

"Well, she did. But I never pay much attention to the boring parts in her letters. Oh, Schani dear, it's all supposed to be terribly secret and Resi isn't supposed to know anything about it, so don't mention it to anyone."

"Scout's honor, Steffi," said Riebeck, who felt he had not as yet heard anything worth repeating. "Let's go home. I have a headache."

"Poor Schani. I'll give you baldrian."

"Thanks, I prefer the headache."

The Baranyis were dining out that night. Riebeck had considerable trouble fighting off all the kind offers of someone to keep him company. He waited until he was sure none of them would be coming back for forgotten gloves, handkerchiefs, scarves, or any of the numerous things the aunts were always leaving behind. Then he went to Steffi's desk and looked through her letters. He had never done anything like this with a relative's property and he did not like it at all. But when he found the letter from Belgium he forgot his scruples. Resi's spelling was terrible, but she was an enthusiastic snoop and she did think like a man.

Riebeck put his feet up on Steffi's desk, lit a cigarette, and settled down to a long session on the telephone. When Katalin stopped by after dinner to see whether he was better and cared to go to the theater he had entirely recovered from his headache, but persuaded her, without much trouble, that it would be more fun to stay home.

Two days later he received a telegram from Paris: "One thousand regrets, Aunt Sylvie dangerously ill. Come at once."

Steffi, another enthusiast for other people's mail, read it over Riebeck's shoulder. "Who's Aunt Sylvie, Schani?"

"I don't think you ever met her. She's religious and has lived a retired life. She is also very rich and she's always said she'd leave me her money, so I suppose I had better go."

"How nice for you. I mean, I do hope she'll get well, but one should always prepare for the worst."

Riebeck thought he could bear the worst with fortitude, since he had never, rich or poor, owned an Aunt Sylvie.

He got leave from the Legation where, until now, he had not made much of a mark, and drove straight to Paris.

He and Latour no longer met at the Deuxième. Though it poured rain, Riebeck went for a walk in the Luxembourg Gardens. Latour also felt the need for fresh air, and they collided, quite accidentally, of course, by the Medici Fountain. "Like Gide's counterfeiters," said Riebeck. "Aren't you being terribly cloak and dagger?"

Latour, who had not expected to be greeted with a literary allusion, was somewhat taken aback. "Not really," he said defensively. "Paris is crawling with so-called German tourists."

"This aunt—"

"Don't worry, we'll supply you with a dead aunt. It will all be quite authentic. Tell me all your troubles."

"Well," said Riebeck, "this thing, if it is true, is so top secret that it hasn't even leaked in Vienna yet, so I didn't like to send it through the legation. According to my Aunt Steffi's Cousin Resi—"

"Jean, I beg of you."

"It's true, but you needn't pass it on like that. Say you have it from the highest authority. Hitler and Schuschnigg are about to sign an agreement."

"About time too."

"Listen first. One of the terms states that Hitler pledges himself—Hitler, I ask you—to keep out of Austrian affairs if Schuschnigg allows the Austrian Nazis into his government."

"And the Austrian Nazis are run from Germany."

"Exactly."

"Schuschnigg is going to sign this?"

"What choice has he left? Mussolini told him to run along and play with Germany, and London and Paris weren't any more helpful. I didn't want to write anything down, so pay attention. These are the terms of the agreement." They walked through the rainy park, Riebeck talking, Latour listening, their hands shoved into pockets, coat collars turned up against the rain. When they passed Verlaine emerging like a genie from the vase that forms the pedestal of his statue Riebeck began to laugh. Ever since his earliest childhood this vase with the emerging poet had filled him with hilarity.

"Why are you laughing? It isn't funny."

"I know. It's Verlaine."

"You're mad. Let me buy you a drink."

"With pleasure. I thought you didn't want to be seen with me."

"Not at the Deuxième. In public it couldn't matter less. I'm in the department of statistics now. What could be more harmless?"

"Latrine inspection."

Three days after their first meeting Latour telephoned Riebeck at Madame de Baro's. "Bump into me accidentally at the Champs Elysées this afternoon."

"What time, which end?"

"About three, Madeleine end. Very accidentally."

83

"All right."

This day the sun shone and the Elysées was full of children. Latour got in first. "Like Proust and Gilberte."

"Quite so."

They stopped to watch Punch belabor a policeman.

"Shall I kill him?"

"Yes," shrieked the children. "Kill him."

"How like the Coliseum," said Riebeck. "You're looking very cheerful, Jacques. Don't tell me somebody is taking an interest in us at last."

"Lean against that tree before I tell you who. You have an appointment with Marshal Pétain at four tomorrow afternoon."

"*Kill him.*"

Riebeck turned his head to look at Latour. "Not me."

"They want you to tell them what you have told me."

"But that is all I know."

Punch beat the policeman and the children urged him on. Latour did not raise his voice over their noise, but he spoke with great intensity. "Jean, perhaps you can get those soldiers in petticoats to act. I think you must, or I don't know what will become of us."

Riebeck turned away without an answer and walked toward the Etoile. He knew that he was not the man for the job. He could describe a situation and outline a course of action. He had no gift for pleading and convincing.

Latour caught up with him. "What's the matter with you? Say something, damn it."

"It's not my sort of job," said Riebeck.

"You're landed with it. What are you going to tell the old pussies?"

"The truth, I suppose."

The truth sounded strangely without force in the room with the green baize table where Riebeck, the next afternoon, repeated once more the tale of the Schuschnigg-Hitler agreement. Marshal Pétain, two generals, and two colonels looked important and busy and professional, but none looked interested. One of the generals said, "I don't quite understand what it is you are concerned about,

84

Colonel. It is surely a desirable thing that Austria and Germany should come to an agreement."

"Yes, but this isn't an agreement. An agreement is something to which both parties consent. This is an ultimatum."

"If it will make for peace and quiet between Austria and Germany, what does that matter?"

"How do we know," the other general wanted to know, "that there is such an agreement at all?"

"That's not really important so long as we are, should there be such an agreement, prepared to act."

"Act, Colonel?"

Riebeck glanced at Marshal Pétain and saw that he had fallen asleep. He said that if Schuschnigg were assured of French support he would not need to sign the agreement. In '34 Mussolini's troops massed at the Brenner Pass and kept the Germans out of Austria. French troops on the Rhine would probably do the same thing. The mention of the Rhine did not go down very well, since Hitler not long ago had taken the Rhineland back without more than a verbal reproof from the French.

"And if just having the troops there is not enough, Colonel?"

"Then it would probably be better to fight them now rather than later."

And there the meeting ended. The last thing these generals wanted to do was fight. Marshal Pétain roused himself sufficiently to thank Colonel Riebeck for his valuable work and, to show that the army was not ungrateful, gave him a medal.

In June Elisabeth was delivered of a fat, healthy daughter whom she called Lisa.

In July the Hitler-Schuschnigg agreement was made public and was hailed everywhere as a great step toward peace.

Since coming to the French Legation Riebeck had not seen very much of Istvan. Istvan's work kept him in Budapest when he was not away with the Hungarian Equestrian Team. They spent their week ends together whenever possible, and Riebeck saw to it at such times that his cousin was provided with plenty of drink and disreputable female company. For things were not going well for Istvan.

Madame de Pogany refused to budge from her position of rich-duke-or-nothing. Eva said she would marry Istvan or remain a spinster, but at the same time held that disobedience to a parent was quite as much a sin as union unblessed by the church and that she did not intend to commit either. Istvan, who was too much in love to think straight, said that he would be willing to wait until Madame de Pogany either changed her mind or died, though he privately confided to Riebeck the fear that by that time he might be too old to consummate the marriage. Riebeck was extremely annoyed with Eva for tormenting Istvan so, but Istvan himself greatly admired Eva's piety and fortitude. They had discussed the problem in every detail and from every possible angle, and had concluded that unless something gave way—Eva's virtue or Eva's mother—it was insoluble.

Madame de Pogany realized at last that she had driven her daughter into a stalemate. Eva remaining a spinster was doing no one any good. So, while Riebeck was trying to budge the French, Madame de Pogany was busy finding a husband for Eva. She succeeded and precipitated one of those crises which the Baranyis and Tiszas so much enjoyed.

When Riebeck came back from Paris he found Baranyi Palace deserted except for Count Xandi, who told him that everyone had gone to Budapest to meddle in Eva's and Istvan's love affair.

"The old harridan's got a husband picked out for Eva," he told Riebeck at dinner. "You'll never guess who it is." Xandi mentioned the name of a gentleman who was indeed a duke and rich, but had nothing else to recommend him, being an old and intimate friend of the Duke de St. Leger.

Eva had announced publicly that rather than marry this choice of a fond mother, she would enter a convent. Istvan, she suggested with the ruthlessness of her romantic nature, could resign his commission and like the knight in the poem waste away in a reed hut outside the convent wall. The aunts, realizing that in his present state Istvan was capable of anything, packed their bags and the uncles and took off for Budapest.

"What a brawl," said Xandi. "You know what Steffi is. If darling Istvan wants something darling Istvan must have it or else. 'But he's a much better family,' she kept shrieking. 'Just look at that Esterhazy nose,' and the old Pogany dragon kept saying, 'Where's his Esterhazy money, I should like to know,' and this went on and on. I got so depressed I came back here."

"Where is Katalin?"

"Schani, you've been away for two weeks. You didn't think she'd sit here and knit until you came back, did you?"

"No, I suppose not."

"How's your aunt?"

"Better."

"Oh, bad luck."

Katalin may have been flighty, but she was not without family feeling, and ever since that summer in Venice she had preserved a special fondness for Istvan. She went to Budapest, though not with the aunts. Once there she took enough time from her momentary preoccupation to remind her mother that it was St. Leger money that allowed her to live so high on the hog and that this money could be withdrawn. Madame de Pogany said something about a serpent's tooth but she was beaten.

In Vienna Riebeck went to bed, wondering whether it was worth a trip to Budapest to watch the comedy. He had been asleep some time when Franz woke him to tell him that he was wanted on the telephone.

"Tell them to call back in the morning, Franz."

"It's long distance, Monsieur Schani."

"Paris?"

"Budapest, Monsieur Schani."

"Oh for Heaven's sakes!" He picked up the telephone. "Is that you, Istvan?"

"*Servus*, Schani, *comment ça va?* I'm getting married."

"Oh, to whom?"

"How very humorous."

"Last I heard Eva was taking the veil and you were joining the Foreign Legion to stand with frozen heart and unflinching face in the heat of battle."

"Schani, what's the matter with you?"

"I'm sleepy. Do you know what time it is?"

"Sorry. You'll be best man, won't you?"

"Of course. When?"

"As soon as possible. I'll let you know. Have you ever been best man?"

"Twice."

"Then you know what to do."

"Get you drunk the night before and sober the morning after."

"I'm scared, Schani."

"Cheer up. I'll come to Budapest and I'll hold your hand till it's all over. Now let me go back to sleep."

"You promise?"

"I swear. Goodnight, Istvan."

Istvan, who had never had any to spare, had lost weight and looked haggard. But he was jubilant when Riebeck arrived at Tisza Palace.

"Do you know, the aunts wanted the wedding at the Stefansdom. I had an awful time to talk them out of it."

"What are the plans now?"

"We're getting married at Hommages day after tomorrow. At least the chapel there doesn't hold a thousand guests. It'll be scary enough without that."

"So are we going to Hommages?"

"Let's go out and get drunk first. Maybe I'll feel braver to-morrow."

Riebeck was agreeable. "Where to?"

"Maria Terezia Barracks. I want you to meet Palko."

"Who is Palko?"

"A friend of mine. He's a Communist."

Riebeck said nothing. That Istvan should have a Communist friend was so out of the ordinary that he wanted to laugh.

"What does he do, this Palko?"

"He's an officer, of course."

"In Horthy's army?"

"He doesn't go about saying so, naturally. But in his father's house he has a party card cemented in the wall behind a brick, waiting for the revolution."

"How charming. And he told you all this?"

"Yes."

"Does he know who your mother was?"

"Yes. I tell you, Schani, you'll like him."

Riebeck was quite prepared to like any friend of Istvan's, but he had no intention of ever liking a Communist; Communists being in his eyes raving maniacs itching to get at the Rosenstil fortune.

"He isn't that kind of Communist," said Istvan, correctly interpreting his friend's silence. "You'll like him, you'll see."

And Riebeck did like him; Lieutenant Pal Donath, short, cocky, and very cheerful. He reminded Riebeck not so much of a Communist as of a large, faithful watchdog. Riebeck had long been uneasy about Horthy and his flirtation with the Nazis, and was glad to see Istvan would have a good friend close by when trouble happened.

Riebeck, Istvan, and Palko had themselves a very enjoyable evening, visiting such bars and brothels as struck their fancy, until Palko remembered that he had to be on duty in an hour. Istvan offered to drive him back in Riebeck's car, claiming that as a native he was more familiar with the short cuts of Budapest. They drove all over Buda without finding the barracks, which are located in Pest. Palko was past noticing and Riebeck lay on the back seat of the car, watching with fascinated interest a drunken moon tumbling amid whirling and bouncing stars in a madcap sky.

Eventually Istvan ran down a policeman who agreed to drive them to the barracks and then back to Tisza Palace, where, protesting loudly that he was an officer of the law and could not possibly accept a reward for doing his duty, he quickly pocketed the banknote Istvan gave him.

Istvan, declaring that he wanted a shower, headed for the park. Riebeck suggested that they might use the bathroom, but Istvan was beyond such palterings with the stern facts and made determinedly for the Tisza Fountains, shedding his clothes on the way. Riebeck laughed and followed him.

"Have Zeus," said Istvan hospitably. "I'll take Neptune."

"Thank you."

They climbed in the moonlight amid the pale spray of water, stepping over Greek gods and using fat wet cupids for footholds, until they arrived on the top of Olympus, high above the water-lily pool.

"Observe," said Istvan, always the good host, "observe the view."

"The view," said Riebeck politely, "is magnificent."

Istvan, balancing with the drunk's undeserved equilibrium, said he was going to dive.

"You'll kill yourself," Riebeck told him, having arrived at the magisterial stage of drunkenness. "You're up too high and the pool is too shallow."

Istvan bent down to look and said again, "I'm going to jump."

"All right, but hurry. I'm cold."

Istvan said between chattering teeth that he was warm.

"Eva," Riebeck pointed out, "will be sad when you kill yourself."

"*La pauvre*," said Istvan with genuine sympathy, and turning vengeful, added, "If you plant lilies on my grave I'll haunt you."

"No lilies, I swear. What would you like instead?"

"Truffles," said Istvan and overcome at the beauty of this thought burst into tears. Then he bent over and held out his hand. "*Servus* Schani. It's been a privilege, knowing you."

"You too." They shook hands solemnly and nearly fell off. At the last moment Riebeck said, "I can't let you do it alone, Istvan. I'm coming with you."

Istvan's gargoyle face twisted into cheerful laughter. He stood for a moment, gaunt and poised, and laughed at his friend. Then they swung out together from the gray gods of Olympus to the water lilies floating on the shallow pool.

The policeman, who had been watching, fascinated, these antics of the aristocracy, jumped from the gate and walked quickly away. He was certain both the foolish young men would be dead and he had no wish to become involved in the subsequent paper work.

The next night Istvan's brother officers gave him a party at Hommages, so that on the morning of the wedding Istvan was in very poor shape. Riebeck, finally remembered his duty as best man, forced Istvan into a cold bath and made him drink a pot of black coffee, none of which diminished Istvan's feeling of utter misery.

"Schani," he pleaded movingly, "tell the bishop I'm in no shape to get married. Look at me."

"Get dressed," said Riebeck unsympathetically. "Thank God we're not civilians or we would have to wear a morning coat and a silk hat."

Istvan said he had always been too poor to own a morning coat and looked depressed.

"Ugly things," Riebeck consoled him. "You'd look hideous in one."

Istvan said he looked hideous in everything and everybody hated him. Riebeck's bracing lack of sympathy finally got him dressed and to the altar.

The wedding followed a slow and stately course. The Uncles looked magnificent in their leopard capes, the aunts wore quite unbelievable hats and blew their noses like trumpeters, Eva was properly radiant, Katalin had returned from her excursion and was among the guests, and if Istvan looked like a temperance poster no one could see it except Archbishop Jarnitz, who in Christian charity attributed it to love.

Finally it was all over and Istvan had survived without falling flat on his face. Riebeck, recalling one of his favorite Kipling stories, whispered: "Dismiss, Break off, Left wheel!" which Istvan automatically obeyed.

At the celebrations which followed Istvan recovered with the aid of a bottle of *palinka* and became very cheerful.

The wedding party lasted for three days, but Istvan and Eva left that first afternoon for Uncle Pipi's yacht on Lake Balaton, seeing no reason for postponing another moment what was at last consecrated by Archbishop Jarnitz.

VIII

In February 1938 von Papen was fired, Aunt Sylvie had a relapse, and Riebeck went to Paris. The situation in Austria had deteriorated to such an extent that even some of the higher-ups in France were now interested. One of them was the general who had been so dense at the interview with Marshal Petain. His name was L'Abbé. He, Latour, and Riebeck had many meetings in a room in a private hospital near the Bois de Boulogne.

"You seem to be very well in with these people," said General L'Abbé after Riebeck had discussed and documented the plans of Xandi's friends.

"They can afford to trust me because I'm compromised. You see, these plans are mine."

"Honestly, Jean, isn't that going too far?" asked Latour.

"They're flashy but not practical. I don't think they'd work. But they have this on me. If I don't behave they can send this stuff to Paris and I'll be in hot water."

"What will you do if they blackmail you into something you can't fake?" asked General L'Abbé.

"Come home?"

The general looked stony.

"Kill myself?"

"Never," protested Latour. "Let them frame you. We'll court-martial you, you escape to Germany, and there you are."

"Colonel Latour," said the general, "the army does not rig courts-martial as a favor to the Deuxième. I think, Riebeck, on the whole suicide would be best."

"I'm so glad you think so," said Riebeck humbly. He glanced at the plans. "We're doing France now. I'm to be Gauleiter of Alsace Lorraine."

"Congratulations."

"That's their great bait, you know. They promised Xandi Hungary."

"Aren't these plans rather grandiose, Riebeck?"

"Oh, I don't know. It wouldn't surprise me if they did it."

Aunt Sylvie lingered. General L'Abbé, Latour, and Riebeck faithfully continued their visits to the hospital.

"Schuschnigg went to Berchtesgaden," General L'Abbé said one afternoon.

"Did he have a nice visit?"

"I don't think so. Hitler screamed at him for eleven hours without pausing for breath."

"What about?"

"He wanted a job for one of his pals. Seyss-Inquart is to be Austrian chief of police."

"Seyss-Inquart? You mean Schuschnigg is to have a Nazi chief of police?"

"He's not a party member, you know."

"Yes, I know. That's their ace in the hole."

"Schuschnigg didn't like it either. But Hitler didn't bother to argue. He simply tore open the door and roared: 'Keitel, where is Keitel?' "

"Keitel was there?"

"Oh yes. And General Reichenau and General Sperrle. He's the head of the Bavarian Luftwaffe, as doubtless you know."

"What did Keitel say?"

"I don't know. They lowered their voices after that. Our man was outside, waxing the stairs, so he couldn't hear any more. But I should imagine it would settle the argument, Keitel and Sperrle being there."

"I hope you give your man the *croix de guerre* with palms," said Riebeck. "He's earned them. I think we ought to let Aunt Sylvie die or recover. I'd better get back to Vienna."

Schuschnigg gave one more wriggle. He called for a plebiscite. When Riebeck returned to Vienna everyone was talking about it.

The uncles were at Baranyi Palace, and were, as always, delighted to see him. "Come into the library, dear boy. The rest of the palace is a madhouse."

"I've noticed it. Are you planning a mass escape?"

Maids and footman, displaying every symptom of hysteria, were dashing about with trunks, their arms full of clothes.

"Steffi and Pepi are going to America."

"Good heavens! It's an excellent idea, really, but a little drastic. Why not Budapest, or Paris?"

"One hears stories," said Count Nikki, "about Gestapo organizations in other countries which manage to bring back the reluctant relatives of those who have opposed the Reich."

Riebeck did not think the Gestapo would consider the uncles as important as all that, but it obviously gave them pleasure to think of themselves as desperate fellows, and the aunts would probably enjoy their holiday in America.

"Don't forget to make them take all their jewelry just in case," he said.

"A good idea. A lot of the diamonds are still at the bank. We'd better get them out, Nikki. And now, Schani, tell us what you think of this plebiscite."

"I think it's come at the worst possible time."

"It was the French consul that suggested it."

"I know. My government is for it. I still think it's a mistake."

"I said as much to Schuschnigg. You know what Xandi says, Schani?" Count Pipi burst out laughing. "He says 'We won't stand for it.' 'You and who else,' I asked him, and he said, 'Me and Herr Hitler.' It's charming to have such a well-connected son."

During the following days everything was confusion. There was a large party to celebrate the departure of the countesses. The actual departure surpassed in madness everything that had gone before. Everyone constantly counted the forty-seven pieces of luggage. They were content when they got more—at one happy instance they counted sixty-one—but when they got forty-six hysteria ensued.

Steffi's maid lost her smelling salts, Pepi couldn't find her Mothersill's, knocked the pheasant off her hat in getting into the motor car, got out again and insisted on searching through forty-seven trunks to make sure the maid had packed her other false fringe, while the maid, having misplaced her statue of the Infant Jesus of Prague, interpreted this as an evil omen and began to say her rosary out loud.

Despite all expectations they were finally stowed into the car while three more were loaded with the luggage, and tearfully protesting that they had changed their minds and were going to stay home, the aunts departed at last.

With much less fuss Riebeck managed to get the uncles into his car and out of Vienna. They left half a day ahead of the Nazis. The car bore on its bonnet the red, white, and blue pennant of the French Legation. Riebeck had his diplomatic passport as well, and they encountered no difficulty at the border.

They ate dinner that night at Tisza Palace with Istvan and Eva. Despite the precarious situation in Austria they were all gay. Uncle Pipi kept them in shouts of laughter with the story of the aunts' departure, and Xandi's lordly Me and Herr Hitler. Riebeck reflected how nice they were to talk in front of him as if he had never expressed a pro-Nazi sentiment. How embarrassing it would have been had they been tactful and considered his supposed feelings!

Laughing, they went into the drawing room for their coffee and liqueurs. Eva switched on the radio and turned the dial to find gypsy music for the uncles. She came instead upon a station which was broadcasting Chancellor Schuschnigg's farewell speech to Austria.

The uncles walked across the room and pretended to look out the window, not noticing the drawn curtains. Istvan Halyi glared at his riding boots. When he had learned that Riebeck was in Budapest he had rushed straight from the barracks, not giving himself time to change. But now he refused to meet his friend's eyes.

Schuschnigg ended his speech: "God protect Austria." For the last time the Austrian national anthem was played and was interrupted suddenly by the *Horst Wessel Lied*. Riebeck reached across the table and switched off the radio.

No one spoke. Istvan was still glaring steadfastly at his boots. Eva glared at Riebeck.

Finally Count Nicolas turned from the window and said, "Thank you, Schani, for making us leave Vienna. You probably saved our lives, but I don't mean that. Pipi and I are both old, and our lives are not very important. But we are grateful that you spared us the sight of this. Nazis in Vienna."

"I am very glad I did. But I think I had better get back myself. The Legation—"

"We quite understand," said Eva. "You will want to celebrate with your Nazi friends." She went out, slamming the door. Katalin would have been more graceful about it, Riebeck thought.

"I apologize for my wife," drawled Istvan. "She's been badly brought up. You know her mother."

"I am sorry you have to leave us so soon," said Count Nikki, overriding with his powerful voice anything that would remain better unsaid. "Before you go, Schani, Pipi and I have something to tell you. We can't be very sure that our lives are safe, even in Budapest. It's unlikely that anything will happen to us, but we have taken it into consideration. In any case we will not be able to return to Vienna for a very long time, if ever. What I am trying to say is that we want you to have Baranyi Palace. Please do not interrupt me, I haven't finished. It is yours provisionally as of now. If we should be able to return to Vienna, we shall of course want it back. When we die it is yours without any further provisions. You'd better see our lawyer when you get back to Vienna—there are things to sign."

Riebeck found himself without a word to say. He looked across at Istvan, who grinned at him like a delighted gargoyle.

"Thank you very much," he said finally. "I am deeply grateful. But I must refuse. If you don't want to let Xandi have the palace it should be Istvan's."

"Good Lord," said Istvan appalled, "I could never afford the taxes on the thing. No, you have it, Schani."

"Istvan will have Tisza Palace when we die," said Count Nikki, "and all the parts of the estate that aren't entailed. The rest will have to go to Xandi. We did think of leaving Baranyi Palace to Istvan, but as he says, he can't afford it and there is another consideration. Istvan is a Hungarian, and an officer in the Hungarian army. I do not think that his being the absentee owner of a house in Vienna would prevent anyone from looting it. When it belongs to you it will be the property of a member of the French Legation. That will be much safer."

Riebeck did not agree with Count Nikki; the Nazis had wrecked diplomatic property before this. He was sure Count Nikki did not believe it either, but he was grateful to him for not stating the obvious truth; that in belonging to Riebeck the Palace would be safe because it would belong to a friend of the Nazis.

"All right," he said. "I accept. And I hope I shall be able to return the palace to you very soon. And now I really must go."

He said goodbye to the uncles, thanked them inadequately—what thanks are adequate for the gift of a house designed by Cuvilliers?—and went downstairs. Istvan came with him.

"I'm sorry Eva was so rude."

"How nice of you."

"I mean it, Schani. I don't say I don't hate what you're doing—"

"I know you do. Istvan, could you just take me on trust for a while?"

Istvan smiled at his friend. "All the trust in the world, Schani."

"Thank you."

They went out into the courtyard where Riebeck had parked his car. "Schani," said Istvan, "would you write me a letter, please, when you get to the Palace. I'd love to know what sort of face Xandi will make when he sees you. He's had his eye on it for years. He wants to sell the Brueghels to pay his gambling debts."

"God forbid. Istvan, are you sure you don't want it yourself?"

"Don't be an ass. I like your having it. Goodbye, Schani. Weep over Vienna for me."

"That I shall. *Servus*, Istvan."

The sun was gold in a golden sky and the Danube was actually blue for once as Colonel Riebeck drove into Vienna. The city was jubilant. Even knowing that the people who had no reason to rejoice had either fled or were lying low, and that crowds are caught up as mindlessly into jubilation as into panic, the amount of enthusiasm astonished him. He decided to have breakfast at the Bristol. It was always full of newspapermen and gossip.

"*Heil Hitler*," said the colorfully uniformed black doorman.

"A merry *Heil Hitler* to you, Batu," Riebeck answered crossly.

Batu opened the car door. It is difficult to see when black people are frightened. They don't turn white with fear. Riebeck guessed it from Batu's eyes. He was showing a good deal of white there.

97

"My poor Batu, how will you ever prove that you are one hundred per cent Aryan?"

The black man shrugged. "At least I am not a Jew."

"That's right," Riebeck agreed. "Always look at the bright side."

"*Heil Hitler,*" the desk clerk greeted him.

"*Heil Hitler,*" said the lift boy.

But the waiter who brought him his breakfast greeted him with the old Viennese: "*Küss die Hand, Herr Baron.*" The title is a meaningless courtesy bestowed on the untitled in the hope that they will tip more generously.

"*Heil Hitler,* Hansl," Riebeck said severely.

"Feh!" said Hansl.

After breakfast he went to the Legation. There were many brown and black uniforms, many swastika armbands in the streets. In the buttonholes of the civilians the diamond-shaped swastika pin had sprouted overnight. Plainly the Viennese had been prepared for the evil day.

Far from being able to weep over Vienna for Istvan Halyi, Riebeck found himself forced to exasperated laughter.

"Quite the stranger here," said the Military Attaché. "Everyone all right?"

"Yes, no thanks to your plebiscite idea."

"It was only a last try. Nothing could have stopped things."

"It was very quick, wasn't it?"

"Quick and quiet."

Though neither said so, the unspoken thought between them was that such prompt surrender was contemptible. There was no fortune-teller to tell them that in two years Paris too would surrender without a shot fired.

"Incidentally, the Gestapo has completely taken over the Austrian police," said the Military Attaché. "They are temporarily quartered at the German Legation."

"That's not surprising."

"I just thought I would mention it."

Count Pipi's lawyer was not one of the cheerful Viennese, though whether he was anti-Nazi or simply professionally lugubrious,

Riebeck could not tell. He signed any number of documents, shocking the lawyer very much by the careless manner in which he refused to read them or have their contents explained to him.

"Much too dull," he said firmly.

"You'll sign your life away one of these days," said the lawyer.

No talk of war had resulted in the world's press from the take-over of Austria. Yet they both knew that war had moved close enough to be touched.

"Supposing," said Riebeck, "that for some reason or other I have to be away from Vienna for a long time, how can I keep the palace from being looted by anyone that fancies it?"

"You can't, if you mean will the law protect you. My advice would be to ask Count Sandor to continue living there."

"I was going to do that anyway. He's a magpie, though."

"Here is a complete inventory. There's another copy of it in my safe. I think Count Sandor can be frightened into respecting other people's property."

"I expect he can. I wonder if I can frighten his pals."

"No, Colonel Riebeck, nobody can do that any more. Which reminds me, I have a piece of bad news for you. Your cook has given notice."

Since Riebeck had always felt that Alphonse, the uncles' French cook, was one of the things that made life worth living, this was definitely a blow. At the same time he had to laugh. It was so typically Viennese to worry about a cook on a day like this.

"Is it money? I'll pay him whatever he likes."

"No. He said he would not cook for Count Sandor."

"What nerve."

"He has the artistic temperament."

Several of Vienna's top restaurants had in the past tried to bribe Alphonse away from the uncles. "Who bagged him?"

"Sacher's."

"To be sure. Did you tell him the Palace was mine, not Count Xandi's?"

"Yes. But I think he felt, as you do yourself, that you might not be in Vienna much longer."

Not till late in the evening did Riebeck manage to get to Baranyi Palace. He found every window lit and black Mercedes saloon cars with swastikas on the doors blocking the Herrengasse. He slammed the knocker against the heavy door, and while he waited, read the inscription above it. *"Mon coeur au dames, ma vie au roi, à dieu mon âme, l'honneur pour moi."* Yes indeed.

Franz was crying silently; the tears ran from his eyes without sound. "Monsieur Schani," he said, "Oh my God."

"You're not crying, Franz."

"Why not?"

"I know. But don't."

"How are their Excellencies, Monsieur Schani?"

"Safe and well in Budapest, Franz. I take it Count Xandi is home. I have news for him."

Franz stopped crying. "We know, Monsieur Schani. The man from the lawyer's office was here this morning. If I may say so, we're all very pleased."

Riebeck interpreted this correctly to mean the staff was pleased, not Xandi. He went upstairs to the dining-room. He could hear the drunken noise from the bottom of the steps. On the dark landing he stopped and lit a cigarette. He forced himself, with the most tremendous effort of will, to control the icy fury that shook him. He had got to the end of the cigarette before he could trust himself to open the door to the dining-room.

The table had all its leaves in. Food was spilled on the damask cloth, candles had been turned over and had scorched brown circles. Everyone was extremely drunk. Everyone was in uniform. The black of the SS dominated the gray of the army.

Riebeck would have given everything he owned to be able to say, in the voice which would make the request a mortal insult: "This is my house, get out!"

When he had returned from Indochina he had despaired of ever finding a task that would demand all his courage and effort. He had not looked for it in this guise, but he recognized it.

He smiled and without raising his voice he said into the drunken roar: *"Servus,* Xandi."

Xandi was very drunk, but his manners were part of him and

drink did not swamp them. He wore the black uniform with the double lightning bolts of the SS on the collar. There was no denying the fact that he looked very handsome in it.

He stood up. "Schani." He was pleased, but inarticulate. "Hey, Schani!"

"My congratulations, Xandi."

Someone from the other end of the table shouted: "Riebeck, have a drink. To a German Austria."

He accepted a glass. "To a German Austria," he said. "And to all of you who worked so hard for it. My congratulations."

Early the next morning Colonel Riebeck, tenderly holding his head between his hands, came down the stairs on his way to the Legation. At the door he stopped and said to Franz, "I'm worried about you."

"Me, Monsieur Schani?"

"All those people you kicked downstairs. I know you can say you did it because you were ordered to, but I'm not sure it's enough of an excuse. Perhaps you'd better go to Budapest."

Franz smiled broadly. "That's all right, Monsieur Schani. I'm a Gestapo spy."

Riebeck wished his head were in better shape to deal with this information. Perhaps he ought to follow Latour's advice and switch to lemonade. But Xandi's friends were not tolerable unless heavily diluted with alcohol.

"I'm surprised at you, Franz. Only yesterday you were crying."

Franz smiled more broadly still. "They pay me. I'd be a fool to turn them down."

"I suppose you would. I'm damned if I'll tip you for this information, Franz."

"Oh no, it's a present, Monsieur Schani. But if there's ever anything I can do for you, I wanted you to know I can be bought."

Riebeck went out into the street. He would have shaken his head, had it not felt too frail to withstand such activity. He supposed every doorman, green-aproned *hausmeister*, and waiter in Vienna was already in Gestapo pay and was at the same time willing to receive money from any other source. It was decent of Franz to tell him. A Gestapo spy! Dear God, what a people.

No one had expected the Austrian Nazi Party to behave well when it came into power. Nor did they. The Jews of Vienna had always led precarious lives; outbreaks of brutal and violent anti-Semitism had been common at various periods of the city's existence. It seemed to be the ambition of Vienna's Nazis to make the previous pogroms seem no more than a bit of good-natured teasing by comparison. But it was not only the Jews who suffered; indeed the rich ones were allowed to leave the country at the cost of leaving behind everything they owned. No such courtesy was extended to the personal enemies of the people now in power. The Austrian Nazis had long memories and now had the opportunity of paying back old debts. It soon became practical to have a local concentration camp rather than deport such large numbers of people to Germany.

Riebeck had a talk with Xandi, in the course of which he assured him that he had no intention of putting him out in the street (he could not have done so had he wanted to; if Xandi fancied the palace his friends would quickly see to it that he got it). He also said, though gagging on the words, that Xandi's friends would now be welcome; that he considered them his friends as well.

Count Xandi took full advantage of this offer. There was only one thing that could be said for his friends: they all talked a lot. Riebeck was not sure how useful their gossip might be. It was increasingly difficult to help people escape, it was not always easy, even, to warn them in time. As for larger plans, he reported them as a matter of form. He knew from experience that nothing would be done.

He hoped that not too many reports of his conduct would travel to Budapest. Gossip had always moved swiftly between the two cities, but now Vienna under its continuing surface pleasantness was beleaguered and there was some justice in his hope that the uncles might not hear of the people who frequented the palace now. Of Istvan Halyi he could no longer bear to think. He knew he had a great deal of credit to exhaust with Istvan, but he would have respected him less had that credit been inexhaustible.

In Budapest a warm summer rain washed the dust from the trees and blew in the open windows of Tisza Palace. The uncles, Eva, and Istvan were at lunch.

"Do shut the window, Eva," said Uncle Nikki. "This is worse than a picnic."

Eva smiled at him. "The lime trees are smelling again. It's been so hot and dry they haven't had any smell at all."

"It smells like Vienna," said Uncle Pipi, sniffing appreciatively.

The butler came in. "Good," said Istvan. "Phipps, would you close the window, please. It's raining in."

Phipps was a piece of swank on Count Nikki's part. Not many families in Budapest had English butlers. Very conscious of his superiority, Phipps did not consider it part of his duties to open or close windows, and said with dignity that he would send up a footman. Three men, he added, turning to the uncles, who had refused to give their names, saying that they would mean nothing to their Excellencies, said that they had messages from the Countesses. Would their Excellencies see them?

"How odd," said Count Nikki. "I suppose we all have to."

"I don't see why. You don't know them," said Istvan.

"But if they have messages."

"I have to get back to the barracks. Come down with me, Eva."

On the stairs they passed Phipps showing up the three visitors. They were in civilian dress and might to someone less discerning than an English butler have looked like gentlemen. Phipps appeared to have a low opinion of them, judging by the angle of his nose. Istvan too had a feeling that there was something about them he did not like. Their eyes, possibly.

"I forgot my cigarettes upstairs," he said to Eva. "So long, darling."

"Don't be late tonight. We're dining with Matyi."

"Right."

Eva went to her own rooms and Istvan went back upstairs. His entrance checked the three visitors in some action they had been about to perform. They asked politely whether they could speak to their Excellencies alone.

"This is our nephew, Captain Halyi," said Count Pipi, and to Istvan added, much as one having heard the doctor's diagnosis might repeat, "It's the Black Death," "They are the Gestapo."

"Throw them out," said Istvan.

"I was about to do so," admitted Count Pipi.

"Pray allow us one moment," said the leader of the group. "We have letters from the Countesses von Tisza and Baranyi, which I am sure you will want to see." He was bored. The Gestapo had evolved a trick that had never failed them, indeed could not fail, considering the people on whom they used it. They had been doing the same thing everywhere through Austria, in Hungary and in Prague, and other places where people had gone before the Nazi invasion. It might have been amusing once or twice but, its infallibility established, it had become a bore.

They put on the table two letters written in the handwriting of the aunts. The wording was almost identical. It always was. It said the Gestapo was holding the aunts as hostages until the Counts should give themselves up.

Istvan read the letters and said, "Forgeries, of course. They left two months ago for America."

"Have you heard from them since?"

"A cable to say they'd arrived."

"It is not," said the Gestapo officer mildly, "beyond human ingenuity to send a cable in someone's name. Have they written?"

"It is not beyond human ingenuity to intercept letters either," said Istvan. "I'm sure you're good at it."

"It's Pepi's handwriting, Istvan," said Count Pipi.

The Countess Josephine wrote as she had been taught by the nuns in the finishing school she had attended almost forty years ago, a beautiful, ornate hand, as illegible as embroidery.

"I can't say it looks much like Steffi's," said Count Pipi. "But then it never does."

Any forger would have had difficulty with the Countess Stephanie's handwriting. It was never the same two days running. Two lines filled a page. Any chicken with ink on its feet could have walked across the page and produced a credible facsimile.

The Counts, who habitually treated the smallest contretemps as a calamity, accepted real calamity with admirable calm. "*Tu viens, Nikki?*" said Count Pipi to his cousin. They had given up speaking German since the Anschluss, to show Hitler what they thought of him.

"Eh? Yes, of course, my dear fellow. Just a moment while I fill my cigar case."

Istvan remained silent with astonishment. It was so manifestly a trick that he had not thought even his uncles, who were admittedly no leading intellectual lights, capable of falling for it.

"You're not going," he shouted at them when he got his voice back. "Don't you realize it's a trick, a stupid, transparent trap to get you into a concentration camp?"

"Very likely it is, my dear," said Count Pipi, while his cousin carefully arranged the cigars in his case. "But one cannot take the chance that it isn't."

Istvan turned on the three Gestapo officers, who had stood silently by. "The Countesses are in America. You couldn't possibly have caught them. Besides, you have no right to be here, and I shall call the police."

"Of course, if you do not care what happens to your aunts, Captain Halyi."

"You are bluffing," said Istvan, but did not pick up the telephone.

"Call the police then and see."

"Istvan, Istvan," said Count Nikki reprovingly, "what a fuss. We're old men, Pipi and I. You're a dear boy to take it so hard, but don't."

"I'll find Schani," said Istvan. "He'll get you out quickly, you'll see."

"Yes, of course. A splendid idea," said the uncles, not because they believed it, but because it appeared to cheer up Istvan. "Good-by, my dear, good-by."

They both embraced him and kissed him and patted his shoulders and fussed over him as if he and not they were in need of comfort.

The Gestapo officers stood aside to let the uncles precede them out the door. Count Nikki took Count Pipi's arm and said in the clear loud voice he used for discussing animals and servants, "They are polite at least, these Boches."

Istvan had let them go, standing still and unmoving for a long moment, numbed by the suddenness of it. Then he caught himself up. Though he was in uniform he was unarmed, but he had his hands, after all, and the house was full of servants. He yanked the bellpull till it tore from the wall, and ran out of the room. The uncles were in the hall, putting on their coats. Istvan tore down the stairs—"Duck, Uncle!"—smashed his riding boots and spurs into the belly of one of the Germans and his fist into the nose of the other, hardly aware of the blow of the third one's fist in his own face.

"They're Gestapo, Phipps," he called to the butler who stood by, frozen with astonishment, holding a coat.

"I see, sir," said Phipps, and with decorum stuck out his foot to trip one of them who was lunging out at Istvan.

"Gestapo," he said to the servants whom the ringing bell had brought. The bootboy tore a support from the banister and hit the butler on the head. He had secretly worn the swastika pin under his lapel for months. This was the first blow he had been able to strike for the Reich.

Janos tackled the bootboy and smashed his head against the marble floor. The others brawled among themselves. The Nazi faction consisted mostly of the younger servants, and had by far the best of it. Istvan brought his knee up into the groin of one of the Germans and laughed to see him double up and yell. Monsieur Dulac, the cook, who had providently arrived with a sharp knife in his hand, lunged for another of the three, but Istvan got in his way and Monsieur Dulac slashed his respected young master from elbow to shoulder.

"Oh good, a knife," said Istvan, took it from the cook and dived back into the brawl.

The uncles were attempting to revive the butler. "Tsk tsk," said Count Pipi.

"Yes," agreed Count Nikki. "Isn't it."

The Gestapo, of course, went everywhere armed. But they were not accustomed to using their revolvers. The need never arose. What with the suddenness of the attack, the general brawl it immediately developed into, and the intense pain of Istvan's unsporting blows, they did not think of drawing their guns for several minutes. The articulate member of the three, the one Monsieur Dulac had meant to eviscerate, finally remembered that brawls are easily stopped with a Luger. He fired into the crowd and killed one of the servants—a Nazi as it happened.

The brawling stopped instantly, falling into a room full of silence, rimmed with the echo of the shot.

Count Nicolas had not seen that anyone had been killed. He was smiling. "There, Istvan, now you will have to stop. Oh, but you are a dear boy. Shall we go, gentlemen?"

Istvan drove straight to Vienna, without stopping, his foot pushing the gas pedal down to the floor, his arm carelessly bandaged with a handkerchief and still bleeding.

Count Xandi's guests were too drunk to be startled by the door's being flung open and Istvan Halyi standing in its frame, his uniform torn and one sleeve soaked with blood.

"You're drunk," Count Xandi greeted him disagreeably. "Go to bed."

Istvan did not answer him. He was not aware that Xandi had spoken. Anger choked him, red-hot in his throat and behind his eyes.

The uncles taken prisoner by the Gestapo, and Schani Riebeck was sitting in the palace—his palace now, thanks to them, drinking with them, laughing. . . . He had been laughing when Istvan had come in, with a red and black German general.

He was not laughing now. He looked at Istvan, the bruised face, the bloody sleeve, the murderous eyes. He looked at him with understanding and affection, and then withdrew both, standing up, leaving on view a mask of courtesy and competence. Istvan knew he was about to be dealt with and it enraged him. He waited.

"Istvan," said Riebeck, going up to him.

Istvan stopped leaning against the door. All his angry strength went into his unhurt arm, and lashing out, he smashed his fist into Riebeck's face.

Riebeck, unprepared, was caught off balance and crashed backward into the table. He had no impulse to return the blow. He sat, holding his jaw. The fat general brought him a glass of brandy. He drank it thankfully.

Count Xandi pleaded again. "Get rid of him, Schani, do."

None of the guests except the general were sufficiently sober to have noticed anything untoward. Riebeck sighed and stood up. He said firmly, "Come to the library, Istvan, Xandi has guests."

Istvan did not hit him again.

"Do you want us?" Count Xandi asked anxiously. He had always been a little frightened of Istvan. At this moment he was terrified.

"No thanks, Xandi."

"Let Johann know if you need anything."

Johann materialized at Riebeck's elbow with that quiet touch of the supernatural good servants manage to give their work. "Brandy, Johann, and iodine and bandages. Bring the stuff to the library, please. Come on, Istvan."

They went to the library and Riebeck pushed Istvan into a chair. "Tell me about it. Is it the uncles?"

"Yes. Can you do something, do you think?"

"Perhaps. Tell me what happened."

Johann came in with the tray. "There isn't any iodine, Monsieur Schani."

"Never mind. Brandy will do as well. Thank you."

Riebeck lit a cigarette and gave it to Istvan. "Hold on, *mon vieux*, this will hurt."

"I'm not sorry I hit you," said Istvan.

"No. It's a nasty gash. You ought to have stitches. Hold on." Riebeck poured brandy into the cut. Istvan yelped and took the bottle away from him. Riebeck bandaged him very professionally, a trick he had learned in Indochina.

"Tell me about the uncles. How did it happen? Why didn't you call the police?"

Istvan told what had happened after lunch, making his way

through his awful, absurd tale steadily until he was quite sick with it and hated himself for not having been able to prevent it and his friend for not having foreseen it and generally feeling so wretched that he had to hurt someone.

"I came to find you, because I thought with all your Nazi pals you might be able to do something. Do you want to?"

"What do you mean, do I want to?"

"I thought perhaps you mightn't. After all, if the uncles are killed the palace will be yours."

Riebeck shoved his hands in his pockets and clenched his fists. This time he did want to hit Istvan.

Istvan, seeing that he had drawn blood, felt better.

"Why are you doing all this?"

Istvan was sorry and too stubborn to admit it. "I didn't much care for the sight of you celebrating with your Nazi friends in the uncles' house while they are on their way to a concentration camp."

"They are Xandi's friends, you know. And none of us knew about the uncles."

"You get on very well with Xandi's friends."

"I'm paid to get on well with people."

"That's fine."

"All the trust in the world has worn thin, *hein?* I give it back to you. I'm sorry I asked you for it. I had no right to put you on that particular spot. If you can't stomach it, don't."

"I can't. I can't stomach what you're doing, not anything about it. I wish I could get to the point where I can't stomach you either," said Istvan angrily.

"I know." Riebeck smiled. "Bad habits die hard. But even if it makes things difficult for you I am glad. It's very important to me that we should not change. I don't know why. For some reason your friendship gives me a very important hold on the world, Istvan. Perhaps it is because I've never really loved anyone else and one must love someone to be a human being. I don't know. I don't even care, so long as I have it."

"Couldn't you give it up, Schani?"

A simple question—it dumbfounded Riebeck. It was the first time in all the years of their friendship that one of them had tried to interfere with the other. Until now both had scrupulously observed that first law of abiding friendships—to leave the other person free to act without pressure or persuasion. One might disapprove, one might fear for his safety and happiness, but one might not stand in the way. A man who is not free to act is no longer free to be a friend. Istvan knew this with all of his sound instincts as well as Riebeck knew it with his mind. Istvan was blackmailing him. Riebeck had never known that he cared so much.

He said, "But I don't want to give it up."

Nothing he had ever had to do had hurt as much as this. Having to shoot Alexandra had been child's play in comparison.

Istvan shrugged. "All right, sorry."

Riebeck lit two cigarettes and handed one over. "About the uncles, I'll see what Xandi can do, and we could try von Fahrenkamp."

"Is that Prussian still here?"

"Yes. He's doing some kind of liaison, intelligence, I shouldn't wonder. Are you supposed to be anywhere?"

"Yes," said Istvan. "At work."

"Call up and make an excuse and then go to bed."

"I'd better go back."

"You're in no shape to drive."

"I'm all right. *Servus* Schani, sorry about the chin."

"Forget it. *Servus* Istvan. My regards to Eva."

Count Xandi resolutely refused to do anything about the uncles. "I know nothing about it except that it's very unwise to interfere in these things. You'd better remember that, Schani."

"Don't be childish."

"Schani, they wouldn't have been arrested if they hadn't conspired against the Reich."

"By kicking your friends downstairs? Xandi, this is your own father in a concentration camp."

Xandi said blandly that these were times of blood and iron and that family considerations must vanish before the greater end for which they were all striving. Riebeck was so sure that his next words would be that Hitler was the father of them all that he left the room, fearing he might say something he would later regret.

He picked up his jacket and ran downstairs. Franz held the door for him.

"Their Excellencies were arrested today, Franz. Any information you can get I'll buy."

"Yes, Monsieur Schani," said Franz, while great crocodile tears ran down his cheeks.

"Colonel Riebeck." Colonel von Fahrenkamp tied the sash of his dressing gown. "Is something wrong?"

"I'm sorry. It's very late, isn't it? The Counts were arrested by the Gestapo in Budapest and I don't know where they are."

Colonel von Fahrenkamp looked distressed but not surprised. "Come in, please. Can I get you a drink?"

"No thanks."

"I don't know how I can ask you to believe this, but I give you my word of honor I had nothing to do with it."

"I never thought you did. It was Xandi's gang, of course. I came to ask your help."

Colonel von Fahrenkamp busied himself with some bottles and glasses and handed Riebeck a drink. Riebeck put it aside. Von Fahrenkamp remained silent. Riebeck trod on his pride. "Please," he said. "Would you?"

Colonel von Fahrenkamp faced his visitor in the dim room. He said in a voice he might have used, passing judgment at a court-martial, "I can't."

Beside Riebeck a window stood open. In the light of a street lamp the dusty leaves stirred, pale like the first leaves of spring. The square was silent; no late walkers, no revelers were abroad. Riebeck thought that he would never grow accustomed to Vienna streets silent at night.

"We have used these people," said von Fahrenkamp to no one, "to gain our ends, we thought. And now—"

Riebeck stood up. "I didn't come to wipe your face in that. I'm sorry."

"You could try bribery. Money sometimes works. I don't know. It's a weakling's excuse to say I never meant things to turn out like this. I never did."

It was humiliating to be powerless in something that concerned him so personally. He had located so many people who were strangers to him; had arranged escapes that were no more than a job. He could do nothing for the uncles.

Franz, greedy though he was, had been able to learn no more than that the Counts were not at Mauthausen. That meant they must have been sent to Germany.

Colonel von Fahrenkamp said, "It can be nothing but a vendetta. If it were anything else there would be an opportunity for bribery somewhere. Have you tried Count Xandi?"

Riebeck had. Knowing that all his life Xandi had suffered from staggering gambling debts, Riebeck had tactfully offered him the use of unlimited funds if there were someone to bribe. Xandi had refused even to discuss it. Obviously he had been threatened and ordered to stay out of it. For all his talk about blood and iron, Xandi was easily frightened.

"I have bad news for you," said Colonel von Fahrenkamp on the telephone.

Riebeck did not turn his eyes from the window. He had been watching the first snow of the winter falling into the Baranyi courtyard. "About the uncles?"

"Yes. They are dead."

"How?"

"I do not know," said Colonel von Fahrenkamp, and Riebeck knew he was lying.

It was difficult to write the aunts. (They were in America: their letters had been coming regularly since the uncles' arrest.) It was worse to write Istvan. Riebeck had thought of telephoning but could not face it. He wrote, knowing that it was the end between them.

No reply came from Budapest. He had not expected any.

IX

In the spring of 1939 Latour sent Riebeck a message asking if he planned to spend the war in Vienna. Though talk of war was everywhere, Riebeck no longer believed in it. He was, however, glad for an excuse to get away from Xandi, so he drove to Paris and went to visit Latour.

He said, "I'll bet you we won't fight. Look at Munich last year."

"We'll fight this time. And I've got a job for you."

"So does my regiment, if there really is a war."

"In Indochina? We've had all this out so many times. Look, Jean, say it starts in August, or September, depending when they get their harvest in. Where will it go?"

"Poland."

"Right. By then it will be too close to winter to start anything new. They'll wait for the spring and then—France."

"Who's going to run this war, you or Hitler?"

"I hope he will run it as I plan it. It will make my job much easier. Now we know that he has his troops massed in the East to overrun Poland. He doesn't need that many troops for that. King Arthur could overrun Poland. Christ, Jean, do you realize their cavalry still fights on horseback?"

"An appropriate thing for cavalry to do."

"Especially against *Panzer* troops. Now in the course of the winter these troops, or a lot of them, will have to be moved back to the Rhine. I want you to be in the middle of Germany to blow them up."

For the first time Riebeck looked interested.

"I thought you might enjoy making a bang. What do you have to do in Vienna to wind up your affairs? What about that palace of yours?"

"There's nothing to wind up about it. I shall have to let Xandi live in it and hope for the best."

"Good. Then write him to send you your stuff because your leave of absence was canceled and you are going back to Indochina."

"You'd better let me go back for a week or so, Jacques. It's taken me all this time to find out who was responsible for killing the uncles. But I do know now, and I want to finish it up. After that I'm all yours."

Latour turned his eyes to heaven and sighed. "Will you never learn that the Deuxième is not run for your private shenanigans? Besides, think of all the reprisals you would cause. It's not worth it."

"I suppose not. But I would have liked to do it."

"I want you to be comfortably settled in Germany before this war starts," said Latour. He unfolded a large map and put it on the table between them. "I'll tell you what all those marks and things mean in a moment. Now this is where you go—" his ruler tapped the center of the map. "Weimar."

"Also Buchenwald."

"Two miles away."

"Why not the bridges over the Rhine?" said Riebeck, not relishing this vicinity.

"They'll be too well guarded and if you fail, the German army will be in France. Besides, this isn't a job you are going to do alone, you know. You're going to run the German end of it for me. I would like people at every railway crossing, every bridge and *Autobahn*, ready to blow things up. I won't get them, of course, but this is an important job and they're supplying me fairly liberally."

"Do you realize that I don't know the first thing about blowing up bridges?"

"We'll teach you. And there's someone I want you to meet in Weimar who will be very helpful. I'll tell you later. I've thought a good deal about who you are going to be. I decided that an American of German ancestry would be best, since you speak English."

"I don't think it's quite the same."

"Germans won't know the difference. Pick a name."

"Jacques, you are too good to be true. John Housman."

"Why?"

"John is my name, Housman's my favorite poet. Besides, I can say it used to be Hausmann."

"I've never heard of him."

"He was an English poet who wrote many beautiful poems about young men being killed in battle, but for himself he lived to be quite old."

"Perhaps you will too," said Latour without conviction.

"Don't be silly. You know an impossible job when you see one. Tell me, how does it feel sending people to certain death?"

Colonel Latour permitted himself an indiscretion. "Marvelous, if you want to know the truth. Like God, arranging people's fate and having them meekly go off to die at my command."

Riebeck laughed. "There is something in La Fontaine about people falling into holes they dig for others. Be careful, Jacques. After you have killed us all off there will come the moment when you say to yourself: 'Latour—' By the way, when you speak to yourself do you say Jacques or Latour?"

"Latour. We are not very intimate."

"You will sternly say to yourself: 'Latour, better men than you have perished in this cause. You can no longer stand back. The time has come.'"

Latour, laughing, held his head. "Stop. I've never heard you talk so much. What's the matter with you?"

"Do you really want to know? I'm scared."

"So you ought to be."

"What if somebody recognizes me?"

"Why should they? People never recognize anyone they don't expect to see. At worst they'll say, 'That fellow looks like that awful Colonel Riebeck we used to know in Vienna.' Well, shall we start picking your rabbits?"

They spent the afternoon going through dossiers and interviewing people. Latour did most of the talking. Very rarely Riebeck threw in a brief question. He sat with his back to the window, so that his face was in the shadow. His questions seemed to Latour the height of irrelevance.

In the evening Latour said: "Well?"

"No good, Jacques. It won't do."

"Not one?"

"You'll have to do better than this if you want me to pick anyone. And don't bother me with civilians. They don't interest me."

"Don't be absurd, Jean. I have mostly civilians working for me."

"I don't want them working for me."

"What do you have against civilians?"

"Nothing. It's just that I don't know many and I can't judge them properly. I feel safer with soldiers."

"Perhaps you'd better have Pierre Bantain, then."

"Who's he?"

"A very conceited young man. One of L'Abbé's boys."

"I'll have a look at him tomorrow. Jacques, what about Vic Cavignac? He ought to be in on this."

"He is. But his German's awful, so we'll have to keep him on this side of the Rhine."

"Yes, I suppose. I miss working with Vic."

"Perhaps later," said Latour. Cavignac had told him of some of his and Riebeck's escapades in Indochina, and Latour privately felt that the further apart those two were kept the better for the Deuxième.

Lieutenant Bantain had merry eyes and a melancholy fold at the edge of the eyelids which made him look like a clown. He moved with crashing energy but spoke with a languid drawl. He wore, under his tunic, a black turtleneck sweater. Riebeck, who disapproved of tampering with any uniform, no matter how unattractive, told him to go home and change.

"L'Abbé's boys wear pretty much what they please," said Latour after Bantain had saluted and left.

"Not when they report to me. I think he's what I want, more or less. Would L'Abbé lend you more than one?"

"As many as I like. We are like this, L'Abbé and I." Latour twisted his second and third fingers together. "In the higher sense of the word, of course."

"Go on."

"As a matter of fact Bantain has three friends. They've been inseparable ever since St. Cyr, a bit like you and me and Vic. L'Abbé calls them his four horsemen, though why, since they're artillery, I don't know."

116

"Death, famine, war, and pestilence."

"Famine must be little Renault. He's the size of an undersized jockey. Then there's Vertot, who likes to play with explosives, and a cousin of yours, I believe. Charles de Valterre?"

"Oh, good."

"Here are their files. Will you devote yourself to their study while I go and have lunch?"

"That seems to me an unfair division of labor."

"I'll have them send you a sandwich."

When Lieutenant Bantain reported back without a turtleneck sweater, Riebeck said, "Have a sandwich."

"Is that an order, *mon colonel?*"

"Of course not. I just thought you would like it."

"No, thanks."

"I think we are going to be friends. Now look. I've got a job for you and your pals. Very noisy and likely to prove fatal. If you're interested, report to me here at two o'clock and I'll tell you all about it. And if I see one single turtleneck sweater among the four of you I will have you locked up until you turn black. That's all."

He returned the beaming lieutenant's salute, chucked the folders back on Latour's desk, and went to join him for lunch.

"I think they'll do, Jacques."

"What decided you so quickly?"

"Bantain doesn't like sandwiches."

The four young artillery officers reported punctually at two. All wore dazzlingly well-tailored and correct uniforms. Riebeck returned their salute and smiled at his cousin. "You are looking well, Charles." They all looked well, he thought with satisfaction. A skinny one, a fat one, a tall one, and a short one, all with the same look that had impressed him about Bantain, a look of self-sufficiency and discipline that was not imposed from the outside.

"You ought to see me in my turtleneck sweater," said the Vicomte de Valterre. "What's all the mystery?"

"Join the army and see the world. I want you to come to Germany with me."

"No thanks," said Valterre. "I had a year in Göttingen and that was enough."

Colonel Riebeck explained what they were going to do, and was so convincing that he soon had their wholehearted support. Even Valterre capitulated. "It sounds all right," he said.

They had a long talk during which it was Riebeck's unpleasant duty to acquaint them fully with the consequences of their actions should they be caught, and also to tell them frankly that their chances of not getting caught were one in a thousand if that. Only then were they free to accept or reject the assignment. They all accepted without hesitation and without fuss.

"Well, that's done," said Latour. "Come and have dinner at my place. As far as I know there are no hidden microphones and we can talk in comfort."

Latour did his own cooking and the dinner was deplorable.

"We could have eaten in a restaurant and talked afterwards," said Riebeck ungratefully.

"If you could stop thinking about your stomach for a bit I would like to tell you about Weimar," said Latour. "There is a doctor there, Dr. Sivan, whom I want you to meet as accidentally as possible. He is French and was a prisoner of war somewhere near Weimar in the last war. After the war was over he married a German widow and to please her became a German citizen. She died at least ten years ago, but he has practiced medicine in Weimar ever since and has therefore a background that is as close to perfect as it is humanly possible to be. In addition to this he happened to be present one time when Goebbels fell ill, and since it was an emergency there was no time to send for Goebbels' private doctor, so Dr. Sivan did the operation. Goebbels took a great fancy to him and sent him all his friends, so that we get all kinds of high-level information from Nazis talking under the ether."

"I shouldn't think things people say under an anesthetic would ever be very interesting."

"Terrible rubbish mostly," said Latour frankly. "The really important thing for you is that Dr. Sivan has a cellar that has been entirely closed off from the rest of the house—the house is on a hill if you follow me—"

"Vaguely."

"Well, anyway, Sivan keeps the explosives and stuff there. For a hobby he has a small stud farm outside Weimar. I daresay you could get together with him over that. If not you could always let him take your appendix out."

"I hate the way you are starting to dispose of bits and pieces of me. Jacques, what about the explosives? We haven't got anyone with more than basic information about them. The people in Vienna had no end of trouble with the stuff. It often didn't work at all, or worse, worked only in parts, which made it embarrassing when the parts that didn't blow up were found."

"Yes, I had thought of that. But I haven't at the moment got anyone I could give you. It's a short-lived profession, you know."

"Do you remember Dupont?"

Latour said nothing.

"He was the one that doctored the grenade for us at St. Cyr."

"Yes, I remember. I could never quite see Dupont as such a great friend of yours, if you don't mind my saying so."

"Friend?"

"He used to tell Vic and me he had been your closest friend when you were children."

"Nonsense. He wasn't even a neighbor. They lived in town, in Nancy. His father taught chemistry at the lycée there."

"Poor Dupont," said Latour. Riebeck never considered how he looked to other people, but Latour could without difficulty picture how the youngest Riebeck boy at Fontaines must have looked to the son of the local chemistry teacher. To René Dupont it must have been a world apart, a world he could never dream of approaching. Yet at St. Cyr it had seemed within his grasp.

Latour, by nature an observer, had never forgotten what Riebeck had doubtless not even noticed: how René Dupont had tried, during those first weeks at St. Cyr, to make a bond of the common home town. His effusiveness had been turned aside with an indifferent politeness that must surely have taught him once and for all that a common home town is no bond for people who do not live in the same world.

It was, Latour supposed, typical that Riebeck remembered of

the grenade incident only Dupont's clever handling of explosives while he—Latour—remembered mainly Dupont's behavior afterward.

During the instruction in the use of grenades, dummies were naturally used. Dummy grenades are painted in bright colors so they can never be confused with the real thing. But in order to impress his pupils with the awful consequences of pulling the pin and not instantly lobbing the grenade toward the enemy, the instructor had evolved a macabre lesson. He had one of the dummy grenades painted to look like a real one. From this he pulled the pin and continued talking to the class. Pedagogically it was a great success.

Both Riebeck and Cavignac had been preceded through St. Cyr by older brothers and therefore knew all about the dummy grenade. Together with Latour they decided that it would be extremely funny if the supposedly harmless grenade were to blow up and surprise the instructor.

"Dupont's father teaches chemistry," Riebeck had said. "I'll ask him if he can doctor the grenade for us."

Dupont had been delighted at the attention and had promised to do his best.

The next day the dummy grenade, painted to look like a real one, lay in front of the instructor. He pulled the pin, and still holding the grenade in his hand, described to the class in glowing terms what would happen to any fool who . . . That was as far as he got. A loud bang, black smoke, and a really awful stink filled the classroom.

"Riebeck, de Cavignac, Latour, report to the Commandant," said the instructor and fainted.

At St. Cyr, whenever something fell down or blew up, when notices acquired a meaning never intended by their authors, when chamberpots were found on the outstretched sword of a general's statue, it was automatically assumed that Riebeck, Cavignac, and Latour were the authors of the outrage. A mathematically inclined cadet had calculated that the distance covered by these three, marching in full kit in the sun by way of punishment, would have taken them comfortably to Saigon.

The Commandant told them earnestly that they were not soldiers but Hottentots.

"Riebeck, I suppose you are responsible."

Latour and Cavignac murmured that the idea had sort of come to the three of them at once.

"Who did up the grenade for you? Your marks in chemistry show no sign of such inventiveness."

But they insisted they had done it all.

The Commandant, remembering nostalgically that an older, tougher generation—his own, in fact—had simply substituted a real grenade for the dummy one, sent them to march in full kit until told to stop. It was a warm day and René Dupont told Latour afterward that he had felt very sorry for them.

"Are you quite sure you want him?" Latour asked now.

"He's sort of dull, isn't he? But I think we'd better have him if he has specialized in explosives, which he told me at the time he was planning to do."

Latour got hold of René Dupont's file the next morning, learned that he had indeed been working with explosives, and sent for him. René Dupont volunteered for the job half-heartedly. He hadn't the nerve to say no.

"It's all laid on," Latour told Riebeck. "You've got Dupont. But you'll have to share him with the others until I can find you some more explosive experts."

"We'll probably be dead by then."

"Don't be so depressing, Jean."

"Why not? Or haven't you considered yet that you are sending six inexperienced people to do a job where no one can afford to make the slightest mistake?"

"Oh yes," said Latour, "I have considered it. But I had rather hoped you hadn't."

John Housman of Philadelphia, Pa., arrived in Weimar in the war-hysterical summer of '39. He took lodgings with a Professor Keller. Latour had intended for his visit the outré reason that he was writing a book about Weimar's great poet, Johann Wolfgang von Goethe. The academic atmosphere seemed therefore appropriate.

The Keller family were in the habit of renting their spare room to students. They had some misgivings about having an American lodger, but John Housman was quickly able to dispel these. Though American he resembled in no way the mental picture the professor had formed of him. He wore well-tailored, unobtrusive tweeds instead of a raccoon coat turned fur side out, he was courteous to ladies and did not call them sister, he addressed gentlemen by their proper titles and surnames, did not chew gum, never called Professor Keller "Mac," and at meals held his fork, as do all decent people, in the left hand.

When he was asked what had made him come to Germany at such a stirring time, he answered that many Americans of German ancestry—his own grandfather's name had been Hausmann—were deeply in sympathy with the aspirations of the German people, and that with a fortunate legacy he had been happy to be able to come to Germany and share, in his humble way, in her march toward the future. It went down awfully well.

He was able to make Dr. Sivan's acquaintance without relinquishing his appendix. As Latour had expected they got together over the stud farm and soon went for daily rides together. After the rides Riebeck usually stayed for tea and not infrequently for dinner. Weimar society was gently amused over this prompt and great friendship between their famous doctor and the young nobody from Philadelphia. What they would have thought if they had known how much of this friendship was spent in a dank, ill-lit cellar, Riebeck did not like to contemplate.

On occasion, so their visits should not look too one-sided, Dr. Sivan visited Riebeck at the Kellers'. To watch them bridle on those occasions was mortifying.

"I find German society very hard to understand," Riebeck said to Dr. Sivan after one of these visits. "Why is a doctor better than a professor? Every time you come to see me there they move a step higher in society."

"It is, I think, that I am a Nazi doctor," said Sivan.

"I used to think they would lose caste by having an American to stay, but apparently not. Everyone seems to think Americans are fascinating. I wish they wouldn't. They ask me so many questions I don't know the answers to."

"It's a peculiar choice of nationality. What made you do it?"

"It was Jacques' idea. But really, what else could I have been? I could get away with pretending to be a German, but my age is a trouble. I should probably find myself in the German army, fighting the French. It had to be a neutral nation, and what is there? Sweden and Switzerland, of course, but I do not think anyone respects them. It had to be a powerful country with a strong embassy."

"But you are so thoroughly un-American."

"Surely all Americans can't be alike. There are so many of them. Besides, it's been a big help, being un-American. People like me for it."

"They won't when they find out how ignorant you are. I'll never forget the day you told Professor Keller that New York was the capital of the United States."

In Dr. Sivan's cellar they listened to the broadcasts from the BBC. The phony war was still in full swing; the French and the Germans were gazing at each other across the Maginot Line. A famous French general had said for the thirty-sixth time that the Maginot Line was impenetrable.

"What an ass," said Riebeck exasperated. "It may be impenetrable but it is not endless. The Germans will walk around it and invade France through Belgium, that's all. If I were Marshal Pétain—"

Dr. Sivan, who did not want to hear again what Riebeck would do if he were Marshal Pétain, said, "Allow me to congratulate you and Monsieur Dupont. You did a nice job on the railway bridge."

"Thank you. I was pleased with it. I think that's the first time all the explosives went off as planned and while the train was on it."

"The Germans, needless to say, are very displeased. Have you seen the paper today?"

"No. I slept till noon."

"They call it the act of a diseased Jewish mentality, but they know damned well it's professional sabotage. All civilians are commanded to help in apprehending the criminal or criminals concerned. In fact," said Dr. Sivan, who had been saving his plum all afternoon, "Herr Major Werner of Buchenwald is offering a reward."

"Really? How much?"

"Five thousand."

Riebeck seemed pleased. "That's not bad."

"Not for a start," Dr. Sivan agreed. "Now I've a pretty good rumor for you. They're going to use passenger trains from now on and load the troops on at the last moment, so the saboteur will not know it until it is too late."

"You can't load a troop train in two minutes. Are they leaving from here?"

"Probably. Tomorrow or the day after."

"Latour was right about the big spring offensive, then. And do you know what that means, Sivan my Sivan?"

"That your mind has been affected, just as it said in the paper."

"It means I go home, put on a uniform, load my revolver, and fight in a real war."

"If you are not caught by the Gestapo."

"If I am not caught by the Gestapo. *Malbrouck s'en va-t-en guerre, mironton, mironton—*"

"Not much of a singer, are you?"

"Sorry. I usually confine it to the privacy of the bathtub."

"They are rerouting the trains over the Saalfeld Bridge."

Riebeck stopped his cheerful, tuneless singing. "Oh no! Are you sure? That means hours in the water. It's the wrong time of year for swimming."

"I'm sure. You'll need help."

"Yes. Will you call Jena for me?"

"I don't like Dupont."

"I know."

"I don't trust him."

"Nonsense, Sivan. We went to St. Cyr together."

Dr. Sivan laughed, but without pleasure. "I happen to know that he has gambling debts and needs money badly. A man with a price on his head must expect to be sold."

"I'll tell you what, Sivan, you turn me in. If someone is going to have the money I'd much rather it was you."

"Thank you very much, but I'm fairly well off already. Dupont isn't."

"Yes. Well, call him up. I want him here tomorrow. He can stay with you until he's needed."

"Yes, *mon colonel.*"

For René Dupont working in Germany had not turned out at all as he had expected. He had envisioned a close partnership of shared work and danger with Colonel Riebeck, extravagant rescues perhaps, and the final recognition on Riebeck's part of who his true friends were.

Instead he was shuffled around between a group of conceited young prigs who treated him like a plumber. "Oh Dupont, the stuff blew up half an hour after the train left, could you have a look at it please. Dupont, none of these fuses work, see what you can do. Dupont, I'm shorthanded. Could you stay tonight and help me mine the railway tracks?" And occasionally a call from Weimar: "Dupont, one o'clock by the Parish Church." At such times he felt that Riebeck liked him because he was competent with explosives. But René Dupont did not want to be liked for being good at his job. He wanted to be liked for himself.

He was always afraid. He had never known that fear could be like this: so constant and unflagging, fear present with every breath he drew, with every bite of food he swallowed, fear the last thought on falling asleep and the first on awakening. None of them had known it would be like this. But it never occurred to Dupont that they were all afraid. He smoked too much and drank too much. He gambled, losing much more than he could afford. He could not get to sleep without barbiturates and could not get up without Benzedrine.

Bantain, who had been working with him most, was sufficiently concerned about it to go to see Riebeck in Weimar. He said, "Dupont ought to be sent home. He's going to crack up soon."

"We're all nervous," said Riebeck. "Besides, I can't spare him just yet."

"He's not so bad when he's working. You don't see him when he's not. He drinks too much, for one thing."

"You're one to talk."

"I haven't been drunk in ages."

"Good boy."

"He's gambling too."

"Is he winning?"

"Do they ever, when they're that desperate? He has bad debts and he's terrified of the Gestapo."

"So am I. And if you have any sense at all, so are you."

"Yes," said Bantain soberly. "I am."

They had none of them enough experience to know that no matter how urgently he is needed, a secret agent who drinks to excess, accumulates debts, and is uncontrollably frightened is dispensable.

When Dr. Sivan sent for Dupont to come and help blow up the Saalfeld Bridge, he nearly refused. It was madness to continue. The police, the Gestapo, the army, everyone was out looking for them. They could not go on here. Riebeck had no right to expose anyone to such danger. He ought to be stopped. It was not fair that he should not be afraid, that he should be able to laugh and make jokes, that his hands, tying explosives to beams, should be so steady.

Dupont had done this kind of job so often now that he was able to think of other things while he worked. He thought of the Gestapo. (They hold your head under water, someone had told him, until you all but drown. Then they pull you out, make you vomit, and start all over again.) He grasped the end of a rope and dived under again. The bridge had been well guarded, but a silent and quick attack had taken care of that. The water was so cold it had numbed him long since. That was a help, in a way, because the ropes took all the skin off the palms of one's wet hands, and tying explosives to beams could become pure torture. He held his head under water until he could no longer bear the pain. Of course the Gestapo would hold you under longer than that.

He thought that it would be Colonel Riebeck's fault if they were caught. No human being had the right to expose another to such a fate. He forgot that he had volunteered for the job. He knew only that Riebeck must be stopped. And suddenly, without wishing to, he thought of his gambling debts.

He wrenched himself around and dived under again to get away from his thoughts.

They walked home, the points of their cigarettes glowing in the dark. "Fear death by water," Riebeck said. "I love it. If I could choose I've always thought I would choose drowning. It must be nice to be utterly exhausted and go down and down. Cold and dark and quiet."

"Ugh," said Dupont. He was chilled to the bone and could not control his voice. Riebeck too was shaking with cold. Bantain or Renault would at such a time have taken his arm, not from affection but merely for mutual warmth. It was so like Riebeck, thought Dupont, to prefer his own cold to someone else's body warmth. And to talk of drowning at the same time.

"Perhaps not," Riebeck agreed politely. "It's only a private idiosyncrasy."

"Aren't idiosyncracies usually private?" Dupont loved to score off Riebeck. He did not get the chance often.

Riebeck laughed. He was feeling fine.

"I think drowning is horrible," said Dupont vehemently.

Amiably, Riebeck gave him a choice. "What would you like?"

"Oh, I don't know. Something quick that I needn't know about. I should like to die in my sleep, I think."

"Mm. Sounds rather uninteresting." The end of the cigarette burnt Riebeck's fingers. He dropped it and swore. "That's one thing I hate," he said. "Burning. I'm terrified of it."

"I quite agree with you. I got a very nasty acid burn in the lab once," said Dupont, and enlarged on this until he became aware of Riebeck's obvious boredom and his words ran down into an angry silence. Why could Bantain talk nonsense to Riebeck by the hour and make him laugh, why did he never withdraw his attention from Bantain in this insulting way?

They separated without speaking again before entering the town. Dupont gave a contemptuous mock salute which Riebeck either did not see or could not be bothered about. Like a child compelled into naughtiness by the inattention of his elders, René Dupont went to the railway station, warmed by continuous explosions of anger in his blood.

The train blew up as it crossed the Saalfeld Bridge and the price on Riebeck's head was doubled.

"Now will you clear out?" asked Dr. Sivan. "Surely you've done all the damage you can here."

"Nonsense. There's lots more. The trains are still going."

"You've done enough. You can't go on, the whole thing has become much too dangerous. They will kill you."

"*Qui ante diem periit,*" quoted Riebeck laughing," "*sed miles sed pro—*"

"Oh, shut up," the doctor interrupted. "I'm sure you'll die in the best Ronald Coleman tradition."

"You've been corrupted by the decadent American films, Sivan. But truly, you worry too much. I'm a soldier and soldiers get killed in wars. I promise you that when my time comes I shall die without embarrassing you with speeches."

"I daresay you won't be able to speak any more by then. Any damned fool can die, you know. That's the one thing that's within the scope of everybody. They die well or badly, but everyone accomplishes the act of dying. I'm not all that worried about your dying. But if you stay here you will not die in battle, you will die in Buchenwald, hanging from a meathook. It will take a long time and you will be in no mood to do it well, I assure you."

"You never told me about the meathooks before, Sivan."

"No."

"What a ray of sunshine you are today. Let's go see what the BBC has for us this morning."

"*Bien, mon colonel.*"

"Poor Sivan, I'm sorry I annoy you so. Shall I make you happy and tell you the truth? Listen, I am not only frightened, I am terrified all the time now. I don't know when I've last been able to sleep through the night. And please don't give me barbiturates, because I'd only throw them away."

"Going to France would cure the insomnia."

"There are worse things than insomnia. Running away from a job before it's finished, for example."

Doctor Sivan looked at him. He felt old and useless. "I never had a son," he said irrelevantly.

"I'm not allowed inside my father's house."

Dr. Sivan smiled. "Do you want some tea? It's hot."

"Please."

The doctor went to get it. When he returned with the steaming cup on a tray, he found Riebeck asleep in his chair, a burning cigarette still between his fingers.

When Riebeck returned to Dr. Keller's house, he was met by a very well-dressed, very handsome member of the Gestapo, who said, "My men are searching your room. I hope you don't mind."

"I do mind. In America—"

"The circumstances are extraordinary, Herr Housman. Could I have your passport, please."

"It's with my things in my room. I should have thought your beavers would have found it by now."

"Shall we get it?"

"If you like." The passport was a faultless forgery.

Riebeck's room was a mess. Clothes and books lay scattered on the floor. "Look here," he said sharply, "you can just pick all that up again."

"Your passport if you please," said the leader of the group. He was annoyed. The Gestapo was not accustomed to being addressed in that tone of voice.

One of the searchers handed it over. The well-dressed Gestapo officer said to his underlings: "Search him. He might be armed."

He was not. But one of the eager underlings had found the French army revolver in the desk drawer, and Riebeck wanted to kick himself. "Whatever happens to me now," he thought, "I deserve it. Why did I never bother to get an American gun?"

The Gestapo officer examined the pistol with some interest.

"The American Embassy is going to be very distressed by all this," said Riebeck to distract him from his contemplation.

"It is regrettable, but we are looking for the saboteur who has been damaging our railways."

"A shocking affair," said Riebeck. "I shouldn't think he'd still be hanging around here, though."

"Where did you get this gun, Herr Housman?"

"In Philadelphia."

"For what purpose?"

"I can see you have never been to America," Riebeck said pityingly. "Gangsters. America is full of gangsters. Dillinger. Baby-face Nelson. Squint-eye Malone," he added imaginatively. "Two-gun Sweetie-pie."

The Gestapo officer refused to be distracted. "But this is a French army pistol," he said.

"Is it? I've no idea what they use in the French army. I bought it in a pawnshop."

"Ah. And why do you need it in Germany? We have no gangsters here."

Riebeck had the impression that the Gestapo officer was playing cat and mouse, that he knew more than he let on but was enjoying himself. Riebeck did not like being the mouse. Nevertheless he went on. "It was the saboteur," he said. "I thought if I met him one night sabotaging or whatever it is saboteurs do, I could shoot him."

"Hardly the job for an amateur, Herr Housman. You would be dealing with desperate men."

"I know," said Riebeck with truth. "May I have my passport back?"

"Not just yet. Herr Major Werner wants to have a look at it and at you too."

"Werner? Oh yes, the little cockatoo that prances around Weimar with spurs on his boots, though no one's ever seen him on horseback."

"He uses the spurs on his prisoners, Herr Housman."

"Well, I'm not going. I'm an American citizen and I don't have to go anywhere I don't want to."

"That is true. You can be carried."

Riebeck decided to test his hands by lighting a cigarette. They were passably steady.

"Well Herr Housman, shall we go?"

"The American Embassy—"

"We will apologize to them—if we are wrong."

"You'll be sorry."

The drive to Buchenwald seemed to Riebeck very short. Before he had even begun to subdue his panic they were passed through the gate by a guard. Riebeck was put in a cell and locked in. Thank God, they had left him alone.

There was no furniture of any sort, so Riebeck sat on the floor with his back against the wall. He lit a cigarette and forced himself to think things over calmly. It was not easy.

Would they check with the American Embassy? He did not know the procedure. He had an arranged alibi, for what that was worth, and except for the French army pistol they had found nothing to incriminate him. Dynamiters have lots of equipment, they must know that.

There was a possibility that they had dropped on the first foreigner they could find in order to satisfy Berlin's demands for a saboteur. In that case they would torture him until he confessed and then kill him. But why pick on an American? A Pole would cause much less fuss, having no government to make a protest.

They had let him keep his cigarettes and matches, probably because very few prisoners try to commit suicide by setting themselves alight with a match. They had not searched him for poison. Surely with a secret agent that was standard procedure. Or did they know—discouraging thought—that he had none?

Abruptly he wearied of the pros and cons. He knew, in spite of all the chances he might have, that he was done for, that somewhere he had slipped up badly.

Awash and nearly drowned in terror, he had no hold now but the remembered touch of his fingers on the damp stone of the Flying Horses, where he had made the decision that had brought him here. Would Coysevox see him through now?

He had a sudden, overwhelming desire to do the thing well if it must be done. It would matter to no one, apart from having to keep quiet about information that mattered, how he carried it off. But he wanted to do it well. He had never included vanity among his failings. Why then this sudden vanity? Or was it something else? Count Nikki had once said, "One must meet disaster with courtesy." Being a Riebeck gave one early lessons in that. As a small boy he had watched his father, superb in the face of calamity, accept the news of his oldest son's death at Ypres with nothing but concern for the messenger. "You have come a long way and must be thirsty. Allow me to offer you a glass of wine."

Terror had exhausted him. He sat against the wall, his eyes shut. A guard thought he was praying. But such a thing would never have occurred to Riebeck. It was not Notre Dame he saw behind closed eyes, but the Salle Napoleon with its banners whose litany read Marengo, Hohenlinden, Austerlitz; the twin battles of Jena and Auerstadt, Friedland, Wagram, Dresden. The patron saint of French officers should be Bonaparte, carrying his eagles across Prussia.

A guard fetched him after an hour. Was that hour, he wondered, a psychological trick to give him time to despair, or was it merely Major Werner's time for lunch?

Werner's office floor was covered with an Aubusson rug. The desk was huge, like a Hollywood tycoon's. There was a Rubens on the wall. Considering its location, the office was in the worst taste.

The man behind the desk matched his office. He was small but marvelously turned out in cavalry uniform. He wore several fourragères and clanked with medals and spurs.

He straightened the Rubens. "From a palace in Poland," he said to Riebeck. His voice was unexpectedly deep and pleasant. "Do you like it?" He picked up the passport. "This is yours?"

"Yes."

"It might interest you to know that the American Ambassador has never heard of you."

Major Werner sighed. "You have nothing to say to me? And I had so looked forward to having a talk. In the end we will find many topics of mutual interest. So why not now?"

Silence could always goad Major Werner into talking too much.

"Let us stop all this nonsense, Colonel Riebeck. Let us bury John Housman."

He dropped the passport ceremonially into the wastebasket.

If Riebeck had asked him how he got all his information, Werner would have been evasive. But Riebeck said nothing.

"A fellow officer of yours, Colonel Riebeck, one Lieutenant Dupont, has told me all about you, in return for money and his own safety. You will object that he may have invented the whole thing."

Werner paused to allow Riebeck to object.

"You may say men will say anything for their safety," Werner prompted.

Riebeck said nothing.

"I assure you, Colonel Riebeck, that Dupont would not have lied to me. I know when men lie and I know how to deal with liars."

"Poor Dupont," thought Riebeck. "Poor fool."

"Would you like to see him?"

"No."

"Ah, success! You have spoken to me. The monologue has become a dialogue and things are looking up."

Riebeck thought that in another moment the bastard would have him laughing, which would never do. He turned his face away and lit a cigarette.

Dupont was sent for. He came, insolent and terrified by turns. He was between two fears, fear of Riebeck and fear of Werner. Though one was prisoner and the other executioner, the balance held.

"Lieutenant Dupont," said Werner kindly, "please look at this man and tell me who he is."

"Dupont," said Riebeck, "I order you not to answer."

"You cannot take orders from my prisoner, Lieutenant. I want you to tell me his name."

"He . . . I . . ."

"Shut up, Dupont," said Riebeck gently. "Stop playing cat and mouse Major, the mouse is too nervous to enjoy it. If you want a confession you can have it. I'm Riebeck and I've been blowing up your damned trains. If you want it written down and signed, I'll do that too."

133

"No," said Werner, who had not missed the look of relief on Dupont's face. "That is not what I want. Lieutenant Dupont, Colonel Riebeck has just robbed you of your financial reward in a very foolish attempt to save that which you do not have: honor. Are you grateful to him?"

Riebeck caught a look of unequivocal hatred in Dupont's eyes, and this time he did laugh.

"However," Werner said, "the reward is still yours if you will, here and now, in front of the man you have betrayed, tell us who he is."

"He's Colonel Riebeck," said Dupont sullenly. "You damn well know it anyway. He works for a Colonel Latour. You can't get Latour because he's in France, but you've got Riebeck. He's the one that's been blowing up the trains. He forced me to help him. I didn't want to do it. He thinks he's better than I am because he's never afraid. But it's human to be afraid, it's nothing to be ashamed of, is it? You'll make him afraid. The Gestapo will, won't it?"

"Yes, Lieutenant, it will. I imagine it already has. And now—"

"He's afraid of fire," said Dupont quickly. "He told me so."

The silence lasted long enough to let Dupont hear his own words echo in his mind. Werner looked mildly interested. But it was the look on Riebeck's face Dupont could not bear. Riebeck looked as if he were sorry for him.

"Treason!" Dupont said to himself. "I've committed treason. Aren't you going to notice me, even now?"

"Thank you, Lieutenant," said Major Werner briskly. "I will keep your suggestion in mind. So no doubt will Colonel Riebeck. And now, if you will excuse us, we have work to do."

"Yes, Herr Major. Thank you." His knees shook now with re-action and there were tears in his eyes. "*Mon colonel*, I didn't—I didn't mean what I said. I'm sorry. I—"

"I know," said Riebeck. "It's all right. Go away now."

When Dupont had closed the door behind him, Riebeck put out his cigarette. Werner looked annoyed. The scene had not gone off as he had expected. "You were much too kind to him, considering."

"Children," said Riebeck, "loose in a man's world. What a miserable sight."

"You are contemptuous of my methods. Why?"

"So much melodrama to corrupt the corruptible."

Werner sighed. His duties often weighed heavily upon him, but he was a German officer and German officers do not shirk. "I took no pleasure at all in breaking Dupont. It was too easy. Most people are too easy. Duty, as I am sure you have noticed, is almost invariably dull. It would have been simple, very simple, to arrest Dupont and to torture him. How long, do you think, before he would name his associates? But a man of Dupont's caliber, how much does he know?"

Riebeck felt sick thinking how much Dupont knew. Sivan, Bantain, Valterre—he knew enough.

"Also it is wise to deal honorably with traitors," Werner went on. "It may encourage other traitors. So you see, the hold I needed over Dupont had to be a moral one. What does a man do, Colonel, when one has seen him at his worst?"

"Kill you?"

Werner laughed. "Not Dupont. Never Dupont. He will follow me like a puppy and wag his tail to please me. What do you say to that?"

"Poor Dupont."

"Ah, you are exasperating. Tell me, how much damage do you think you have done? Do you think you have stopped us?"

"No, of course not."

"Did you think you could?"

"No."

"How futile. And I do hope you are going to say something besides no."

"All Intelligence work is futile."

"Then why, I always wonder, do you people take such dreadful risks? It's not really worth it, is it?"

"Yes, it is."

"Do you think we will win in the end?"

"No."

"Do you think you will?"

"No. Not in any way that matters."

"Then it is futile."

"No."

"Colonel Riebeck, you will presently discover that the thing I punish most severely is an uncooperative attitude. A steady stream of noes is hardly going to incline me to clemency. You look unimpressed. I have had much experience, and I assure you, every man can be broken."

"Nonsense. I don't believe it."

"You can be broken, Colonel Riebeck."

"That I believe."

"The only question is how."

"That," said Riebeck as amiably as he could under the circumstances, "is your problem." He yawned, suddenly and uncontrollably. A better psychologist than Werner would have recognized that yawn for what it was. Werner was merely angry. "I think I shall introduce you to Sergeant Schlosser."

The sight of Schlosser, when he came into the office, was not reassuring, and Riebeck yawned again.

"Colonel Riebeck, will you make a bargain with us?"

"Depends on what you want."

Werner's face fell. "I'm surprised at you, Colonel," he said sadly. "I never thought you would bargain with the Gestapo. I thought you were a man of principle. But you have no stamina, you French. Still, I suppose it is better to keep things pleasant."

"What do you want?"

"I want to know the things you have not told me. That noble confession you made was not after all about anything we did not already know. Otherwise I imagine you would not have made it, Lieutenant Dupont or no Lieutenant Dupont. I am not such a fool as to believe that you and your intrepid friend did all this work. No one can be in Weimar and in Jena at the same time. So I want to know where you keep your equipment, who is in this operation with you, and where they can be found. And do not imagine, pray, that you will save your self-respect by not telling us the easy way. When Schlosser gets started self-respect is the very first thing that goes. Isn't that so, Schlosser?"

Schlosser laughed.

"Dear Schlosser, he does so enjoy his work. I don't like to disappoint him, but all the same, Colonel Riebeck, I hope you will be sensible. Have a cigarette, make yourself comfortable, and tell me where you keep the dynamite."

Riebeck said: "No."

He continued to say no through the following days. When even such a brief word became too difficult he set his teeth and said nothing at all.

Four days after Colonel Riebeck's arrest three men in the black uniform of the SS entered Dr. Sivan's house under the cover of darkness. They climbed without noise down the cellar stairs, though it was generally known in Weimar that Dr. Sivan's house had no cellar. Dr. Sivan, who was entertaining a group of medical students, had apparently not heard anything, and it must be said that the visitors were very quiet. He gave his full attention to the students and did nothing to make them suppose he wanted them gone. They left very late, and Dr. Sivan went upstairs. He turned on his bedroom light and the light in the bathroom. There were small chinks in the blackout, not enough to violate regulations, but enough to make anyone who might be interested realize that the doctor was on his way to bed. In a short time the lights went out and the house was quiet. Dr. Sivan, in pyjamas and bathrobe, groped his way downstairs in the dark. He went to the cellar, which had neither cracks nor windows, and could therefore be lighted without causing suspicion. In the light of the bare bulb he looked at the three young faces, drawn and tired and apprehensive.

"Why the masquerade?"

Renault said sulkily that black was useful in the dark.

"Very clever. Why aren't you where you're supposed to be? Don't think you can do as you like just because the Colonel's been caught. I'm in charge until someone comes to take his place."

The young men simply continued to look at him as if nothing he had said could be of any possible consequence.

"Do you know anything?" Valterre finally asked.

"Yes. He is still alive and he has not talked."

Valterre looked ready to break into physical violence at this. Pierre Bantain held him back. "Of course he hasn't," he said. "There is no need to point it out. We're here to get him out."

"Are you going to get the moon too while you are at it? You know the Colonel's orders."

"Never mind the Colonel's orders."

Riebeck had strictly forbidden any rescue attempts. They were too unsafe, and their small group could not afford to lose any men. Dr. Sivan knew Riebeck well enough to realize that he would not consider changing an order simply because he was now the one to be rescued.

"I am not going to allow you to commit suicide," he said. "You have work to do. Now more than ever."

"Look." Valterre took a piece of paper from his pocket and showed it to Dr. Sivan. It was an order from the Gestapo chief Heinrich Himmler to have Riebeck brought at once and alive to Berlin for questioning. It bore Himmler's signature and even more convincing, since signatures can be forged, his seal.

"Great God," said Dr. Sivan, "it looks authentic."

"It isn't. I used to forge my Papa's signature on my report cards," said Valterre, with a flash of his old laughter, "and from there to a life of crime was only a step. The seal's a copy. Whoever staffed Berlin did a marvelous job. He had no trouble getting it. Now, Dr. Sivan, you'll have to get Werner out of the way, because he would be quite capable of ringing up Himmler and giving him hell."

"I can do that for you," said Dr. Sivan, suddenly very fond of the serious young men who had done something while he had sat biting his nails. "Werner is a patient of mine and I've cultivated him as a friend as well—very *contre coeur*, but I'm glad of it now. He should have to blow off steam by tomorrow. I'll invite him for a game of cards. Whenever he feels frustrated he tells me his tales of woe because I am such a sympathetic listener. Perhaps after all we have a chance. Where is Vertot?"

"He's hiding out with our staff car. That also comes compliments of Berlin, by the way. Somebody there is a wheel, I can tell you."

"I'll send you down some food and beer," said Dr. Sivan, who disliked such speculation. "You can't smoke, I'm afraid. The cellar is full of explosives. Then get some sleep. Do you have Demerol?"

They nodded. They could no longer sleep without it.

⚜ TWO ⚜

*But in the very midst of our indignation with the gentleman, we have
a consciousness that his preposterous inertia and negativeness in the
actual emergency is, somehow or other, allied with his general superiority
to ourselves. It is not only that the gentleman ignores considerations relative to conduct, sordid suspicions, fears, calculations, etc., which the
vulgarian is fated to entertain; it is that he is silent where the vulgarian
talks, that he gives nothing but results where the vulgarian is profuse of
reasons; that he does not explain or apologize; that he uses one sentence
instead of twenty, and that, in a word, there is an amount of interstitial
thinking, so to call it, which it is quite impossible to get him to perform,
but which is nearly all that the vulgarian mind performs at all.*

William James: Psychology

X

"*Give him an overdose of morphine*," said a man's voice, speaking English, "and let him go in comfort. He'll never pull through."

"If you do"—a woman's voice, this, a nice one—"I'll report you
to the police."

"Now Jenny—"

"And the British Medical Association."

"Jenny," said the man's voice, "if he were a horse you would
shoot him."

Pain was complete, but never for long. The cold touch of alcohol,
the sting of a hypodermic, and pain would recede to form a
square about him, moving slowly closer again. Always he wanted
to say, "No thank you, I can manage this time," and always he was
too late. Or they would not listen. Anodyne followed pain and

there was no escape. One does not escape from Buchenwald, Colonel Riebeck. One does not even try.

Their latest invention; a whirling room. Somewhere a door closed and hammers pounded his head. He forced his eyes to open. The room stood still.

"Christ, what a hangover."

It was his first coherent sentence. They never afterward let him forget it.

A girl turned from the window and smiled. *"Ça va?"*

"Je me défends."

"So I see. Do you know where you are?"

"Did. Forgot. England?"

"Yes. London. You were late getting out of France. All the coast hospitals were full."

He could not even remember how he had gotten *into* France, but it was too much trouble to ask her, and probably she would not know. She spoke French like a Frenchwoman, but her voice stirred a memory of words spoken in English, and he dredged up a name. "Jenny?"

She smiled. "How did you know?"

" 'If he were a horse you would shoot him.' "

"Oh dear. People aren't supposed to remember what they hear under an anesthetic. You'll forget it, won't you?"

"Surely." He saw that she had a hypodermic in her hand and said quickly: "Take it away, please. I don't want it. I can manage without, truly."

She did not argue. "If you change your mind later, tell me." She gave him two white pills and a glass of water. "You don't have any moral objection to APC, do you? I imagine your head hurts."

"You imagine right." He took the pills and water. His hands were bandaged. He remembered about that.

The nurse—Jenny—went back to the window and took up some mending. The APC helped a little. By lying absolutely still and not breathing too deeply he could manage, just.

London! By way of a beach brown with soldiers, Stukas diving down with their siren howl, and Bantain battling with an English naval captain who had not wanted to clutter up his boat with as poor a risk as Riebeck had evidently looked.

The morphine Dr. Sivan had given him had hardly touched the pain, but had caused him to react to everything with a sublime insouciance. Hurt away, shoot away, argue about whether you'll take me away or leave me to die on this awful beach, I don't care one bit.

Bantain appeared to be under the impression that an English naval captain was equal to a captain of French artillery. It was a misapprehension the Englishman did not share.

Must remember to tell Bantain a naval captain's equal to full colonel. Important.

"Did you want something?" asked the nurse. Not Jenny this time. Older. Different uniform.

"No. Sorry. Was I making a noise?"

"Have this." Another white pill. Not aspirin, evidently, because it put him to sleep.

China clattered on a tray. "I've brought you your tea, Jenny."

"How nice of you."

So Jenny was back. Good. He opened his eyes and found that though his head hurt as much as ever, the room was at last stationary.

"Hullo," said Jenny. "I hope we didn't wake you. Would you like a cup of tea?"

She was, he decided, a very odd nurse. Previous hospital experience in Indochina had taught him that nurses never offer patients cups of tea. Only pills and thermometers.

"It's foul tea," she said as she handed him the cup. "It always is here."

He was clumsy with his bandaged hands and grateful that she did not offer to help him. The tea was very bad; even Riebeck, not ordinarily a tea drinker, could recognize this. But it was boiling hot, scalding his mouth, and as exhilarating as drink.

"Could I have a cigarette, do you think?"

She took cigarettes from her pocket and gave him one. As she bent over to light it for him he realized that she was different from the army nurses in Hué in another respect; she was beautiful. Her eyes were of a grey so dark they looked black in the dim room.

Her hair was tied back, but a strand of it had slipped down and he could see that it was very fair; pale silk in color and texture. Snow Queen hair.

"There isn't an ashtray," she said. "You can use the saucer. If matron comes in, hide the cigarette under the blanket or I shall be in hideous trouble."

"Thank you," said Riebeck. "Tell me about the war."

"You lost."

"So quickly?"

"Pétain capitulated."

"Oh, that. That was to be expected. We shall simply have to use England and Africa as bases and keep on fighting."

She laughed, suddenly sympathetic. "Do you know a General de Gaulle?"

"I've read his books."

"He had the same idea as you. In fact he is in England now, getting together a Free French army."

"Good. Did you have much trouble getting out of France?"

"No. I was already here. I live in England. It's only my father's people who are French. My mother's are English and so is my husband."

"Husband? Sorry, that was silly. You look rather young to boast a husband, though."

"I do assure you I wasn't dragged screaming with terror to the altar. I am twenty."

"My abject apologies, Madame."

"Oh all right, sorry. But I get awfully fed up with all that child-bride nonsense."

It was not, he now realized, only her youth that had disconcerted him, but her beauty. Whom do Snow Queens marry?

"What is he like, your husband?"

"But you know him. Captain Falconer. The surgeon who's been taking care of you."

He had no very clear recollection of him. "The one who shoots horses?"

"You promised to forget that." She took back his empty teacup and the remains of his cigarette. "Better look tidy. Jonathan—

Captain Falconer—makes his rounds about now. Surgeons are dreadfully fussy people."

Captain Falconer, wearing the uniform of the Royal Army Medical Corps, met Riebeck's exacting standards of what Jenny's husband ought to look like. He was a little old for her perhaps, around forty at a guess, but he had a well-made, intelligent face, fine hands, and a marvelous Harley Street manner.

Jenny introduced her husband and then said to him, "Colonel Riebeck remembers you wanting to send him to the knacker's."

"Nonsense." They never show they are disconcerted in Harley Street. (It was Wimpole Street, actually, Riebeck found out later, but the manner is the same.) "People don't remember what they hear under an anesthetic."

"He does though."

Captain Falconer said to Riebeck: "Did Jenny tell you that she bet me five pounds you would pull through, so that now I have to keep you alive against my best interests?"

"What is much worse," said Riebeck, "is that if I die of natural causes, everyone will suspect you did me in for five pounds."

"Take very good care of him," said Captain Falconer to his wife. He saluted and left.

Riebeck, rather tired by so much society, accepted two aspirins and went to sleep.

"What is that uniform?"

They had switched Jenny to night duty, which pleased him. He could sometimes get to sleep during the day (though even daytime sleeping is no insurance against nightmares) but he never managed it at night. When Jenny was not busy she often brought her knitting to his room and stayed to gossip.

"The uniform? VAD. Voluntary Aid. One gets paid for it, though."

"It's a hideous uniform."

"Yes," said Jenny agreeably, "isn't it. My uncle, Admiral Tavistock—you may have heard of him, he's the one that almost lost us the Battle of Jutland—wanted me to be a Wren, and I almost did because they have a very pretty hat. But if the war lasts a long time I imagine I should get very tired of the hat, no matter how pretty. Jonathan thought the VAD would be a good idea, but it's turned out to be rather embarrassing because in public he has to call me VAD Falconer and I have to call him sir, and it makes him have the giggles."

"I cannot imagine Dr. Falconer giggling under any circumstances."

"You mustn't call him doctor. English surgeons are mister."

"Are they? Doesn't it depress them after working so hard to become doctors?"

"Well, if they don't kill too many rich patients they usually become sir sooner or later."

"And then you will be lady sooner or later."

"Yes, isn't it awful?"

He was willing to chat like this for hours. It passed the nights.

When he did not feel like talking he could fill the time with speculations about her. It was difficult to make much judgment of the person behind the ugly uniform. She gave him the feeling that there was much money in her background, and that it was not her husband's but her own. In the fall, when the nights grew cold, she often wore a dark mink coat over the uniform. This she would bundle quickly out of sight when matron made her rounds. People to whom mink is a luxury don't stuff it under the bed, matron or no matron.

She wore no jewelry, not even a wedding ring. Her hands were as rough as a housemaid's, for nursing entails a great deal of scrubbing, and the white-veiled languid lady who dabs the patient's brow with a cloth exists only in films. Watching her work reminded him of his own year as a private in the French army. She was competent enough, but it was obvious that she had never had to work before, and as soon as the war ended, would never work again.

Then one night a few words of idle chatter gave him her background, and he felt that like everything about her it was perfect and could not have been otherwise. Speaking idly of various friends and relatives who had escaped from occupied France and come to England, she said how much her father would have enjoyed a Scarlet Pimpernel escape across the Channel.

He remembered that she had spoken only of her father's people, never directly of him. Since fathers in these days might be Pétainists and collaborators, it was all too easy to put a foot wrong. He moved with care.

"Do you think perhaps he will?"

"He's dead. Otherwise I am sure he would have."

"I'm sorry."

"He and my mother were killed in a plane crash just before the war. If you like music you've probably heard of him. François Vaucaire."

The possession of a famous name, he thought, probably forces one into this exaggerated modesty. For next to Casadesus, François Vaucaire had certainly been France's most famous pianist, and as a national possession he had probably been the most popular, having been a poor boy from Brittany who made good and married, like the third son in a fairy tale, the gilt-haired only daughter of an earl from Cornwall.

Riebeck remembered dimly from more than twenty years ago the Sunday supplement romance, revived in the double (yet still somehow romantic) tragedy of the flaming private plane quenched and lost forever somewhere between Finisterre and Land's End.

He made his apologies to Jenny for having revived sad memories, but she brushed this aside. "I hardly ever saw my parents, you know. I usually lived with my uncle in Cornwall or else in finishing schools in Paris. I went on tour with my father just before the accident and I found I liked him very much, but that was really the first time I got to know him at all well. It's a film star life, being a virtuoso," she added contemptuously.

He liked her for being honest about this. She could have posed becomingly against the background of tragic orphan, and counted on anyone's sympathy. But he had already had occasion to learn that for all her fair and slender beauty there was nothing of the lily maid about Jenny. Vaguely he remembered newspaper photographs of her mother: a delicate, doll-like shepherdess. Jenny resembled her not at all. She had a Breton width of brow and cheekbone, and a Breton toughness of mind which she concealed,

147

not always successfully, under the charming manners of the gently reared.

In the fall of 1940 the air raids started. The big Sunday raid in September caught him by surprise. He had been asleep, still finding sleeping easier in the daytime, and awoke to shaking walls, the shriek of air as bombs tore their way down, the blasts that rocked the town. "What is it?" he asked Jenny who was looking out the windows. "Have the Germans come?"

"An air raid. It just started."

"I didn't imagine I had slept through much of it. Come away from the window."

"It's all right, I opened it."

"It's not all right. Come away."

She turned and came to stand by his bed. She was not smiling, but it cost her an effort. He knew then that she loved destruction with a childish wilfulness, taking no account of the suffering it involved, and the loss, loving it for its violence and magnitude.

During that first great raid all the windows were blown out at the hospital, and after that it was safe to stand by the open windows and watch. Riebeck sat there many nights looking at the flame-smeared sky, listening to the roar of holes torn into resistant air. It was impossible to think of people involved in this; of suffering and hardship caused. It was a spectacle merely, of death-dealing largesse.

And there were moments of comedy to sharpen the edge of disaster. Matron especially, who had the unreflecting courage of a very stupid lion, performed prodigies of useless valor. She rescued pregnant cats, molting canaries, and once somebody's very nasty mother-in-law, who had obviously been left behind deliberately. She even appeared in a Sunday paper once, with some of the members of the bedraggled menagerie for which she had so many times risked her life. The caption mentioned both Florence Nightingale and St. Francis of Assisi, and considerably brightened Riebeck's and Jenny's Sunday.

Among those who made their way from France to England was Vic de Cavignac. He arrived at the hospital one day, carrying a battered pigskin case.

"It belongs to your aunt," he said. "She'll have a fit. I came over in a little fishing boat from Brittany to Cornwall and there was a wind. Too sick-making, as my English friend said. It's your uniforms."

"What a kind thought. Thank you."

"I'll have you know I risked my life to get them. Madame de Baro is a terrific Nazi, did you know? An SS colonel who says he's a cousin of yours is staying at the Hotel de Baro and Paris gossip has it that they're madly in love with each other. She must be at least a hundred."

"Good God, it must be Xandi."

"Count Baranyi or something like that. Anyway she was understandably eager to have me out of the house."

"Come and sit down and tell me all about it," said Riebeck.

"Just a moment." From the bottom of the suitcase Vic produced a bottle. "Cognac from the Chateau Cavignac. What do you say, *mon lapin?*"

"I shall recommend you for instant promotion to marshal of France. Dammit, I'm glad to see you, Vic."

"Me too. When they told me you'd turned up in London I fainted. Do you realize I'd already had masses read for your black soul?"

Riebeck yelped.

"How are you, really? You look like hell."

"I know. Amaranthus all his beauty shed," said Riebeck, whom boredom in the hospital had driven into reading books he would not ordinarily have considered entertaining. "They tell me a lot of those scars will disappear, but not all. I'm hoping to keep the ones that look like Heidelberg dueling scars. Tell me about the world, Vic. I only get the *Times* and I had one very depressing talk with General de Gaulle when he brought me a little green and red ribbon to pin on my pajamas."

"The man lacks judgment. Nobody ever gives me anything."

"I would call that judgment. How is Jacques?"

"Damn," said Vic, "I forgot the corkscrew."

"Push it in. Did you bring cigarettes?"

"Here," said Vic, throwing Gauloises from every pocket on the bed. He poured the cognac into tooth glasses and they both drank.

"I'd forgotten how good the Cavignac cognac is, Vic. Tell me about Latour."

"Jacques' having a marvelous time. He's teamed up with General L'Abbé and they're conspiring in the sewers. They said to tell you they're saving a desk for you."

"Not in the sewers," said Riebeck decidedly. "Anyway, I'm going back on operational as soon as I learn to walk without falling flat on my face."

"Good. Jacques says to tell you he's got Bantain and Valterre safe. Dr. Sivan is still in Weimar, enjoying his unspotted reputation."

"What about Renault and Vertot?"

Cavignac said, "They were caught. I don't know any more than that and I don't want to. You forgot to ask after Dupont, Jean."

"So I did."

"Tell me something. How were you caught?"

"Easily. I walked right in on the Gestapo searching my room, which among other things contained my French army revolver."

"I don't mean that. Why were they searching your room? Latour says Dr. Sivan is certain you were betrayed."

"Tell Latour to tell Dr. Sivan someone overheard him calling me 'mon colonel.' "

"Be serious for a moment. What happened to Dupont?"

"I don't know. Do you know anything about the Kellers? I've often thought that it must have been very unpleasant for them, having me for a lodger."

"They were arrested and questioned, but evidently their ignorance and sincerity convinced the Gestapo, so they were told to go home and be a little more careful about their roomers in the future. Socially of course they are ruined. And now stop treating me as if I were a tame rabbit, Jean. Tell me about Dupont. It won't go any further if you don't want it to. I promise."

"I made a prize ass of myself," said Riebeck. "What do you want to talk about it for?"

"Because we've been friends since St. Cyr, and I think you should talk about it."

Riebeck sat silent for a moment, biting his thumbnail. This was one of the things that kept him awake nights. He had never intended to tell anyone about it. But Vic was an officer and wouldn't say anything stupid, probably.

"It was my fault, all of it," he said at last. "You know they warned me about him. Dr. Sivan warned me and Bantain warned me and here was I, running around like a busy little beaver, paying no attention. I was damned lucky at that. We were pretty nearly at the end of those train jobs, I imagine, and Werner wasted so much time on me everyone else had a chance to get out. Much, much luckier than I deserve."

"I wouldn't say that. I lost five of my people."

"Not through carelessness on your part."

"One. I know, Jean. It keeps me awake nights too."

"What happened?"

"Bad planning on my part. We bitched up the timing and he went up with the explosives. I was the one who made up the schedule."

"I see. At least he only died, Vic. I'm responsible for a man under my command having committed treason."

"Yes."

"Well, thank God you didn't try to tell me it wasn't my fault."

"It's going to be a long war, Jean. By the time it's over we'll all have things on our consciences that won't bear talking about."

"We'll probably be dead by then."

"We'll be in good company."

"What have you been doing, Vic? Why are you in London?"

"I've been in France setting up underground organizations and all that sort of thing. Then they wanted me to report here and now I don't know when I'll be able to get back. London's a lot harder to get out of than France. Wait till you see the War Office, Jean. Rows upon rows of generals what-whatting into telephones. Oh, I almost forgot to tell you. The Riebecks are in Brazzaville and I'm afraid there's a German general living at Fontaines."

"Pouagh! Well, it isn't the first time."

"I must go, Jean. I have to be at the War Office at five ack emma, whatever that means. I wish I spoke English a little better. I don't know it well enough to be really offensive."

"I know," said Riebeck, laughing like a schoolboy. "I heard your little speech on the BBC. 'Sirs and Madams' indeed."

"How anyone with your intelligence can listen to the BBC—I really have to go. Whenever I'm two minutes late they ask me if I realize there's a war on. What a people! Au revoir, *mon lapin.*"

That evening, when Jenny came to collect Riebeck's dinner tray, she handed him a letter. "Major de Cavignac left this for you just now. He said he forgot to give it to you this afternoon and to tell you that your Nazi cousin gave it to him. Do you have a Nazi cousin?"

"SS even." He had recognized the writing on the envelope and for the first time wished that Jenny would go away.

She picked up his tray and looked at it with disapproval. "You haven't touched your food again, though I've told you that whatever the patients don't eat gets made into shepherd's pie for the nurses."

"And when the nurses don't eat it, it comes back to the patients with tomato sauce. Please don't let me keep you from your work."

"How tactful. It looked like a man's handwriting, or I would have left you to it at once."

"It is a man's," said Riebeck, causing Jenny to leave the room with raised eyebrows.

Istvan wrote:

Schani, what can I say? If I could put lentils in my shoes, not cooked ones, the hard kind, and make a pilgrimage for penance, I would do so gladly.

I think there ought not to be too much apologizing and forgiving between friends, but nevertheless I must ask you to forgive me.

I can't write in a letter what I feel. Probably, if we were to meet, I couldn't say it either. And who knows when we will be able to meet again.

If it is at all possible for you, could you send me a letter and let me know how you are. Perhaps through Xandi. He's a wart, but I honestly don't think he'd give you away.

Eva is at Hommages and is well. For myself I am more and more torn between the devil and H. (Horthy) Where does an officer's duty leave off and his conscience begin? I don't know. I am certain you do.

With all my concern and love, Istvan.

Riebeck wrote back: "Don't worry so much, Istvan, I'm all right. Please don't apologize. It was your duty to dislike me so long as you thought me a Nazi. It was probably nastier for you than it was for me." He gave such family news as he had and ended: "Save your lentils. As they never cease to remind us here, there is a war on, and we will presently be glad of all the food we can get." He did not say anything about the question of an officer's duty and conscience. It was not one he felt he could competently answer for anyone but himself.

XI

He had been prepared for pain and exhaustion in learning to walk again, but nothing Captain Falconer had said or he had pictured was as bad as the real thing. Through the winter-frozen halls of the hospital he hobbled between two canes, nauseated with pain, sweat running between his shoulder blades.

Captain Falconer said daily, "Don't overdo it; it looks like being a long war," and Riebeck swore silently to himself that as soon as he could get about with only one cane he would use the other to brain Captain Falconer.

"You can't expect to walk on it overnight," said Captain Falconer, reasonable as always. "It was a very bad break. I have never understood quite how you did it."

"I didn't do it."

"No, of course not. Though it doesn't make much sense even then."

"It serves the purpose of a ball and chain, doctor."

Jenny, knowing that Riebeck only called her husband doctor when he wanted to annoy him, would have recognized the danger signal, but Captain Falconer went blandly on. "Broken leg or no broken leg, I shouldn't think one could get out of Buchenwald in any case."

Riebeck's temper, understandably short these days, snapped. He said, "I don't know about the RAMC, Doctor, but in the French Army officers are at least supposed to try to escape."

The Harley Street manner was after all not indestructible.

"In the *English* army," said Captain Falconer kindly, "we are not supposed to get caught, Colonel Riebeck."

Fury sent him halfway down the hallway before he caught hold of his temper. He looked around. Captain Falconer still stood there. Now he smiled. "You walked that extremely well, Riebeck."

He began to laugh suddenly, leaning against the wall for support. "You mustn't judge the French army by me," he said at last. "We aren't supposed to get caught either."

He walked on, but Captain Falconer caught him up in a few steps. "Dirt-eating apologies," he said. "There's every reason for you to feel cross and none whatever for me, except that I get very bored in London and the War Office won't send me abroad. They keep saying I'm too old, which is rubbish. There aren't any young surgeons, the training takes too long. Speaking of the War Office reminds me. General Burkey rang up to ask whether he might come and see you."

"Who is he?"

"Jenny thinks he's an old dear. I think he's a vile bore. He heads one of those hush-hush War Office Intelligence things."

"It must be hush-hush if even the RAMC knows about it."

"One of Jenny's friends works for Burkey."

"I suppose that's an explanation, of sorts. You wouldn't tell him I'm dead, would you?"

"Dead patients are a poor recommendation for a surgeon."

"So different from veterinarians. All right, I'll see your hush-hush general."

General Burkey arrived the next afternoon. He was in his fifties and beautifully turned out. He was handsome in a silly-looking way, like a film star pretending to be a general. His rise in the army had been regular and unexciting; had there not been a war he would without doubt have died a colonel. It was not easy to associate him with any form of intelligence, but he was eager to do the right thing and in his witless way he tried to be helpful. It was this eagerness to help his department that had brought him, he explained, to see Colonel Riebeck. He was French, he had lived in Germany, and if he would, he could undoubtedly be of great help to the general. "Of course I quite realize I mustn't tire you," Burkey added to this explanation. In an exasperating way he was rather endearing.

"I should be very happy to help you in any way I can, sir," said Riebeck. Burkey beamed upon him his most grateful smile.

From wanting information General Burkey returned many times to ask for advice. When Jenny first heard of his visits—she had been on night duty for several weeks and had thus missed him— she was, for the first time, extremely angry with Riebeck. It was typical of her that she should snap at him with a quotation from Kipling. "The burnt fool's bandaged finger goes wabbling back to the fire."

Riebeck looked at the burn-scarred palms of his hands and murmured, "Must you be quite so appropriate?"

Convicted of tactlessness, Jenny was forced into apology, as Riebeck had meant her to be. But she never relented about Burkey.

"He's a leech. I don't know why you let him pick your brains like that. It's gotten so he can't blow his nose without coming to consult you first. He'll get all the CBE's and OBE's for your work, you'll see."

"It's interesting work, you know. And I don't want a CBE, whatever it is."

"You had your light on again all night, working on those blasted maps for Burkey. Jonathan says you simply must take your pills and go to sleep."

"Captain Falconer needs enemies better able to defend themselves than I am. I shall be so glad when they send him abroad."

"They finally decided to, you know. He just got his orders today."

"Good. Oh sorry, I suppose you don't feel that way."

"A husband at home who wants to be abroad is much worse than a husband abroad."

"I imagine that's true. And now I shall go for a little walk."

"You've already had your walk for today."

"I went all the way down the stairs and back without having to sit down."

"Good for you. But that's enough for one day."

"Just a small walk. Not all the way downstairs." He put his trench coat on and grasped his cane. He had graduated to walking with only one, and the pleasure of this accomplishment balanced the pain it entailed.

In the hall there was a knot of doctors and nurses, whom Jenny joined. Riebeck turned in the other direction, having had a surfeit of doctors these last months, but was called back by Captain Falconer.

"I have news," he said. "I am leaving on Monday, and they've promoted me to major. I'm not supposed to know where I'm going but they said tropical kit, so wherever it is, I shall be warm."

"Don't be too sure. When I was sent to Indochina they said tropical kit, apparently under the assumption that the entire country was a steaming jungle. The only trouble was we were on top of the Annamese mountains, and until we could send home for our winter uniforms we nearly froze to death. However, there aren't too many places one can be sent to right now, so I wish you luck."

"Thank you. It's probably Narvik. Jenny tells me you made it down the stairs this morning."

"With the greatest of ease. Shall I show you?"

"No, thank you. I know you'll be playing hopscotch all over the hospital the moment I've gone, but spare me the sight, please."

Later that afternoon General Burkey arrived in despair. He almost had tears in his eyes as he explained his errand. General Partridge sent his compliments. Would it be at all possible for Colonel Riebeck to come for a conference to the War Office? He would of course be picked up and driven back. "I told him you were not fit to go out yet," said Burkey, almost weeping, "but General Partridge . . ." loyalty prevented him from going on.

General Partridge was the head of the Intelligence Section for which Burkey worked. Riebeck had heard a great deal about him. Even a man as taciturn as General de Gaulle had been moved to speech on the subject. Riebeck had heard him described as out-and-out fascist by Vic, a blot on humanity by Partridge's opposite number in Foreign Office Intelligence, and most accurately by Captain Falconer, who had once had a tussle with the General's gall bladder, and said that like Major Yammerton, General Partridge was a rather peculiar man inasmuch as he was an ass without being a fool.

Riebeck had long wanted to get a look at this paragon and was rather cock-a-hoop about his progress with only one stick, so he said gleefully, "But I am fit, and I would love to come, sir."

General Burkey was much relieved and promised to come by in the evening and pick him up.

When Major Falconer came round for his evening visit, Riebeck said, "Could I go out tonight? I'm being taken in a car."

"You don't have to be so mysterious. Burkey asked my permission. When have I ever tried to stop you from killing yourself? If you think you can manage it, go ahead."

"Thank you. If I do manage it tonight, I'll be out of here in a week."

"You're mad," said Major Falconer, but looking back from the door he was no longer sure. A face with far too many reticences, he had always thought, but what he saw now was a schoolboy's face, full of laughter and excitement.

Riebeck dressed in his uniform. Vic had neglected to bring his medal ribbons, so he only wore the *croix de Lorraine* and the *croix de guerre*, which he had acquired since coming to London. Had he spent hours planning to infuriate General Partridge, he could not have succeeded better.

When Sister Fuller reported the staff car from the War Office, he limped downstairs, so excited about getting out that he scarcely noticed how much it hurt. He was followed by the nurse's litany of apprehensions; did Major Falconer know about this, was he sure of the man who had come to meet him, it wasn't the Gestapo, was it?"

"Not in a War Office car, Sister," he said consolingly and shut the door behind himself before she could offer to call Scotland Yard.

There was another flight of stairs outside the hospital. He hadn't counted on those and had for the moment quite enough of stairs, but in the pleasure of standing outside in the icy rain he managed them passably well.

"Good show," said General Burkey, who had long since learned not to offer help.

Riebeck, who had been curious about London, was balked in his intention of sightseeing by the combination of blackout and rain. Foreigner though he was, he did not believe the shabby office building in front of which they stopped could be the War Office.

"Certainly not," said General Burkey indignantly. "Our various sections have their own offices. We move them about quite often. Safer that way."

Safer possibly, but as Riebeck was to learn, very annoying for the operational personnel, who often found their old office gone and had no place to report when they returned from France.

"You won't mind General Partridge, will you, Riebeck?" said Burkey anxiously, putting a hand on Riebeck's sleeve. "People say he's rude, but I don't think he means to be. It's just his manner."

Riebeck wondered how this peaceable soul, so eager to create good will all around, had ever gotten into the army. He said, "I shan't mind."

General Burkey led the way and opened the door to an ordinary conference room with a green baize table. At its head General Partridge came to his feet and instantly regretted it. He looked exactly as Riebeck had expected him to, with a conceited moustache and pale pig's eyes; a representative of the British Empire forced to meet a French—French, oh my Gad!—colonel.

Riebeck took his time, looking over the other people in the room, ignoring Partridge's pig stare. There was a toady, Partridge's ADC, no doubt, who peered worriedly through thick spectacles, and a stocky, red-haired captain with a broad, lined face and merry eyes. Riebeck smiled at him and returned his glance to General Partridge. He moved his cane from his right hand to his left and saluted.

General Burkey, rattled by the fact that for the first time in living memory someone had set down Partridge, and by the sudden wail of the air raid sirens, got his sentence upside down and said, "Colonel Riebeck, may I present General Partridge."

Into the purple silence he blithely continued, pointing to the red-haired captain, "Captain Tyrell, who has just returned from France." He ignored the ADC.

General Partridge made noises in the back of his throat, like a turkey on Christmas Eve.

"Hello," said Captain Tyrell cheerfully. General Partridge turned on him a blue flash that should have killed him.

Riebeck was enjoying it all, but his leg hurt abominably. He could feel his shirt stick to his shoulder blades. Partridge was still standing. Riebeck wondered how much longer he would be able to keep on his feet, but he was damned if he asked Partridge's permission to sit.

Jeremy Tyrell hooked a chair with his foot, shoved it across to Riebeck and said, "Let's all sit down." Riebeck made a noise which he pretended was a cough, but which had sounded to General Partridge remarkably like a snort. Finding that he was still standing while his inferiors sat, Partridge made another noise in the back of his throat, smoothed his feathers and, pretending that nothing had happened, sat down.

He moved his forces into a new formation for attack. "Why was French Section never notified that you were in London, Colonel Riebeck?"

Riebeck took out his cigarettes, looked for permission to General Partridge, who did not himself smoke and did not believe any soldier ought to, but could not at the moment refuse, waited while Captain Tyrell lit his pipe and then said, "General de Gaulle was informed that I was here, sir."

The turkey noises were louder now. There was a ruffling of feathers and protesting slap of wings. The mention of General de Gaulle always did this to General Partridge.

Riebeck continued as placidly as if he were discussing the weather: "I have General de Gaulle's permission, sir, to help you as much as I can, within the limits of my own discretion."

"Your own discretion?" said Partridge with the greatest contempt. He did not believe that any officer acquired discretion until he became a brigadier.

Riebeck's eyes narrowed. He was smiling, and General Partridge did not like that smile at all. "Oh, but I am very discreet, you know," he said gently.

The man with the axe could be seen approaching the turkey yard. General Partridge retired to the second line of the trenches, leaving the defense for the moment to his second-in-command.

"Tell him what we want, Burkey."

"It's the escape routes for the RAF," said General Burkey. "Tyrell has been over there, in France I mean, trying to set up routes for RAF men who are shot down and have to parachute. The trouble is—I mean to say—er—the difficulty we encounter—ah, we—"

"The trouble," said Captain Tyrell firmly, "is that there are too damned many collaborators."

"Our trouble too, Captain," said Riebeck mildly.

"I daresay. But it complicates things," said Tyrell. "I expect you frogs are better informed—"

"Really, Jeremy—" General Burkey murmured weakly.

"What we want," said General Partridge, "is a list of people who are reliable and who will pass our fliers on until they can be brought across by boat."

Riebeck had heard many stories of General Partridge's gall, but this exceeded all expectations. Forgetting diplomacy he said bluntly, "I can't give you a list, sir. Surely you know that."

The man with the axe was in the turkey pen now, looking directly at Partridge, whose feathers were all on end with indignation. When was the last time a mere colonel had said to him: "I can't"?

Outside the sirens howled the all clear. "What happens to the names the pilots are given?" Riebeck asked. "Are they written down?"

"They memorize them the night before, and the lists are destroyed," said Captail Tyrell.

"Good. I would do much for the RAF, but of course I cannot give you lists. What I can do is have a talk with Captain Tyrell and put him in touch with some of our people who have been in France from the beginning and know their way about."

This struck everyone as practical and they relaxed, tossing the shopworn topic of invasion back and forth once more.

"You were in Germany, Colonel," said General Partridge, "what do you think? Are they going to invade us?"

Riebeck shrugged. "They might mess about in the Balkans for a bit yet. Yugoslavia perhaps. Countries who announce they are neutral are usually asking for trouble. But I really think they will march into Russia."

"Russia!" exclaimed General Partridge in profound disgust. "Absolute tosh."

General Burkey insisted on driving Riebeck back to the hospital, which was nice of him, everything considered. He was silent, rather frightened of this new Colonel Riebeck, so different from the amiable man who had done his homework for him.

Riebeck too was silent, thinking over the extraordinary evening. What had happened in this meeting that could not have been handled as well by Burkey as a go-between from the hospital to the War Office? Was it simply chicanery on Partridge's part? In spite of the bad impression the general had made, Riebeck did not believe it.

Did Partridge by any chance dislike go-betweens? Had he refused to deal with a man he had not seen face to face?

A prize ass, undeniably, but not, at any time, a fool.

"Is Captain Tyrell the one that writes poetry?" Riebeck asked his silent companion.

General Burkey was very fond of Jeremy Tyrell and wanted Colonel Riebeck to think well of him, but he was incapable of telling a lie. "He used to. But I am sure he has quite stopped since he came to work for us."

"I read some once. I thought it was very good."

"Oh, really," said General Burkey, much relieved.

They had arrived at the hospital. "If Captain Tyrell will come here tomorrow afternoon," said Riebeck, "I shall be glad to see him. Thank you for my first evening out, sir. It was delightful."

General Burkey blushed with pleasure.

Sister Fuller, glad to see Riebeck alive, made him a "nice cup of tea," very strong and sweet and perfectly nauseating. Worn out, Riebeck went to bed, and for the first time in many months slept through the night.

The next morning a larcenous young officer in French Intelligence procured Tyrell's file for Riebeck. From the bare statistics (Born January 1, 1900, in Sligo, ran away from school and joined the army with a borrowed birth certificate in 1916, emerged two years later with the rank of private) Riebeck thought he scented regret that Jeremy Tyrell should be so spectacularly good at his work. For he was good; that was obvious from the brief assignment reports, each ending with the laconic conclusion: "Successfully carried out."

Riebeck had read hundreds of files in his day and he knew, as plainly as the recorded facts, the things that remained unsaid. The picture he made for himself from the report was the same he had formed of the person he had met the night before: clever, fearless, and most important, consistently lucky. Also unorthodox in his methods, undisciplined in his manners, and incurably civilian. The report told him nothing new, except a small note on the bottom which he had almost overlooked. Married to the Honourable Pamela Tregaskis, with a Cornwall address. Two children. So *he* was Jenny's great friend who worked for General Burkey. "How very interesting," he thought, making sure that it was a purely noncommittal comment.

Jeremy Tyrell arrived punctually and was shown into Riebeck's room by Jenny, with whom he appeared to be on excellent terms. He brought with him a cold draught of London air, and all his unbounded energy and health. It was like letting a snowstorm into a morgue. Riebeck said he was glad to see him and meant it.

"I am honored," said Jeremy quite seriously. "But I would prefer to see you almost anywhere else. There is a smell about hospitals that depresses me at once."

"I expect to be out in a week," said Riebeck. "Do sit down."

Jeremy complied. Riebeck looked him over, taking his time about it.

Jeremy Tyrell was less than middle height and what his friends called "portly." His numerous enemies described him simply as short and fat. He had a broad, freckled face that had been left out in the rain and wind too long, a big nose that had seen better days before it was broken, outrageously red hair, and the most astonishing china-blue eyes, as opaque and cheerful as a baby's. He might, Riebeck thought, be many things; a sailor, a mercenary, a smuggler. He did not look like his idea of a poet.

"So you know Madame Falconer," he said.

"My father-in-law is the neighbor, in Cornwall, of Lord Allanbank who is Jenny's uncle. I've known her for years. I'm the only man under eighty in London who isn't in love with her. Not but what in a platonic way I'm very fond of her indeed. Of course Falconer is a bounder."

"Is he? I find it hard to tell with the English, but he is always very *comme-il-faut*."

The suggestion that in England it is difficult to tell the gentlemen from the bounders would have been taken up very warmly by anyone less intent on his gossip than Jeremy.

"Too *comme-il-faut* if you ask me. Anyway we were at the same school and I remember his transformation. His name used to be Sokol in those days."

Riebeck laughed. "Now that is clever."

"Lord yes. Clever's his middle name. He became great friends with Gerry Allanbank, Jenny's cousin that is, and used to go home for holidays with him. I don't for a moment suppose Lord Allanbank would have let him marry Jenny if they'd been of the same class, but the English aristocracy is utterly pathetic about this sort of thing. Lord Allanbank is the rudest man I know, but he would never dream of telling an ex-Jew he isn't good enough to marry his niece."

And what of the niece?

While Riebeck was still debating with his lower self whether he ought to ask, Jeremy, ploughing on with his piece of gossip, answered it. "Of course he must have been a great temptation for Jenny, one can see that."

Mere politeness now required Riebeck to say, "Why?"

"You don't know what an English debutante season is like, do you? It's to society what spring is to the barnyard. Only nothing as lusty as a cock or a bull ever turns up at a deb dance. The males consist entirely of Young Young Men and Old Young Men. The Young Young Men have spots and no chins, the Old Young Men have no spots and two chins. After a London season Jonathan Falconer must have been very nearly irresistible. Jenny may have been slumming when she married him, but who can blame her. All the same, it's a pity."

Riebeck reflected that this habit of Jeremy Tyrell's, of stopping his stories with a remark like this, was extremely annoying.

"Why a pity?"

"I think," said Jeremy, "that if you are born with looks like Jenny's, your function in life is to inspire a *grande passion*. To make someone fling away the world for your sake, or wreck his life for love of you; to make the grand gesture. Not to marry a half-warmed fish like Falconer. Does it strike you that he's a queer?"

Riebeck, startled, said, "Surely not. No, I'm certain he's not."

"No, I suppose not. Much too definite. He's just an enigma. Whatever answer you find for him, it doesn't fit. Everyone has a ruling passion. It may not be an obvious or even recognizable one, but it's the thing that gives life its direction. What is Falconer's? Not his wife. His career? I doubt it. He's clever and he would have been good at most things, but surgery is a socially acceptable profession and he picked that. He hasn't got one."

"Perhaps he merely hides it well."

"There's nothing to hide. I tell you, I've known him since we were boys. What there is, is out in front. His looks, his brains, his manner. Do you like him?"

"Yes. No." Riebeck thought about it for a moment. "I don't know. Which is odd, because I am not usually vague about these things."

"There is nothing there to like or dislike. What is your ruling passion, by the way?"

"Not to be bored," said Riebeck promptly. Jeremy burst out laughing.

"I accept the rebuke. For forty years I've been told I talk too much. It hasn't done a bit of good, as you can see."

Riebeck said, "You haven't bored me. I meant it exactly as an answer to your question. Now I'll do the talking, and I hope you will find it interesting." He described the best escape routes and the chain of people who could be relied on to pass the RAF men on to the coast; the way it was worked with separate places of *rendez-vous* so that each member of the chain knew only his own part and if caught could talk to the Gestapo to his heart's content.

At this Jeremy protested.

"They are civilians," said Riebeck. "Believe me, it is better so."

"You make them sound like an inferior breed. I think it's marvelous of them to take all these risks. Why should you assume that they are more cowardly than professional soldiers?"

"I don't assume it. They may very well be braver, but we have no right to endanger the lives of the other members of the chain, as well as the freedom of your pilots—of whom you have so few— on a flattering assumption."

"Being a civilian at heart, this whole attitude puts my back up."

"It shouldn't. Every profession entails certain risks and rewards. A bull-fighter may not protest if he gets gored, whereas a bank clerk would be quite within his rights to complain bitterly about such an incident. A professional soldier accept risks to his body and his mind as part of the job."

"Why his mind?"

"Because wars are the ultimate exercise of the belief that the end justifies the means. If you engage regularly in a paranoiac profession it may well affect you eventually."

"What are the rewards?"

"I can't tell you."

"You mean they're too rarefied and olympian for a mere civilian to understand?"

"No. I meant that I do not know."

Jeremy began to laugh.

"Why is that funny?" asked Riebeck.

"Because things that are typical usually are funny. You see, I heard stories about you long before I met you, and you match them perfectly. I'd say it's also typical that you don't ask what the stories were."

"What were they?"

"Now you're being polite. You don't give a damn, really. When I get back, may I come to see you again?"

"What optimism. You mean *if* you get back."

"I've a hunch I'll make it."

"How wonderful," said Riebeck.

"You don't believe in hunches?"

"In Indochina the natives used to stand in the middle of the road and jump aside from oncoming cars at the last moment because they believed that any evil spirits following them would then get run over. The only things that got run over, unfortunately, were the less agile natives."

"But that is primitive superstition," said Jeremy. "Mine is quite different. You see, I am Irish, and my grandmother is a witch."

"And what did you think of our Jeremy?" asked Jenny when she brought Riebeck's dinner.

"Very entertaining."

"That means he gossiped. He's the biggest gossip I know."

"He says his wife's people are your uncle's neighbors in Cornwall. I must say I've rarely seen anyone who looked less like a husband."

"He's the world's worst. He hasn't lived with his wife since about two days after they were married."

Riebeck, remembering under the next-of-kin the two sons, Patrick and Terrence, said, "Surely not two days."

"Well, two years then. How pedantic you are. As a matter of fact he's quite domesticated now. When he was in America just before the war he fell in love with a girl called Barbara Leigh, who is a great friend of mine. Her husband used to be an actor but is in the RAF now and is a great friend of Jeremy's."

"Now I would call that gossip."

"Only like telling fairy tales to babies so they don't notice how awful Benger's tastes."

Riebeck turned the food on his plate with his fork and said, "What is Benger's?"

"Baby food. Come on, finish up, or we'll get shepherd's pie tomorrow."

"I thought this was shepherd's pie. What's the dessert?"

"Custard powder custard and tinned peaches."

Colonel Riebeck said a bad word and lit a cigarette.

"I know," said Jenny with resignation. "You are getting out of here within the week."

Riebeck left the hospital exactly one week after his meeting with General Partridge. Major Falconer refused all responsibility for his future, but Riebeck, lying fluently, said he felt absolutely marvelous.

He moved in with Vic de Cavignac, who had a large unfurnished flat in Duke Street.

"You can keep the place," said Vic, who was about to go back to France, "on the condition that you will let me stay with you when I come back," which, considering it was Cavignac's apartment, seemed to Riebeck a very reasonable request. "I'm sorry I never got around to buying furniture."

Riebeck said it didn't matter. There was a bed and a chair. He stacked his books on the chair and used the bed as bed, dining table, closet, and desk.

Cavignac bequeathed him the remains of the Chateau Cavignac cognac and an introduction to the Cardinal Richelieu, a black-market restaurant where the food was plentiful, excellent, astronomically expensive, and entirely illegal.

When Riebeck reported at French Intelligence that he was well and ready for anything, they laughed, promoted him to full colonel, and gave him his assignment. It was known officially as liaison between their office and General Partridge's. Unofficially his orders were to infiltrate behind their lines, bring them to heel, and give no quarter. Since Riebeck himself was forced to admit that he was in no shape as yet to go abroad, he said, "How amusing," and accepted.

There began a war of attrition with General Partridge from which the Psychological Warfare Department might have learned valuable lessons. General Partridge held his ground by employing the great genius of the British for losing all the battles and winning the war.

The basic conflict was one of personality. General Partridge held sacred the British Empire and despised all foreigners for not being English. Colonel Riebeck sincerely believed that there was only one civilized nation on earth, and that all others were second rate if they imitated France, or barbarian if they did not. From this sprang endless irritations from General Partridge: Riebeck's unshakable admiration for General de Gaulle, General de Gaulle's refusal to cooperate with the British (it was not reasonable to expect it; he could not even cooperate with the French) and British Intelligence's steadfast refusal to cooperate with anybody at all.

The liaison job soon evolved into something more definite. Even before Riebeck had taken it over, there had been talk about setting up a new department in order to coordinate a certain type of intelligence work: jobs which had to involve members of several nationalities almost invariably ran into trouble and ended in jealousies, bickerings, and feuds carried on with as much leisure and venom as though the respective countries had been at peace.

"What we need," said General Burkey to Colonel Riebeck, "is a department of combined operations, which concerns itself with those jobs which cannot be done by the agents of one country alone."

"Yes indeed," said Colonel Riebeck.

"What you need," said General Burkey to General Partridge, "is . someone with a great deal of tact, for whom people will work willingly, because he will always do more than they. There is really only one logical person to run this new department of yours."

"I will not have Riebeck," said General Partridge with great firmness.

"But my dear fellow," said the meek General Burkey, "of course you will," and he was right.

Riebeck talked it over with General de Gaulle, who considered it infiltration on a grand scale and gave his permission. Riebeck was given a very small office between those of General Partridge and General Burkey (Jeremy claimed it had originally been the drinks cupboard), hung a picture of General de Gaulle on the wall, and went to work exercising (according to General Partridge) an evil influence on General Partridge's young men.

He did not do this intentionally, even Partridge had to admit, but it was annoying to have to hear fine English boys speak with a French accent, to watch them walk with a limp whenever they remembered to, and worst of all, to see them kiss ladies' hands and murmur "*enchanté.*" It was too much.

Riebeck laughed and said he could not help either his accent or his limp, but promised not to kiss any more ladies' hands. "Once they're sent abroad it will all be forgotten, sir."

"Let's hope so. That young ass Hilary asked me yesterday what one has to do to get one of those sissy braids to wear on one's uniform. I sent him to the decoding room for a week."

"The fourragère? It's a regimental citation, not a personal one."

"Then why the devil are you wearing it now? You're not with your regiment."

"I'm on leave of absence from my regiment, sir. Besides," added Riebeck, "I think it's rather pretty," and had the pleasure of seeing General Partridge turn purple once more.

General Partridge's department was officially designated as St 2. No one at the War Office knew what the initials stood for. Jeremy Tyrell maintained that the S was for espionage, and for the rest unrefined people filled the initials as they pleased. The department consisted of a German section and a French section. The French section functioned reasonably well; the German one was almost moribund.

Riebeck who, thanks to the Gestapo, had plenty of time to think about things, arrived at conclusions that were in most cases directly opposed to the accepted Intelligence theories. He believed that no German-occupied country was cut off from any other. Intelligence operations in no matter what country were to be considered as an integrated whole. In England, where the French section wasn't talking to the German section wasn't talking to the Poles wasn't talking to the Czechs *ad nauseam,* this was a revolutionary innovation and one to be distrusted. It was, incidentally, a theory General Partridge had advocated for years. But, unable to agree on any

169

subject with Colonel Riebeck, he now pretended he had never heard of it.

Riebeck held that the best security a secret agent can have is his mobility. He disliked the idea of resident agents. He had disliked it even before his own disastrous Weimar experience. A resident agent was a sitting duck.

He supported wholeheartedly any and all activities that could annoy the Germans, from sabotage to arson and murder, but these he felt should be left to the local resistance, organized by a few trained and mobile agents with an escape hatch always ready; a waiting submarine, a Lysander, and since these were hard to come by, at least a new identity.

While it was England's good fortune to be an island, it was most unfortunate from Riebeck's point of view. He demanded airplanes and submarines. What he got was a frosty question from the Admiralty. Was he aware that there was a war on?

His relations with the Royal Navy were at all times thorny. Jeremy, who had been at Dunkirk, too, thought he could guess the reason. He too had at that time felt the humiliation of the defeated army having to be rescued by the undefeated navy. But it was the navy of his own country and he was a generous person and had long since forgiven the Royal Navy for saving him. But for Riebeck things were not so simple. The undefeated navy was not his own, and he was at no time a person who took kindly to being helped. He therefore treated the Admiralty with icy, unforgiving politeness, and they replied in kind.

With the RAF his relations were *frère et cochon* from the start. The Air Marshal declared himself perfectly willing to give him planes and pilots just as soon as he could spare them, and for the rest they would simply have to pig along.

After endless badgering Riebeck talked a French pilot and plane out of General de Gaulle. The RAF was wonderful and helped him as much as they could. And if everything else failed there were always the fishing boats from Brittany to Cornwall. They obligingly ferried secret agents, escaped prisoners of war, and shot-down pilots. But since the boats, in order to evade German vigilance, preferred to sail in foul weather, these trips were usually a trying business to all but hardened seamen. Even Jeremy Tyrell, who had grown up on the Irish coast and had before the war sailed his own boat all over the Mediterranean, felt the distress of those journeys and once radioed back: "Psalm 45." Riebeck thought at first something had gone wrong in the decoding room, but was enlightened when he looked it up and discovered that this is the psalm that begins: *"Eructavit cor meum."*

Riebeck had no regular staff of his own, since he would draw on the personnel of the other departments as the situation dictated. He made the fullest use of this arrangement. His first step was to annex Jeremy Tyrell on a permanent basis. With less enthusiasm he accepted the small group of friends General Partridge described trenchantly as "Tyrell's gang." They were actors, poets, and esthetes (to give them no harsher name), and Riebeck considered them something of a trial. They all looked alike, talked constantly about Russia, read the *New Statesman,* and all of them seemed to be called Lionel.

"They're all right, really," said Jeremy when Riebeck complained that he would never learn to tell them apart. "I mean if they ever saw a Russian Commie they'd probably faint."

As it seemed to be impossible to have Jeremy Tyrell without his entourage, Riebeck tolerated the Lionels until he discovered that they had all spent many years abroad (often at the urgent request of their families) and spoke French fluently though with very strange accents. Knowing that Latour and L'Abbé would never forgive him, Riebeck at once sent every single Lionel to work in France, where to his astonishment they did extremely well.

Far more useful than the Lionels was Colonel Simon Cook, another friend of Jeremy's, and the only member of the Department who was even-tempered enough to serve as General Partridge's second-in-command. He was a most unlikely friend for Jeremy to have, for he was earnest, intelligent, and conscientious, and had in private life been a schoolmaster. He was good at his job and saved Riebeck endless hours of trouble by standing between him and General Partridge whenever necessary.

From the Poles Riebeck borrowed Captain Novotny who was so unremarkable that one could barely remember his face while one was talking to him. This lack of distinction made him as valuable to Riebeck as he had been to the Polish section.

From the Norwegians he borrowed Major Danny, who was their best explosives expert, and from Latour he abstracted Cavignac with entourage. He called it borrowing and did it so gradually that the heads of various departments realized only when it was too late that they had lost their top people to Riebeck.

His favorite was and remained Jeremy Tyrell. He was fun to work with and he could deal with the people with whom they had constantly to associate now; the fishermen and farmers and waiters, the clerks and shopkeepers who were the base of the resistance.

It was not snobbery that made Riebeck ill at ease with these people. It was the fact that their lives were circumscribed differently from his own. Manners are a protection only among equals. With soldiers military etiquette and an unbreakable system of caste had kept him safe from personal involvement, but there were no fences here, they were not soldiers, but they were all fighting. It was not of Riebeck's choosing that around his person legends had grown. A resistance movement is a romantic affair and largely an amateur one. It needs its heroes and legends. And who could serve better than the aloof colonel with his thin, scarred face and lame leg, and that touch of miracle which gives such comforting invincibility to legendary heroes: he had survived Buchenwald.

So Jeremy became his go-between. Jeremy got along splendidly with everybody. He consumed admirable quantities of wine, told dirty jokes in his terrible French, and gave satisfaction.

There was indeed only one thing wrong with Jeremy Tyrell—the way he spoke French.

"It is one of the marvels of the war to me," Riebeck said to him once, "how the War Office ever came to think that you could pass for a Frenchman."

"Did you ever see that thing in *Punch* where an Englishman is all dressed and made up to look like Hitler, and one Intelligence officer says to the other: 'Of course to carry it off properly he would have to learn German.' "

"Yes," agreed Riebeck, "that's it."

"It's the way Intelligence works, you know. My languages are German and Greek, so naturally I was sent to France."

"I didn't know about the German," said Riebeck.

"I spent a year there as a kid. My mother had a friend who was a moldy old professor at Heidelberg. *He* had a kid that played the violin."

"How dreadful," said Riebeck. "Would you prefer working in Germany?"

"I would in a way. I frankly prefer Huns to Frogs," said Jeremy, whom no consideration of what was fitting kept from speaking his mind. "But as long as you're mucking about in France, I daresay I can stick it."

XII

Having an office next door to General Burkey's presented Riebeck with the constant temptation to poke his fingers in the General's pies. It was not a temptation he resisted often, for Burkey was hopeless, knew it, and was grateful for any help he could get, and Riebeck had met and come to like many of Burkey's people, and did not wish the hazards they met to be any greater than absolutely necessary.

With fewer losses than ever before, General Burkey's section began to pull off jobs that turned General Partridge green with envy.

Then the hazards, reduced to the necessary minimum in competent and experienced hands, increased again. Colonel Cook parachuted into a German ambush, some of the local French people were dropped on for no apparent reason, and Jeremy Tyrell was forced to spend two weeks hiding from the Gestapo instead of rescuing an English general from a prisoner-of-war camp. The general, who had been pretending to be a corporal, and had been forced to dig potatoes by the Germans, had many bitter things to say to Colonel Riebeck when he finally arrived in London. Riebeck passed his comments along to General Partridge with a comment of his own: "It's got to be someone in the department, sir," he said. "No one outside could know all these things."

General Partridge became red and warm at this suggestion. "Colonel Riebeck," he said, "there are no traitors in the *English* army."

Belonging, as he did, to an army that could boast Marshal Pétain, it was now Riebeck's turn to get hot under the collar. Burkey obliged only with a few distressed tut tuts and handed the problem back to Riebeck. "What do *you* think we ought to do?"

Riebeck thought the time had come to test his nerve by going to Germany where he had a contact who occupied a high-ranking post in German Military Intelligence.

He telephoned Squadron Leader Laurence Leigh, Jeremy's protégé by virtue of being Jeremy's mistress' husband, and the department's more or less private pilot, and asked him if he could drop him within walking distance of Berlin.

"Sure," said Larry Leigh. "Can you parachute?"

As a matter of fact he could. As a lieutenant at Chalons he, Vic de Cavignac, and several other young officers whose high spirits had got on their general's nerves had been sent on a parachute course.

The general had hit on parachute training as a form of punishment, little guessing that his lieutenants would probably have been happy to volunteer to make the jumps without parachute simply to escape for a little the boredom of garrison life. Nor did he see anything bizarre in having, in his regiment, a number of young officers who could correctly wear paratroop wings on the sleeves of their cavalry uniforms.

But that was long ago, and all Riebeck now remembered was that he and Vic had mostly been very drunk and had frequently landed in trees. Also he had not then had a lame leg.

To Squadron Leader Leigh he said, "Lord yes, I've done the whole course in France," and then proceeded to prepare himself for the coming adventure by reading with passionate interest everything the instruction book on parachuting had to say.

The night before he left he took Jenny Falconer out to dinner. They had seen each other frequently since he had left the hospital, and going out in the evening with Jenny was one of his favorite leisure occupations. After the VAD uniform it was a great pleasure for him to see her in clothes which were prewar but had come from the good French houses, her pale Snow Queen hair piled high and caught with diamonds. He liked her sable coat and her jewelry, but he also liked the rough housemaid's hands, which she tried to hide from view. He enjoyed the fact that she was so rich and made use of her money, thinking of his own fortune and how little he had done with it. Except for Baranyi Palace and the horses and cars he had occasionally bought he might as easily have lived on his officer's pay.

They usually ate at the Richelieu. Jenny invariably felt obliged to protest against the black-market food, but he had noticed that her protests never extended to not eating. After dinner they went to a film both had wanted to see, yet the evening was somehow not a success. There was a certain lack of attention on Riebeck's part, and this Jenny silently resented. He took her home early, refused to come in for a drink, and hurried back to his apartment. The truth was, he wanted to get home and read the parachuting books again.

Before dawn he was driven to the airfield, where bombers stood in shining rows, waiting to fly to Berlin. Riebeck regarded them with satisfaction. The fact that he might be in Berlin when all those bombs would arrive bothered him not at all.

Squadron Leader Leigh came up and saluted. He was conspicuously handsome, very dark, with hazel eyes, a nose just long enough for character but not too long for beauty, a well-cut mouth, and a real, half-inch dimple in his chin. In other days film fans had swooned at the sight of him and teenage girls had slept with his photograph under their pillows.

Women who knew him were curiously immune to his looks. His wife had left him for Jeremy Tyrell who was certainly no beauty, and Jenny, who could often be seen dancing with him at night clubs (probably unable to resist being half of such a singularly handsome couple), said he was an angel in a voice that betokened very little interest.

He had been a good actor, and so long as he fancied himself in the part of British Airman, Jeremy assured Riebeck, he would be an excellent pilot. Riebeck had not been reassured. He did not want his agents flown into enemy territory by this ultimate in civilian development, a film star. But Larry Leigh's excellent record in the Battle of Britain and later for the department had put his doubts to rest. In all fairness one must give him credit. He could have been an RAF pilot in Hollywood with far less danger and much more pay and adulation.

They walked to the plane while Larry gave the latest weather reports; foul for pilots, fair for spies.

"This is our navigator," he then said, pointing to an elderly man who must have done some ingenious cheating to get into the RAF, "and this is Herb. You do what he tells you and I'll put you down exactly where you want to be."

"Have you parachuted much, sir?" asked Herb, helping him into his parachute.

"Never from an English plane," said Riebeck, which within limits was the truth.

"Remember not to look down, sir. People forget and then they leave their teeth."

Riebeck remembered that in English planes one dropped through a hole in the fuselage instead of jumping out the door, and promised to hold on to his teeth.

The night was very cold and rough over the Channel, but the RAF had provided hot coffee laced with rum, and Riebeck felt that Jeremy had for once not exaggerated when he had called them angels.

Larry Leigh had a DFC and fifteen German planes to his credit. When he came back for a short visit and said, "I don't know how you can do it, I wouldn't go to Germany for anything in the world," Riebeck had to laugh.

"Please," said Larry, "when you are ready to be picked up, would you find a nice flat field for me to land on. The boys in your department seem to think nothing of sending me a message that says: 'Am on highest peak of the Dolomites, come and get me.'"

Riebeck was much cheered by Larry Leigh's innocent assumption that he would be coming back.

To his surprise the parachuting was not only simple but fun. (Beginner's luck, he later discovered.) The meeting between himself and General Koenig, the French officer who had been on the German General Staff in World War I and was now a big wheel in Nazi Military Intelligence, was managed after a few minor difficulties. General Koenig was able to tell him that the leak had come from a man in the decoding room of General Partridge's section. He was no one Riebeck knew, which was a distinct relief.

"After all the trouble I had getting you out of Germany last time," General Koenig then said, "I do wish you'd stay out."

"I gathered I had you to thank for the staff car and forged papers. I wish you'd tell me what happened, exactly. I was too doped to notice at the time."

"When this war is over," said Koenig, "you can buy me an eight-course dinner at Lapérouse if we are still alive, and I will tell you then. It is much too long for now. There was a message for you from London, saying could you go back by way of France. Your Captain Tyrell parachuted near Nancy a week ago and has not been heard from since. There could be many reasons," he added seeing Riebeck's face. "You don't have to imagine the worst yet."

"I try not to."

"Are you all right for papers?"

"Yes, thanks. I can get about Germany and France. I'd better leave at once."

"Don't be a fool. Sleep first."

"I am well supplied with Benzedrine," said Riebeck. "They worship that stuff in London. Good-by and thank you."

"Take care of yourself," said General Koenig. "Things have tightened up a lot. I couldn't get anybody out of Buchenwald now."

"Don't rub it in."

The German railways had been disrupted by bombings and a coal shortage. Riebeck decided it would be quickest if he hitched a ride with someone. Since the only people who were still driving cars were staff officers of high rank, it was with a German staff officer that he traveled to France.

Riebeck knew about Tyrell's assignment and had a general idea of his whereabouts. There was in the countryside not far from

177

Nancy a factory so well camouflaged that the English discovered its existence purely by accident. No amount of tactful questioning had elicited information about what was manufactured there. Secret factories like this always made General Partridge extremely nervous, and Jeremy Tyrell, with a radio operator and an assistant, had been sent to blow it up. Jeremy had remarked insultingly that it was probably a place where woolen socks were knitted for the Russian campaign, but had not protested any further, for he dearly loved loud noises, whether necessary or not. It was Riebeck who had protested against the whole operation, which was of the kind he most disapproved. Instead of dropping explosives and at most one agent and letting the local maquis do the job, three English officers who did not know the terrain or the local setup well were being endangered for the sake of blowing up one mysterious factory.

There could be several reasons for the silence. Difficulties often cropped up on this type of job, and there was then nothing to do but lie low and bide one's time. Still, if he had a wireless operator along it was strange that Tyrell had not informed London of his whereabouts. Unless of course the wireless didn't work, which had been known to happen.

The German staff officer was on a secret mission—evidently his first—and very proud of it. Riebeck hinted that he too was doing top-secret work for the Reich, and since he invariably looked like an officer no matter what he wore, his new acquaintance believed him without difficulty. They shared a bottle of brandy the German had thoughtfully brought with him, and became very cheerful. When they arrived in Strasbourg they swore eternal friendship with an ardor hampered only by the fact that neither was at liberty to give his name.

"You have been more than kind already," said Riebeck to his host, "but there is one more favor I must ask."

"Ask away, dear fellow."

"If you should ever see me again after today, in no matter what circumstances, you must pretend that you do not know me. It might easily," said Riebeck with truth, "be a matter of life and death for me."

"My dear fellow, I quite understand and I give you my word. But perhaps after the war is over . . ."

Riebeck said they must, absolutely. They arranged to meet at a restaurant in Berlin one month after the cowardly English had been brought to heel and finished the rest of the brandy to that happy day.

From Strasbourg Riebeck was obliged to walk, which did not do his leg any good. After an hour or so he got a ride on a lorry as far as St. Nicolas. Finding himself so near Fontaines, he could not resist going to see what it was like with Germans living there.

Avoiding the avenue of poplars that led to the front of the house, Colonel Riebeck walked on Dr. St. Pierre's bridle path till he came to the wall that separated the two parks. He swung himself up on the wall and looked about him. In the spring sun the exacting design of the park looked at first untouched. Curious, he jumped down on the Riebeck side and walked toward the house. Then he wished he had not come. His eyes, ready to greet the fountain, saw only rusty pipes. All the Pigalle figures were gone. And in the middle of a park built with a river as its center, a German family was admiring its latest folly; a large, green swimming pool.

There was an elderly man whose tunic hung over the back of his chair, a woman in a hideous silk dress looking friendly and tired, and a girl, wearing premature shorts, dangling her feet in the icy water.

Perhaps she felt someone looking at her, for she turned and saw a tall man who for all his dark, shabby clothes had the air—she told herself so, indignantly—of owning the place. She got up and walked toward him. Her parents too were looking at him now, but they made no move. Evidently they were accustomed to letting their daughter handle such things.

"I am trespassing," said Colonel Riebeck when she came up to him. "I used to know the people who had this house, and I was curious. I shall go now. I'm sorry I disturbed your *apéritif*."

"Don't go," said the girl, liking his looks. "This is fascinating. Come and have a drink with us. What is your name?"

"Etienne Regnier," said Riebeck, who had an obscure and boring cousin by that name.

"I'm Susanne Wagenmuller. My father is a general."

"Yes, I can see that from his tunic."

"Please come and meet him. Papa, this is Monsieur Regnier. He used to know the Riebecks."

"Which is no excuse for disturbing you," said Riebeck, turning on the charm. "Please forgive me, Madame."

"But it's very interesting," said the Frau General.

"Sit down and have a glass of wine," said her husband, overriding anything else she might have cared to say. "I will say for old Riebeck, he kept a good cellar."

Colonel Riebeck, accepting what he rightly felt to be his wine, agreed.

"How did you happen to know the Riebecks?" the general wanted to know.

"Jean, their youngest boy, and I went to St. Cyr together. I used to come here often during the summer holidays."

"Oh, then could you tell me," asked the general's wife, risking one more foray, "where the curtains to the library are? I found most of the others packed away in the attic, but I could not find those."

They were Gobelins and valuable, and Riebeck knew that they were hidden in the gardener's cottage, because Elisabeth in one of her endless letters from Brazzaville had told him all about it. His eyes involuntarily went to the raped fountain.

"I regret, Madame, I have no idea."

"We sold the figures," said the general, intercepting his glance. "I thought them terrible rubbish myself, but our neighbor, the young Monsieur St. Pierre, Bertrand—do you know him?—told us they were by Pigalle and valuable, and as it turned out he was right."

"Yes. Pigalle came here after he had finished the tomb of the Marshal de Saxe in Strasbourg. He made the fountain to cheer up a very sad young Vicomte de Rebeque who lived here in exile from Versailles. Unfortunately the young vicomte did not like country life and died of a broken heart."

"I never knew the Riebecks had a title," said Susanne, who had seized upon this as the most interesting part of the story.

"It was lost in the Revolution."

"Along with the spelling of the name, eh?" said the General.

"I suppose if one settles in a country where three quarters of the people speak German that is to be expected."

"It's a pity not everyone in Elsass Lothringen expected it," said the General. "Down by the river there is a deer and a fawn. St. Pierre says they're by Coysevox. You seem to know a lot about this place. Would you happen to know if it is true?"

Riebeck had ridden that deer before he had ever owned a pony. He laughed. "Poor Bertrand, I'm afraid he took the Riebecks too much at face value. They always called it 'our Coysevox' but you know what French country houses are."

"Good," said the General. "I have grown very fond of them and I shall be glad to be able to keep them here."

"Would you like to see what we've done with the house?" the General's wife asked kindly. "These French houses are so large and bare, but I brought a lot of my things from Germany and I think I have made it really *gemütlich*."

Riebeck, knowing his limits, thanked them for the wine and left. It had, he said truthfully, been very interesting.

He felt in large measure consoled by the visit. Cavignac's "There are Germans living at Fontaines" had sounded final. But these Boches with their despoiled fountain and their swimming pool had restored it to a slapstick comedy, painful at times to the man who slips on the banana skin, but all the same, a comedy.

He came to Nancy with no very clear idea of how to find Tyrell. There was no one in the area whom he considered reliable enough to ask for information. Perhaps it would have been best to go straight to Paris and ask Latour for help. But he could work up no enthusiasm for this or any other plan, for he was convinced—he admitted it at last—that it was already too late, that Tyrell had been caught, that his silence was part of the pattern of treason that had been hounding the department and which was now ended, too late.

He was so depressed that he walked through the Pépinière without looking about him and nearly passed Jeremy Tyrell, who was sitting on a bench in the spring sun, reading a German war novel.

Riebeck's first reaction was not relief but anger. "What the devil do you think you are doing?"

Amiably, Jeremy said, "Hullo. I thought someone would turn up sooner or later."

Riebeck's vocabulary was always extensive when he was angry. He cursed fluently for some time. Jeremy never turned a hair.

"I know," he said, when Riebeck was forced to stop to breathe, "I know. When Patrick—my oldest son—ran away from home we were all dreadfully worried. We live by the coast and it's very dangerous for a little boy alone in the dark. But when a neighbor brought him back, instead of being grateful to see him, I gave him the worst spanking of his life."

"Don't flatter yourself," said Riebeck coldly. "If you wanted to sit in the park and read tripe you could have done it in England without wasting my time."

"Keep your hair on," said Jeremy, "and listen to me for a change. This is the third time in a row that we've parachuted into a German ambush, and I for one am fed up with it. There is nothing that makes one feel sillier than to fall languidly from the sky into the fire of accurate and unsportsmanlike German machine gunners. Your damned local maquis had lit the fires before the Germans arrived. They buggered off, which was all right, but they forgot to put out the fire, so that we jumped all innocently smack into the arms of the Germans. Timmy was shot, by the way. He's dead."

Riebeck sat down on the bench next to Jeremy and lit a cigarette. Timmy was Lieutenant Timothy Foyle and Riebeck had chosen him from a stack of files and three interviews to go to France for the first time. Tim Foyle, and how many others?

The pick of the lot, the clever, brave, imaginative ones. "Fellows who were good and brave and died because they were." How delighted they always looked when one told them they had been picked to go abroad. It was an accolade, to be sure. It was also, often, the first lap of a journey to a brutal death.

They were told that, of course. Their life expectancy was brief, their statistics hopeless. But it was salve only to the conscience of those who read the death sentence: "You have been chosen for a mission in France." No one believes that the statistics work against him. If 999 die out of 1000, each man thinks he is going to be the lucky one.

Riebeck pointed out to himself every time this happened that they were volunteers. They were warned of the danger and told what to expect. No one asked the soldier in the trenches if he was ready to die. But Tim Foyle had been asked.

"No one will think the worse of you if you feel you can't do it." That was the formula. It gave them their out, the generals and colonels who had to do the choosing, the officers who became executioners.

Had there ever existed a young lieutenant who had admitted to a superior officer that he did not feel equal to dying in a concentration camp? Riebeck had never come across one yet.

Well, they survived to people one's nightmares. Add another name.

"I am sorry," said Colonel Riebeck. "Why didn't you use the radio?"

"I didn't have it. The Germans picked up all our stuff."

"You could have got in touch with local maquis, surely."

"That is what I have been trying to do. I couldn't find them, so I thought if I sat conspicuously in the middle of the town, they might find me. No success so far. I could have made my way back by way of Finisterre or Spain, but it takes a long time and it's not very safe, and I was fairly sure if you didn't hear from me you'd send someone to see why. I really didn't expect you to come yourself."

"It was on my way," said Riebeck tactfully. "I'll get on to Paris and see that you get some explosives and help. And for heaven's sakes stop sitting in the middle of the town for any German to pick up."

"There's safety in being conspicuous. Before you go to Paris, could you use some food?"

"I could indeed. You really have established yourself, haven't you?"

"Food and drink," said Jeremy, patting his stomach, "are at all times my first concern."

"Why, hullo, Colonel Riebeck," said Jenny. "Have you been abroad? Nobody's seen you for simply ages. Good evening, General Burkey."

Riebeck, who had been standing outside the War Office wondering whether Burkey's flow of conversation would ever cease, was grateful for the interruption.

"Now, now, Mrs. Falconer," said Burkey earnestly, "careless talk loses lives."

"Yes, I know. But it's the only kind that's really interesting. Are you busy, Colonel Riebeck?"

He wasn't, but a colonel cannot say out loud that the conversation of a brigadier is an idle waste of time.

"Because if you aren't," Jenny went on, "you might come with me. I do hate walking alone through the blackout."

Burkey, seeing beauty in distress, gallantly dismissed Riebeck.

"Come back and have dinner with me," said Jenny. "You really ought to see Allanbank House. Queen Victoria Gothic."

The Falconers' house in Wimpole Street had been damaged by bombs, and Jenny had moved into her uncle's London house which had no central heating and, apart from its architectural peculiarities, little to recommend it.

Riebeck would have liked to accept Jenny's invitation, but reflecting that with rationing an unforeseen dinner guest was a complication rather than a pleasure, said he was busy.

"If it's rations you're worried about you needn't be. I have a pig."

"For a pet, do you mean?"

"No, to eat. Last time Uncle Ambrose butchered a pig he gave me a bit. I would advise you to come. It's real pork with crackling on it, not that grey stuff we get in the shops in London."

Riebeck was amused at this materialistic aspect of one who looked as if she lived on nothing more substantial than wild strawberries and champagne, but he was not surprised. At the hospital the shepherd's pie had often engaged her thoughts for days on end.

"Thank you," he said. "I should like to see Allanbank House and real pork with crackling."

"The house is rather awful, but that's a comfort in a way."

"How?"

"I don't know if I can explain properly. One always half feels it's unpatriotic now to be warm and comfortable, so that one really welcomes all the bother and discomfort; you know, queues, and no heat, and the food."

"How civilian. All soldiers ever want is to be warm, fed, and comfortable."

"Yes, but they get to do the fighting. Here we are, Allanbank House. It's a pity you can't see the outside properly in the black-out. It's a nice blend of Victoria Station and the Crystal Palace. Good evening, Bessie," said Jenny to the maid who opened the door.

Bessie stumbled over her own feet and said "Good evening, Miss."

"I should keep my coat on if I were you," said Jenny to Riebeck.

He was too busy admiring the house to answer. Above him was a huge glass dome painted black to comply with wartime regulations. Stairways formed narrow balconies, twisted themselves round aimlessly, and did not appear to arrive anywhere in particular. The furniture was grained oak with twiddles and turrets.

"How do you like it?" asked Jenny proudly.

"Victoria Station may be bigger, but I really think this is uglier."

"One thing," said Jenny gratified, "is that one feels so safe here during air raids. It would be such a pleasure to see the Germans smash it to pieces. And I'm sure Germans would never do anyone a kindness. Though I did use to have nightmares about nuns parachuting through the glass dome."

"You would simply let them all come down, lock the doors, and keep them here to the end of the war. That would teach them to invade people."

"Goodness, I don't think the Geneva Convention would allow us to keep prisoners of war in this cold. Come to the library. We usually have a fire going there, and books do seem to keep out the drafts a bit. Would you like some sherry? It's Spanish, not South African."

"In that case, yes, please."

"It isn't that we approve of Franco," said Jenny seriously, "but

Uncle Ambrose bought a whole lot of sherry before the Civil War and there is still some left."

There was a loud clatter of breaking china in the next room. "That's Bessie," explained Jenny. "She breaks a lot of dishes. Still, she's cross-eyed and deaf, so she won't get called up or put in munitions. I expect all that noise means dinner is ready."

The dining-room had a gothic vaulted ceiling, cathedral windows with purple panes, pitch-pine paneling, and a row of still-life paintings over the sideboard.

"There," said Jenny proudly.

"It's very impressive. Though the purple windows rather lead one to expect a corpse on the sideboard. How nice this pork smells. The meat they call pork in restaurants doesn't smell at all."

"Not when it's cooked. You ought to get a nose full at the butcher's. I do miss proper dinner parties."

"Are you old enough to remember them?"

"Oh yes. I came out two years before the war. I didn't like London parties very much because the men were so silly, but in Paris they were lovely."

"I wish I could have been there. I was in Vienna then, and Budapest. I must say they did their parties well."

"I was in Budapest once, with Papa when he gave a concert there. They gave us a lovely dinner at Tisza Palace."

"But that is where I used to live when I was in Budapest. It belonged to my uncle, and it now belongs to Istvan Halyi who is my cousin. How did I come to miss you?"

"I remember Captain Halyi. He is very ugly and he has a pretty, buxom wife. He's madly attractive for all he has a face like a gargoyle. I expect if I had stayed in Budapest another day I would have fallen in love with him."

"I have no doubt he would have enjoyed that very much. He and I have been each other's best friend since we were six. I am so glad you liked him."

"I adored him," said Jenny with her customary social hyperbole. "And Count Nikki and Count Pipi. Really, the Nazis are beasts, killing off people like that. How quickly dinners are over these days. One's hardly sat down and it's done. I think Count Pipi's was

186

the only twelve-course dinner I've ever been to. We ate for hours."

"I know."

"I swear," said Jenny, poking ungratefully at a sardine lying on a burnt triangle of toast," when this war is over I will never eat another sardine again. Isn't it dreadful how one talks about nothing but food now? I often think about the famous lovers in books and what they would talk about if they were alive now."

"Romeo and Juliet discussing roast peacock."

"Yes. And Cyrano telling Roxanne about goose liver and truffles."

"Natasha and Prince Andrey would talk about caviar."

"Dante and Beatrice could discuss spaghetti."

"Do you know," said Riebeck, "I can't think of a single pair of English lovers."

"Lancelot and Guinevere."

"Lancelot was French."

"Yes, I'm afraid we do have to import them. Like wine. Elizabeth Barrett and Robert Browning."

"How very dull. Very well, let Elizabeth Barrett write sonnets about steak and kidney pie, which is something I have only read about but never tasted."

"It's very good," said Jenny, her eyes shining at the memory. "Let's go have our coffee in the library. At least the fire will be warm because I promise you the coffee won't be."

One end of the library was almost entirely taken up by a grand piano.

"Papa used to practice in the drawing room here when he was in England," Jenny explained. "He said the acoustics were exactly like the Albert Hall. We had to move the piano in here, though, because the drawing room is much too cold."

"Do you play too, or does being a pianist's daughter put one off music forever?"

"No, I play. What would you like?"

"The Mozart A major sonata, please."

Jenny smiled and went to the piano. There isn't a child with a year of piano lessons who hasn't thumped through it. "Are you being kind or is it really your favorite piece?"

"It is my favorite piece."

"*Eh, bien,*" she said and began to play.

Riebeck listened, elbows on the piano, chin on fists. It took him the length of the sonata to deal with his astonishment. Jenny's playing had no touch of the amateur about it. She had all the authority and technique of François Vaucaire. That explained, he supposed, her offer to play what he liked without the fuss amateur musical hostesses like to indulge in. And it explained how in this cold house the piano was perfectly tuned.

When she was finished she put her hands in her lap and smiled at him.

"Why the violet by the mossy stone?"

She did not pretend not to understand him. "I have everything but the need to produce myself in public. Applause and approval don't mean enough to me to put up with all the drawbacks of the profession. It's a disciplined life, you know. Almost as disciplined as your own, I should imagine."

"Do you think applause and approval are all the rewards one gets?"

"Yes. That's what fame is, isn't it?"

"Do you practice every day?"

"I used to, of course. Now I often haven't the time. I try to do as much as I can."

"Perfection only for yourself. I suppose that is the ultimate in luxury."

She got up and went back to the fire. She sat down and put the mink coat over her feet. A book fell from the pocket. Riebeck picked it up. "*Les Liaisons dangéreuses.* This was my favorite book for years and years. Valmont was my ideal when I was a boy. I wanted nothing so much as to grow up and be like him. But when I was seventeen I read *La Princesse de Clèves* and fell in love with my brother's wife, fancying myself as the Monsieur de Nemours. Nine years later I discovered I did not love her after all, so I returned to Valmont."

"He suits you much better. Do you conduct all your love affairs according to the books you read?"

"Of course. Romantic love is a literary invention. Was it La

Rochefoucauld who said many people would never fall in love if they had not read about it in a book?"

"Yet love kept him in hot water most of his life."

"Love and gout. What do you think of love? Not the sleeping-around kind like Valmont. That is very easily achieved if one has the time. The other kind. The *grande passion.*"

"I don't know."

"I should have thought you would be an authority. You can't have met many men who didn't fall in love with you on sight."

"That is silly. I thought we were talking about the *grande passion*. I am one of La Rochefoucauld's people, I know it only from books."

"You are very young. It will come later."

"I hope not," said Jenny. "I haven't the temperament for great pleasure and great pain. I prefer the untroubled surface."

"Do you?" said Riebeck, pleased. In the hospital, he remembered, during those long idle talks during night duty he could often afterward not remember whether she had voiced a thought or he had, so much did their minds march together. "Then we are both Rochefoucauld people, doomed to everlasting safety. What a comfort that is."

A log fell from the fire. She bent to push it back with the tongs. Her hair fell forward and hid her face. He thought that it would be pleasant to the touch, like the fine silk one sees in Eastern bazaars.

"Snow Queen," he said. "I haven't read those stories since I was a boy, but they keep coming back to me now. There was a little mermaid who felt as if she were walking on knives."

"And Kay who had splinter in his heart so that it turned to ice," she said. "He was a La Rochefoucauld person too."

"Yes. But the Snow Queen kissed him and he no longer felt cold and he loved her."

He spoke idly, out of his detached mood, and found instantly that even for La Rochefoucauld people such conversations were dangerous. Jenny pushed her hair back and looked at him, her eyes full of mockery and resistance.

There are times when even soldiers must run. Riebeck got to his feet. "It's late, Madame," he said, "and I still have work to do. Thank you for the dinner. It was delightful."

She was as polite as he. "Goodnight, Colonel Riebeck. I am so glad you could come."

The next morning he sent her a bunch of violets with a card: "Thank you for the Mozart." She sent him her own copy of the *Maximes* of La Rochefoucauld, but though he looked through it with care he could find no note.

XIII

In 1941 Hungary, promised the return of its lost provinces, joined the war on the side of Germany. Istvan Halyi went to fight in Russia. He did so with distinction, insofar as this is possible when one has to command oxcarts instead of tanks. He was flamingly indignant all the time at the treatment the Hungarians received from the German strategists. They were not equipped with arms and were thrown in to fight as well as they could wherever the going was worst.

Istvan resented bitterly the use of his men's lives as a barricade between the Russians and the Germans, and finally lost his temper at Headquarters. He demanded, in a strong French accent, horses and arms for his men. German Headquarters was not accustomed to having a mere captain of an inferior race come yelling at them, and so startled were they that they issued Istvan's regiment with horses and carbines before they realized what they were doing. That there was hardly ever any ammunition did not matter. The Russians had no ammunition either, and the carbines did very well for hitting them over the head. It was not magnificent, but it was war, and Istvan enjoyed it.

Colonel Riebeck sometimes wondered whether Istvan had considered the morality of fighting with the Germans, but usually decided that the higher philosophic aspects of anything would not interest Istvan Halyi. So long as he had a horse to ride and an enemy to kill, Istvan would care very little for the justice of his actions. (A good war, says Nietzsche, hallows any cause.)

It is probable that Istvan might have continued to fight for the Germans in Russia until he was killed or taken prisoner, had his first leave not coincided with the German occupation of Hungary.

Like everyone else in Russia, Istvan had not the faintest idea what was going on anywhere in the world except in his immediate area of command. About a year before, Palko Donath had disappeared in the night without a word of farewell. This was not rudeness but tact. Explanations would have put Istvan, as his commanding officer, on the spot between duty and friendship. This way he could enter next to Palko's name: Missing, believed dead, and write Madame Donath a reassuring letter. Palko's case was not the first.

Istvan returned from Russia to find German soldiers swaggering through the streets of Budapest like conquerors, Count Xandi, returned from France, nearer than ever to his dream of becoming Gauleiter of Hungary, relatives who had been high in government circles the victims of inexplicable suicides and accidents. He went to look up Palko's wife and found the house locked and shuttered and the neighbors too frightened to talk. He remembered then that Madame Donath was Jewish. Race defilement, Xandi called it, rejoicing in his blond hair and blue eyes.

Istvan called on Admiral Horthy and told him exactly what he thought of him. Horthy, a prisoner in all but name, had come down a long way from the arrogant regent Istvan had loved, and this defeat more than anything goaded Istvan into being not only unfair but also extremely offensive. After his interview with Horthy Istvan disappeared. When he did not return to his regiment, his second-in-command put next to his name: Missing, believed dead, and carried on for a while.

Riebeck was in Austria on a job for General Burkey when one of his contacts told him that Istvan wanted to see him. At first he laughed, then he was annoyed, finally he agreed to go to Vienna for a few days and meet Istvan, who wanted advice on the manner in which he was to lead his new life. Istvan had not yet arrived, so Riebeck moved into Baranyi Palace, which had stood empty since 1940.

He checked the blackout, found most of it in good condition, and settled down in the rooms that faced the park. He found the keys to the wine cellar and pantry, both of which were well stocked. There were plenty of books in the library and the beds were comfortable. He caught up on his sleep, read, ate the delicious food the prudent Alphonse had put up in gleaming glass jars, and drank the late Count Nikki's excellent wine.

He was alone for three days. On the evening of the third day he heard footsteps across the courtyard and the creak of the heavy back door. He went to the head of the stairs and saw, in the pale light of the early evening, Istvan Halyi standing in the hall.

The last time they had met it had been with Istvan's fist in his face. He had borne the purple mark along his jawbone for several weeks, and in one place, where Istvan's knuckles had split the skin, a small scar had remained, narrow and colorless, but still visible. He had acquired far more spectacular scars since, but he found himself absurdly hoping that Istvan would not notice the one that was his doing.

Happy as he was about the meeting, Riebeck wished it were half an hour later, past whatever was going to be said about his limp, his scarred face and hands. Whatever it was, it would be embarrassing and awkward to deal with.

But Istvan said nothing. His vital, ugly face spoke for him.

"*Servus* Istvan."

"*Servus* Schani. *Comment ça va?*"

The volumes of sympathy, anger, explanation, justification, and mutual apology had been circumvented and were already forgotten. They were back where they had always been: friends with perfectly synchronized minds and the experienced tact that kept them from overstepping the borderlines whose existence friendship forbade them to acknowledge.

Istvan grinned. Though he had left the army he was still in uniform and very dirty. Riebeck wore the dark trousers and black shirt, with black plimsolls, which were practically a uniform for St 2. In these clothes they could move without noise, and with dirt rubbed on their faces they were invisible in the dark.

"I am starved," said Istvan. "Is there any of Alphonse's food left or did you hog it all?"

"I've been gorging but there's plenty. Come along to the pantry. There seem to be a lot of truffles in jars. They taste very strange."

"I remember them. Alphonse used to get them from Perigord and bottle them. They must be ancient."

"I'll heat some pheasant for you. Only I'm not very good at it. By the time the top gets even slightly warm the bottom always burns."

"How do you heat things without showing smoke?"

"There's some bottled gas left. I don't know how much. It may run out any time."

Istvan went to explore the wine cellar and returned with a bottle of 1934 Chambertin. "Schani, did you know you still have some of the 34s left?"

"Mhm. I was saving them for myself."

"I think it most unwise. Supposing we get killed or something. We'd better drink it now."

"True enough," agreed Riebeck and threw the corkscrew across to Istvan who caught it. "The wine cellar's full of stuff that ought to be drunk soon."

Istvan said he would do his best. "It was a splendid idea of yours, coming here," he said, opening the wine and sniffing the cork.

"It's my house, after all. Eat now and then tell me what you have done."

Istvan pitched into the pheasant, too hungry to complain that it was burnt on one side and cold on the other. Finally he caught his breath and lit a cigarette. "Lord, I was hungry."

"Tell me what happened to you," said Riebeck and listened with a frown to Istvan's tale of his interview with Admiral Horthy.

"What did you do about Eva?"

"She's at Hommages."

"Is that safe?"

"Oh yes. I am listed as missing, not as a deserter, you know."

"What are you going to do now?" Riebeck asked severely.

"Annoy the Germans, preferably. I was hoping you could give me some ideas."

"I'd rather give you some advice, though I know it's a waste of time and in your case also about a month too late. But if this sort of thing should ever happen to you again, Istvan, for heaven's sake stay in the army. You're of precious little use to me like this, and you could have helped me a great deal if you'd kept your mouth shut and made friends with Xandi's gang. I don't suppose you can go back now?"

Istvan, remembering some of the juicier bits of his quarrel with Horthy, said sulkily that he did not think so. He had expected praise, not good advice.

"Yes. Well, we'll do what we can. Come into the library and bring the wine."

For the next week Istvan was put through an intensive course in various criminal arts; he learned how to use a knife rather than a gun, and was carefully instructed in the use of explosives. He was allowed very little time in the kitchen and even less in the wine cellar, and he never got near a bed. Finally he complained.

"Don't you ever sleep, Schani?"

"You slept till five this morning," said Riebeck, surprised that anyone should ask for more.

"Do you always work like this?"

"When there's work. I don't always get this much done, though. Now fuse this *plastique* again, and then we'll eat. Afterwards I'll teach you how to set up a proper underground organization where practically nobody knows anybody else. There are two groups in Hungary you can work with. One is very bad; they're mostly monarchists and they don't really know what they're doing and why. The other is better, but they're Communists. They're run by Palko, as a matter of fact. To be frank, neither of them is terribly much use. Hungarians are hopeless when it comes to getting organized. For example, since you are scowling so, we knew to the minute when the Germans would march into Hungary. There is only one main road from Vienna to Budapest, and this was supposed to be mined. I don't know what happened to all the stuff I sent, but not a single German was blown up. Well yes, I do know as a matter of fact. The Monarchists said they'd do it and Palko's Commies said no, they would, and they both talked so much it never got done at all."

"Very likely," admitted Istvan. "I don't much want to be a

Communist, but if it's a question of working with Palko I'd like it very much."

"Naturally. But you can be in both camps and that may turn out to be a help to me. Will you try?"

"Sure," said Istvan, throwing the *plastique* to his cousin who caught it.

"Don't throw those things when they're fused, you ass." Riebeck looked at it, defused it and handed it back. "They take months in England to teach you all this. I had three weeks in Paris. I don't believe it matters. Some of our best people never had any theoretical training. You'll learn by trial and error, we all did. Mostly error, I'm bound to admit. If you err once too often you'll find yourself on the wrong side of a concentration camp. It's wonderful what an incentive it gives one to do things properly. Let's eat."

They went to the kitchen and looked sadly at the nearly empty shelves. "We've about eaten our way through here," said Riebeck. "Just as well, I really have to get back to London."

"You make it sound so easy."

"It is for me. I have all kinds of forged papers and special passes, and with my idiotic leg no one asks me why I am not at the front fighting the Red Hordes."

"It's a very handsome limp. I'll bet the women fall for it."

"Yes. But in England I don't fall for them very much."

"Oh come. I remember once you spent five weeks doing absolutely nothing but chase an English girl."

Riebeck laughed. "God, what ages ago. I can't even remember her name. Sylvia, Sally, Susan—"

"Olivia."

"That's right. I don't have five weeks to seduce people in now, you know. Much too busy."

"Marriage has quite ruined my sex life," said Istvan cheerfully. "I find now if I can't have Eva I am simply not interested. Have we any cigarettes left? I can't find them."

"I think we finished the ones I brought. But there are still some of yours."

"Ah," said Istvan, "the Spartan life begins. No food and Hungarian cigarettes."

"There is still lots of wine."

"That's true." Istvan went to the cellar and came back upstairs with his choice in bottles. They returned to the library and opened the wine.

"I hope Eva is keeping up Hommages," said Riebeck. "After the war I shall want my children to come and play with yours."

"What children? I thought you were so busy."

"I hadn't meant it that literally. Though there is a possibility that I may have a daughter, only fortunately the lady in question is married so I can't be sure. Anyway it was ages ago, before the war."

"That's funny. I have a bastard too. Only mine is a boy."

"Good. Perhaps he can marry my daughter. What's his name?"

"Peter. And I imagine he's too young for your daughter. He's only four."

"Really, Istvan. I thought you were off other women since you married Eva."

"It was sort of an accident."

"It usually is. Why Peter?"

"That was the lady's husband's name. Unfortunately it convinced nobody. Big Peter has a great lumpy nose growing in all directions and little Peter is going to have the Esterhazy nose. All right, laugh. It's true. So there was a lot of squabbling and I finally said I'd take him home to Eva. She was always wanting a baby anyway. I thought she'd be pleased," said Istvan.

"Instead she went off the deep end?"

"And how. I'll never understand women."

"No," agreed Riebeck. "I don't think you ever will. So what did you do with the child?"

"Janos is taking care of him."

"Hm," said Riebeck. He did not care for the situation. Certainly Janos had taken excellent care of Istvan when he was a boy, but it was nevertheless unsatisfactory. Peter was Istvan Halyi's son, with an Esterhazy grandmother, and it was wrong that he should be raised by servants. Riebeck felt a moment's annoyance with Eva, but had to admit that few women would have behaved differently. Oh well, let it go. For the moment Istvan's child was as safe with

Janos as with anybody, and there was little purpose in worrying about the future.

"It will do very well while the war lasts," he said. "And that, I imagine, will be a while yet."

"Do you think we'll win, Schani?"

"I don't know. I don't care."

Istvan, unable to believe the words, looked at his friend's face for confirmation and found it. A strange face, he thought suddenly, a face he knew well and was not in the habit of regarding with attention. Strange because it had not changed. It had never really changed. No, that was nonsense. Of course it was changed with all the ordinary marks of growing older, the scars of Buchenwald, the lines of habitual pain, the tiredness of never enough sleep and rarely enough to eat. But the feature that gives a face its expression, the eyes, had not changed. They were those of a man at home in the world and capable of dealing with it.

Riebeck, who had borne his friend's scrutiny with patience, said, "Satisfied?"

"I'm not sure. There must be some sort of hope in a fight or how could one go on? Don't you care at all?"

"I do care, in a way, because I know I should." He was not very clear in his own mind about this and was not given to discussing his thoughts, but talking to Istvan was so much like talking to himself that he went on. "I cannot convince myself that all this is important. To Europe, yes, but not to me. It doesn't matter to me whether I win or lose. The thing that does matter is having made one's stand."

"Schani, can I ask you something?"

Riebeck looked up and smiled. "About Buchenwald? That's just morbid curiosity, Istvan."

Istvan made a face at his friend.

"I'm not funny about it or anything," said Riebeck. "I mean I could talk about it if I wanted to. Only I don't want to. I can't find the *grandeur de souffrances humaines*. That's the stupid sort of thing only a poet would say. If there is any *grandeur* it is in happiness. So one must learn to be happy again as quickly as possible."

Istvan was certain that Riebeck had told him the truth, just as he knew that all kinds of dreadful nonsense had been told to other sympathetic inquirers. That locution, "one must be happy," was certainly a Riebeck one. Anyone else would have said, "I want to be happy." It was the explanation for the untamed eyes and the arrogant mouth. The must in conjunction with happiness.

They were silent, comfortably so on Riebeck's part, uneasily on Istvan's. At last he said, "Schani, what did you think of my fighting for the Germans?"

"I never judge anyone's actions but my own. How much less then yours, Istvan."

"When you get all pompous like that it's bad. In plain language, if it had been anyone but your fair-haired boy you would have disapproved strenuously."

"No. If it had been anyone else I would not have worried."

"About my getting killed?"

"No. I thought you might not be very happy fighting on the German side."

"I wasn't. Are you going to keep the stiff upper lip or are you going to ask me why I did it?"

"If you want me to. Why did you?"

"An error in judgment. I felt responsible for the regiment. It's not boasting, Schani, to say that I took better care of them than anyone else might have. I didn't realize until I saw the Germans in Budapest how wrong I'd been to put the regiment first. You must have known it long ago. Why didn't you tell me?"

"How could I do that?"

"It seems to me the least you could have done."

"It is the one thing I cannot do for you, Istvan. I can't think for you. I can't be anyone's conscience but my own. Speaking of conscience, do you want an L pill?"

"What's that?"

"L for lethal."

Take it, Riebeck wanted to say. No one's endurance is without limits. If they caught you, that would be the end of mine. You didn't like seeing me with a scarred face and a lame leg. But I was safe in London before you ever knew I had been caught. You don't know anything about it. I do. I have no ignorance left to spare me.

But he knew that he had no right to burden Istvan with his own weakness. He said, "When you hear an ominous knock on the door in the middle of the night you take your pill and by the time the Gestapo breaks down the door you're dead. Only it won't be the Gestapo. It is the air raid warden, to tell you you're showing a light."

"Be serious for a moment, Schani. It isn't so much what one thinks the proper thing to do, but what one ought to do. Suppose—"

Riebeck had heard that suppose a hundred times. He always advised the pill, simply to be on the safe side. But to Istvan he said, "You're all right, don't worry."

"How do you know?"

"You're not afraid to die."

"Like hell I'm not. Besides, the people who take the pill die too."

"That's not what I mean. The pill's a last resort. I mean you are not afraid of dying to the extent that a threat of death would force you into doing something you don't want to do. If you were, you'd be in a different profession. You have no idea how much torture is self-inflicted. The principle behind it is to make the prisoner choose the rubber hose with which he will be beaten and to have him dig the grave in which he will be buried. I mean this literally, though there is an infinite variety of method. It's invariably painful, humiliating, disgusting, and always enforced with the threat of death. It is never done because the Gestapo is too witless to choose its own rubber hose or too lazy to dig a grave. It is done to make the prisoner take part in his own punishment and thereby make him lose all sense of what is reasonable, proper, or indeed possible. There are two answers to it; you can refuse, which is hard, or you can take the pill, which is easy."

"I see what you mean."

Riebeck stood up and moved about the room, coming to rest at last with his back to Istvan and his arms on the mantel. "I was afraid you would say no. If you change your mind, Palko'll give you a pill. And please, whatever you do, don't get the idea that there is something creditable about doing without."

Above the mantel was a pale square where a picture had been removed to the cellar for safekeeping. Riebeck looked up at it, remembering that since his first visit to the palace it had been his favorite, the Messina painting of the Renaissance captain, which, but for the dark hair and costume, might as easily have been a portrait of Istvan Halyi.

"I am going to take the Messina back to England with me," Riebeck said suddenly.

"What for?" asked Istvan suspiciously. All his life the family had teased him with the resemblance. Istvan alone refused to see it. "Nonsense."

"Not nonsense at all. He even has the Esterhazy nose. I want him."

"How are you going to get out of Austria with a portrait under your arm?"

"I'll take the canvas off the frame and roll it up in a newspaper."

"It will look as if you're smuggling out top-secret maps."

"Or a salami. Speaking of which, I must get over to Sacher's before I leave. I'm going to liberate Alphonse."

"You're mad, Schani. Do you realize how fat he is? What are you going to do with him, wrap him inside the Messina?"

"He can walk."

"I don't suppose Alphonse has walked for the last thirty years. Anyway, he'd never come to England."

"I need him," said Riebeck piteously. "You don't know what the food is like in England."

"He'll never come."

"I expect there'll be an air raid tonight. There's a full moon. I'll take a chance on it and pay him a call then."

"In a million years, Alphonse would never go to England."

What Istvan did not know was that Riebeck did not take chances. Alphonse, as he had expected, was tearfully grateful for the chance to get out of Austria. Several months earlier he had recklessly allowed a mysterious man to leave a letter with him, which had later been picked up by another mysterious man. He had lived in mortal fear of the Gestapo ever since. He said he would be delighted to come and cook for Monsieur Schani.

But, he said, he must have his special knives, his pots, and his soufflé molds. Without them he could not do himself justice.

Colonel Riebeck protested that one could not cross a carefully guarded border while clattering with pots and pans like a tinker, but Alphonse was firm. Riebeck capitulated and, as they clanked their way across Austria, reflected that if they were caught and killed his funeral sermon ought justly to deal with the deadly sin of greed.

Back in London he was obliged to plough his way through all the paperwork that invariably piled up whenever he was away, and always seemed so trivial after being abroad. But sustained by Alphonse's meals he managed with fairly good grace.

D Day was supposed to be top secret, but no one in London was talking about anything else. "Even in Germany there were rumors," said Riebeck to Jeremy Tyrell, "though they're far more discreet than we are and no one's been able to find out much. They seem to be up to something nasty themselves. A new kind of bomb, Vic thinks."

"Much good that will do them, with the state their Luftwaffe's in."

"Vic is coming over soon, I am glad to say. L'Abbé wants us to hatch plans."

"The Last Offensive," said Jeremy optimistically.

"I hope so. What we need is to round up papers and personnel that will be important later, and to have lots of sabotage and demoralization ahead of the invading armies. You'll enjoy that bit."

D Day came and killed, among so many others, two French colonels: Lucien and Pierre Riebeck.

A week later de Cavignac sent a message on the radio that he was on his way. Riebeck sent a staff car to the airfield to meet him. He knew it would cause an outcry. Jeremy, especially, could get lengthy on the subject of preferential treatment given to graduates of the Ecole Spéciale Militaire. But this was Vic de Cavignac, after all, and if Riebeck had owned a red carpet he would without doubt have sent that too.

Only Vic did not arrive. His plane was shot down over the Channel. There were no survivors.

Riebeck's first feeling was one of overwhelming gratitude that

Vic had been allowed a decent death. Later he was shocked at himself. Was the Gestapo so much on his mind that the first thought at a friend's death by another agency was gratitude?

"You may have to shoot me one of these days," he said to Jeremy, who had dropped in to offer his condolences and to demand how it was L'Abbé's boys were met by staff cars. "I'm losing my nerve."

"How?"

Riebeck told him and Jeremy laughed. "You're not alone. This war's been going on for five years and we've all lost what nerve we had. And these damned buzz bombs they've been sending over haven't exactly helped."

"They are a nuisance," Riebeck agreed. "Half my staff sits under their desks all day and the other half keeps running back and forth from the cellar."

"I hate them," said Jeremy vehemently. "If they want to kill me, let them fly over and drop a bomb. This is so impersonal."

"Would you feel any happier if you were blown up by one that had inscribed on it: 'To Captain Tyrell with love'?"

Jeremy laughed and said, "Talk about nerve. One manages without, you know. There goes the siren. Care to join me under the desk?"

The bombs arrived almost as soon as the siren stopped. "I think it's because they sound so much like a dentist's drill that they make people so nervous," said Jeremy.

"It's when they don't sound you'd better say your prayers. Someone tells me they're going to send over silent ones next."

"Christ," swore Jeremy, as a buzz bomb drilled over the roof and exploded farther down the street, "give me the bloody Gestapo any day."

"I'm glad you feel that way, because we're leaving almost at once," said Riebeck. "I meant to tell you. Austria. You, Cook, and me. Next week sometime, if the weather is bad."

A week after Vic's plane had crashed, another of General L'Abbé's young men stopped off to give Riebeck a letter. A letter from Vic de Cavignac.

"I was supposed to bring it several weeks ago," said the messenger, "but I got stuck in Brittany."

"That's quite all right, thank you."

Of course it was no message from the dead. It was a letter written two weeks ago and said among other things that Vic was looking forward to one of Alphonse's dinners and a night's sleep in a bed.

Knowing it to be a last letter, Riebeck had expected a portentousness that Cavignac, not sharing his knowledge, had failed to give it. It was an unemphatic letter, trivial even, friendly and cheerful. Not the letter of a man at whom death had pointed a finger, saying: "You next."

And finally, with the letter between his fingers, Riebeck understood that Cavignac would never come to London again, would not reclaim his apartment, drink Chateau Cavignac brandy, dine at the Cardinal Richelieu, find himself a girl to fall in love with for a day or two. Vic was dead, and Riebeck felt as forsaken, for that one moment, as an orphan on Christmas Eve.

"We will be in good company," Vic had once said when Riebeck had pointed out to him that it was unlikely any of them would survive the war. Tim Foyle, Bantain and Valterre caught last year in Germany and dead on a meathook in Buchenwald, Lucien and Pierre Riebeck; the best, the most select company in the world.

XIV

Cardinal Jarnitz had become blasé about air raids. At first he had rushed into the cellar and been severely frightened by the sound of sirens, but now, unless his particular area of Budapest was being bombed, he went serenely about his business. He had never liked the Nazis and had at great risk to his person refused to cooperate with them, and though the Russian and American pilots dropping bombs on the city had no way of knowing this, Cardinal Jarnitz had an obscure and touching faith in their discernment and trusted he would not be hit.

This afternoon they were bombing the Pest side of town, and

His Eminence continued on his way to pay a call at Tisza Palace, ignoring the fracas across the river.

The Russians were getting ready to enter Pest. The Cardinal would have preferred Americans, but he was not discontent. The Russians would put an end to the German occupation, and that was the important thing. He said a prayer for all those in battle. Christian charity bade him include the Germans, but it was his private and secular opinion that they were past redemption and not worth praying for.

The doors to Tisza Palace were locked, but Cardinal Jarnitz knew that the house was not empty and beat his fist against the door. At last Janos looked suspiciously out the window, and recognizing a prince of the church hastily came to let him in.

Above them Eva rushed to the stairs and called out! "Istvan, darling."

"I am so sorry to disappoint you, my dear," said the Cardinal, "not Istvan."

"Your Eminence, how nice to see you." She knelt and kissed the Cardinal's ring. "I had no idea you were in Budapest. You must forgive us for locking the door, but Istvan insisted. He says there are Undesirable Characters about."

"He is quite right."

"How did you know I was here?"

"I saw Istvan in Pest. He told me you were leaving tomorrow, so I decided to see you first. Yes, thank you, I will have a glass of wine with pleasure."

"Istvan is making me go back to the country," said Eva. "I came in with the Ford van. Janos wouldn't bring me, so I hid in the back. I had no idea what Istvan wanted it for, and when it was too late I found it was loaded with machine guns and grenades and things. I was terrified and Istvan was furious for quite five minutes. Did he tell you why I came?"

"He did indeed. He announced it at the top of his voice from the middle of the Petofi Bridge for all of Budapest to hear. I am very pleased indeed. I christened you and married you, and now I shall look forward to christening your child. But certainly you must go to the country and take care of yourself. Budapest is no place for you now."

"I promise. From tomorrow I'll be very good and quiet and live at Hommages and drink milk. Do you like milk, Eminence?"

"No."

"I don't either."

"I am sorry Istvan is not here," said the Cardinal. "I have something for him. But I would really rather give it to you, for I fear that Istvan would laugh at me." He put two fingers in his vest pocket and brought out a silver medallion on a chain. "It is St. Stephen," he said. "The patron saint of Hungary and also of your husband. I thought, perhaps, in a battle for his country's freedom, Istvan might find it helpful."

"You're quite right, Eminence, Istvan would laugh. But he will wear it if I ask him to. Will it still work that way?"

"I do not see how St. Stephen could refuse you anything, my dear. I must go."

Carefully the Cardinal pushed himself out of the chair. "I hope you never get rheumatism, dear child."

"Do you think God will count it toward your years in purgatory?"

"I hope so. Good-by, my child. God bless you. Don't come outside with me, it isn't safe."

Istvan came home in the evening, flung his carbine on a delicate rosewood table, and grinned at his wife's delighted, "Darling, you pig."

"I'm a pig in more ways than one. Don't touch me, I'm filthy. I must have a bath."

"There isn't any hot water."

"Cold then. It doesn't matter."

"How did you get so dirty?"

Istvan burst into his great, scowling laugh. "I've been digging, like a peasant. Look at my hands."

"Darling," said Eva blowing him a kiss from the distance. "Come, we'll get your bath. Why were you digging? Are we going to be peasants after the war?"

"You'd make a fine peasant's wife with your silk frocks and

mink coat. No, we shan't be peasants, I hope. Come upstairs and I'll tell you while I have my bath."

"You know I can never hear anything you say when you're in the tub, you wallow so. I'll just go and tell Janos to get dinner and then I'll come up."

In the days of Count Nikki the Tiszas and their guests had bathed in tin baths placed before the fire in their bedrooms and filled with boiling water which the footmen and housemaids had been obliged to carry in huge cans up three flights of stairs. Count Nikki's wedding present to Istvan's bride had been, at her special request, a bathroom adjoining her bedroom. Here, among Eva's flagons of scent and bath salts Istvan flung his muddy boots, threw his pistol on the dressing table and his dirty clothes all over the floor, and with a yell of indignation plunged into the cold water.

Eva dodged the tidal wave and said, "So tell about the digging?"

"Last year Janos buried a whole lot of explosives behind the stud farm. He must have dug a hole halfway to China. Today we had to dig it out. We didn't notice until we got there that the whole lot of us were officers and we didn't have any underlings to do the dirty work, so we had to do it ourselves. Lord, how we dug. I don't know how peasants do it. It must be a terrible life. Do you remember that picture *The Man with the Hoe?* Fellow that stands with his hands dragging on the ground and his teeth hanging out? I know exactly how he felt."

While Istvan got out of the tub Eva retired to the bedroom to avoid being drenched. "What do you want to wear, darling?"

Istvan followed her, toweling himself and dripping water all over the white mink rug that was Eva's pride and joy.

"Nothing at the moment. I am going to bed and so are you."

"But dinner is all ready."

Istvan knew it was a token protest. "Dinner can wait," he said. "I can't."

To be with Eva was like walking into a past that no longer existed for him. It continued, this past, he knew, at Hommages, where Eva ignored the war. His own world was very far from hers now, but whether the anachronism was his or hers he did not know.

"Underground," a word in the past holding romantic connotations, had turned out to mean, for Istvan Halyi and his men, just that. They lived like creatures of the dark, far removed from the lives of decent soldiers. They died and killed secretly, without honor. Istvan hated it every moment, and when he could bear it no longer he allowed himself to step back into the past and went to Hommages to visit his wife. But the longer the war lasted, the more difficult this step grew. He carried with him a burden of experience he could not share with Eva, and could not leave behind. More and more he felt like the swineherd who has inadvertently married the princess. But now he was beginning to see the end of the fight. Somehow he would learn to forget, and Eva would learn too that her world had ended forever, learn to live in whatever world the war would leave them. These lessons would not be easy, but Istvan did not mind how difficult things were as long as he and Eva were together.

"You will go back to Hommages tomorrow, my dearest love," he said. "You must promise. You see, the Russians are here and there is going to be a very nasty fight. The Germans have decided to defend us whether we like it or not."

"Is that guns, all that noise?"

"Yes, dear idiot, that is guns. That's why I want you to go to Hommages and wait for me there. I will come to you as soon as I can. And you must take good care of little Eva too."

"Not little Eva," Eva protested. "It reminds me of something nasty, I can't quite remember what. Bloodhounds chewing someone's heels."

"Bloodhounds don't eat meat, darling."

"Don't they? Oh well, it doesn't matter. It's not going to be a girl. It's going to be a boy and we'll call him Istvan."

"If it's a boy we'll call him Jean Nicolas Istvan Halyi."

"Too many names for a little boy."

He knew which one she considered superfluous. It seemed a pity, thought Istvan, only mildly distressed at that moment, that of the three people who anchored him to love—Jean Riebeck, Eva, and the lost, small boy growing up in Janos' house at Hommages—she should dislike two. He might devote his postwar leisure to teaching her to love without jealousy. It would be a full-time occupation, as futile, without doubt, as all other high-minded postwar projects. "Maybe you'll have triplets," he said, declining the opening for a quarrel.

"I wish you'd let me stay in Budapest, Istvan."

"No."

"Bully. Why not?"

"Because if anything were to happen to you I would die of a broken heart. Satisfied?"

"I'll bet you would. You'd go about as a romantic young widower and let all your old mistresses console you until you dropped dead from overexertion, and that's what you'd call dying of a broken heart."

"Don't joke about it, dearest. I really think I would die, or at least I'd want to, which is worse."

"All right, don't worry. I'll go to Hommages and pine for you. Istvan, what are the Russians like? You don't seem to be worried about them."

"You've been listening to the German radio," said Istvan.

The Germans had been busy broadcasting tales of Russian atrocities. Russians, according to the German Propaganda Ministry, raped any and all women, bayoneted babies, and burnt old and sick people in their houses. The broadcasts were not very successful. After a year of German occupation the Hungarians optimistically felt that things could not get worse.

"They're fine," said Istvan. "Really. They're wonderful fighters and very good fellows." Here he stopped, realizing that his luxury-loving Eva might find some drawbacks in his new friends. "They're not overly fond of washing and they steal like magpies," he added. "You've hidden all the silver and the paintings, haven't you?"

"All safely down the dried-up well," said Eva. "Janos threw a dead rat on top of all the stuff, to discourage searching. It will be such a mess, getting things up again. Oh dear, I don't think I am going to like your new friends as much as your old ones, Istvan."

"You don't have to like them. Just let them have Hommages. You'll be quite comfortable in the Dower House for the time being. It's all been arranged."

"All right, darling, don't worry about me, I'll be nice to them, I promise. Will we have to be Communists after the war?"

"Not unless you like the idea. I'm an officer, not a politician. I don't see why I should have to get mixed up in it at all. You'll go into the cellar if there is shooting, won't you? Did you put the cots and tinned food down as I told you?"

"Yes, darling," said Eva untruthfully. "Don't worry so."

"Do you know something," said Istvan, "I am atrociously hungry."

"Dinner's been ready for hours, darling."

"Has it? Why didn't you say so? I'm starved."

They dressed and went down to the dining-room where Janos served them silently, pretending hard not to guess why they were two hours late for their meal.

They spent the night making plans for their lives after the war, and Eva forgot the medallion the Cardinal had given her to keep Istvan safe. She was not an imaginative person and it never occurred to her to worry about Istvan. She remembered it again when there was another air raid just before dawn as Istvan left the house. This time the planes were over Buda and the bombs fell very near.

Eva put on her fur coat and ran downstairs. The rosewood table had a deep gash where Istvan had thrown his carbine, and she determined to take him to task for it at some quieter time.

A bomb blast nearly tore the heavy front door from her hand. She looked about her, but the hit was farther down the hill. She had never been in such a bad raid before, but like most unimaginative people she could not conceive of personal danger. Istvan had not turned the corner yet and she called his name and ran out into the street.

Istvan turned and shouted at her to get back into the house. He never heard the explosion of the bomb in the house across the street, but he saw the wall tumble very slowly, all of a piece, so slowly that it seemed to him that if he ran he would have time to reach Eva and pull her to safety. But the street was filled with rubble and stones and dust. Frantically he ran to where Eva had stood and began to dig with his bare hands, quickly, without hope.

After a while he found he was not alone. Janos had come out to help him.

Nightmares are like this, filled with terror but without pain and without time. They found her eventually, a nightmare creature of fur and dust and blood, like the animals the hounds had hunted for sport at Hommages.

In the rubble beside her, wet with blood, lay the medallion of St. Stephen. Janos bent and picked it up. He held it out to Istvan, who looked at it without comprehension. He bent and picked up his carbine and walked off without a word.

Palko and the others cursed him roundly when he arrived for having kept them waiting, but they were too excited to notice his appearance. The moment they saw him they exploded with the news: The Russians had entered Pest.

It had fallen to their lot to make sure that no Germans in responsible positions left Budapest alive. Desiring no second Lidice, they had waited until it would be too late for reprisals. The work was a butcher's, but Istvan no longer cared.

The waiting, which Colonel Riebeck had advised and which they had all found so difficult, now proved its merit. They knew every underground passage in the old town, knew where the Germans would hide from the Russians, and found them and killed them. The Hungarians were badly outnumbered and many of them were killed. Istvan was as invulnerable as death itself. He walked untouched through arcs of bullets, turned away bayonets with his bare hands and was not cut.

His men said, "He is in form today," and only Palko Donath realized that something was wrong. It was not like Istvan to be so grim about fighting. Usually he would have enjoyed his part in this destruction; powers falling apart like a house of cards and armies tumbled about like tin soldiers on a nursery table. And Istvan would have made them take prisoners, though he might have laughed along with his men, shouted and roared with laughter when a fat Gestapo officer pleaded with Palko for his life, for the sake of his wife and children. Palko of all people, whose own wife had not long ago stood for hours in the rain at Auschwitz, awaiting her turn at the gas chamber.

Palko laughed harder than anyone. He could not stop; tears of laughter ran down his cheeks and he was still laughing when he cut the German's throat.

They hunted, caught, and made mock gestures of letting go, like a cat who is so sure of his mouse that he wants to play first. They were drunk on pillaged food and wine, and drunker on enemy blood.

Istvan Halyi took no part in their drunken, cruel games, nor did he attempt to stop them. He only killed, day and night, not like an enemy but like one who steps on an ant or swats a fly.

He was about to murder another Gestapo officer who was blubbing with fright and attempting to look dignified at the same time; a spectacle which would have delighted Istvan Halyi at any other time, when a hand held his back and Riebeck's voice said, "That's enough for now, Istvan." To the German Riebeck said, "Run for it if you can," but paid no attention when he fainted.

Istvan turned and Riebeck saw the drawn, exhausted face, the green eyes drunk with pain, which had frightened Palko enough to send to Vienna for him.

"Palko told me about Eva, Istvan. I am very sorry."

It was a brutal thing to say, but only a calculated brutality would get through to Istvan now, and Riebeck was in a desperate hurry to get back to Vienna.

Into Istvan's face there slowly came the memory of that unspeakable pain that he had pushed away by murdering until he could not even remember what he was avenging. Now he remembered. With infinite care, as if he had forgotten how to do even so simple a thing, Istvan sat down. And then, choking and inept, he began to cry.

Colonel Riebeck lived in a world and practiced a profession that had given him many opportunities to learn that grown men can cry, but he knew that there are some who cannot, and that Istvan was one of them. He would have put his arms around him and held him like a child, but he knew he had no warmth and comfort left to give. He had lost track of how long he had gone without a meal or sleep, he no longer cared about it; he was empty of everything but weariness now. He stood, his hand tight on Istvan's shoulder, hating the work that had left him without comfort when he most wanted to give it.

Later he lit a cigarette and handed it to Istvan. "You must come home and sleep now," he said. "You can't stay here, you'll be caught."

Istvan did not move. Riebeck bent down to pull him to his feet, and though he gritted his teeth against the pain, his bad leg gave under him.

He cursed and argued and at last he begged. "I can't move you with this blasted leg of mine, Istvan. Please get up and come along."

Istvan looked up slowly and finally saw him. "Schani, are you supposed to be here?"

"No. You're doing a marvelous job, but you must come home and sleep now, and then have something to eat. Come along."

Istvan got up obediently and followed his cousin to a German staff car, not very safe in Budapest any more, but still effective at the border.

"It belongs to a General von Fahrenkamp who fancies vainly that I am his friend," Riebeck explained.

Istvan started a grin, and his head slid against Riebeck's shoulder. He was asleep.

Riebeck took the half-smoked cigarette from Istvan's fingers and threw it into the street, where a famished child scrabbled for it. Riebeck dug in his pocket, found the crumpled pack of cigarettes and threw them to the boy, who laughed and gave him a military salute.

Riebeck thought gloomily that now he wouldn't get another cigarette till he was back in Vienna.

At Tisza Palace Janos came to the door and burst into tears.

"You've found him, God be praised."

"Yes. Help me get him into the house, will you, Janos. I don't want to wake him. Give me a hand."

"Poor Monsieur Istvan," said Janos and the tears started again.

"Poor? He is one of the lucky ones, Janos." They carried Istvan upstairs and put him on the bed where he continued to sleep in his dirty blood-stained trench coat. Riebeck picked up Eva's mink rug and covered him.

"Lucky, Monsieur Schani?"

Riebeck smiled his wintry smile. "How many of us, when we need it, get the chance of murdering the Boches for three days?"

"You used to be such a nice boy, Monsieur Schani."

"Very likely I was. Can you spare any food and some cigarettes, Janos? Don't bother if you haven't got enough."

Janos said they still had food from the farm at Hommages and Monsieur Istvan had Russian cigarettes, which he was sure he would like Monsieur Schani to take.

"I'll take half, thanks, Janos. Give Istvan a drink when he wakes up and see to it that he eats something. Thanks for the food. I'll eat it on the way."

"At least sit down and eat in peace, Monsieur Schani."

"I don't think I'd better. If I sit down I'll fall asleep and you'd never get me awake again. Goodbye, Janos. Take care of Istvan."

"Take care of yourself, Monsieur Schani."

Riebeck smiled and nodded. Then he got into General von Fahrenkamp's car and tore back to Vienna.

He was not able to be in Paris on the first day of its freedom, nor had he any wish to be. Since the Germans had been driven out of France he had turned his back on her. For France, deprived of her liberty and ownership of herself, he had willingly given all his mind and time and would as willingly have given his life, but France, bloated with a victory not of her own achieving, he could not countenance.

That small collaborators are shot while traitors go on to grow fat on the black market, that those who have fought the least make the most belligerent speeches, that those who have suffered nothing are the loudest complainers; all these things he knew. But it is difficult to be tolerant with things loved, and Colonel Riebeck had a very great love for France.

He did go to Berlin a day or so ahead of the Russians, partly to round things off neatly, but mostly to get his man in German Military Intelligence out of the country. He was unfortunately obliged to spend most of his time in Herr Jahncke's cellar. Ernst Jahncke wore a *pince-nez* and six long hairs distributed equidistantly across a bald skull. He was the first to admit that he was not one of nature's d'Artagnans, but throughout the war his cellar had been open to Riebeck and his men, at the risk of his life. He was, as the six hairs indicated, a romantic, and Riebeck was his link with the world of adventure, where men wore dirty trench coats with the collars turned up, had as much hair as they liked, and a scar quirking one eyebrow into a look of amused disbelief. Herr Jahncke had been a discreet and self-effacing host, and his guests had given him no trouble and had always, to his great relief, refused his poor offers of food, though they had often looked half starved.

"If you have no immediate business, mein Herr," he said to Riebeck, "may I share the cellar with you? The upstairs is not healthy today."

"Please do. It's your cellar, after all. Will you try an American cigarette?"

Herr Jahncke turned the cigarette unbelieving in his fingers, read out loud the magic syllables, Chesterfield, and tried to recall when he had last smoked a cigarette not made from tobacco grown in a window box: a most unappetizing affair.

"You ought not to smoke these," he said. "For a packet you could probably buy the Krupp works."

"Whatever would I do with the Krupp works?" said Riebeck, displaying a lack of business acumen that would have caused his late, rich testator, Uncle Rosenstil, to turn in his grave.

Herr Jahncke bowed over the flame of a match cupped in a thin, scarred hand, and ceremonially bowed again in thanks. He smoked the cigarette in religious silence. When the butt burned his fingers, he speared it on the silver toothpick he carried on his watch chain, and smoked it to the end.

In the midst of the Russian shelling a fat man in the uniform of a German general sedately pushed a wheelbarrow through the rubbled streets. He seemed more concerned with this wheelbarrow than with his own safety. He had some trouble finding the house he sought. The street names were down with the walls that had held them. Finally he located Herr Jahncke's small villa and banged on the door. There was no answer. The fat general pushed the door open and pulled his wheelbarrow in after him. He clunked it down the stairs, knowing well that no one these days remained above ground. The noise was formidable and brought Herr Jahncke to the stairs. Seeing a dusty German uniform he turned perfectly white, but said with dignity, "It will do you little good to arrest me, Herr General. The war is lost. Even you must realize that."

The General set his wheelbarrow down with a final clunk and asked, "Is Riebeck here?"

"No," said Herr Jahncke, very pale. "I am alone," and felt like a reward Riebeck's reassuring hand on his shoulder, Riebeck's voice: "I am sorry if it frightened you. Of course you haven't met Koenig. Come in, *mon vieux*, it's the right address. This is Herr Jahncke who has so heroically allowed us the use of his cellar all these years."

Herr Jahncke watched with breathless interest the fat German general kissing Riebeck on both cheeks, and Riebeck laughing like a schoolboy. "So you have lasted. Never, never did I think you would."

"I had no hopes for you either," said the General, laughing heartily. "I used to look through the list of caught spies every day expecting to see your name. I am sorry I never could do anything for those poor bastards, Riebeck. These last few years it became impossible."

"I quite understood that. By the way, what is your real name?"

"Koenig," said the General. "Also I am a Jew."

"Good God."

"I hope you do not mind," said Koenig acidly.

Riebeck, whose prejudice, if any, was all in favor of the race that had produced rich Uncle Rosenstil, said patiently, "When I said good God, I did not mean good God, here I have treated Koenig as an equal and he turns out to be a member of an inferior race. I merely meant good God, how did you get away with it."

Koenig laughed. "I apologize. I don't look it for one thing, and I have no family to give me away. I do not think it even occurred to Streicher that I was not one hundred per cent Aryan, though he did use to tell me he could smell Jews from a long way off."

"What's in the wheelbarrow?"

"Files. Bedtime reading for the Counterintelligence boys. Wonderful files, as many as I could rescue before they were burned."

"What other news?"

"Hitler and Eva got married and then took poison. So did Goebbels, Magda, the children, and the dogs. Very thorough. You know what Goebbels was like. What brings you to Berlin, Riebeck?"

"You. You and your wheelbarrow, to be exact. Someone, I fear, has bungled this business badly and the Russians are going to get Berlin."

"They are allies."

"This is one of those cases where an enemy is preferable to an ally. Well, never mind. As usual, instead of putting their minds to winning the war, the generals are sowing dragon's teeth. Oh, sorry, Koenig."

"I am only a major, really. All my promotions after that were Wehrmacht ones," said General Koenig sadly. "In France I shall have to salute you first."

"That uniform! Why the devil couldn't you wear civilian clothes?"

"Too much of a hurry."

"Well, you can't borrow from Jahncke. It wouldn't fit. Honestly, Koenig, after six years of war it's unpatriotic to be so fat. At least throw your epaulettes and your *Ritterkreuz* away. No, not in Herr Jahncke's dustbin, he'll get into trouble with the Russians if they find them. We'd better get going. Thanks for everything, Jahncke. I'll look you up one day when things have quieted down a bit."

"Before you go," said Herr Jahncke, who had discreetly retired with a book and a candle into the far corner of the cellar, "please tell me, is this really the end? There are no more secret weapons? No chance of anything like that?"

"Oh Christ, you Krauts and your secret weapons," said General Koenig.

"Then it is definitely over."

"That's right, Jahncke. It's over. You lost."

"Then, *meine Herren*, will you do me the honor of drinking with me to the end of the war and to your victory. I have waited for this day for a long time, and I have a bottle of champagne put aside which I bought for this purpose on September 1, 1939."

"You are an extraordinarily good fellow," said Koenig.

Herr Jahncke squirreled upstairs and returned shortly with the champagne bottle, two jam glasses, and a coffee cup. "I have no ice and no champagne glasses, unfortunately."

"War is hell," said Koenig sympathetically.

Riebeck, who had glanced at the label of the bottle and seen at once that the champagne was of a bad year and an inferior brand, silently agreed.

"To your victory," said Herr Jahncke solemnly, "and to peace for us at last."

"God, wasn't the champagne awful," said Koenig, pushing his wheelbarrow along a muddy lane and belching loudly.

"Yes. Poor Jahncke. He thinks things end."

"Poor fish. Do you feel as if we had won? Did you feel it when the Allies marched into Paris?"

"No."

They slept that night in the woods and the next in a village that had been recently taken by the French. The initial suspicion caused by Koenig's German uniform was fortunately dispelled by the regimental commander who knew Riebeck from Indochina and Koenig from the Polytechnique. They were given French battle dress—Koenig promptly split the pants—bully beef, known to the French army as monkey meat, and the unexpected luxury of beds.

Late at night, weary with unaccustomed food and drink, they went outside with the battalion commander. In the courtyard a very drunk French soldier was riding a German woman's bicycle and singing *Madelon* at the top of his voice. "*Et pourquoi prendrai-je un seul homme, quand j'aime tout un regiment.*"

The battalion commander laughed and Riebeck said to Koenig, "Now I believe it. We have won the war."

"*Nunc dimittis,*" said Koenig.

In February '45 General Partridge was told to come to the War Office for an interview with the Grand Panjandrum of Military

217

Intelligence; a personage so top secret that hardly anyone knew he existed. The interview was not a pleasant one.

The Grand Panjandrum was very complimentary about General Partridge's work, but praised particularly the splendid idea of setting up the Combined Operations Department with Colonel Riebeck at its head. And this brought him to the reason for this interview. He could not afford to lose someone like Riebeck to the French at the end of the war, and General Partridge would, it was hoped, use all means at his disposal, up to and including a brigadier's third pip, to get Colonel Riebeck to exchange his French uniform for an English one.

General Partridge said that this was highly irregular. The Grand Panjandrum replied that they were here to be irregular and conveyed, politely, that the interview was at an end.

General Partridge passed a bad week, with his mind dwelling constantly on the possibility of being condemned to work forever with Colonel Riebeck. He was not quite mean enough to wish that the Gestapo would catch Riebeck and that this time they would not bungle the job, but if Heaven would arrange for a swift and painless death, General Partridge would be grateful.

Heaven did not see fit to answer the General's prayer. Late in April Colonel Riebeck reported to the office, looking deadly tired, ragged, and starved, but alive.

General Partridge, asking death where his sting was, said he would like to have a talk. Riebeck, with the unshakable courtesy that so annoyed General Partridge, dismissed from his mind at once all thought of his overwhelming need for a bath, food, and bed, and turned his entire attention to what General Partridge had to say.

"Oh," said General Partridge. "Ah."

"Sir?"

General Partridge, reminding himself that these were stirring times and that no sacrifice was too great for King and Country said, "Have you any idea what you are going to do when peace is declared, Riebeck?"

Colonel Riebeck said that his future was not his own to decide. Perhaps he would continue in Intelligence. Or he might be permitted to rejoin his regiment, still fighting in Indochina.

General Partridge, feeling like the poet Keats that now more than ever seemed it rich to die, repeated the Panjandrum's order. Colonel Riebeck was surprised, not to say stunned, but he had over the years learned to control his features and annoyed General Partridge very much by neither confounding himself in tearful gratitude nor refusing point blank. He said he would certainly consider the suggestion, that he was honored, that he would like a little time to talk it over with General de Gaulle, that he would let General Partridge know as soon as possible.

General Partridge, left alone, feverishly attempted to look at the bright side. The question of the third pip had not been broached, General de Gaulle would certainly not look kindly upon the Grand Panjandrum's plan, nothing was as yet settled, and the war was not entirely over. Colonel Riebeck might yet be allowed to lay down his life on the field of honor.

Riebeck himself was too tired to think anything reasonable. He went home, had a bath, and, half asleep, ate without noticing what he was doing, Alphonse's delicious black market *sole au sauce crevette*. Alphonse stood over him, bemoaning his lack of awareness.

"This is too much. You don't eat, you don't sleep, and then you come home too tired to appreciate my cooking. War is all very well, but there is no need to overdo it like this."

Riebeck went to bed and was asleep before he finished pulling up the covers.

He awakened early from habit, and lay motionless in the wonderful knowledge that he did not have to get up until he wanted to. After the last few weeks, when sleep had been snatched for an hour, waking had been sheer physical agony, and breakfast had consisted mostly of Benzedrine, the simple pleasure of staying in bed turned into luxury.

He was happy. He had done an impossible job well, it was over, and after weeks he was lying, clean in a clean bed, with the sun on his back and breakfast and the London *Times* on the way. He lay like a drowned man on a beach, face down, his arms spread wide, the exhausted lines of his face ready to change into lines of laughter. There was something amusing that had not yet surfaced in his

219

mind. It was waiting somewhere at the bottom, contributing to his sense of well-being. And then suddenly he remembered General Partridge's offer and his shoulders began to shake with silent laughter.

Alphonse found him like this when he brought in the tea.

"Good morning," he said sternly. He had not yet forgotten his slighted *sole au sauce crevette*. "I don't know what you think you've got to laugh about."

Riebeck turned on his back and Alphonse was suddenly reminded of something he had not thought to see again: the face of young Monsieur Schani up to his tricks, wanting people to make him laugh and champagne for his breakfast.

"They want me to become an English officer, Alphonse."

"What is that, an honor or an insult?"

"I don't know. I think it's a joke."

Alphonse picked up the teapot and solemnly carried it out of the room. Riebeck, who did not really like tea so early in the day looked after him, surprised but not dismayed. He unfolded the morning paper and idly read the front page. Alphonse returned with a tray on which he carried a glass, an ice bucket, and a bottle of champagne.

Riebeck had no intention of discussing anything with General de Gaulle, whose reaction he could easily guess. Instead, when his work brought him to Paris, he looked up Latour and asked his advice.

The war years had caused Latour to assume the expression and speech of an elder statesman; cynical but not unkind. He did this very well, quite as well as he had played the part of ruthless and mysterious spy in the Thirties. It never failed to delight Riebeck.

He listened with gravity to Riebeck's story and then said, "What have you decided?"

"I thought I wouldn't decide anything till after I'd talked to you."

"Liar."

"Well, I don't mind admitting I'm tempted. Those English uniforms are very smart."

Latour threw up his hands in laughing protest. "Don't, don't, don't fill my mind with your nonsense so you will not have to tell me the real reason. I know our peacetime Intelligence was dull, but—"

"Oh no. I was frightened all the time and when one is frightened one isn't bored."

"Fear is the one drug that never wears off. What would we do without it?"

"*Timeo, ergo sum?* How depressing."

"Now," said Latour.

"I don't know. I like working with the English, I suppose."

"Yes, of course. Who doesn't? And then you've never forgiven us for 1940, which was a year when we behaved very badly and the English extremely well."

"I am not," said Riebeck, annoyed, "so conceited that I go about sitting in judgment on my country."

"Oh yes you are," said the cynical elder statesman, "and why not? It is a terribly difficult thing to forgive. I admit that by and large we all behaved badly and will without a doubt behave very badly again in the future. And I grant you that the English were magnificent. They always are when they are losing a war. To get the best out of an Englishman you must have him pushed against a wall with a knife at his throat."

"The sure testing of a man is in peril, mark him as he is in adversity."

"Ah," said Latour, unflaggingly charming, "there is nothing like a solid classical education for answering people back. But a very unfair statement, you must admit, Jean. Many people who are very amusing and entirely admirable under normal circumstances are of no use in adversity at all. And the converse holds true as well. People who are splendid in trouble are usually vile bores in times of peace. Your English are like that."

"Do you really think we shall have times of peace?"

"I can see that your mind is made up. And I am not so conceited as to imagine I can change it. What would you like for a farewell present from your grateful government? I don't know what medal you don't already have. Or how about a promotion. Partridge wouldn't like to see you a general."

"I'll tell you what I would like if I may."

"Please."

"I would like permission to continue wearing the fourragère. It's a regimental citation, you see, and I shall have to give it up when I leave my regiment. It's a terrible thorn in Partridge's side; he turns purple every time he looks at it."

"If it gives the old ass apoplexy," said Latour, forgetting his elder statesman role for the moment, "you shall wear your fourragère or my name is mud."

"Thank you."

"And now," said Latour, "tell me the real reason why you are changing sides."

"Not sides. Only the base of operations. All right, I'll tell you. I want to run the Department some day. I'm after Partridge's job."

"If I were you, Jean," the elder statesman advised kindly, "I would think up a more convincing lie than that before I went to see General de Gaulle."

❧ THREE ❧

All this suppression of the secondary leaves the field clear—for higher flights, should they choose to come. But if they never came, what thoughts there were would still manifest the aristocratic type and wear the well-bred form. So great is our sense of harmony and ease in passing from the company of a philistine to that of an aristocratic temperament, that we are almost tempted to deem the falsest views and tastes as held by a man of the world, truer than the truest as held by a common person.

William James: Psychology

XV

As soon as the war ended, England embroiled itself in a general election. Colonel Riebeck, who had garnered all his ideas of English politics from Mr. Slumkey's election at Eatanswill, was in for a few surprises. The Falconers were expectedly Conservative, though they didn't make a fuss about it, but Simon Cook, all the Lionels, and Jeremy Tyrell were Labour in the noisiest way. Jeremy especially embarrassed everyone by his vigorous canvassing. He preached to his friends, harangued complete strangers, and gave mortal offense to Jenny's cook, who said she had voted Tory all her life and did not hold with gentlemen in her kitchen if gentlemen you could call it.

Jenny was obliged to visit her uncle and aunt in Cornwall for several weeks so she would not be available for the cook to give notice to. Anyone else would thereafter have been forever exiled from the Falconer guest list, but since the culprit was Jeremy, Jenny merely said, "You are a nuisance, darling," and took him and his Barbara off to Cornwall with her.

Jeremy had removed himself from the army with a dispatch that impressed even Riebeck. After his great success of bringing the Labour Party into office (for which he took the fullest credit) he came to make his farewells to Riebeck. He seemed disappointed that no peace treaty contemplated giving back to England her rightful possessions of Anjou, Maine, and Aquitaine, and aired his views on the venality of politicians at some length. This was the sort of thing for which Riebeck would, in other days, have sent Jeremy to the decoding room for weeks, but he held no authority over a Jeremy Tyrell in an ancient tweed jacket and flannel trousers with shabby fringes on the cuffs, and had to confine himself to a cool good-by.

Simon Cook went back to his job as modern languages master at Wellington. Others of his former officers had retired from the Service to write, to Riebeck's distressed amusement, their memoirs. The man who had fallen among thieves could hardly have been more unpleasantly surprised than Riebeck when he discovered that he had been working for years with disguised authors.

They invariably sent him their typescripts and hoped, bashfully, that they might be allowed to dedicate their masterpieces to him. Riebeck read these fabrications with shouts of laughter, but refused all dedications. Truth had never flourished in Intelligence circles, and had been completely routed in the memoirs.

His French colleagues too were busy with their typewriters, but while the English concentrated mainly on hair-raising adventures they had met without a twitch of the stiff upper lip, the French, while never denying that they too had encountered peril with *sang-froid* and panache, preferred to concentrate on romance. Considering the large amounts of creditable work these people had accomplished, Riebeck found the quantities of time they had been able to devote to sex absolutely amazing.

As he read these inventions, which had about as much to do with their real work as Vultz, the mad German inventor, and Captain Zoom, Birdman of the RAF, had to do with a real war, he found he missed their authors, and above all he missed the war.

This was no doubt very shocking, but there it was. It was his profession to fight a war, not to punish afterwards the enemy survivors. And for all that he was swamped with work he was bored by London now (Jenny was in Paris). When Major Bryant protested for the sixty-seventh time that he was not the person to run the Berlin office and would resign unless it was at once taken over by someone who was, Riebeck said to General Partridge that he would like to go.

General Partridge was delighted to get him out of the way. And, for that matter, Riebeck was delighted to go, for he and General Partridge simply could not help disagreeing about almost everything.

The German scientists for whom Colonel Riebeck had been looking (without any encouragement from Partridge) since they had left Peenemunde had turned up near Kochel, in Bavaria, where they had docilely surrendered to the Americans, by whom they were now employed.

"They are more than welcome to them," said General Partridge when Riebeck once again deplored the fact that the English had no organization similar to the American "Paperclip," which was picking up Hitler's physicists all over the place, "wouldn't want a lot of Nazis in England, you know."

"You'd want these, if only you knew," muttered Riebeck under his breath and picked up his telephone to ask Larry Leigh if he could fly him to Berlin.

"Piece of cake, old boy," said Larry.

Riebeck laughed. "I see you have been learning the language by leaps and bounds."

"It'll come in handy in Hollywood. You sound like Ronald Colman, you've got it made."

"How is it you aren't back yet?"

"I have time. So far the only parts I've been offered were two; one a gallant flight lieutenant and one a gallant squadron leader. Have you heard from Jeremy?"

"Yes. He's in Ireland and apparently not liking it much."

("Do you know sweety milk?" Jeremy had written from his home. "Probably not. It's a nauseating mixture, as nauseating as its name, of hot milk, cinnamon, and sugar. My mother insists that as a child I was fond of it. It seems improbable, but even if it is true, must I, at the age of forty-five, return from the wars to be met with sweety milk?")

"They are making him drink milk," said Riebeck. Larry choked into the telephone and rang off.

In the scramble for buildings still usable for office space Major Bryant had come off worst. The Americans lived in luxury, the French had a roof over their heads, Major Bryant had what was formerly a fashionable address on the Kurfürstendamm. All the windows were blown out, the ceilings were cracked, and several walls were down. From one of the remaining walls the absent-minded Bryant had forgotten to remove the portrait of Hitler.

Here Riebeck set to work, close to the Russians, within Russian territory, watching with interest and amusement their peculiar behavior. Here a nation had broken apart and in the debris many interesting things came to light. Riebeck did not stay in Berlin all the time; he used it as a jumping-off place, but it became his headquarters and he enjoyed it. There was never enough time for all the things that had to be done. He hoped all that talk about planes flying faster than sound would prove true.

The Russians, after their first cheerful meeting with the Americans at the Elbe river, had crept back into their shells and had become increasingly secretive, annoying, and suspicious. Colonel Riebeck wanted an opening wedge of some sort, a Russian friend, preferably one in Intelligence circles. To this end he had done something of which he usually disapproved; he had gone out of his way to capture a former SS officer who had in '41 made a nuisance of himself in Kiev, and whom the Russians therefore wanted very much. The SS officer had been caught two weeks before, and Riebeck had allowed rumor of his capture to leak out.

Riebeck had been in Berlin for several months before the first nibble came from East Berlin. Major Bryant told him that a Major Dyelik had rung up while Riebeck had been out to lunch, and would call back at four.

"He's supposed to be with the Russian Counterespionage people, but I think he's MVD."

"Thank you," said Riebeck. "Have we a file on him?"

Major Bryant, who was a wonderful second-in-command even if he would never be able to run the Berlin office by himself, handed Riebeck the file and left. Riebeck lit a cigarette and read through it.

"It's not very informative," he said when Bryant came in with a cup of coffee.

"It's all the information we have. I've heard he was one of Beria's Rote Kapelle. They were all caught and most of them were executed. Dyelik wasn't because he knew an awful lot and wouldn't talk. He spent two years in Dachau."

"How depressing. Did he say what he wanted when he rang up?"

"No. But I think they've bitten."

"About time, too."

When the telephone rang at four o'clock, Riebeck looked at his watch and said to Bryant: "A punctual Russian."

"Major Dyelik from Russian Headquarters here," said a pleasant deep voice. "Can you understand my English, Colonel Riebeck? My French is even worse."

"And my Russian worst of all," said Riebeck. "Your English is fine. How do you do, Major Dyelik. What can we do for you?"

"I believe you are holding prisoner one former SS officer by the name of Stallman."

"Are we? I should have to check."

Major Dyelik—who had heard that Colonel Riebeck had imperturbably walked into the German's carbine fire, armed only with his revolver, until he was close enough to shoot the gun out of the German's hand; that a brawl had ensued in the course of which Riebeck had managed to hit Stallmann over the head with the discarded carbine, thus disabling him—chuckled appreciatively. He said, "I understand. If you do have him, I wonder whether we might borrow him. We'll return the carcass if you like."

Riebeck said cautiously that some kind of trade might perhaps be worked out. "Are you free to come here and talk things over with me, Major Dyelik?"

"Right now if you like."

Riebeck gave him a good mark for not asking for safe-conduct.

"Good. I'll arrange the official business on our side." He rang off after several polite exchanges of farewell and said to Bryant, "He's coming here. Whether it will lead to anything remains to be seen."

"It's a damn good start, sir. They must want Stallmann very badly. Whom are you going to ask for in return?"

"Jennings, I suppose," said Riebeck without much enthusiasm.

Lionel Jennings was one of the members of Jeremy's entourage who had been so enthralled by his wartime adventures that he had decided to spend the rest of his life working for Colonel Riebeck. No arguments to the contrary Riebeck could invent managed to deter him.

He had been dropped on during an exploratory walk in the Russian zone two weeks previously and had steadfastly maintained that his name was Smith, that he was the son of a distinguished English peer, that a deeply concerned embassy might at any moment begin to ask agonized questions about him, and that he had been innocently drunk and had walked into the Russian zone purely by accident. He had been wearing civilian dress at the time and the whole thing was not implausible except that the Russians were moved to wonder what an English civilian was doing in Berlin at this particular time.

"Walking tour, don't you know," said Mr. Smith blandly.

Evidently Russians knew nothing about walking tours, for they continued to hold on to him and as yet no questions had been asked in the House of Lords.

"Thanks, I do need him rather," said Bryant.

"Yes, I know. Otherwise I should leave him there indefinitely. Really I can't see why Tyrell couldn't take his Lionels with him when he left. There's another one in France."

"He's very good, you know."

"I know, I know," said Riebeck. "That's the trouble. Will you please arrange all the necessaries here, so that Dyelik doesn't get arrested. That would put a damper on things."

"Right ho," said Bryant, who, though in uniform, was an incurable civilian and could never learn that there was only one answer to all of Riebeck's questions: a brisk, "Yes, sir."

Major Dyelik arrived a little after five. He wore a Russian uniform without any badges on the collar. He had a jolly round face, merry black eyes that could turn as mean as a shark's, and a cheerful disposition. From the moment of their meeting Riebeck felt that he had possibly come on the only Russian alive with whom he could get somewhere. They spoke the same language about many things.

Most Russians had peculiar ideas about saluting, feeling that an English colonel should salute a Russian lieutenant first. Dyelik was not of this breed. He saluted promptly and smiled.

"I am happy to meet you, Comrade Colonel."

There was a gut-shriveling silence until Riebeck decided that more important things were at stake than his dislike of being called comrade.

"Even in Russia I heard about you," Major Dyelik went on, amused. "You see, I know your cousin, Colonel Halyi."

"Oh. Have they made him a colonel? Please sit down."

"Only a lieutenant-colonel. We all come to it sooner or later. At least I hope so." .

"Assuredly. It's getting to be a general that's difficult."

"It is the same in every army in the world."

They lit cigarettes and settled back to talk.

Colonel Riebeck had in his occasional dealings with Russians noted two things: they hate telephones, and they have a national inability to come to the point. If Major Dyelik had come to discuss an exchange of prisoners, he would without a doubt talk about anything but the purpose of his visit. Though lots of work awaited Riebeck's attention, he put it out of his mind and tried to pretend to himself that he too came of a country that had unlimited space and unlimited time. For a European this is a curiously difficult exercise.

They spoke of the recently ended war, of course, and Dyelik had very sound ideas about the Germans, saying that if he had his way they would all be lined up against a wall and shot. He spoke highly of the English army and Riebeck returned his courtesy. Dyelik asked how a Frenchman came to be an English officer, told concentration camp jokes, enlarged on the mental failings of his general, quoted Mayakovski on the Brooklyn Bridge and Tolstoi on the Russian peasantry. When Riebeck could bear it no longer he said, "How is it you know Istvan Halyi?"

Major Dyelik said that the Hungarian officers who had fought in the Communist underground at war's end had been taken to Moscow and feted everywhere as Communist heroes.

"I liked Colonel Halyi very much," said Dyelik. "And the little Pavel Donath. We drank each other under the table every night. What hard heads those Hungarians have."

"Speaking of drink, may I offer you some Scotch?"

Dyelik said he would try anything once and if he liked it he would try it again. He liked the Scotch very much and repeated the experiment several times.

"I cannot tell you how funny it was," he said, aided in this indiscretion by Scotch, "when someone accidentally stumbled on the fact that Colonel Halyi's mother was the Princess Kira Esterhazy."

Riebeck smiled. "It must have been." A Communist who could find other Communists funny was a being as doomed for extinction as the great auk. A sense of humor was the worst affliction a good party member could suffer.

"I must explain first," said Dyelik, "that Colonel Halyi had taken Marshal Zhukov's fancy and that the two were the most tremendous friends. Well then, this Esterhazy canard came out and they at once called a staff meeting and everyone pounced on me—how was it that I hadn't known the general staff were making themselves ridiculous by feting a disguised Esterhazy all over town?"

Not only Istvan's but Dyelik's life had at that moment been in danger. Dyelik did not say so, but Riebeck could fill in the missing pieces for himself. A quiet disappearance for Istvan, which could either mean years forgotten in a Russian prison, or with luck, instant death, and for Dyelik a secret trial, were certainly contemplated by most members of the general staff and the MVD. But Marshal Zhukov had embarrassingly invited himself to the meeting. Marshall Zhukov liked Istvan Halyi. And so Marshal Zhukov looked at the incompetents in general's uniform and said: "Good officers are hard to find. Colonel Halyi is one." Then, looking at a general whose mother had spent years abroad with Trotsky, he said, "We cannot help how we are born and who our mothers are." Several other generals cringed at this tactless remark. "So let us say no more about Esterhazys. If Colonel Halyi shows any aristocratic tendencies the army will know how to take care of the matter."

The MVD acquiesced. For one thing they were frightened of Marshal Zhukov, for another they realized that Colonel Halyi would be a good man to hold in reserve. When a purge of Hungarian officers became necessary, who could better demonstrate that the officers' corps was riddled with aristocrats and imperialist warmonger spies than the tall elegant Horthy officer with his Esterhazy nose?

Dyelik did not of course mention this final thought, but Riebeck could guess. He did not like it at all. But it was Istvan's soup and Istvan would have to eat it. Riebeck could only hope that Marshal Zhukov was steady in his affections and took good care of his health.

"To Marshal Zhukov," said Riebeck, lifting his Scotch, "a long and successful life. And now, Major Dyelik, will you give me the pleasure of dining with me at our officer's mess, though I must warn you before you accept that the only thing that can be said for the food is that it is not poisonous."

Having thus put Dyelik in the position where he could not refuse without appearing critical of English cooking, Riebeck led the way downstairs.

Dinner was an extremely nasty shepherd's pie and a soggy trifle. Dyelik, casting about in his mind for vengeance, said Riebeck must dine with him on the Russian side sometime soon.

If such an invitation was what Riebeck had been angling for he gave no sign. He merely said that he would have loved to, but that, owing to a slight misunderstanding at the crossing into the Russian sector he had lost his pass. He could of course cross over any day in civilian clothes, but that, as Lionel Jennings' case proved, could have its disadvantages.

"Bureaucrats," said Dyelik vengefully. "I'll send you a special pass and then there will be no more trouble."

Back at Riebeck's office they had another Scotch, discussed the futility of the Nuremberg Trials (though Riebeck forbore to say that having Russian judges try Nazis seemed to him a travesty of justice) and some further mental limitations of Dyelik's general. Riebeck, who could have told a tale or two on the subject, knew better than to criticize a superior officer and confined himself to making sympathetic noises.

Finally, the amenities having been fully met, Dyelik appeared willing to get down to business.

Colonel Riebeck was holding prisoner one Herr Stallmann who was of no use to him, but was very much wanted by the Russians. They in turn had a Mr. Smith, whom they did not particularly want, but who was Major Bryant's much needed Captain Jennings. The whole thing could have been settled in three minutes by a mental defective, but not by a Russian.

Major Dyelik went from saying that there was no Mr. Smith to the suspicion that Mr. Smith was a spy and ought to be questioned before he was released (a suggestion with which Riebeck heartily though silently concurred) to the rumor that Mr. Smith had already been questioned and was now digging salt in Siberia, to the sad news that Mr. Smith had been shot dead while trying to escape, and overcome by shame for spying on the People's Republic had hanged himself in jail.

Colonel Riebeck, concealing his impatience and a headache, countered Major Dyelik's moves by claiming that there was no Herr Stallmann, that he was a spy, was in Dartmoor, had been shot while trying to escape and had then committed suicide. To Dyelik's ultimate lie that Mr. Smith had learned to love life in a true democracy and chosen to remain, Riebeck replied with perfect truth that Stallmann wished for nothing more than to spend the rest of his life as far away from Russia as possible.

This last apparently struck Dyelik favorably, for he promised to return Mr. Smith in good health and at the same time to take away the SS officer who had left such lively memories in Kiev.

With expressions of unlimited mutual confidence they parted. Riebeck took an aspirin and went to bed.

Two days later he found in his mail a pass signed by Major Dyelik authorizing him to cross into the Soviet zone at any time and a letter suggesting a time and meeting place for the exchange of prisoners.

Stallmann was reluctant to come and eloquent in his pleas.

"Nauseatin'," said the sergeant who guarded him.

Stallmann thereupon burst into tears and, finding his captors unmoved, told them what would happen to them when the glorious day of the Nazi renaissance arrived.

"Which will be never if I have anything to say about it," said the sergeant who had fought from Normandy to Torgau and was not impressed by Germans. He took Stallmann by the scruff of the neck and packed him ungently into the back of the jeep.

Major Dyelik once again surprised Riebeck by being punctual. Jennings looked sheepish but unharmed, and Stallmann once again wept.

"You promised to have dinner with me, Colonel," said Dyelik.

"Any time you say."

"Tomorrow? Tonight I shall be busy." Dyelik turned his shark's glance on Stallmann, who flinched.

"Tomorrow then. *Au revoir*, Major. You drive now, sergeant," said Riebeck and got into the back with Lionel Jennings.

"I'm frightfully sorry, sir," said Jennings.

"How did they treat you?"

"Not too badly. They questioned me a lot, but not unkindly. The food was almost as bad as our and the cots were very hard, but on the whole they were very decent. I almost liked Dyelik. He had a long talk with me last night. I gathered I was being sent to points East unless I told him all my little secrets, so I'm quite glad to be back."

"I expect you'd like a bath," said Riebeck.

Jennings moved apologetically to the furthest corner of the jeep. "I'm sorry, sir."

"Quite all right, not your fault. I'll drop you at the house then. The geyser collapsed again last week so the bath water is like ice. I sometimes wonder whether cleanliness is all it's cracked up to be."

"The Russians don't care for it much. Who was the weepy chap you gave to Dyelik?"

"A former SS officer who had a hobby of torturing hostages in Kiev."

"Oh I say," Jennings exclaimed in distress, "won't Dyelik be rather unkind to him?"

It was the sort of Lionel remark that Riebeck found hard to tolerate. Had Major Dyelik still been there, he might have been tempted to return Captain Jennings to him.

"Teach him not to monkey with hostages next time," he said unsympathetically.

The next evening he put on a freshly pressed uniform, his fourragère, all his medal ribbons, and his Webley, and drove himself to Russian Intelligence (so-called) Headquarters. He was looked at like the man from Mars and shown to Dyelick's office, which was decorated by a huge picture of Stalin and had a large piece of ceiling hanging down.

"I am delighted, Comrade Colonel," said Dyelik, coming around the desk to shake hands. "Do you like vodka?"

"Love it."

Major Dyelik brought out a bottle from a locked file drawer and two exquisitely thin crystal glasses. "*Za vashe zdorovye*," he said.

Riebeck, who had progressed to page 96 of his Russian primer, made an inspired guess and replied, "Cheers."

The Russian food was not quite as bad as the English, and Dyelik's fellow officers, while somewhat surprised to see the enemy in their midst, were friendly and polite and touchingly pleased with Riebeck's bits of Russian. Dyelik talked pleasantly about administrative problems in Berlin, about the shortage of coal and the severity of the winter, and then asked Riebeck whether he would care to visit the unfortunate Stallmann. Riebeck refused firmly.

"You gave him to us," Dyelik reminded him.

"I know."

"Captain Smith must be of great value to you."

"Who is Captain Smith?"

"I hear our Mr. Smith now wears an English uniform with the rank insignia of a captain."

"Oh Lord, you mean Lionel," said Riebeck. "You can have him back any time."

Dyelik, not knowing what a Lionel was and quite at sea at his visitor's eccentric offer, tactfully changed the subject. "Have you ever been to Russia, Colonel? You ought to visit us. Such a wonderful country, so big. In Germany I feel that I am in a cage. I come from Leningrad. A beautiful city. Have you ever been there?"

"No. I have never been in Russia at all."

"I did not spend much time in Leningrad myself, but I think I have lived in every garrison town we have. My father was a cavalry officer. I was in the cavalry myself until I changed to Intelligence."

"How interesting," said Riebeck and set himself to exploiting this happy coincidence shamelessly to cement his lucky friendship with the Russian secret police.

They saw a good deal of each other after this, though not usually for business reasons. They genuinely liked each other, and Dyelik felt the need to blow off steam about his job and his general, which he could not very well do on the Russian side. Colonel Riebeck, whose code forbade him ever to criticize a superior officer, even if that officer happened to be General Partridge, confined himself to being a sympathetic listener and plying his Russian friend with Scotch. Dyelik had a hard head, but Riebeck's was harder, and he learned quite a bit more about the workings of Russian counter-espionage than Dyelik intended. Mainly, however, he learned of the trials life was inflicting on the major's soul. He was, he said, an officer, not a butcher, and he hated his present job. It was not only degrading but also, in the long run, destructive of a man's finer sensibilities. Besides, Major Dyelik had a vocation which his chief was too stupid to recognize. Major Dyelik wanted to sit up with a wet towel around his head and decode things.

"Look here," Riebeck said once, after having listened to another harangue, "if you ever get fed up enough I can get you a job decoding for me."

Major Dyelik was sincerely shocked at this suggestion, but Riebeck thought that if he were left to think it over he might in the end come to consider it not a bad idea. To have a member of the

MVD on his staff would be unorthodox but useful. Certain precautions would of course be necessary to make sure Dyelik was not working both sides of the fence at once—many people did— but that was not a serious problem.

Having set everything up so neatly, Colonel Riebeck was not at all surprised when Major Dyelik, instead of defecting to the West, was recalled to Russia. He could only sigh and begin to look around for another Russian.

Fearing that Dyelik might want his pass back, Riebeck decided to drive to Weimar for a day and visit Dr. Sivan, a thing he had meant to do since May but had never found the time for.

Dr. Sivan still lived in the same house and still cared for his undernourished patients. Slowly and with tact he was living down his reputation as a Nazi doctor. Riebeck had, in May, written him a thank-you note which had caused the old doctor to grumble: "You're too charming by half." But he had decided, though he would have died rather than admit it, to remain in Weimar instead of going home to France, as he had meant to do.

Riebeck found Weimar unchanged and the doctor's door, as always, unlocked. When his knock was not answered he went in and followed the sound from the gramophone. Dr. Sivan was playing Schubert *Lieder*. *"Wandrer du müder, du bist zuhaus."*

"Hello, Sivan."

The doctor jumped creakily from his chair and hugged Riebeck.

"Jean, *ach, mon dieu,* how glad I am to see you. How are you? Let me look at you. You are looking well, much better than I've ever dared to hope."

"I'm all right," said Riebeck. "Don't fuss. You look thin. Not enough food, *hein?* I've brought you all the American cigarettes I could get my hands on."

"You're very thin yourself. Don't they feed you in Berlin?"

"I'm fine, Sivan."

"You're all bones and beak."

"Very flattering."

"It's an improvement over last time I saw you. Come, sit down. Tell me about yourself."

Colonel Riebeck's idea of telling about himself was to ask Sivan about General Patton's victorious entry into Weimar.

Dr. Sivan laughed. "Oh, those Americans. It was very hard, you know, to believe that these fat, cheerful young men could be an army. They wear rubber-soled boots, you know, and they slouched into town with no more noise than a regiment of cats. We stood in the street to watch them, and though they had fought across France and halfway across Germany we all said, 'But they must be a very bad army, look how they march.' Also they always eat chocolates and ices like little children, and that is not very military. Then they went all over town by twos and asked people to turn in their guns. Well naturally I had a gun, but I couldn't very well explain to them that I kept it in case the Gestapo should come for me. I lied and told them I hadn't got one. They were delighted with my rusty school English and never bothered to search the house. Later I discovered that someone had hidden a machine gun in my raspberry bushes. Can you imagine the German army behaving like that? And yet they win wars."

"Not all by themselves, Sivan. Were you one of those whom Patton gave a guided tour through Buchenwald?"

"No. I had half of Buchenwald in my cellar. Your Major Tyrell brought them here in a van. It seems he simply marched in, wearing an SS uniform and an eyeglass and said he had orders to remove all the British and French spies to an extermination camp further South and drove out again."

"Considering that I merely told him to see what he could do he managed very nicely."

"Poor boy, he was very sick when he came here. I thought he should never get done retching."

"And the Weimarers who toured Buchenwald? Were they sick?"

"They looked the other way. And many said, 'They were only Jews, after all.' All of them said they hadn't known."

"I know. Nobody knew anything. It's almost remarkable, that."

"They are telling the truth in a way, you know. It's like people not knowing they have cancer. They do, really, but anything is more bearable than the truth."

"Thank you for taking such good care of my people. They are all most grateful, and so am I."

"Oh, please. I can't tell you what a pleasure it is to see you again. Never did I think you would survive the war."

"Neither did I. It's rather an anticlimax, to tell you the truth."

"Don't be ungrateful. Good God," eclaimed Dr. Sivan suddenly, "I must be getting senile. I forgot. I have a surprise for you." .

"Good. I like surprises."

He left the room. When next the door opened Riebeck looked up to see a young man with a melancholy, handsome face, wearing a shabby French uniform and under it a black turtleneck sweater. He blinked once with surprise and then with a whoop of pleasure threw himself upon Colonel Riebeck.

"Bantain, I thought you were dead."

Lieutenant Bantain pulled himself together and apologized. "I was carried away for a moment. I know how you dislike emotional outbursts. But yes, I am alive and I am extremely happy to see you again."

"Just for being alive you can burst emotionally as much as you like. Why didn't you write to tell me, Sivan?"

"I did. In May."

"I never got it. This is marvelous, Bantain. Were you in Buchenwald all the time? You're looking well."

"Yes. I didn't look like this last April. Dr. Sivan's been patching me up."

"He looks better than I do," said Riebeck.

"The war taught us a lot of new surgery. I could probably do something about your leg now, you know. I don't know if I could fix it so you wouldn't limp at all, but it could certainly be improved."

"How nice. I'll try and take a week end off soon and drive down here."

Bantain laughed and Dr. Sivan said, "A week end will not do it, I'm afraid. It would take months."

"Are you mad? I haven't got months. Baintain, how would you like to get back to work? I'm in Berlin now, working for the English of all people, and I could use you."

"Now, *mon colonel*," said Dr. Sivan, "you can't tank over people like that. Pierre's not all that well yet, and if he comes with you it will mean working twenty hours a day and chasing women and getting drunk the other four. I won't let him go."

"You overestimate me, I assure you," said Riebeck. "Besides, in Berlin the women chase us."

"May I remind you, Riebeck," said Dr. Sivan in despair, "that you are no longer in the French army and have no right at all to order Pierre to go to Berlin."

"Oh, that's all right. I'll arrange it with L'Abbé. I pulled off a rather nice job for him last week and he's eating out of my hand at the moment. Don't be mean, Sivan. If you could see the Lionels I have working for me you'd realize I've got to have Bantain."

"What are Lionels?" asked Bantain.

"Come to Berlin with me, and you'll find out."

"Now Pierre," Dr. Sivan implored weakly.

"Don't fuss. I must see what a Lionel looks like. Besides, I feel awfully well now."

"You look it," said Riebeck approvingly. "How does it happen that you are still alive?"

"I was the only one left who knew where the cyclonite came from. So whenever Werner said 'Hang that bastard Bantain on the meathook,' or, 'Throw that bastard Bantain alive in the oven' I said, 'Oh please, nice, kind Herr Major, don't do that and I'll tell you where all the stuff is.' So then I'd send them off digging in the Harz mountains or something equally time-consuming and when they came back the whole business started over again. Werner didn't take very kindly to liars and I'm a fluent one. Luckily he was sent to the Russian front, and the fellow who succeeded him didn't know me from Goering, so I was more or less left alone. There was some talk at the end about shooting all the spies, but your red-haired Irishman came and got us all out."

"God," said Riebeck, "you're wonderful."

"When I think," Dr. Sivan said, "that my safety was in the hands of two madmen like you I get cold all over even now."

"Well, you're still here," Bantain said bracingly.

"Let's go," Riebeck told him. "I've got work to do. I'll see you again one day. Sivan, when I have a little more time. Come along, Bantain. You do," he asked belatedly, "want to come?"

"Don't ask silly questions."

"Good. Sivan was right about working twenty hours a day. What you do with the rest is your business."

Lieutenant Bantain went to put on his coat and said a quick good-by to the bewildered Dr. Sivan.

They drove north on what had once been a perfectly good Autobahn. Riebeck was silent, concentrating on avoiding the shell holes which the Russians could see no reason for filling. When they came into a fairly clear stretch he looked at Bantain and said, "Oh, by the way, thanks for getting me out of Buchenwald."

Bantain snorted but was not offended. If that was all his life was worth to him, a five-years-belated "Oh, by the way, thanks," that was all there was to it and one expected it from Riebeck.

Misunderstanding the snort, Riebeck said, "I meant to thank you earlier than this." (Cleaning up and bandaging, though deftly and carefully done, had been a small Buchenwald in itself and, in spite of the morphine, sweat had stung his eyes and blasphemy his tongue. When afterward he had asked for Bantain, Sivan had said, "He has gone to the WC to be sick and to cry, I think.") "If I didn't thank you at the time," Riebeck said, "it was the morphine. You must forgive me."

"That sounds encouraging."

"How?"

"You don't remember what you said?"

"No. What?"

"You said with what might easily have been your last breath: 'Sivan, tell that bastard Bantain that he disobeyed my orders and that if I live to see him again I shall have him locked up until he turns black."

Riebeck laughed. "I would much rather have that for my last words than the bilge people go down in history for. There was an English writer who said: 'See in what peace a Christian can die.'"

"That," said Bantain, "would have been highly inappropriate. Your language at the time was most unchristian. I never thought much of the cavalry, but when Sivan was working on you I realized that when it comes to swearing the fashionable regiments have it all over the artillery."

"Naturally. By the way, we must do something about that uniform of yours. That turtleneck sweater has got to go, and I daresay there's a promotion waiting for you at home. You shouldn't still be a lieutenant."

"Not much promotion in being thought dead, I guess," said Bantain laughing. "That was a large assumption to make, you know."

"We had a supposed eyewitness. And he was right about the others, unfortunately."

"Yes. Tell me about Berlin. Have you really got twenty hours a day of work for me? I can't tell you how grateful I am. Sivan's been very kind, but one has so much time with him, and so little to do except think."

"If you come to work for me you won't think again for the next five years."

After that they talked shop.

XVI

Riebeck had been in Berlin for four years when General Partridge expressed a sudden desire to have him back in London. What had caused this wish Riebeck could not discover, for General Partridge, when asked, muttered: "Busy now, some other time," and became unavailable.

"He's mad, you know," said Captain Jennings, whom Riebeck had recently succeeded in palming off on General Partridge. "He probably can't remember what it was he wanted to see you about, and he won't admit that he's forgotten, so he goes beetling off till he thinks up another reason."

"That's all right. I shan't mind a few weeks of Alphonse's cooking."

For several weeks General Partridge pretended to be out of town, while Riebeck, almost automatically, slipped back into doing General Burkey's work as well as his own. Finally General Partridge poured himself a stiff whisky and asked Riebeck to come to his office.

"Sit down," he said, "tell me about Berlin."

Riebeck gave his report. General Partridge listened patiently, asked a lot of questions, and even went so far as to tell Riebeck that he seemed to have done a good job. But finally there was nothing more to be said.

"I suppose you've heard that General Burkey is leaving us."

Since he had heard it only as part of the everlasting gossip around the office, Riebeck thought it more judicious to say, "No, sir."

"It's been a problem, finding someone to replace him."

"Yes, sir."

"But it's finally been decided," said General Partridge, with a face that made it perfectly clear that the decision had been made without him and was to be considered a major disaster. "We'd like you to take over the job."

A scowl cut a straight line between Riebeck's brows. He said, "I'm sorry, sir, but I don't want it. I want to stay in operational."

Instead of being relieved, General Partridge felt a strong desire to murder Riebeck.

"Think it over," he said. "Can't stay in operational forever. Not getting any younger, you know."

"I shall be dead long before I get too old to do my work," said Riebeck, and with this small comfort General Partridge had to be content.

When Riebeck came out from General Partridge's office, Lionel Jennings removed his ear from the keyhole and said, "Jeremy called, sir."

"I hope you didn't let him reverse the charges."

Jeremy Tyrell had the amiable habit of keeping in touch by telephone from such far-off places as Famagusta or Trebizond. As an economy measure he charged all such calls to his friends.

"He's in London, sir."

"Is he really."

"He's got a new book of poetry coming out. It's called *Saints in Crystal Buckets*."

"Are you sure?"

"He told me so himself. It's from a poem of Sir Walter Raleigh's. 'And then to taste those nectar suckets, At the clear wells where sweetness dwells, Drawn up by saints in crystal buckets.' "

"I see," said Riebeck, congratulating himself once more on having got rid of Lionel Jennings. It occurred to him that Jeremy Tyrell would be just the person to appreciate the joke of Colonel Riebeck being offered General Burkey's job. He rang him up and asked him to dinner. "There's something I have to tell you."

"Funny, I hope."

"I think so. Bring Mrs. Leigh."

"Can't. She's dining with her husband."

"Oh," said Riebeck. "I see."

Jeremy appeared at Duke Street, tanned, shabby, more portly than ever and very cheerful.

"How's the book?"

"Splendid, thank you. It's called," said Jeremy proudly, *"Saints in Crystal Buckets."*

"Ah," said Riebeck, seizing his opportunity. "Sir Walter Raleigh."

Alphonse's lobster bisque soothed Jeremy's disappointment. He said, "Barbara was crushed she couldn't come. Jenny's always talking about your Alphonse. Barbara hated Greek food. She says it tastes like vaseline and the wine's like cough medicine. It's quite true, you know. It's nice to get back to London cooking."

Alphonse, hearing his art described as London cooking, kept back for his own dinner the crème brulée he had meant to serve for dessert and instead put before Jeremy a piece of cheese he had been saving for the mousetrap.

Still unreconciled, he made mud instead of coffee and brought it to the library. While Riebeck poured brandy Jeremy read several letters not addressed to him, put a log on the fire which at once went out, and choked on the coffee. When he had recovered he said, "What was the funny thing you had to tell me?"

"Oh yes. General Burkey is resigning and they have offered me his job."

Jeremy did not bother to look surprised. "Why not? You've done his work for years."

"Be sensible. What would I do with a department?"

"Become a general, for one thing."

"That is the last of my worries. Partridge would never allow it."

"You should have been one long ago. Why aren't you?"

"Because in the French army anyone who's good at his job can become a colonel, but to become a general one has to suck up to the politicians and I can't do it. In England of course it's Partridge who blocks my promotion. It's just as well, really. My Papa would not like it at all."

"I should think he'd be proud of you."

"No. You see, he retired as a colonel. I'm considered the black sheep of the family, so it would hardly be tactful for me to end by outranking him."

"Do you care that much for your father's feelings?"

"Of course. He is after all my father. But all that is beside the point. I very simply don't want to get stuck behind a desk and that is what running Burkey's department would mean."

"What you need," said Jeremy thoughtfully, "is a flunky like Burkey to do your paper work. I'm going to Wellington tomorrow, by the way. My sons are there now and it appears the headmaster wants urgently to see me. Do you know, after all these years I still feel squeamish about it. Head's office, Tyrell *minimus*. Not even the Gestapo scared me as much."

"Why *minimus?* Were you so little?"

"No. I was the youngest of three brothers there. *Major, minor,* and *minimus.* Get it?"

"Oh, I see. In *Stalky,* which was my only contact with English public school life, they called them *tertius.*"

"Whichever way you look at it, it's depressing. Why don't you ride down with me tomorrow?"

Colonel Riebeck, who had acquired considerable skill in following Jeremy's processes of thought, said, "Are you thinking of Simon Cook?"

"It can't be much of a life, schoolmastering, after working for St 2."

"I'd rather have you," said Riebeck.

Jeremy blushed, but said instantly, "I haven't got the time."

Riebeck laughed. "You've nothing but time. What are you doing besides writing poetry?"

"I consider that a perfectly respectable occupation."

"I don't. I consider it a waste of time."

"Philistine! Besides, writing poetry is not all I do. You forget that I am in love. I have all the war years to make up for. And I've had a feeling lately that time is running out. I can't quite explain."

Riebeck was unimpressed. "One of the celebrated Tyrell hunches, no doubt."

"They work. I expect I'll die soon," said Jeremy cheerfully.

"Don't you dare. I need you."

"Uh-uh. My girl's my full-time occupation."

"If Mrs. Leigh ever gets fed up with these persistent attentions, let me know."

"If she ever gets fed up," said Jeremy, "I'll drown myself."

They drove to Wellington two days later. General Partridge had for once been delighted with an idea of Riebeck's and had ordered him to bring Colonel Cook back, with his shield or on it. To have Simon Cook, so serious, so reliable, so English, in General Burkey's office while Riebeck continued abroad, being shot at by resentful Gestapo and eager Russians, restored to General Partridge, despite Mr. Attlee, a certain order and serenity.

General Burkey was not quite so pleased. "Cook's a very good chap," he said, "but he will never run the department the way Riebeck would. Riebeck's got the only quality that's indispensable to running a department; his officers will do anything for him."

With this General Partridge was forced to agree. "Chap's a bloody inspiration," he said. "Blessed if I know why. Dreadful feller, really."

Colonel Riebeck professed himself impressed by Wellington but read the school's motto: "The path of duty is the way to glory," a little skeptically, saying he had never noticed this to be particularly true. He did however admire the cricket fields.

"So this is where the battle of Waterloo was won. How very interesting."

"You're all mixed up," said Jeremy. "The battle of Waterloo was won *by* the Duke of Wellington *on* the playing fields of Eton. I'd better go see the headmaster before my nerve gives way entirely. Good luck with Cooky."

While Jeremy had his talk with the headmaster Riebeck drank tea with Simon Cook, who was eager to hear all the news of the department. He sounded homesick, which Riebeck considered a good thing.

"How do you like schoolmastering, after all the excitement of the war, Cook?"

"Frankly, I find it dull. You'll think me silly, no doubt, after all the talking I used to do about getting back to Wellington. But either it isn't what it used to be or I'm not."

"More likely you are not. War spoils one."

"I like you in English uniform. It becomes you."

Riebeck, whose Anglophilia was his best-kept secret, felt privately very flattered. To Cook he said merely, "How would you like to run Burkey's Department?"

Simon Cook spilled his tea. "Is that what you're here for?"

"Yes. Errand boy for General Partridge."

Cook busied himself for at least five minutes in wiping up his spilled tea. At last he said, "How I envy whoever it was who had the strength to say *nolo episcopari* when he was elected pope. I ought to, you know. I can't really run that kind of thing."

"Why not? You're a good bit brighter in the head than Burkey ever was, and he's run it very well."

"I was in the department for several years before you came, Riebeck, and I assure you, it was not run well until you started to do the running."

"I did not—"

"It's quite understood that you have to go about saying that, but it doesn't change the facts."

"Don't disappoint me, Cook. I'm looking forward to working under you."

There are things that need not be put too plainly. Simon Cook understood perfectly well what Riebeck meant. As with the witless General Burkey, Colonel Riebeck would do whatever it was one had to do to give the department that shine and dash it had acquired since he had come to England. Simon Cook would sit in the office and do all the slow and painstaking jobs that also have to be done to keep the works efficient. Was it a fair arrangement? Simon Cook did not like to ask and Riebeck never would.

"Very well," he said. "And thank you."

"Thank General Partridge. It's his gift. And now I must find Tyrell. He had to see the headmaster and was shaking in his boots about it."

"Never, never in my life," exulted Jeremy, as they were driving back to London, "did I think that I would ever sit in the head's office and be given tea. He only called me Tyrell *minimus* once by mistake, and then he apologized. He's perfectly all right, you know. A very good egg indeed. And to think I used to accuse him of watering our milk when he was my housemaster. Did you suborn Cooky?"

"He's going to take Burkey's job."

"You're mad, Riebeck. You're completely out of your head. Cooky can't run a department."

"Certainly he can. Better than Burkey any day."

"With you holding his hand and blowing his nose?"

"Why not? I like being an *éminence grise*, you know. I have an idea with Cook taking over here, and if Bryant keeps quiet a bit longer in Berlin, I'm going to take a week off and go home."

"Home?"

"To Fontaines."

"You are a displaced person, aren't you? When you said home I simply couldn't imagine what you meant."

As the plane came down into a rainy Paris morning Riebeck felt a shock of familiarity, love, and homecoming that made him dismiss Jeremy's remark. He had decided that he would not stay at the Hôtel de Baro this time. He had never taken Albertine seriously enough to have found her collaborating objectionable, but her continued liaison with Count Xandi he could not forgive, for he had never forgotten that Xandi had refused to do anything to rescue the uncles.

He stayed instead with Latour, who had no care for comfort and did his own cooking. And though he had not given any serious

247

thought to Katalin de St. Leger for years, it was almost a reflex for him, as soon as he arrived in Paris, to pick up the telephone and call her.

She was home and sounded pleased. "There isn't a soul here," she said. "Poor old Jean is in Antibes. Do come, I'll give you lunch."

"Love to," said Riebeck and suddenly wondered if he did. He had not the temperament for being kind to people for old times' sake. Ten years was a long time not to see someone. And so much had happened these ten years, most of it sad.

The Duke de St. Leger, though rather addled in his wits at times, had come out, like all the Riebecks, strongly anti-German. While he was a harmless soul as far as politics were concerned, he was also a duke, and the Germans had thought him sufficiently important to send him to jail for several years. Albertine de Baro, remembering that poor old Jean was a relation and extremely rich, had been as kind to Katalin as she dared, but Katalin, always loyal to a husband she did not very much like but to whom she owed the delectable fact of being a rich duchess, had refused Albertine's advances and had gone to live with Riebeck relations in Brazzaville. For a woman as bent on the cosmopolitan pleasures as Katalin, Brazzaville proved a trying place. Getting the Duke back after three years in a German prison must have been an additional blow, and it was quite possible that Katalin, so beset, might have given up. It seemed to Riebeck the height of folly to exchange the memory of what had been his favorite love affair for lunch with —possibly—a middle-aged frump. At least he might have waited till he had seen her at someone else's party.

Yet when she came down the stairs of the Hôtel St. Leger to greet him, he instantly forgot his doubts and could no longer even explain them. For Katalin was Katalin still, his dark-haired, black-eyed enchantress.

"Schani, my dear."

They stood, not touching, not even quite smiling. He said: "This morning, when my plane came down, I looked at Paris and I thought 'There is no place on earth I love as much as this. Why am I always letting things keep me away from here?' And now I look at you and I feel the same thing. In Vienna I used to think you would never be more beautiful. But you are."

"Oh, Schani, I'm afraid it's a triumph of art over nature now."

"Good. I'm for that. That is civilization."

"Is that how you think of it?"

"Yes. What do you think civilization is?"

She considered this. "To make pleasures of one's necessities. Food, clothes, sex. To invest them with elegance, rather than accepting them as a covering against cold, hunger, and loneliness."

"It comes to the same thing. You said it better."

She laughed suddenly. "I thought we'd have a drink and talk about when we were young. But it isn't like that at all, is it?"

He reached out and touched her beautiful face. "No," he said. "It's just as it always was."

"This is disgraceful," said Katalin. "Do you think if we meet again forty years from now we shall go staggering off to bed in bath-chairs?"

"I certainly hope so. Don't move, Kat, I want to look at you. People say one tires of beauty. I never have."

"Do you still get bored very quickly?"

"Always."

"Me too. Frantically. You know, after you telephoned I had second thoughts and then when I saw you that was the first thing I remembered, that we never bored each other."

"I know. I had second thoughts too."

"Of course. Tell me about England. Do you have many love affairs there?"

"Not so many. None that take time and attention. I'm too busy for anything serious."

"Do you ever think we made a mistake not to get married?"

"No," said Riebeck with decision. Katalin made a sound that was hard to define; amused and outraged together.

"I don't mean to be rude. If I could live with anyone I could live with you. But I am simply not a domestic person. I think if I felt I wanted to marry someone, to live with someone, it would be a way of being in love entirely different from any I have ever experienced. But I don't believe that such a thing exists outside of romantic literature."

"It doesn't there either. Have you never noticed that the great lovers in books are never condemned by their authors to lives of domestic bliss? What are your feelings about lunch?"

"Approval. I came over courtesy of the RAF and their idea of breakfast is a stale sandwich and coffee kept hot in a thermos from the night before."

Over lunch Riebeck was willing to discuss briefly the health of his godfather.

"It's strange, isn't it," said Katalin, "all the young people that died, and there is poor old Jean, on his last legs for years, surviving a German prison camp."

"Bad luck."

"Oh, he's all right," said Katalin, always loyal. "Don't laugh, Schani. He's writing his memoirs. And he's having fearful trouble with his secretaries because they all give notice. And the ones who don't mind the stuff he dictates usually can't type. Yes, darling, do laugh. I'd forgotten how one always used to say of everything funny that happened, 'I must save that for Schani, it will make him laugh.'"

"Poor old Jean. If he had wit as well as vices he might have been another Marquis de Sade."

Katalin said loyally, "I wouldn't have liked being married to the Marquis de Sade. If Jean weren't so stupid he'd be intolerable. You do have silly relatives, Schani. So do I. My Papa was so stupid even the other Honved officers noticed it. And you knew Maman. Wasn't it dreadful, poor Eva living in a fool's paradise like that and being killed? Poor Istvan."

"It was terrible. I was there a few days later. But you know, Kat, I don't believe the fool's paradise could have lasted much longer, and it's worse if things go to pieces slowly."

"But I thought they were so happy."

"Oh yes, they were happy. But Eva was incapable of change. Istvan was very much changed by the war, I suppose all of us are, but it never came near Eva. While the fighting lasted it worked very well; they saw each other rarely and when they did I suppose it was a sort of respite for him, going back to better days. But that couldn't have survived the peace. Imagine Eva as the wife of a Communist army colonel." Katalin laughed. "You see."

"All the same, it's sad. Poor Istvan, I did love him."

"I still do."

"Let's get all the depressing things out of the way at once. I was so sorry about Baranyi Palace being bombed."

"So was I. I was damned careless, you know. All the paintings were packed up and put in the cellar, but apparently the bombs went right through. Why did I never have them sent to Switzerland? I can't remember. I suppose I never expected anything to go wrong with any property of mine. All I have is the Messina *condottiere* that looks so much like Istvan."

"It's a pity and I'm sure it's no consolation at all that so much else was destroyed too. Are you staying with Albertine?"

"Not this time."

"Oh?"

"I'm still annoyed with Xandi. I think I always shall be."

"Dear Xandi. You can't imagine what a success he's been in Paris. The moment he took off his SS uniform and came to dinner in a white tie everyone fell in love with him. Of course Albertine was simply wild about him, but I rather think that's about to come to an end. There's a long waiting list for Xandi, so I imagine he will always have a roof over his head."

"I shall be very glad," said Riebeck, "when it is no longer the de Baro roof."

Before he left her, at five in the morning, he said, "Later in the day, will you come to Père Lachaise with me? I want to bring flowers to the twins."

"Much later in the day, Schani, please."

"I'll call you around noon and we'll see about lunch."

The sun shone through the gray filigree of Paris when they came to Père Lachaise. "Dear twins," said Katalin. "They were killed together, weren't they?"

"Yes, on D Day. Give me the flowers for them. They aren't

buried here, you know. Nobody knows where they are. But perhaps they will accept the thought."

"People always say identical twins aren't really alike except in looks, that you can tell them apart by their mannerisms and personality. But Pierre and Lucien were not different in anything, were they? They were truly one person split in half."

"I think that's why they never married," said Riebeck. "They always fell in love with the same girl at the same time. I'm glad they died together. I cannot imagine how they would have borne being separated."

They turned to look down at Paris from the cliff. Riebeck said, "Katalin, one shouldn't ask anyone who has the good fortune to live here to visit Berlin. But will you?"

"You know I will. When are you going to Fontaines?"

"Tomorrow."

"To see Elisabeth?"

"To see my father. And Lisa, whom I've not yet met."

"Does it make you nervous?"

"Meeting Lisa? A little. I'm wondering whether I'll know for certain when I see her. And if so, what I want to know."

"Even if you do know, what can you do?"

"Nothing while Robert is alive. I wouldn't in any case. Good heavens, Kat, what would I do with a daughter in London?"

"I have enjoyed your visit so much," said Latour when Riebeck stopped at his apartment long enough to borrow his car.

"It's been delightful," said Riebeck with conviction.

"We must do it again one day."

"Sorry, Jacques. Come see me in Berlin. Not so many distractions. Can I have the car?"

"Yes, of course you can. Only don't fall asleep while you're driving. You look as if you might."

"It must be the change of air," said Riebeck demurely.

A German general had spent four years at Fontaines, had sold the Pigalle sculptures, and had built a swimming pool. Then the Riebecks had returned, had swept out the knickknacks and furniture with which the Germans had cosied up the rambling French country house, had filled the pool with dirt and thrown grass seed on top. They left the fountain as it was. It was the only thing changed.

Riebeck liked the permanence of Fontaines. It would drive him mad to have to live there, but since there was no danger of that he was able to rejoice in the drive he could have made with his eyes shut, to Nancy, and then south along the river and down the avenue of poplars into the stable yard where Marthe promptly burst into tears because he was much too thin.

Colonel Riebeck had long since forgiven his son for leaving the cavalry. He could not forever hold a grudge against anyone who had been such a thorn in the Germans' side, and then there were the outward symbols of respectability; the *croix de guerre*, the *médaille de la résistance*, the purple and white MC. So he shook hands cordially enough and almost managed to smile.

Because stupid people do not age quickly, Elisabeth looked very much as she always had. There were grey streaks in her hair and she was plumper, but her smile was as sweet as ever and her sapphire eyes were still starry blue. She told Riebeck that three of her sons were away in school. He met the other two who were so like Robert that it seemed unbelievable that anyone would go through all the bother of having a child to produce anything so dull. It was plain, however, that to their parents and their grandfather they were eminently satisfactory.

Being by nature a nettle grasper, Riebeck said, "And Lisa?"

Elisabeth blushed a little. "She is at school. She ought to be home at any moment."

"You will hear her when she arrives," said the Colonel. "She is a very noisy child."

"She goes to school with the nuns at Nancy and they are working very hard to make a lady of her," said Elisabeth.

"Without success," added the Colonel.

Elisabeth said, "She has a great admiration for you, Jean. She insisted on having your room and she keeps it like a shrine, no one's allowed to touch anything. She won't even let me change the curtains and they are so old they hang in shreds."

"It is easy to be admirable *in absentia*," said the Colonel.

Whatever Lisa's admiration for him, Riebeck was amused to see through the window that it could not compete with her interest in Latour's car. She poked her head under the bonnet for a moment and then wiped her greasy hand on the skirt of her school uniform. She was a tall, skinny girl, with her hair straight and untidy. There was no denying that she did not look like Robert.

She came into the room and shook hands abruptly, like a boy. She was shy. She sat down, with her feet hooked around the feet of the chair, and looked silently at Riebeck. He hoped she would not find him too disappointing. It was safer, really, to chose one's idols among the dead, as he had done with the Marshal. He had wondered for so long if anything would tell him, once and for all, when he met her whether or not she was his daughter. But nothing special happened.

"Do change your clothes, darling," said Elisabeth.

Lisa unhooked her feet, got up, knocked over the chair, and with a furious scowl left the room.

"You see," said Elisabeth.

"She is only fourteen."

"She is not pretty."

"No. But I don't think that will matter."

She returned in a very short time, wearing a pair of denim pants and a shirt that obviously belonged to an older brother. "Oh, darling," said Elisabeth, but Riebeck thought the boy's things became her better than a skirt.

After another silence she got up enough courage to say hoarsely, "I've got your room."

"It's a nice room. I used to like the fountain."

"I don't remember it. I have your books."

"Kipling?"

"Yes."

"There's one called *Only a Subaltern* that used to be my favorite."

She nodded, fearing that if she agreed she might be suspected of time-serving.

"And Prinz Krafft."

He did not look as if he considered this unsuitable reading for a girl. He almost had her confidence now. But there was one more trap waiting for him. Stupid people, contemptible people, often asked her if she liked to ride. A question as ignorant as asking someone if they liked to breathe.

Riebeck said, "Do you ride?"

"Yes."

"Well?"

"Yes." She could not lie about something so important, though politeness demanded it.

"So do I. We must ride together tomorrow."

I like her, he thought, but I still don't feel like a father. I'd like her as much if she were the child of strangers. I suppose it's practice. One can't just blow in and talk for five minutes to someone who may or may not be one's daughter and feel paternal. Pity.

"Would you like to see your room again?" she asked. "I haven't let her change anything." She gave Elisabeth a look which showed Riebeck that the battle of the curtains had been a searing one.

"Yes," he said, "I would."

"Wash your hands while you're upstairs, Lisa," said Elisabeth. "It's almost dinner time."

His tin soldiers stood on their shelf. He recognized his books at a glance, even those he had long forgotten. The little Augarten porcelain of Alexandra was on the desk. But the walls were bare.

"Where is the Marshal?"

"In Germany somewhere," Lisa said sadly. "Bertrand St. Pierre told the German general Gros portraits were worth money."

"Excuse me a moment, Lisa. I have an errand I must do at once." He went quickly downstairs and across the park, while Lisa watched him out the window. From the St. Pierre house she presently heard a crash of glass. Then Riebeck returned, the knuckles of his left hand scraped bloody.

Lisa leaned out of her window. "What did you do?"

"Knocked St. Pierre through his dining-room window. I hope he broke his neck."

"I hope so too. He's a toadstool."

"I could forgive the fountain. But the Marshal was too much."

"I wish I could have seen his silly face."

"I wish you could have too."

After Lisa and Elisabeth had gone to bed, Riebeck went up to the library to find something to read, knowing that it would never occur to Elisabeth to put books in a bedroom, or if it did, that they would be Bedside Books in the most depressing sense of the word.

He found his father at his desk, going over the accounts. He took down a volume of Stendhal and with a brief "Good night, Papa," was about to leave when the Colonel said, "Please stay if you want to read, Jean. You won't disturb me."

Riebeck, remembering from his youth the howls of anger that met anyone venturing to use the library while his father was doing the accounts, realized that the diffident invitation was in fact an order. Probably an explanation for the change of uniform would presently be demanded.

He sat down, stretching his long legs to the fire, and fingered the pages of his book. But he did not read. He listened idly to the familiar night noises of the house and gave himself over to the pull of his memories.

Much of his youth had been spent in Paris, but it was here that his roots were, here that he could go upstairs into the room where he had been born, and his father before him and his grandfather— his great-grandfather too, probably, and every Riebeck except the one who had built the house. This is a powerful anchor, difficult to comprehend for city dwellers who are born in a hospital, live in an apartment, and die in a hospital. He felt it this night very strongly, perhaps because he had been away so many years.

So many familiar sounds were caught in the library; the yell of the wind imprisoned in the chimney, the tree branches fingering the window, the scratch of his father's old-fashioned pen on paper, Marthe lumbering upstairs, grunting and wheezing. And something else, long gone, existing only in his mind: the fragrance of camellia, the crackle of taffeta, and the whisper of silk, which was all he could remember of his mother.

Over the fireplace hung her portrait; a face trapped in time, an arrogant and mindless beauty, robbed in the painting of the predatory charm which she had carried in life. He thought, "She is half of me, and I don't know her at all. Ancestors, ancestors. This house is full of them. The sad Vicomte, the Marshal, the generations of dull, dutiful officers and their wives, the fighters and gentlemen riders and money-grubbers and gamblers; it's like living in a spiderweb of ancestors. Doesn't Papa mind it at all?"

The Colonel put down his pen, sighed, pushed the accounts away, lit a cigar, and looked with embarrassment across to his son.

"Ah," he said. "Ahem. Here we are."

"Yes, Papa," said Riebeck obediently.

Both stared into the fire. The Colonel had always found talking to his sons a difficulty and avoided it as much as possible.

"Brandy?" he asked to break up the silence before it could wrap them so completely that they would never escape.

"With pleasure."

"It is nice to have you here," said the Colonel, taking advantage of the moment when he could turn his back to pour out the drinks. "I hope you will be able to stay a while."

"I don't know, Papa," said Riebeck cautiously. "I'm sorry I wasn't able to come sooner. It simply wasn't possible."

"I understand. A soldier's time is not his own. I am glad you are here now. This house needs young people in it."

"But I am not young people, Papa," he protested. "I am forty-two."

"I know. But you are my youngest. François would be sixty this year."

"The lads that will never grow old."

"What's that?"

" 'They carry back bright to the coiner the mintage of man, the lads that will die in their glory and never grow old.' It's an English poem."

"They had the best of it, the young men like François. Still, it is a pity. They are the ones who should have married and had children. So should you, Jean."

"Well, there are Robert's six," said Riebeck evasively.

"With six sons I might have expected more than six grand-children."

"It's a very poor idea, having a family in my sort of work, Papa. The fewer hostages one gives to fortune the better."

"Perhaps you are right. There is nothing worse for a parent than to know that his child is being hurt. And that that child is arrogant, wayward, and grown-up makes very little difference."

"I am sorry, Papa."

"Well," said the Colonel, taking this as mere social formula, "it is over. And I was proud of you, afterwards. I haven't approved of a single thing you have done since you left the cavalry. But then I was proud of you."

"Take the credit for it then. It was something you taught me as a child that saw me through."

"What can that have been?"

"Do you remember, when I was little, and the twins and I would pester you for something, we would say, 'Oh Papa, you must.' Do you remember what you used to tell us?"

The Colonel shook his head.

"You used to say, 'The only thing I *must* do is die, and even that I must only do once.' I cannot tell you what a help it was."

"Oh Jean," said the Colonel bewildered, "will you never make sense? And surely there is no need to continue that kind of work now that the war is over."

"But I like it, Papa."

"You used to like the cavalry."

"With all my heart. But cavalry is gone past recall. And even if it weren't, I don't think I could go back to it any more."

"Why? What is there about Intelligence work that makes it so impossible to leave it? You're not the only young man who got himself hopelessly lost in it, Jean. I know many others."

"It is so very much like the Grand Guignol."

"The Grand Guignol!" The Colonel gave his derisive bark.

"Yes. The way it affected one as a child, you know, not as a grown-up. The way one was all doubled up with laughter one moment, and then instantly frozen into terror, still in the pose of laughter. When it is good, Intelligence work is like that. There is nothing else like it, certainly not peacetime cavalry."

"I see. No, I don't really, but I'll try to understand. I so often wonder about you, Jean. Are you happy?"

Riebeck was brought up short by the question, not because he did not know the answer, but because it was so completely out of character for his father to ask it.

"Yes," he said.

"I am glad to hear it. Though I would have preferred to see you happy in a French uniform."

"Ah," said Riebeck, "we have arrived."

"Arrived?"

"At the explanation for the English uniform. The trouble is I could give you ten different explanations, all of them true."

"One will do, Jean."

He cast about the number of reasons that had affected his decision for one his father could accept. He said, "There is a lady."

The Colonel snorted. "That is hardly something new, Jean."

"Well, it is new for me. She is married to someone else, for one thing, and if she weren't I could still not marry her. I have never had an affair with her and I don't think I ever shall. She travels a lot and of course I am often away from London for years on end, so I do not see her very often. Sometimes we have lunch together in a very public restaurant or we have a cocktail in the Ritz bar, and at other times we write long letters without saying anything. I am very happy, and if ten years ago someone had told me I would ever behave like this about a woman I would have howled with laughter."

The Colonel seized on the one fact he had been able to grasp. "Jean," he said, "you are not to marry a divorced Englishwoman."

"No, Papa." Before his father had time to realize that he had not really been given an explanation that was at all satisfactory, Riebeck changed the subject. "The house looks well," he said. "The German general cannot have done much damage."

"Not inside. Marthe gave it a good cleaning when we came back and threw out all the knickknacks and their furniture. For the rest there was no difficulty. But the park! They ruined the fountain—you saw that—and, here, you'd better have another drink before I tell you this, they built a swimming pool right in the middle of the park. I ask you. A swimming pool."

Riebeck laughed. "I know. I saw it. I came by here once during the war, and couldn't resist the temptation to look around. I was caught trespassing by their daughter, who was quite large and masterful. She took me to meet her parents. They were very nice and invited me to have a drink. I rescued our Coysevox, by the way. The General wanted to sell it but I told him it was only a copy. Then the Frau General offered to show me how nice she had made the house. She thought it would interest me because I'd told her I was an old friend of Jean Riebeck's and had known the house before the war. But I hadn't been out of the hospital for very long and I didn't think I would be strong enough, so I left."

The Colonel gave his bark of laughter. "Really, Jean, I am beginning to see why you like your work. It must be funny. Tell me some more."

For the pleasure of hearing his grumpy father laugh, Riebeck told him funny stories for nearly an hour. The Colonel laughed haltingly at first, as one adventuring into a foreign language, not sure of the vocabulary. As the stories grew more and more outrageous he gained courage; eventually he relaxed and roared. In the end he had to beg his son to stop. The unaccustomed exercise had given him a painful stitch in his side.

In high good humor they went upstairs to bed, for the first time completely satisfied with each other. At the top of the stairs Colonel Riebeck, saying, "Well, good night my boy," put out his hand to touch his son's arm in an awkward gesture of tenderness and quickly withdrew it, overcome with embarrassment. Jean said, "Good night, Papa," and bending down, kissed his father's cheek. The Colonel accepted it stiffly, too awkward to respond. Unlike his son he had not the correct gesture at any moment. "Good night," he said again and stumped off to bed. Lying in the dark he realized suddenly that he could not remember ever having one of his sons kiss him. Not even when they had been little boys.

"Impertinent show-off," he said to himself, immensely gratified.

Fontaines was the haven Riebeck had never used. He would have said he was happy here now, busy with the horses, riding with Lisa, at rest on the river, walking with his father, still mostly in silence but no longer a silence that excluded. Yet, when in a few days he received the telephone call from Berlin, he knew that he had been waiting for it with unacknowledged impatience.

In Berlin Bantain met him with the news that the head of the Vienna office had been found floating dead in his bathtub, whether by accident, murder, or suicide it was impossible to say, since he had been engaged in perilous work, was extremely drunk at the time of his death, and miserable about a love affair gone wrong. At the same time Frederick Townsend, the distrait, amiable, and nearsighted English master at a girl's school in Nicosia, was handing in his resignation, having met and married an American heiress who did not believe that husbands ought to have secrets from their wives.

Riebeck said he hoped in his next incarnation he would become the abbot of a monastery, being sick and tired of grown men behaving like infatuated teenagers, and that he wished he had stayed at Fontaines.

"You've been drinking RAF coffee again," said Bantain. "You know it always makes you cross. I'll go and make you some fresh. Here's your mail."

Riebeck, reflecting that he would have to send Bantain to Vienna, flicked sadly through his letters until he came on one with Jenny's writing on the envelope. He slit it open and read:

Did you ever meet Jeremy's Barbara? I think not. She was a darling and a great friend of mine. Last Thursday she ran her car into a level crossing.

It's so damned ironic, she was the best driver I've ever known, much better than me, and infinitely better than Jeremy. She drove an ambulance all through the blitz and the blackout with never a scratch.

Jeremy is behaving very badly. You may remember how he hates all things to do with illness and death; hospital, doctors, weeping willows, cemeteries, and all the *pompes maladives et funèbres.* In any case he became unavailable and if Larry Leigh had not so well played the part of bereaved young widower it would all have been rather awkward.

Have you ever read a thing Jeremy once wrote, called *Conversations with a Swami?* In the section where they discuss death Jeremy says: "To contemplate my extinction with serenity merely because it is inevitable seems to me profoundly immoral." They have a long talk about the various aspects of death and in the end the Swami hopes he has been of help. Jeremy assures him that he has. He says: "I am now able to contemplate with equanimity everyone's death but my own." Dear Jeremy.

Riebeck, keeping his mind a decent blank after his first thought, of which he had at once been ashamed, but which undeniably had been, "Thank goodness, Tyrell can take over Nicosia," folded Jenny's letter and put it away in the drawer in which he kept mail he considered worth saving. There we stacks of scrawled air mails from the aunts in America, pages covered with Jeremy's unexpectedly legible writing, a few sheets of cheap paper from Istvan, and a bundle of letters on Jenny's grey writing paper with postmarks from many places.

Jenny's traveling was as compulsive as is it was conventional. Paris for the fashions, St. Moritz or Kitzbuehel for the winter, Scotland in the fall, Biarritz in the summer. Letters postmarked Athens, Alexandria, or Famagusta indicated visits to Jeremy and Barbara. It would never have occurred to her to go there otherwise.

She never stayed anywhere long. Her pleasure lay in arrivals and departures. The number of letters in Riebeck's desk drawer might have astonished Mr. Falconer.

When next he flew to London Riebeck went without much enthusiasm to call on Jeremy. "He is suffering with a determination that does him credit," Jenny had written, "and drunk most of the time." Such Dostoyevskian gloom was definitely not Riebeck's thing.

He climbed the stairs to Jeremy's flat and knocked on the door. Jeremy shouted, "Come in," and far from entering on a scene of drunkenness and despair Riebeck found Jeremy before the fire rocking back and forth with laughter.

"So many aspiring young fools think that since I have written *Saints* I am qualified to judge their silly poems. This boy compares sunsets to squashed tomatoes and now he wants to know why he can't find a publisher. Have a drink."

Jeremy was working on what plainly was not the first drink of the morning. Riebeck wondered whether he had bothered to eat breakfast.

"You look awful," he said.

"I know," Jeremy agreed. "Comes from drinking. However, since I am not about to enter a beauty contest, it is of little consequence. Has Jenny sent you to scold me?"

"Mrs. Falconer says you're behaving badly."

"Mrs. Falconer," said Jeremy, clutching at a red herring, "is Lady Falconer now. Didn't you know."

"I haven't had time to read the *Times* for weeks, and she didn't mention it."

"Now how," said Jeremy, "do you expect her to mention it. Dear Colonel Riebeck, please note that the proper form of address is your ladyship? I mean really. Falconer was on the last honors list for removing all the insides from some minor royalty without actually killing the poor chap. What a life it is to be a surgeon."

Riebeck, knowing from experience that Jeremy could drivel on like this forever, said, "Lady Falconer says you are behaving badly."

Jeremy nodded solemnly. "I know. No stiff upper lip. Not playing the game. Letting down the side. Bloody awful."

"I think it is, rather," said Riebeck, trying not to grin. "You can't go on like this."

"Why not?"

Riebeck, who did not know, said vaguely that a grown man could not spend his life reading manuscripts by people who compared sunsets to squashed tomatoes.

Jeremy said comfortably that he had done nothing for many years before Riebeck had ever met him, and did not see what was wrong with it. "I have a large talent for idleness, you know. Why is it that you, so tolerant of every other vice, should disapprove of this one?"

Riebeck said, "Because you are getting fat."

Jeremy indignantly squared his shoulders and pulled in his stomach. "I am not."

"Indeed you are. I'll bet you can't button your uniform any more."

"There is no reason why I should," said Jeremy with dignity.

"There is, as a matter of fact. Townsend is marrying an American heiress and leaving us."

"Dear Lord!"

"And I want you to take his job."

"I am not about to teach English in a girl's school," said Jeremy, pouring himself another large drink.

Riebeck, trying to visualize it, had to suppress his laughter.

"Hardly. After all, you've lived in Cyprus before, there is no reason why you should not do so again. You might write a travel book."

"Oh yes," agreed Jeremy. "The last one sold all of two hundred and seventy-six copies."

"That is between you and your publisher. For me, will you take the job?"

"You've come at a bad time," said Jeremy. "I'm not overly fond of the department at this point. Indeed I've been spending much time thinking that I wasted five years dashing about abroad when I might have been right here with Barbara, writing colorful leaflets for the Ministry of Information."

Riebeck, feeling that he had had about enough of this, said, "In that case the competition with Squadron Leader Leigh might have been a little stiff. As my favorite poet has said, 'Oh who would not sleep with the brave?' "

Jeremy looked really shocked at the outrageousness of this insult. "I swear I wish I were on your shit list, Riebeck. You're always so much kinder to your enemies than to your friends."

"Enemies! I dote on my enemies, I pamper them. How would one ever get out of bed in the morning in a world full of friends. Come, stop behaving like a prima donna. If you are determined to go to the dogs you can do it as well in Cyprus."

"All right," said Jeremy.

"Good. Get your coat, I'm going to buy you breakfast somewhere. You'll have to stop using Scotch for meals, Cooky doesn't allow it."

"You must come visit me in Cyprus," said Jeremy politely. "You haven't really lived until you've tasted Greek wine."

XVII

"*This is a silly town,*" said Bantain to Riebeck. "There is almost no employment for the professional agent, since all of Vienna is cluttered with amateurs. They drink coffee and eat pastries in great amiability and practically all the information is bought, not fought for. I have a bit of news that might interest you. Have you ever heard of a Dr. Kerenyi?"

"No. Hungarian?"

"Yes. A scientist. He works on missiles and such. In fact he is a Peenemunde graduate. He's also a sort of scientific quack. His brains are for sale to the highest bidder."

"He should be content. The Russians treat their scientists well."

"He was, for a while. He is, however, a very ill-tempered man and apt to discuss his dissatisfactions in public. Even a Peenemunde scientist can step on Russian toes once too often, and Kerenyi has exhausted his credit. They wouldn't kill him, because they need him too badly, but they are thinking of a vacation in Siberia. He wants to get out before that happens."

"I can understand that. But if he is for sale to the highest bidder he will go to the Americans."

"Not Kerenyi. He plays safe. He's let it be known that he will work for whichever country rescues him. Since he lives in Budapest I thought it might as well be you."

"How nice of you. I haven't been there for seven years."

In Vienna, where the walls ooze secrets, Dr. Kerenyi's offer was known to everyone, and Riebeck was not surprised when he went to lunch at Sacher's to find Jacques Latour and Chuck Wallace there before him. Wallace was a former member of the OSS and since that organization had ceased to exist had turned up in various places claiming that he was collecting local color for a spy story.

"Ah Jean," said Latour, "we were just wondering when you would arrive."

"How delightful to meet so many old friends," said Riebeck courteously. "Hello, Wallace. How's the book?"

"Coming along," said Chuck complacently. "Sit down and join us. We were just saying that it's a wild goose chase. I hate to be defeatist, but we were thinking we might as well go home again. Do you know what it's like getting into Hungary these days? The entire border crossing is mined and they have the most trigger-happy guards since *Birth of a Nation*."

"What a shame," said Riebeck sympathetically.

"I tried to get in with a guide," said Wallace. "Arpad Szabo his name was, God rest his soul. It seems he used to take people across the border, Out, usually, not In. But he offered to take me back with him. He walked us right into a patrol and said, 'Here is another capitalist imperialist American spy.' Of all the embarrassing things to happen."

Latour exhorted Wallace not to be so secretive in the future as everyone but the CIA had known about Szabo for years. Wallace made a routine protest about belonging to the CIA and added that now they really might as well go home because if anyone could get Dr. Kerenyi Riebeck could, being the owner of a cousin who was a Communist army colonel.

"How the devil did you know that?" Riebeck asked.

"The CIA knows everything," said Wallace.

"Of course," said Latour. "I'd forgotten about Colonel Halyi. Don't look now, Jean, but I think there's a Russian looking for you."

Riebeck turned and saw Major Dyelik make his way across the restaurant.

Riebeck would have preferred to see Dyelik at some more private occasion, but nevertheless was delighted and introduced Monsieur Latour, a textile manufacturer from Lyons, and Mr. Wallace, the celebrated author of spy thrillers from New York. "Won't you join us, Dyelik?"

"Thank you, I shall be delighted. How have you been since we last met in Berlin?"

Riebeck said he had been fine. His colleagues pulled together as one man in an effort to bore the Russian to death. Wallace asked stupid questions for the background of the book on which he was supposedly working, and Latour discoursed on textile manufacture. Riebeck sat back and listened, his eyes narrowed with silent laughter. When Dyelik showed distinct signs of going mad, he invited him to dinner and they left together. The two men left behind agreed that Riebeck had the damnedest friends and speculated on the various ways in which death would befall Major Dyelik this evening, from a lethal pill in his after-dinner coffee to a gory throat-cutting in a dark alley. But Latour, who knew Colonel Riebeck very well indeed, said that either Major Dyelik would be arrested by his own MVD with lots of damning evidence on him or else would turn up presently in St 2 working for Riebeck.

At dinner Dyelik enlarged once again on the mental and moral deficiencies of his general, on the soul-destroying effects of his work, the lack of promotion, and the boorishness and venality of his comrades.

Riebeck said, "My former offer is still open."

This time Dyelik was neither shocked nor indignant. "It would be too complicated," he said. "I should never be allowed to work for you."

"General Partridge is on my side for once. I think it can be arranged."

"And just how much do you think my life would be worth to my side if I turned up in London?"

"My dear Dyelik," said Riebeck laughing, "what a time to begin worrying about your safety."

Dyelik laughed too and changed the subject. Dinner ended without any further mention of defection. Riebeck tactfully shook off his companion and returned to Bantain, who gave him brandy, got a roaring fire going, and solved all his problems.

"Of course you can get in," he said when Riebeck repeated Latour's and Wallace's conversation. "We have a very good guide—"

"Not Arpad Szabo?"

Bantain laughed. "Arpad Szabo is no more, I fear. Those OSS tactics are brutal. Our guide is called Miklos. I can't pronounce his second name. He's one of the comrades left over from '44. He's a Red, but he doesn't like Russians."

"Bantain, I don't want a Communist guide."

"He's perfectly reliable. His first aim is to get the Russians out of Hungary, and then," mimicked Bantain, " 'we will get you aristos.' I don't know what makes him think I'm so aristocratic unless he mistakes my natural superiority for the advantages of birth."

"Hm," said Riebeck. "Do you think I could see Istvan Halyi without compromising him too much?"

"The Red Colonel?"

"Good Heavens!"

"It's what Miklos calls him. He hates all the officers who've sold out to the Russians."

"Sold out?"

"Sorry. Listen, the important thing about Miklos is that he fought in '44 under Colonel Halyi and he knows underground Budapest like a sewer rat. And that's what you need. You can't walk through the streets to visit him. It would be much too dangerous for both of you."

"Good enough. What time is the train?"

"5:26 A.M."

"How awful."

"Sleep here tonight. It'll save you time in the morning."

Riebeck realized on his way to the railroad station that he was being followed. Dyelik, he supposed, though Wallace or Latour was quite capable of having someone tail him to see how he got across the mined border. No, definitely Dyelik. Those eyes and cheekbones were Russian.

Riebeck rid himself of his unwanted companion by locking him in the men's room of the station. Even the Russian secret police are only human.

With Miklos to guide him, there was no great difficulty in crossing the mined border fields, though it was a nerve-wracking walk. On the Hungarian side they took the train to Budapest. Riebeck had fake papers made out for one Reszo Komyadi, and could only hope nobody would address him in Hungarian.

He had to admit that, considering what the town had been in '44, the Russians had done well by it. There were hideous monuments as memorials of the war, and an appalling statue of Stalin. Patriotically named streets were lined with apartment houses which, Miklos said, were actually inhabited by workers.

"Captain Bantain says you want to visit Colonel Halyi."

"That's right. Also Dr. Kerenyi."

"After dark. You can stay in an apartment we have here while I have a look at Kerenyi's house. We have some soups in tins from America."

Riebeck's opinion of soups in tins was exceedingly low, but he was touched to see how kindly Miklos was treating him after having made it clear that when the revolution came he would be one of the first to go.

The apartment was in an unreconstructed slum. "It's a little shabby," said Miklos, "but less conspicuous."

"Nonsense. When the police look for people, do they go to the best part of town or to the slums? I stayed in Baranyi Palace when I was in Vienna during the war, and nobody thought to bother me."

"There isn't any Baranyi Palace now," said Miklos severely, "and the Russians have taken over Tisza Palace for offices."

"I like their nerve," said Riebeck indignantly. They had been climbing a narrow and dirty stairway apparently forever, and now came to a door which Miklos unlocked with an enormous key. The apartment was small but not as dirty as Riebeck had expected. He walked across it, looked out all the windows and said. "I suppose you realize you're completely cut off here. If the police come in one door, where are you going to leave?"

Evidently this problem had never occurred to anyone before, for Miklos scratched his head and said, "I suppose that's true."

Feeling that at the moment nothing could be done about it Riebeck gave it up, lay down on the cot in the corner, and resumed his interrupted sleep. He awoke a few hours later, feeling so hungry that he even ate the tinned soup. Miklos had not yet returned from whatever errand he was on, so Riebeck poked about the apartment and found very little of interest except a trapdoor, which hid a small cache of arms, a few carbines, a machine gun, and four automatic rifles.

He had finished snooping and was smoking a cigarette when there was a knock on the door. Miklos would not knock. Who then, was this? Riebeck kept silence, hoping they would go away. But the knock was repeated. He released the safety catch of his gun, and keeping his hand on it in his pocket, watched the door handle turn. Fine, that ass Miklos had not even thought to lock the door. (Miklos, Riebeck was presently to discover, was not such an ass. The lavatory, such as it was, was out in the hall.)

The door swung open and to Riebeck's surprise showed a little man in uniform, whose round face was split from ear to ear by a joyous grin.

Riebeck, relieved and delighted, said happily, "Palko Donath. How nice to see you."

"*Servus* Colonel. Istvan is busy so he told me to look after you. He thought, staying with Miklos, you might be in need of some lunch. I brought it." He displayed a loaf of bread, a Hungarian salami (most delicious of all salamis, redolent of garlic and spices) and from a bulging pocket drew a bottle of red Dalmatian wine.

"You have without exaggeration saved my life, Palko," said Riebeck gratefully. "Bantain's way of living here is too Spartan for words. Tinned soup!"

They sat across from each other at the wooden table, sharing the food and wine, and afterward Riebeck's American cigarettes. While they smoked and finished the wine, Palko brought Riebeck up to date, beginning with the months of the siege in '44.

"Never again will I dabble in underground activities," he said. "You can't imagine how many resistance groups we had, all with their own ideas, and no two of them able to agree. Ours, being military and run by Istvan, did fairly well. We worked very closely with the Russians. Istvan would sneak into Pest to learn where they were going to attack next. As soon as they had started and had the full attention of the Germans, we would start needling them from the rear. It doesn't sound like much, I know, but we were quite effective. You know, when you're fighting a lion in front, it's disconcerting to have mosquitoes biting your ass."

"Would one notice mosquitoes while fighting a lion?"

"They noticed."

Adding story to story and joke to joke while they emptied the wine bottle, Pal Donath painted his picture of a bomb-gutted Buda, its citizens living in cellars, venturing forth only at night in search of food, using the dirty, blood-soaked snow for water. Buda's renaissance palaces became German fortresses. Battles raged from house to house, while in the cellars the civilians huddled and prayed.

Istvan's little army was composed of odds and ends; Horthy officers, members of bright red resistance groups, brave as maniacs and almost as nasty, and aristocrats of the dual monarchy fighting for they knew not what.

"Goodness, we were hungry," said Palko, cutting a hunk of salami, made hungry once again by the memory. "There was no food coming into the city, you know. Janos had hoarded a lot of stuff from the farm, but he was too damned soft-hearted and gave it all to the people in the cellars." Palko laughed. "The animals from the zoo all escaped and ran wild in Budapest. I'd hate to tell you the things we ate. Once we had monkey stew, which wasn't bad, but other times we didn't have the nerve to ask what we were eating. The Russians often gave us part of their rations, but they were starving themselves, poor devils."

And finally the Russians crossed the Danube into Buda, where Istvan Halyi met them with his small army. General Altosov embraced Istvan with tears in his eyes. He and Istvan had seen each other often during the siege, but this meeting was different. The Russians stood on the soil of Buda. Altosov was happy, the Russians

271

were happy, and so were the people of Budapest who crept out of their cellars, and seeing that it was true, that the Russians had really arrived, began to shout a Russian sentence they had learned as a politeness to their liberators. "Long live the Red Army."

Istvan Halyi returned General Altosov's embrace with more reserve than enthusiasm. They were both crawling with lice, but Istvan preferred his own, fed as they were on blue Esterhazy blood.

General Altosov looked around him at the burnt-out houses, the bloody, dirty snow under his boots, and the dead, frozen stiff.

"I believe you have a house here, Ivan Pavlovich," he said.

Istvan had at first protested against the Russian habit of making Ivan of Istvan, but was by now resigned to it.

"On Disz Ter, if it's still standing. I don't know."

"If you agree I shall use it for my headquarters. That will save it from the ravages of having troops quartered in it."

Istvan had seen General Altosov's headquarters in Pest, and inwardly he quailed. But hospitality is strong in Hungarians, and he said he would be honored.

The fighting continued. General Altosov, knowing that Istvan was familiar with every underground passage and every twisting alley of Buda, was glad to leave his division in such experienced hands, while he retired to the renaissance palace and made a shambles of it.

Conferences between them were no longer so frequent. The battle of Buda was taken care of. Also their conferences were a strain. Istvan spoke only rudimentary Russian, and while the General spoke a little German and French, he disliked the feeling of making a fool of himself in those languages. Thus Istvan did not see what had become of his house for several days. When he and Palko finally found time to go there, the first sight of the transformation the pretty jewel box of a palace had undergone was so appalling that Istvan, forgetting sorrow and dismay, burst out laughing.

General Altosov had quartered his horses in the ballroom. The star-patterned parquet floor had been torn up for firewood. Portraits were cut into shreds, chairs and sofas disemboweled, clocks taken apart and their works scattered in the straw that covered the floor. Eva's white mink rug (no longer white) covered a sleeping Russian colonel; two lieutenants were amiably sharing her second mink coat.

The circle of drawing rooms had become offices. Dirty officers came and went behind their beards, picking up any sparkling oddment they found in the straw. In the center of the confusion a Russian captain was sunk in a chair whose stuffing was pouring out all around him. His flat face blissful and idiotic, he was listening to the tinkle of one of Stefanie's music boxes.

Istvan laughed so hard he had to clutch the doorpost for support.

"Istvan hold up, do," pleaded Palko. "This is no time for hysterics."

"I'm not having hysterics, really not." He wiped his streaming eyes on the sleeve of his tunic. "Do you realize that this is a barbarian invasion, Palko? We're lucky to see it. It only happens about every thousand years or so. It's fascinating, isn't it, the impact civilization has on barbarians?"

Palko looked around doubtfully. "You mean the impact the barbarians have on civilization."

"No, I don't."

"Well, here comes Attila. Posh, isn't he."

General Altosov had shaved (perhaps even washed, certainly he smelled strongly of Eva's Chanel) and had put on a clean uniform. Among the dirty rabble of his own army and his ragged visitors he moved like a king among beggars.

Though clean himself he again embraced Istvan warmly and shook hands with Palko.

"Ivan Pavlovich," he said sadly, "it is impossible to explain this mess."

Hungarian hospitality had always been Asiatic in its lavishness. Such hospitality presupposes a certain breeding and restraint on the part of the guest. General Altosov had been entirely lacking in this restraint, but Istvan probably intended no sarcasm when he said, "My house and everything in it is yours."

General Altosov bowed.

"Shall we go to my private office? It is quieter there."

He had chosen the Countess Pepi's sitting room, perhaps because it contained a small desk. It could hardly have been for privacy for the doors had been torn off their hinges for firewood and the adjoining bedroom was jammed with sleeping Russians.

General Altosov threw everybody out. "And stay out," he shouted. "This is a private conference. Top secret. Ivan Pavlovich, be pleased to sit down."

There were no chairs. "Thank you," said Istvan gravely. "I prefer to stand."

Through the open door the Russians surged back into the room and fought for places on the bed. Others moved about the office, chopping up a Riesener commode and feeding the pieces to the fire. In the midst of it all stood General Altosov, creating for his guests through sheer power of will an island of the most gracious hospitality. He wore a cloak that touched the tips of his boots (he being rather shorter than the late Count Nikki.) Now that he had shaved it could be seen that he was a very handsome man. Palko, literate and middle-class, was reminded vividly of an illustration of Prince Andrey in his copy of *War and Peace*. Istvan, who had not read *War and Peace* but had spent his youth among princes, made no such comparison.

"You are tired and hungry," said the General, and at once produced the remedy, a bottle of vodka from which he filled three chipped kitchen mugs.

"*Egeszegere,*" he said.

"*Zdorovye,*" said Istvan and Palko politely. These were some of the words they had of each other's languages.

"This looting," said the General, "is most regrettable. There are the strictest rules against it, but Ivan Pavlovich—" one gentleman to another, "—if I punish everyone who loots I shall have no army left." He sneezed.

"Your health," said Istvan.

"I have caught cold. Not that it is surprising, with not a single door in the house to keep out drafts."

But he was a gentleman, this Russian general. He did not blow his nose with his fingers the way his officers did; he was the owner of a handkerchief. This handkerchief was of the finest linen and in the corner bore the nine-pointed coronet of the Baranyi crest.

274

Caught on the handkerchief there emerged unfortunately from General Altosov's pocket a diamond rivière, property of the Countess Pepi, long since out of fashion and hideous beyond description. Despite a lot of vodka on an empty stomach, Istvan Halyi was superb. In the ugly face not a muscle moved; he might have been blind for all the attention he paid the glittering diamonds. His green tartar eyes were fixed on the General with the most courteous gravity.

"Soon it will be spring," he said gently. "Spring in Budapest is very beautiful, Mikhail Ivanovich. But I fear this time it will be mainly a problem of disposing of the corpses before they thaw out."

Palko snorted and pretended he had sneezed. "I too have a cold," he said apologetically to the General.

"Well, messieurs," said General Altosov severely, having disposed of the diamonds in a deep pocket, "to work, to work."

There was no need for Palko to tell Colonel Riebeck that Istvan had worked, had kept going until he could drop down in a corner, turn up the collar of his coat and fall at once asleep. The war had taken Eva, but it had given him these months of unremitting fighting, of being able to go for weeks without a single thought in his head beside hunger, cold, and the Germans.

Then, Moscow!

Parties and vodka, speeches, war's end and victory, children lying in the street, asleep or starved to death, who knows. Istvan, in his new Russian uniform, with the colonel's epaulettes on his shoulders, two rows of medal ribbons over his left breast pocket, the partisan star over the right, the hero of the siege of Budapest and Marshal Zhukov's fair-haired boy. Moscow was magnificent, and so was Budapest when they returned. Budapest, liberated from the Germans, beaver-busy rebuilding its houses, its businesses, its army. Vienna and Berlin lay in rubble, but Budapest was building. Budapest was magnificent, the weary old order gone and a new one beginning, with a chance for everyone. Had Istvan Halyi not gone to Moscow, he might have observed once again the interesting social phenomenon that, when people are left to themselves to start

275

from scratch, it is over and over again the same people who rise to the top.

They were not left to themselves for long. Land reforms were instituted. Peasants who had for generations worked land not their own now owned their houses and acres. The large estates were split up. Landowners who had possessed more than ten thousand acres were not allowed to keep a single one. And one day Janos came to Istvan in tears. He had been given a farm and ten acres of Baranyi land. He would not take it. Not while Istvan could not call a single acre of his property his own.

"Don't be an ass, Janos," said Istvan. "What do I want with a farm? Take your ten acres and when I'm an old gouty general I'll come and live with you."

Janos need not have felt so many scruples. Within three years the Baranyi estate was a model collective farm and he was back keeping house for Istvan Halyi.

"Do I take it that you are fed up with the Communists now, Palko?" asked Riebeck.

"No. I'm fed up with the way the Russians are treating us. It has as little to do with Communism as it does with their so-called democracy."

"I think it is the imperfections of the Russian system that make Communism bearable. If it were ever possible to create a truly Communist society—and to the credit of human nature I must say that I don't think it can be done—then you would see what a monster you have been defending all these years."

Palko only laughed. "I don't talk politics with you any more than I do with Istvan. I know a hopeless cause when I see one. If we ever achieve a truly Communist society, Colonel, I'm afraid we'll just have to liquidate you."

"Assuredly. But I think you will have a very nasty surprise, Palko, when you discover that it is precisely your kind that a truly Communist society would do away with first."

"We'll see. I'd better go now. If Miklos finds a Commie officer here there's no telling what he might think."

"Goodbye, Palko. I hope I shall see you again one day."

"I expect you will. Weeds don't perish. So long, Colonel."

When Miklos returned, Colonel Riebeck was smoking a cigarette and looking out the window. "Did you sleep well?"

"Yes, thank you."

"Colonel Halyi said to tell you that he is delighted, and that, while he wouldn't care about himself, it would be best if you waited till dark to visit him."

"It's almost dark now."

"In another half hour it should be safe to leave. There is nothing to be done about Kerenyi tonight. He's at his villa on Lake Balaton for the week end, but he should be back by tomorrow."

"A lenient house arrest," said Riebeck, pleased to have this night for himself and Istvan.

"Those missile boys," said Miklos, "they get away with murder."

As soon as it was dark they left the apartment, walking in the shadows of buildings and avoiding the well-lit main streets. Eventually they entered an underground passage that looked and smelled like a former sewer. Miklos lit a strong torch, explaining that the rats were afraid of the light and would keep away. Riebeck sincerely hoped that the battery would hold out.

"We used this passage a lot during the Nazi occupation," said Miklos. "Actually I think it dates back to the Turks."

After a walk that seemed to Riebeck to have taken several days, though in fact it had lasted only ten minutes, they emerged in the cellar of a house. Miklos switched off his light. They stood for a moment at the bottom of the badly lit stairs, listening. All was silent, so they went up. The house was a large one and it looked familiar to Riebeck. Surely he had come here for a dinner during the happy Christmas holiday when Istvan had fallen in love with Eva. It had now been split up into many apartments and was grimy.

Miklos, who had gone ahead, stopped and rapped on a door. Istvan Halyi opened it himself, standing in the dark hallway of his apartment.

"Hello, Miklos. If you'll go to the kitchen, Janos will give you a beer for what that's worth." He shut the door behind them and switched on the light. Miklos went away and the two friends, left alone, stood looking at each other in a silence that was filled with the years behind them, their last sad meeting and their long separation. Istvan, wearing a badly tailored uniform with a colonel's badges on the shoulders and a leather strap across his chest, looked unchanged, scowling, hideous, his green eyes alive with laughter.

"Schani," he said, touching Riebeck's shoulder lightly with his hand. "*Servus.*"

"*Servus* Istvan." They might have been boys at the railway station in Budapest or young officers meeting in Vienna. When Istvan was very tired or very happy he grew silent, but Riebeck usually took it out in talk. Now he said, "I am glad I have broken the chain. From the time the Nazis annexed Austria till now it has always taken war and catastrophe to bring us together. Now it is only Dr. Kerenyi, whose being sent to Siberia cannot be in any way considered a catastrophe except for the Siberians."

Istvan said, "Come in, Schani," and led the way into a beautiful room with high windows and a large fireplace. "Do you remember this house? We came here for a dance once on Christmas. It belonged to poor Matyi."

"I remember him. He and his wife didn't like each other. He used to spend six months in the house in Vienna while his wife was here, and then they switched for the next six months. I saw them once, changing houses. Matyi came upstairs just as his wife was coming down. He stopped, kissed her hand, said '*Bon jour*, Madame.' She said, '*Bon jour*, Matyi; and went on. I have never forgotten it. Aunt Steffi said, 'Such a nice marriage. In ten years they have not had a single quarrel.' " And remembering that in Hungary poor meant dead, he asked, "Was he killed in the war?"

"Oh no," said Istvan placidly. "He was hanged later. You might say he died of incurable aristocracy."

"Poor Matyi indeed," said Riebeck, accepting a cigarette and a glass of wine, which turned out to be very old, Imperial Tokay.

"If it gets out I have this they'll hang me too. It was Uncle Nikki's. This my last bottle. I was saving it in case you ever managed to get to Budapest."

"How nice of you. I've never tasted Tokay like Uncle Nikki's anywhere else."

"They used to lay the grapes on a wire grill and only the juice that dripped down of itself was used to make this wine. After that the grapes were pressed, of course, and that wine was sold. But the stuff that dripped down of itself was very little, and people like Uncle Nikki who owned the Tokay vineyards always kept it for themselves. It was never sold."

Riebeck became gradually aware of the fact that Istvan was shocking him. His unease had begun, he now realized, with the placid admission that Matyi had been hanged for incurable aristocracy and had become more intense as he had heard Istvan speak of the Tokay and the privilege of certain lucky aristocrats in keeping the best bottles for themselves. Istvan, who had been so much a part of that system that one could not, in those days, have imagined him in any other context, sat by the fire in his badly cut Russian uniform and spoke (still drawling through his nose like all Dual Monarchy aristocrats) as if he were telling tales of the days of King Arthur.

"I like your apartment," said Riebeck. "But the man who makes your uniforms is either incompetent or a traitor."

"One must be adaptable now and look like the masses."

"There is still the Esterhazy nose."

Istvan scowled and rubbed his nose with his forefinger. "That I cannot help. If they want to hang me for my nose they must go ahead and please themselves. By the way, Dyelik is in Budapest. He came by the barracks just as I was leaving and bought me a drink. Very much by the way he mentioned that it must be a great pleasure for me to see my old friend again. I said I was delighted to have met him again and that I often fondly remembered the good times we had shared in Moscow. He said he had not meant his unworthy self, but my old friend Colonel Riebeck. So I got very huffy and said 'Look, Dyelik, I know I'm a degenerate Esterhazy on my mother's side, but I do draw the line somewhere.' He was very polite about it, but I don't think he believed me. Poor Dyelik, I fear he won't last. There is something delightfully *ancien régime* about him."

Riebeck, thinking of the way Dyelik treated his prisoners, said, "Sympathy with the MVD is as a rule misplaced, Istvan."

"I know, Schani."

"I wish you could get him out of my hair."

"I wish I could. Schani, please be very careful. I should not be able to help you if you were caught. We, the Hungarian army, I mean, are not you trusted very far by the Russians, and as far as the secret police go we have of course no influence whatever."

"Yes, I quite understand that. Istvan, forgive me, but I must ask. This being a Communist colonel, is it real?"

Istvan burst out laughing. "How funny you are. Of course it is real. What did you think, that it was all a pose? For what?"

"Simply because it seems so incredible that you should ever be a Communist, I suppose."

Istvan shrugged. "One cannot be an officer in the Hungarian army without being a member of the party. And I am an officer, Schani. Do you hate it very much, my being a party member?"

"I don't know. You see, I wasn't sure before. Do you remember in Vienna, when you quit Horthy, I told you how much more good you would have done me if you had stayed in the army pretending to be a fascist. I thought perhaps you'd followed my advice."

"I haven't," said Istvan, scowling. "I don't know why you imagine people arrange their lives solely so they can be of use to you."

"Don't be insulting."

"Why not? You were. I'm not one of your tame rabbits who go through life pretending God knows what merely so they can be ready to be used by you when the occasion requires it."

"Istvan, you know I don't expect that from you. I didn't come here to ask you to help me in any way. I only came to see you. In fact Kerenyi could have been gotten out much better by someone who knows Hungarian. I only took it on to see you again."

Istvan smiled and said, "I'm sorry. Have another glass of wine."

"Thank you." Riebeck realized that he had rarely seen Istvan smile before. He laughed easily in his scowling, furious way, but he rarely smiled. His smile, breaking through the scowl, was incredibly young and unused and a little shy.

"I'm a prig," Riebeck said contritely. "Be a Communist. It doesn't matter a damn."

"I let you be a Nazi once. Only believe me that I am not doing it because it is a good thing for me or because I am afraid of them."

"I know. Tell me about Peter."

"He is living with me since I came back from Moscow. I like him, but I don't think he likes me. He's never forgiven me for boarding him out with Janos."

"No," said Riebeck. "One wouldn't."

"He wants to go to the University," said Istvan.

"Not the army?"

"He says he wants to be a doctor. Can you think of anything more disgusting? Perhaps if I weren't army he wouldn't be so against it. I don't really understand him, but I try to take him as he comes and we get on well enough. Would you like to see him? He sleeps like the dead."

"With the greatest pleasure."

Istvan led the way to Peter's room and switched on the light. The first thing that struck Riebeck was the bareness of the room. There were no photographs of horses, no rosettes and silver cups from horse shows, no studbooks on the table.

"Poor Peter, no horses?"

"No, how could he? They've made all the horses into salami by now."

Riebeck looked at what was visible of the sleeping boy; a shock of brown hair streaked with blond, triangle eyebrows, and a perfect nose.

"How nice. He has the Esterhazy nose."

"Naturally." Istvan switched off the light. "I am happy to say that he doesn't look like his mother. Though that awful snobbery he must have from her. When I think how we loved living in the stables with Janos when we were children, and how Peter resents it—"

"But we never lived in the stables because we weren't considered good enough to live at the palace."

"I know, Schani."

They went back to the wine and Riebeck's American cigarettes and talked for hours. When it was almost morning Riebeck said he must go.

"Yes, I suppose you must. I hope we'll be able to meet again one day."

"I don't know. I hope so, Istvan. Will you do something for me?"

"Of course."

"If being a comrade palls on you, or if there is any kind of trouble at all, will you come to London and stay with me? There is nothing I should like better."

"I would like to stay with you, but not in London, Schani. I won't leave Budapest again."

"How odd. I always thought of you as a true Hungarian, happiest away from home. I know that exiled Hungarians suffer terribly or say they do, but those that are able to come and go, it has always seemed to me, are happier going. When did you discover this great passion for Budapest?"

"When I came back from Russia in '44. I never knew myself that one can feel about a city as one does about a person, but during the siege and the air raids I found it intolerable that Budapest should be hurt. I used to think, sometimes, that if I could somehow interpose my body between the bombs and take the beating intended for the city I would have been truly grateful." He stopped, ashamed, because he was not usually a fanciful person.

But Riebeck said, "The trouble is that it doesn't work. It doesn't and indeed shouldn't stop one from trying."

"Do you never miss France, Schani?"

"I miss it terribly all the time. But when I go there I find that this is not the France I have missed. I think the France I miss had ceased to exist even before the war. What was left of it came to England with General de Gaulle."

"You set a very high standard of behavior, Schani."

"Latour said that too. He thinks I can't forgive the 1940 armistice. I hope that isn't true."

Istvan grinned and said he considered it quite possible. "But I don't feel like that, you know, Schani. I've often been ashamed of Hungary, but I shall never leave here again. I am determined to die here."

"You sound like your national anthem," said Riebeck sarcastically. "You must live here and you must die here."

"The *Zozat*, you mean. It's not the national anthem."

"Well, you'll probably get your wish at the rate Hungarian officers are being liquidated."

"As long as Zhukov holds on, I will. I'm his pet Hungarian, you know. He thinks he's made a Commie of an Esterhazy through example and precept and it appeals to his sense of humor. He's a very good sort, you know."

"Long life and prosperity to Marshal Zhukov," said Riebeck, finishing his wine.

"One thing though, Schani. If anything should go wrong, could I send Peter to you?"

"Please do. Even if nothing goes wrong and Peter would like to come to England. I must go."

"*Au revoir*," said Istvan smiling. "Just in case."

"*Au revoir* then. Perhaps it will come true."

They stood for a moment in that silent embarrassment that overcomes people who are not given to grand gestures even when they are called for.

Riebeck said irritably, "Where the devil is Miklos?"

"Kitchen, I imagine, drinking beer with Janos. It's a pity you can't say hello to Janos, he would have liked it, but I think the fewer people know you are here the better."

"With Dyelik knowing it hardly matters, but I expect you're right."

Miklos came in answer to a shout from Istvan, touched his cap contemptuously to show what he thought of the turncoat colonel, a gesture that made Istvan grin with genuine amusement. They parted, protected now by a third from showing how bitter this new separation was to them.

Istvan Halyi returned to his sitting room and sat down to finish his glass of wine. He sat for a long time very still, unaware of the dawn growing grey outside his window, his mind back on a dinner party in this house, Schani Riebeck across the table from him next to Eva, careless of her beauty, able to laugh and talk with her in a way Istvan, desperately in love, could not. He did not look at the portrait of Eva over the chimney piece; he rarely noticed it. It was not a bad painting as formal portraits go. Janos had saved it from Tisza Palace as an act of piety, and Istvan kept it not to hurt his feelings. It was meaningless to him, giving neither pleasure nor pain. He needed no picture of her to remember. Time, everyone said, obliterated the strongest memories, but this was not true for Istvan. She was always there, his beloved familiar, and there were moments still when the pain was bad as at first.

Riebeck and Miklos emerged from their sewer into an empty street. Riebeck watched carefully to see if he was being followed, but the streets were empty. They returned to the apartment unobserved and Riebeck went to bed but could not sleep.

He was deeply worried about Istvan, who said, and spoke the truth, that he was not afraid of the Russians. What would happen to Istvan when he came to the end of the system for which he was now working? How near was he to that end? Loyalty would prevent him from speaking ill of a system to which he had given his allegiance; it would never stop him from acting against this system. Riebeck knew all too well what happens to those who act unsuccessfully against Russia. And such actions were in their very nature doomed to be unsuccessful.

He slept badly and was glad to get up and drink the stuff Miklos had made from another American tin called Instant Coffee.

"It's not so bad," said Miklos, "if you think of it as an entirely new drink that has no resemblance to coffee."

Riebeck, who had during the darkest days of France even drunk some stuff called instant wine, agreed politely.

They waited for dark and then left by way of another sewer for Dr. Kerenyi's house.

Dr. Kerenyi turned out to be a disagreeable individual who demanded identification papers and proof that they were not *agents provocateurs*.

Riebeck said, "Even if I did travel in Hungary with papers identifying me as a British Intelligence Officer you would have no way of knowing that these were not forged by the Russians."

"It is all very confusing," said Dr. Kerenyi, who spoke fluent French with a disagreeable accent. "I wish I knew what to do."

"That is for you to decide. If you trust me to take you to England, pack up your things and come along. We have a long trip ahead of us. If you don't trust me, call one of your guards outside and have me arrested. Only make up your mind."

"There is no need to be nasty," said the scientist, and Riebeck, who felt that he was keeping his temper very well, reminded himself that Kipling had called scientists beasts without background and cheered up a little.

"How did you get in here?" Dr. Kerenyi wanted to know. "There are guards around the house. If you are not a Russian *agent provocateur*, why did they let you through?"

"Dr. Kerenyi, I have been in Intelligence for nearly twenty years. I have learned to get through guards without arousing attention. And if you will trust me and do just as I say I can get you past them and across the border."

Dr. Kerenyi said nothing. He tried to light a cigar and had to give it up because his hands shook too much. Riebeck, seeing this and realizing how much fear lay behind the scientist's manners, at once became more patient; a patience that was not so much condescension as the politeness of the professional for the amateur. He lit Dr. Kerenyi's cigar for him and said, "I shall do my best to get you safely to England. I have done this sort of thing before. Believe me, it isn't as difficult as you think."

"I suppose I shall have to trust you," Dr. Kerenyi said ungraciously. "I have no other choice."

"Well, you could go to Siberia."

"You must realize that my kind of brains would be completely wasted in Siberia."

"Of course. Could you get ready quickly? The more time we have for traveling in the dark, the better. It would be simplest if we could get across the frontier before they have discovered that you are missing. Do they check up on you or do they merely watch that you don't leave the house? Are you alone here?"

"My good man, you may be good at escaping, but you obviously have no idea of the needs of scientists. I must get my papers together for if I do not bring them I shall have wasted years of work. I shall be ready tomorrow night."

"Are you joking? I'll probably be dead by tomorrow night. I've already got the MVD on my tail. You come now or never."

"Impossible."

"Very well. Good-by."

"When I get to England I shall have serious complaints to make to your chief, whoever he is. I am not accustomed to such behavior."

"Fine. I'll introduce you to him. Now come on."

Dr. Kerenyi sighed, put his hat on his invaluable brain, emptied his desk drawers into a brief case, put on an overcoat with an astrakhan collar, and said he was ready. Riebeck instructed him briefly in the art of leaving a guarded house, told him not to make a noise no matter what happened and to leave his lights burning to give his guards the comforting belief that he was working late. The drawing-room windows through which Riebeck had entered were still unwatched, there were some useful bushes in the well-tended little city garden, and the moon obligingly retired behind a cloud. It was simplicity itself to get away, thought Riebeck, and walked directly into the arms and revolver of Major Dyelik.

Riebeck pushed Dr. Kerenyi back into the window, took a deep breath and recovered his voice. "Dyelik, you turn up in the damnedest places."

"I might say the same for you. Please go back into the house."

"I can't. Dr. Kerenyi just threw me out."

The scientist, who had put his powerful mind to work, caught this broad hint, leaned out the window and began yelling for help. Guards rushed toward him from several directions, learned that a tool of imperialism had climbed into Dr. Kerenyi's window and had attempted to suborn him to work for the capitalist imperialist West, that Dr. Kerenyi had refused him with moral indignation and wanted him arrested. Torches went on and the guards closed in. Major Dyelik turned on them his frightening dark eyes. "Report to your barracks at once," he said. "Tomorrow you shall have serious charges to answer."

They slunk off. Major Dyelik climbed into the drawing room window, said courteously, "Come in, Colonel Riebeck," and held the curtain aside for him. Riebeck, being confronted with a gun, could not but obey the invitation.

"Thanks," he said. "I think you saved me from a lynching."

"Russians," Dyelik told him severely, "do not lynch. It is an American custom. Dr. Kerenyi, could you offer us a glass of vodka? I think we could all do with a drink. Colonel Riebeck, on your honor, are you armed?"

Riebeck, his left hand in his pocket, his forefinger on the trigger of his gun, said, "On my honor, I am not."

Dyelik took the vodka bottle from Dr. Kerenyi, poured a drink for himself and one for Riebeck, gave Riebeck a cigarette and ignoring his host said, "Where the devil did you hide out? I couldn't find you anywhere. Fortunately I knew what you had come for, so I waited for you here. Colonel Halyi was very secretive about you."

"Colonel Halyi and I have not been on speaking terms since he joined the Communist Party. He did not know I was here." Riebeck wondered how he could dispose of Dyelik before he became a danger to Istvan as well. Kerenyi would be no help. He supposed he would have to shoot, even if it woke the neighborhood. But at least Dyelik had sent the guards away. Why had he done that? It was stupid. Did he want the credit of capturing Colonel Riebeck single-handedly? Major Dyelik, hero of the Soviet Union.

Had Dyelik a motor car so that they could get away quickly? The question was in any case academic. Colonel Riebeck's gun was in his pocket while Dyelik's was in his hand. Unless something happened to distract Dyelik's attention. . . . Better to be shot anyhow than to be taken to Russia. He hoped Dyelik had believed him about Istvan.

"Did you come by car?" he asked.

"Yes."

Riebeck finished his drink and threw his cigarette stub into the immaculate fireplace. Dr. Kerenyi fidgeted. If only he would talk, faint, have hysterics, do anything that would make Dyelik turn his head. But he only sat, twisting his fingers in mute agony. Riebeck made a hideous face at him and stuck out his tongue. Anything to create a diversion.

Dr. Kerenyi looked merely puzzled. He opened his mouth, snapped for air, and shut it again. Riebeck, annoyed, turned back to the laughing Dyelik.

287

"Idiot," said Dyelik with a contemptuous glance at Dr. Kerenyi. He turned his pistol around and handed it to Riebeck. "Here."

It was now Riebeck's turn to open his mouth and, unable to speak, shut it again.

"Take it. I did not come here to arrest you. That little performance with the guards was made necessary by Dr. Kerenyi's shrieks for help. I thought you realized that. I am accepting your offer, Colonel Riebeck. I want to come with you to London."

Riebeck's fingers closed around the pistol and Dyelik let go. He laughed. "Did I deprive you of speech?"

"Yes. I was just planning to shoot you. Of course you would have shot at me first and at this distance you couldn't have missed. Instead of sitting here and talking to you, I thought I would by now be dead."

"And your final act in this life was to stick your tongue out at Dr. Kerenyi?"

Colonel Riebeck turned to the still gasping scientist and apologized. "I was hoping you'd jump and yell at me or something. Anything to make Dyelik turn his head. Then I could have shot him."

"Oh," said Dr. Kerenyi.

"You gave me your word you were not armed," said Dyelik.

Riebeck smiled.

"I shall like working for you," Dyelik exclaimed, delighted with so much duplicity. Since Dr. Kerenyi's powerful mind was obviously not made to grapple with events, Dyelik possessed himself of the vodka bottle again and gave everyone a drink. "And now to business. I have an old mother in Russia, so I would appreciate it if you would kidnap me. We'll toss the furniture around a little, spatter a bullet or two into the walls and smash the bottle. At the border you will discreetly poke a gun in my back, should anybody look into the car. I have papers showing that I am urgently needed in Vienna. And there we are."

"What happens in England?"

"I will be asked many stupid questions, I know. And no one will ever trust me, but they will say, Dyelik is Riebeck's friend. Let's give the poor blighter a chance."

Riebeck winced at this accurate assessment of English security. He said, "I mean what happens to your old mother in Russia when you are discovered working for me?"

"I shall get in touch with the Embassy. No, they will get in touch with me. And I shall be very haughty and say, "Keep away, do you want to ruin everything, you ham-handed fools. I shall say I am working for Smersh, that will frighten them."

"Fine," said Riebeck, who did not believe in either the Smersh assignment or the old mother in Russia. He suspected that Dyelik wanted to leave himself an escape hatch in case life in England did not please him. It would be simple to compromise him sufficiently to make a return to Russia impossible.

"If I am wrong," he thought, "my days are numbered. But I am not often wrong about such things." Aloud he said, "Let's go. Who's driving your car?"

"My driver. I think we will allow him to escape back here once we are across the border. He can tell everyone how I was kidnaped."

"Good idea," said Riebeck, finishing the vodka.

Under Dr. Kerenyi's mute, agonized gaze they broke several chairs, smashed a window, pulled down a curtain, and fired two bullets into the wall. Then they led Dyelik captive from the room.

The driver responded obligingly to the pressure of Riebeck's gun against his neck and turned the car toward Vienna. They drove through dark, pouring rain, covering themselves and anyone they passed with a thick layer of mud. No one followed them or attempted to stop them. The frontier guards, reluctant to come out of their dry little huts, and in any case familiar with Dyelik's car, waved them through.

"Well, that's it," said Riebeck. "I think we'd better not stop in Vienna but drive as far west as we can and pick up a plane tonight. Dyelik, please tell your driver to get out now and make his way back to the frontier."

Major Dyelik spoke to his driver in Russian. Riebeck, who understood Russian much better than he spoke it, gathered that Dyelik was telling him to go home. The young soldier said he was very glad to be in the West and that nothing would make him go back to the Russian army now that he was out. Riebeck burst out laughing, but Dyelik was furious.

They caught a plane in Munich. For the rest of his days, thought Riebeck, he would cherish the memory of General Partridge's face when he arrived in London not only with Dr. Kerenyi but with a Russian soldier and an MVD major as well.

XVIII

The telephone rang inside the flat as Riebeck put his key in the door. He waited until he heard Alphonse say that he was not at home and then went in. Alphonse looked at him in surprise and disapproval. He did not appreciate an employer who cluttered up his apartment in the daytime hours.

"That was General Cook on the phone," he said. "You're to call him back."

"He'll ring back in five minutes," said Riebeck. "I won't be home."

"What's the matter. Are you sick?"

"No. Just through."

"Do you want some tea?"

Riebeck gave him a long, nasty look. For Alphonse the withholding of his employer's title was the assertion of his status as an artist instead of a servant; the modern equivalent of those painters who had their brushes picked up from the floor by reigning monarchs. Usually Riebeck recognized this and tolerated it good-humoredly. But these last weeks Riebeck had not been in a good humor, and Alphonse, though normally as rude as any kitchen prima donna could hope to be, had made a sincere effort to walk on eggs and cook soothing foods. But now he was fed up too. One word out of Riebeck about proper forms of address and he—Alphonse—would be through.

His black eyes, set in yellow pouches of fat, did not waver under a look that had made generals quail. It was the grey eyes, not the black, that gave in.

"No tea, thanks," said Riebeck. "I wouldn't mind a Scotch though."

"All right," said Alphonse, much relieved. "There's the telephone again. Shall I say you aren't home?"

"No, better not. Otherwise it will keep on all afternoon. Here, give it to me. Colonel Riebeck speaking."

As he had expected, it was Simon, playing nursemaid.

"I say, what happened to you? Did you get sick?"

"I'm quite well, thank you."

"Then why did you get up and walk out in the middle of a conference? Partridge's livid, I don't mind telling you."

"I warned you last week," said Riebeck, "that if you told me once more we mustn't rock the boat I'd quit. You did and I have."

"Oh come, that's a bit drastic, isn't it?"

"I want to be drastic."

"You need a vacation."

"I need a boat to rock."

"When was your last vacation?"

"Five years ago, in '49, when I went to Fontaines."

"There, you see."

Riebeck said nothing. Alphonse handed him a drink. At the other end of the line he heard the rattle of crockery. The tea trolley was making its rounds at St 2. From the folded *Times* the headline word "Geneva" caught his eye. It was enough these days to set him raging. He forced himself to rage in silence. Simon was telling him not to do anything hasty or unconsidered.

"Of course not," Riebeck promised sweetly through clenched teeth. "That might rock the boat and wake the baby."

"You know," said Simon in his most schoolmasterly, quelling manner, "Indochina would have been lost even if you instead of General Lattre had commanded Dienbienphu." And having had the last word, he rang off.

"*Tiens*," said Riebeck, replacing the phone. It was true enough that he had been intolerable ever since the siege of Dienbienphu (not because he thought he could have done better than General Lattre but because it was his Indochina and his army that was being thrown away) but he had not credited Simon with the perception to connect the two.

A basic dissatisfaction had been with him since the end of the war. At times it had become overlaid with activity. Not until the fall of Indochina had he become clearly aware of how he felt.

He was tired of being cautious, fed to the teeth with not rocking the boat. The tightrope of the war had turned into a baize conference table, the swift and silent raiders were replaced by gabblers and golfers and old men with a new slogan: It is better to talk than to fight. The West was losing move after move, through timidity, caution, and cold-war nerves. It was a humiliating and unnecessary performance. For the advantage was not entirely on the other side. The Russians were sitting on a powder keg too. The satellite nations were kept from explosion only by rigorous suppression. All Riebeck wanted to do was to toss a few lit matches.

"You know," he had argued this afternoon and not for the first time, "that all you need is some very small provocations. These people will do our fighting for us. You're wasting a lot of energy. Those riots last year in East Berlin; why if we'd had even two or three trained troublemakers there I bet we could have worked it up into a full-scale uprising."

"Yes, and maybe a full-scale war after that," said Simon Cook. "I don't believe it. Dyelik, what do you think?"

"I think it very peculiar of Westerners to assume that only they have sufficient sensitivity to be afraid of the Bomb. I assure you, Russians are afraid too."

"I don't think we want to take chances on that," said Simon. "This is not the time to rock the boat," at which point Riebeck had wished everyone good afternoon and had left.

How like Simon to ring up half an hour later and suggest a vacation. Where would he go? Fontaines? That was a place for people with their minds at rest. Paris? Not in this mood. In Paris you sing for your supper. If you want to be amused you must be amusing.

When the telephone rang again, he decided not to answer it. It was probably Simon with a list of spas for disgruntled people. He said, "I'm not home, Alphonse. I don't want to talk to anybody."

"All right, if you say so. But it's Lady Falconer."

"Oh. That's different. Give it to me."

He reached for the telephone. "Hullo," said Jenny. "If you aren't doing anything, come and have a drink. Uncle Amby is in town and I want you to meet him. He'll probably be terribly rude, he never likes people unless he's known them all his life, and he hates foreigners, but he'll make you laugh."

Riebeck, feeling that he was overdue for some amusement, said, "Thank you, I would like to come."

Bessie, falling over her own feet, opened the door of the Wimpole Street house for him and showed him to the drawing room. "How nice," said Jenny. "I haven't seen you for ages. Come and meet my Uncle. Amby, may I introduce Colonel Riebeck. Lord Allanbank."

Lord Allanbank looked terrifying in the best tradition of Mad English Squire. Riebeck was fascinated by him. He had always supposed this to be a purely literary creation. Yet here he was. With his bandy legs and small blue eyes one could easily picture him in all the classic situations: chasing an erring daughter and her baby into a snowstorm, telling a son never to darken his doorstep again, horse-whipping a poor tenant with ten starving children for poaching a rabbit.

Jenny, who much preferred fiction to truth, claimed that he lived in a mansion resembling that of Count Dracula. Ghosts, she said, could be heard wailing in the housemaid's cupboard, and phantom chains rattled in the kitchen passage. The only thing missing, apparently, was the ghost of Heathcliff moaning on the moor.

For the sake of versimilitude Jenny concealed from Lord Allanbank's admirers that he had no daughter, erring or otherwise, that he was on affectionate terms with his son, and was much too nearsighted ever to catch a poacher.

Lord Allanbank seemed pleased to meet Colonel Riebeck. "I've heard about you," he said. "The feller that gives Partridge apoplexy. Have a drink."

"Thank you, sir."

Giving General Partridge apoplexy seemed to make one Lord Allanbank's friend for life. He ignored the Falconers and at length told Riebeck all about the wonderful time he had had as a young man chopping up Pathans (he pronounced it P'tawns) on the Northwest Frontier and Huns in France. He and General Partridge had been in the same regiment, and Lord Allanbank had many a tale to tell of the General's idiocy, venality, inhumanity, and bungling. He expressed unprintable but colorful opinions about those in power at the War Office who had not seen fit to send him, well over sixty and with a stiff knee, to fight the Germans in '39, and of General Partridge, who had firmly refused to allow him to become a secret agent for the same reasons, with the added disadvantage that Lord Allanbank spoke nothing but English and that almost unintelligibly.

Jenny wrenched the conversation away from her uncle and said, "We were just talking about taking a holiday at Mary's Rue."

"What is Mary's Rue?"

"Amby's place in Cornwall."

"What an unusual name."

"Back in the good old papist days the house overlooked the only road leading to a famous shrine of the Virgin. She worked a lot of miracles and cures and things, but one couldn't get to her without a tip to the Baron Allanbank of the day. He did very well out of it."

"Life must have been very satisfying in those days. Your holiday sounds delightful."

"Why don't you come too, Riebeck," said Lord Allanbank, eager to see more of his new friend.

"Because," Sir Jonathan told him, "Riebeck believes that the Department will collapse if he is away for even one day."

"On the contrary, they are rather eager to get rid of me at the moment. I have five years' leave due to me."

"Do come," said Jenny.

"All right. Thank you very much, Lord Allanbank. If I can arrange to get away, I should like to come."

"Splendid," said Lord Allanbank. "That's settled then. Come along and have dinner with me at my club, Riebeck. Dreadful food. I think they buy their meat from the knacker. But the clart is first rate. D'you like clart?"

Riebeck, having by now guessed that Lord Allanbank was speaking of claret, said, "You ask a Frenchman that?"

"That's right, Jenny told me you were a Frog. Dreadful fellers, always losing the war. Come along then."

Over sherry at his club, Lord Allanbank said, "Never dine with Jenny. I've got a perfectly good family at home to dine with. When I come to London I want some fun. Know Molly Cato's place?"

It was London's most exclusive and most expensive bawdy house; a place for ambassadors, film stars, and millionaires.

"Surely," said Riebeck.

"Home away from home," Lord Allanbank told him complacently. "After dinner, that's where we'll go, right?"

"All right," said Riebeck, though privately he would have preferred to spend the evening with Jenny.

They left London a few days later driving in Sir Jonathan's Daimler west into a beautiful, crisp October landscape.

"We're not the summer vacation part of Cornwall," Jenny told Riebeck, and as in the late afternoon they approached Mary's Rue he could see that in this harsh landscape no pleasure resorts would fit. The shelves of rock were worn hollow by the sea, the trees were bent forever to one side by the wind, and the grass was swept uphill. It was grim and demanding and beautiful.

The houses were built in hollows between the hills to protect them from the ever-present wind, but Mary's Rue crested its hill; an open rectangle, its face turned to the storm. In the misty distance, against a pigeon-egg sky, on a shelf of rock, stood the ruins of a castle. "That's Allanbank Castle," said Jenny. "Cromwell wrecked it, or we'd have to live in it. Let's ride up to it tomorrow. It's full of rats."

"What an inducement," said Riebeck.

They drove through a toy village, sheltered in a valley, and then up through a neglected park to the manor house. The door was opened to them by Kelly, the butler, who was said to be a hundred years old.

"He won't retire," said Jenny, "and Aunt Melissa hasn't the heart to make him. I don't think he tells the truth about his age, really. He's probably no more than ninety-five."

"Welcome to the Maison Dracula," said Sir Jonathan, standing aside for Riebeck to go in first.

Riebeck looked around him. There were no bats suspended from the ceiling, nor were the doorways filled with spiderwebs. Those details aside, Mary's Rue was rather intimidating, with very high, ice-cold rooms and the wail of the wind in the chimneys.

The bedrooms upstairs were arranged in a labyrinth; bathrooms had usually been added as an afterthought in unlikely corners, so that visitors getting ready for dinner found themselves disconsolately walking about in search of hot water, finding neither the bathroom nor their own bedroom until they were rescued by one of the servants.

The smallest of the sitting rooms the family used in the winter had a huge fire, all the curtains drawn against the wind, and was very slightly warm. Lady Allanbank was very pretty and kind, and at once offered him whisky for the cold.

She said, "Was your bath at all warm?"

"No," said Colonel Riebeck, "it wasn't."

"Oh dear. It never seems to be."

"Darling," said Jenny, "this is Colonel Riebeck."

"The baths are too dreadful," sighed Lady Allanbank. "How do you do?"

Jenny said, "Our hot water system was installed at vast expense in 1882. So you see, it is now a valuable antique and the Georgian Society won't let us rip it out."

"Really, Jenny," said Lady Allanbank, "you do tell the most dreadful lies. Did you have a good drive down, Colonel Riebeck? I always think Jonathan's Daimler makes one so sick."

Riebeck said he did not get carsick, only seasick, and that indeed until now Cornwall had held only distressing memories for him, for during the war there had been a ferry service between Pencanze and Finisterre, which was the most sickening form of transportation ever invented. Since seasickness is a subject on which everyone has something to say (either to boast of their hadihood or else of the fact that they get sicker than anyone) they were embarked on an animated conversation by the time Lord Allanbank, in riding breeches and muddy boots, strode into the room and glared about himself in his best mad squire manner. When he remembered who Riebeck was and why Jenny and Jonathan were here, he delightedly refilled everyone's glass and, stretching his boots to the fire, discoursed on hunting.

"You hunt, don't you, Riebeck?"

Colonel Riebeck, unaware of the enormity of what he was saying, told him, "No. I'm much too fond of foxes for that."

Lord Allanbank, looking like a grand inquisitor in whose house someone had innocently declared himself to be a Lutheran, glared madly at his guests and began: "Good Gad—" when Kelly shuffled in and in a dying voice announced that dinner was ready.

The dining room was cold, badly lit, and depressing. The food was also cold and very bad. The wine, however, was excellent. After dinner the ladies returned to the sitting room and Riebeck committed the second enormity of the evening by refusing both port and cigars on the simple grounds that he did not like them.

Sir Jonathan, who had had many occasions to observe Lord Allanbank's rudeness to people who ventured to disagree with him on anything, no matter how trivial, accepted the port and a cigar, and sat back, ready to enjoy himself. He was, however, cheated of his fun, for Lord Allanbank had taken a great fancy to Riebeck at their first meeting, and he was consistent in that he always made up his mind at once and never swerved from his first idea, no matter how wrong he was subsequently proved to be. Riebeck could be sentimental about foxes, refuse port, prefer cigarettes to cigars, be French, perhaps even vote Labour. In Lord Allanbank's eyes he was and would forever remain perfect. Sir Jonathan, who also disliked port and cigars but had never had the nerve to refuse them, wished, not for the first time, that he were not such a martyr to his own opinion of what a gentleman ought to do.

From Mary's Rue the sea looked as smooth as oil the next morning, but at the bottom of the cliffs, where there were no flats of sand for the waves' sleek somersaults to run themselves to earth, they broke with unexpected force. Riebeck, Sir Jonathan, and Jenny, on their way to the castle, stopped their horses at the edge of a gully where the rocks had cracked open long ago. In the narrow passage the water, trapped in the rock, cast up a cold spray.

"This is the great dare for all Allanbank children," said Jenny. "To jump the gully. When I was about twelve Jeremy and I used to jump it blindfolded. Of course Jeremy was a grown-up even then. It didn't strike me as a child that what is very daring at twelve is extremely foolish at thirty. Do you think you could jump it, Colonel Riebeck?"

He looked down at it, assessing the danger of the broken, wet rock and the unknown horse. Then he laughed, spurred the horse over the slippery stones and across the long drop, to hear the horse's hoofs catch on the other side, to hear also another horse behind him. He did not need to look back to know that it was Jenny's. Laughing still, he cantered across the sand down to the beach and stopped where the overhanging rocks made a sunny and warm shelter on this chilly day. Sir Jonathan joined them by the more conventional path, saying ungallantly to his wife that what was foolish at thirty was downright idiotic at thirty-four.

They dismounted and sat down in the sun to smoke a cigarette and look out over the slate water into the dazzle of sun on its surface. Sometimes a forward wave crept to their feet and soaked the sand.

"I think," said Riebeck, lying back lazily, "that I would rather visit the rats in the castle another day. It looks very nice and I shall stay here and soak up sun like a lizard."

"I have to lunch at the Pennimans'," said Sir Jonathan. "I promised in a weak moment. You wouldn't come and keep me in countenance, would you, Jenny? You know how Lady Penniman frightens me."

"No darling, I'm afraid I wouldn't. I'm much too comfortable here to keep anyone in countenance."

"Till tea then."

He mounted his horse and rode up the narrow path to the manor.

"Wasn't he coming to the castle?" asked Riebeck.

"No. He was suddenly going to remember Lady Penniman before we got there. He's afraid of rats but he doesn't like to admit it."

"He has my sympathy. I'm afraid of them too."

"Are you?"

"Yes. They had some very aggressive ones at Buchenwald. There must be something you are afraid of. What?"

Jenny took off her jacket and put it under her head. "Intangibles."

"What intangibles?"

"Growing dependent on something undependable."

"Or someone?"

"Well yes, someone." She closed her eyes and sighed a little. "I'm half asleep."

"Don't mind me, I'm half asleep myself."

They were silent. Behind her sunglasses, Jenny kept her eyes closed. Perhaps she really was drowsy. "Funny," thought Riebeck, "how I always used to wonder why on earth she'd marry Falconer. And there's the answer. You'd never grow to depend on him except as a distinguished-looking escort. And I suppose for that he's dependable enough. Tyrell called him a half-warmed fish. It's what he is, of course. Is she satisfied with that? There's never any talk about her having a lover, for all the men that run after her. Dear Jenny, I'm not a half-warmed fish at all. This is terribly dangerous. Were you warning me off? I don't need warning, I'm doing my best to keep away."

"It was very foolhardy of you to jump the gully," said Jenny suddenly, cutting across his thoughts. "You might have been killed."

"Yes," said Riebeck, "I suppose so. I didn't think about it."

"I do like the way you don't fuss about things like breaking all your bones or getting killed."

Riebeck opened his eyes and looked across at her. It was difficult to judge her expression; her eyes were still hidden behind the dark glasses. But she had sounded—he did not think he was mistaken about it—very wide awake and decidedly peevish. He remembered how annoyed she had been with him at the hospital when he had begun to help General Burkey. It was amusing, this universal female desire not to let the boy stray from the apron string. Especially as neither the boy nor the apron were hers.

"Boys will be boys," he remarked, being deliberately annoying.

"A most original observation, Colonel Riebeck."

"Wasn't it. Do look at the clouds. So much better than quarreling."

"I never quarrel," said Jenny with dignity.

The clouds were doubly shelved against the misty blue horizon. The bottom layer, like hastily bundled featherbeds, was scurrying to the other side of the sky. The top layer had spread itself across the horizon and lay unmoving, like spiderwebs, across the sun. In the blue haze hung the ruined castle. The word Lyonesse came to his mind, sunk into the sea somewhere near here, Tristan and Iseult bewitched by the magic potion between Ireland and Cornwall. Wagner had so teutonized the story that Riebeck had not until now remembered that Iseult was an Irish girl and Tristan a local boy.

" '*Qui Tristan aime bien loyallement, sans s'amie na'a que tourment,*' " he said. "I've only just remembered that it's a local story."

"*Chèvrefeuille?*" Jenny opened her eyes and removed her sunglasses. "Of course it's a local story. '*A Cournouailles il s'en retourne . . . tous les barons sont appelés; A Tintagel ils vont venir—*' It's quite near here. Cornwall is full of love stories that ended badly."

"Of course they would. So many cliffs to jump from. Is it time for lunch, do you think? Not that your uncle's meals are exactly a pleasure, but I would not like to keep Lady Allanbank waiting."

Colonel Riebeck was extremely fond of Lady Allanbank. She was almost old enough to be his mother, but by dint of considerable effort and taste looked much younger. She was a charmer and Riebeck approved of her conversation, which was often about Jenny. On days when the others went hunting he usually stayed with her, for Lady Allanbank did not hunt, saying that it was hard on the skin and in any case she was afraid of horses.

Riebeck, who was usually nervous of holidays, found himself enjoying this one.

Simon Cook rang him up every day to ask how much longer he intended to stay away ("Until you find me a boat I can rock," Riebeck invariably told him.) and get advice on various matters of departmental politics. These calls made Riebeck feel safe. Whenever he got bored he could turn one of them into an urgent summons and return to work.

But in the end it was not boredom that forced him to leave. He soon had to acknowledge that it was a mistake to have come to Cornwall, for it broke down the restrictive fences he had built in his relationship to Jenny, and this he could not afford. In London it had not been difficult to limit their encounters; an occasional lunch, a chat at someone's party, a smile across the theater as the house lights went down. These he had doled out to himself as one does with one's last cigarettes, knowing that there will be no more for days.

London had been his *mise en scène*, Cornwall was hers. He found her disturbingly in his way. He could not but delight in her Snow Queen beauty against these new settings; the gray madcap sea, the blue ruins of the castle, the hunting print colors of horses streaked against the landscape. But it was too dangerous a pleasure. No man can bear two bondages without neglecting both, and in spite of his dissatisfactions Colonel Riebeck preferred work to love. Jenny held the power of a very strong bondage, as he had finally to admit on a night about which he tried not to think, though it seemed to him at times that there were no other memories in the world save that full moon he had gone down to the beach to admire.

As he had stopped to light a cigarette he noticed a shadow on the sand below and the shimmer of pale hair in the dark. She turned to look up. "Jonathan?"

"All cats are grey in evening dress. No, not Jonathan. How do I come down to the beach from here? I've always come through the park before."

"You have to jump off the ledge here. Come, I'll show you."

She moved out of the shadows into the stream of moonlight. She wore a long hooded coat of dark green velvet. Riebeck had seen

301

her huddled in it after dinner, in the corner chair by the fire. It became her beautifully. She said, "I was just about to go to bed when I looked out the window and there was the moon." She held out her hand for him to jump. "Jeremy calls it a madman's moon."

They stood side by side then, and he thought that he must let go of her hand, that something of no consequence must at once be said. Which of them made the final move that brought them into each other's arms and down on the wind-streaked sand he never after remembered, remembered only the warmth of her throat and breasts under his mouth and that she had touched, with lips and tongue, the scarred palm of his hand.

Up at the house a door opened and shut. Jenny said, "Damn!"

"Is it your husband?"

"Yes, naturally."

"Can he see us?"

"Not till he comes down the cliff."

"Let us run away then."

"You've only to make noises like a lovesick cat and he'll discreetly go away."

"Never mind. The moment has evidently passed."

"It's hardly polite to make it sound so much like a reprieve," said Jenny, laughing at him.

"For you too, surely."

"Assuredly." They both laughed then, and he let her go.

"Hullo, Jonathan. We're down here, darling."

"We?" Sir Jonathan turned on the ledge and swung himself down to the sand. "Oh, hullo, Riebeck. Is this insomnia or sex?"

Riebeck said, "Insomnia."

"If I were a witch doctor I should say it's the moon."

"I think you would be very effective with bleached bones twisted in your hair, waving a feather duster," said Riebeck.

"I should have to raise my fees."

Jenny stood away from them both, smiling and drawing the collar of her coat across her bruised throat. What a lot men always talked.

"Goodness but it's cold," said Sir Jonathan. "Moon or no moon,

I am going back to bed. Are you coming, Jenny? You are shivering."

"Yes, darling."

"Riebeck?"

"No, I'm not sleepy. I'll stay down here for a while."

"You'd better have my burberry then."

"Thank you, but I'm quite comfortable." Riebeck felt obscurely that one could not take a man's overcoat after so nearly having taken his wife. He remained leaning against the ledge after they had gone, watching absently the shelves of moonlight on the water. He was horrified at himself. He must get away and quickly too.

The Allanbanks were sorry the next morning when he told them that something had come up at the office and he must leave at once. Jenny's smile said plainly that the man who runs away lives to die another day.

Driving back to London, Riebeck tried to convince himself that he was not only doing the proper thing, but the thing he really wanted to do. But this attempt failed.

XIX

Colonel Riebeck's lie to the Allanbanks came true with a vengeance. He arrived at the office to find every telephone gibbering; L'Abbé from Paris, Simon Cook to Cornwall, Bantain from Vienna, and Partridge meddling into all of them with the sound advice: "Find Riebeck and get him here instantly."

Several dogs who had been sleeping so peacefully that they had been allowed to lie had awakened at once. Partridge made it all sound like a novel by John Buchan, with the fate of the Empire (such as it was) depending on Colonel Riebeck. It was nothing so drastic, being a strictly departmental affair, but there were some boats to be rocked and Riebeck was profoundly annoyed with himself for being able to bring to the most exciting assignment since the war only a divided mind.

He was out of England for five months. Even then he was able to return to London only for a day; a stop that was, as far as the assignment was concerned, entirely unnecessary. He came for one purpose only and would have come sooner if he had had the time.

He stepped off the plane into a day of unclouded skies, a lucky day, a day on which nothing could go wrong for any man on earth.

At the office he threw his papers on Partridge's desk, learned with pleasure but without surprise—this was after all his lucky day —that the General was not in and would like to see him tomorrow.

"He'll have to get up rather early in the morning to do that," said Riebeck cheerfully to Lionel Jennings. "I'm off at dawn."

"Major Tyrell's been asking for you."

"I thought he was in Cyprus."

"He's here for a day or two. The Foreign Office wanted to ask questions again."

"I don't know why Cook allows it. We're not a public information service after all. Let the F.O. send its own people if they are so interested. I am going to lunch now, and I don't think I shall be back. If anyone wants to know where I am you haven't seen me in ages."

"Right. Even Major Tyrell?"

"Especially Major Tyrell."

But he ran into Jeremy coming up the stairs. Jeremy wore a uniform that looked as if it had been worn at Dunkirk and nonstop ever since, and had a dark tan which indicated that much of his work was done on Cyprus beaches. "Watching for gun runners from Greece," he blandly explained.

"I know," said Riebeck. "You too have written a book about the Cyprus situation and you are here to see your publisher."

"I don't know why you have to make it sound like a felony. Have lunch with me?"

"Not today, thank you."

"Dinner?"

"Not if I am lucky. I feel lucky."

"You don't look lucky. You look the very picture of a man about to commit a blithering, monstrous *bêtise*."

"Why not?"

"Why not indeed. Have fun."

304

"I have to leave very early tomorrow morning, so I shan't see you. But I might stop off at Nicosia and catch up on the lunch."

"Do. The food will surprise you."

Riebeck found a taxi and went home. There he told Alphonse to take the day off and then rang up Jenny.

"Lunch with me at the Richelieu," he said when she answered.

"I am so sorry but I can't. I am lunching at the Savoy with Reggie Fortescue."

Reggie Fortescue was a generic name Riebeck had invented for the large group of idle and hapless young men who had nothing better to do with themselves than to fall in love with Lady Falconer and take her to lunch.

He said nothing. He was certain that given a moment to think it over she would see how infinitely preferable lunch with Colonel Riebeck at the Richelieu would be to lunch at the Savoy with a Reggie.

"Oh," she said into his amused silence, "all right. I have to go with Amby to the Army and Navy, so I'll meet you at the Richelieu at one-thirty."

"Good." He rang off and thought with malicious pleasure of Jenny picking up her telephone again and call the luckless Reggie. He looked without interest through his mail. There was an invitation to a cocktail party at the American Embassy for this afternoon, but he expected to be more interestingly occupied by then. He had a shower, put on clean clothes, looked at his watch—1:10—optimistically told Alphonse he could stay out all night as well, and was on his way.

Whistling was an art he had never properly mastered. Nevertheless he whistled, cheerfully if tunelessly, as he got out his battered car, which on this lucky day was obliging enough to start.

Jenny was not at the Richelieu when he got there, which was not surprising. He had never known her to be anywhere on time. He waited, with a martini cold between his fingers, in no hurry now, though he had come across a continent to see her.

Through the window he saw Lord Allenbank's huge Rolls Royce pull up and hoped that Jenny's uncle would not lunch with them.

He watched her lean back into the car to kiss Lord Allanbank good-by. But of course, it was a lucky day.

Someone opened the door for her and she came in, standing for a moment with the sun behind her in the open door. She had dressed for the occasion in the severest and slimmest of black Balenciaga *tailleurs*. Her hair was pulled straight back and wound into a knot. It would not have surprised Riebeck if she had put on her spectacles for his benefit.

She said primly, "How do you do, Colonel Riebeck."

Properly he bowed.

"Why are you laughing?"

"If schoolmistresses could afford clothes by Balenciaga, I would say you look like a schoolmistress."

She took out her spectacles and put them on, ostensibly to look at the menu but in fact to look at him severely through them.

"Ah," he said, "now you are quite perfect."

"May I have some sherry, please."

He ordered her drink and said, "Take them off. I've never believed that you need them."

"I have very long sight," she said, but put them away.

"I was thinking, when I saw you come in, that for weeks and weeks when I first knew you, I never saw you in anything but that VAD uniform and the blue cloak. Never let it be said that fine feathers don't make fine birds."

"I never do say it."

"That," he said reminiscently, "was a damned ugly uniform."

"I know. Yet even the very plainest VADs caught husbands."

"It's always like that in a war. People get married thinking they won't live long enough to have to face the awful consequences. What will you eat?"

"You pick it. I didn't know you were in England."

Colonel Riebeck chose the lunch with the help of the head waiter who had appeared in person to take his order, as indeed head waiters all over the world usually did. "I'm not really here," he said then to Jenny. "Even unreally I have only till tomorrow morning. But that gives us loads of time to amuse ourselves."

"What a pity," said Jenny sweetly, leaning back to let the waiter put the food in front of her. "If I'd only known. But I have a charity tea—very tedious—and a cocktail party at the American Embassy."

"The only cocktails I really like are vodka martinis," said Riebeck, "and I don't like to ask for vodka at the American Embassy. They always give one such a sad look. Let's compromise. You ditch charity and we'll both ditch the Yanks."

"I don't know embassies considered you *salonfähig*."

"Oh you know what embassy people are like. I've known some of them since my own Legation days in Vienna and they will go on inviting me, unless of course I do something dreadful like reading the *New Statesman* or not recognizing the wife of the fifth undersecretary at Harrod's. And when I die they will all put on top hats and come to my funeral. Embassies are like that."

"Well, you can ditch them if you like. I can't. I most particularly promised the Ambassador I wouldn't."

"Oh my dear, American Ambassadors!"

"Well, this one happens to be rather a dear, though he will call me Lady Jenny. Anyway, I promised."

"What did you tell Reggie? Verbatim, I mean."

Jenny shrugged. Riebeck said, "Never mind, I'll tell you. You said, 'Reggie darling, this is the most frightful bore, but an old friend of Amby's is in London and one must do the civil. I couldn't be sadder.' "

Against her will Jenny giggled.

"I knew it," said Riebeck. "Now, you see there is the telephone over there. You go and ring up the American Embassy, and you say, 'Darling Ambassador, this is the most frightful bore but—' "

"Oh, do stop."

"Don't interrupt. I'm just coming to the most interesting part."

"Sorry."

"This is the most frightful bore, but Colonel Riebeck has come to London especially to seduce me, and since he has to leave again very early tomorrow morning. I don't believe I'll have time to come to your party."

"I don't think you're a bit funny."

"No? All right, I'll try again and make it more acceptable. Sup-

307

pose you say, "Darling Ambassador, Colonel Riebeck, who has no business being in London at all, has most inconveniently arrived on the afternoon of your cocktail party. He claims that since I kissed him five months ago in Cornwall he has been completely unable to keep his mind on his work, and that if he does not get his mind back to his work the West will lose the cold war.' That ought to appeal to him."

"Is it true?"

"That the West will lose the cold war? Of course not."

"The other."

He stopped laughing at her and said, "Yes."

She looked rather frightened at that. He put his hand in his pocket and brought out some change which he held out to her. "Make your phone call."

"All right."

When she came back he put out his cigarette and got up.

"Come. I've got my car."

They sat next to each other in the car, he not touching her, with both hands on the steering wheel and his eyes on the traffic. Not the way to travel to an assignation, she thought wryly.

She had no clue to him.

After Cornwall she had lived with the memory of his physical presence, knowing he would have to come back, waiting without impatience and without doubt.

His present attention to the traffic was an insult. What was traffic at a time like this?

The lines at the corners of his eyes deepened. He turned and smiled at her. And now that she had his attention she was not sure she wanted it. One does not, even by a lover, wish to have one's thoughts read like a primer.

She frowned and laughed and finally fell back on conversation. "What about Alphonse?"

"I gave him the day off."

"Did you indeed."

An American car, the size of an ocean liner, cut in front of them and Riebeck, with an oath, turned his attention back to traffic.

At the apartment he led the way down the hall and opened a

door for her. Jenny stepped into a sunny room, her eyes at once caught and enchanted by the glowing spectrum of Canella's Paris street scenes on the wall.

"How nice," said Jenny.

"They were Vic's. He was the most homesick soul on earth away from Paris."

All the luxury was on the walls; the Canellas and the Messina captain. For the rest there was a battered desk, an overflowing bookshelf, and a very narrow, monastic looking, and probably uncomfortable bed with a brown corduroy cover.

"This was the room Vic used," Riebeck said. "When I moved in with him it had the only bed in the apartment. I am rather attached to it . . . Oh, damn the phone. Cook, I told Lionel I wasn't at home. Tell them I've left the country. In that case I have certainly left the country. Oh all right, tell me about it."

Jenny, to show that she was not listening, walked over to the bookshelf and studied the titles. Proust and the *Princesse de Clèves*, Brantome, Moltke and Prince Kraft, Housman, Kipling, Jeremy's Famagusta book and poems, her La Rochefoucauld which she had sent him so long ago; the jumble of an insomniac's bedside shelf.

"Don't ring me up again because I'm leaving the phone off the hook," said Riebeck and rang off. "Idiots!" He went to the window and lit a cigarette. He stood looking down into the sun-flooded street as if he were alone. She was amused by his temper and said smiling, " 'He that hath business and makes love doth do such wrong as when a married man doth woo.' "

Riebeck smiled at her briefly and turned back to the window.

"I do like your room," said Jenny, and was uncomfortably aware that she had already told him.

"Thank you for coming to see it."

He disconcerted her, standing by the window without apparently any further wish than to have her here with him. She wished she knew a little more about the manner in which men conduct love affairs. She had never bothered to find out, always having found the men who fell in love with her pallid and uninteresting. It occurred to her now that she had for years unconsciously compared them with Riebeck in her mind.

"Could I have a cigarette too, please," she said, merely to say something.

He gave her one and lit it for her. Then he went back to his perch on the window sill, and now she made no further attempt at conversation. She could not see him very well, for he leaned against the window frame and when she looked at him the sun blinded her eyes. She wondered if he was laughing at her or at both of them. He was a restless creature, usually, more apt to pace a room than to sit down, but now he was still, like a cat with the sun on his back. Had he arrived at serenity, or merely indolence? Serenity, assuredly, for she too felt herself growing quiet and thought with derision that they would become transfixed like Donne's lovers without having first loved.

"And what," she said, "are you thinking of?"

He came to life at once, getting up with a shake of the shoulders, throwing out his cigarette and laughing. "I do apologize. How boring for you. I was thinking about you. I've loved you for so long, Jenny. I can't say since I first saw you because I wasn't seeing very straight, but a long time nevertheless. Since the night you gave me dinner at Allanbank House, I suppose, and you looked so like a Snow Queen. And all that time I knew I could not have two masters; you and my work, and I knew that I preferred my work. I loved you so much that for fifteen years it seemed quite enough to live in the same town with you and to see you now and then. Even in Cornwall I believed I could make a run for it and be safe. Even today I still thought I could use you as a cure—homeopathy, is it—"

"Hair of the dog," Jenny suggested spikily.

"To have you and get it out of my system. But when you walked into the Richelieu I knew how much I had lied to myself. I love you and there is, I am afraid, no cure for that."

She thought how strange it was to hear love spoken of like this, as a self-sufficient thing, requiring nothing from her. He was the first man who had ever loved her without begging to know that she returned his feelings, who had not even asked her what her feelings were. Yet she too had known without talk, and it dismayed her to hear what she had known for years. What is spoken in love cannot be retracted. She felt that her life had been kicked into new ways without her consent and she was frightened.

He had asked nothing of her and had left her free to act for herself. If she spoke the truth it would an unconditional surrender, and all the safety she had built round herself by her affectionate, unemotional marriage would be broken forever.

But there was no possibility of remaining outside. She loved him, and even more, at this moment, with the width of the room between them, she wanted him as she had never wanted anyone, with a rowel of pain in her body. This too frightened her, not for the future but the moment. The violence of it was too great and terrified her as if its end could not be joy but death. She said, "I am afraid."

He knew what she meant. He said, "Jenny."

Her eyes were as bottomless and dark as those Narcissus saw in the pool and loved and drowned. "Yes," she said obediently.

"It takes eight steps to cross this room." He held out his hand. "That is all the distance left between us. Come."

Afterwards they laughed, clinging together, shaken with laughter, lying happy, tiger-striped in the sun coming through the blinds.

"Damn damn damn," said Riebeck. "What am I to do with you?"

"You could just keep on with what you have been doing," said Jenny. After years of Sir Jonathan's polite conjugal advances, making love with a man who was not polite but had passion, skill, and experience, had proved a revelation.

"Well, naturally. But Jenny, I don't only want to do with you what I have so often done with someone else. In love one wants to make the extravagant exception. I want to marry you."

"Oh my dear, how nice. I would like that very much."

"But I don't see how I can. In my sort of job it simply doesn't work. I've seen it time and again."

Jenny said, "You could quit your job, couldn't you?"

What surprised him was not that she could suggest it. Women would suggest anything. What surprised him was the fact that the solution was simple, and that he had not seen it before. Let them keep their careful, unrocked boats, their humiliating negotiations in nine copies. He would have Jenny.

He began to laugh. "What a brilliant idea. It's something that wouldn't have occurred to me in a million years. I'll tell Partridge to go to the devil, and you shall tell Sir Jonathan—"

"Poor Jonathan."

"—and we'll get written about in the Sunday papers, and then you and I will become very respectable again and be married in the Caxton Hall. Then we will buy a yacht."

"Why?"

"Because with a yacht we can go wherever we like and if we invite boring guests by mistake we can throw them to the sharks and float away. Jenny—what is your name really? Jennifer?"

"Much, more worse. Guenevere."

"No," he said, "I like that."

"It was because of something in my grandmother's will. She was Guenevere, and she decided to leave all her money to the first Allanbank girl to be called after her. So I've got the name, but I also have ten thousand a year, which makes it bearable."

"Ten thousand," said Riebeck delighted. "My dearest, what nice presents you will be able to buy me when we are married."

"What would you like?"

"At the moment, nothing. But when I'm not in bed with you, I want a Vermeer. There were two in Baranyi Palace."

"Denham's going to have to sell his soon, he says."

"I know, that's what put it in my head. He told me last year that he couldn't afford the insurance on it anymore. I even played chemin de fer with him, hoping he'd lose everything he had left. Unfortunately it was the other way round. He won his insurance money and then some." He began to laugh again.

"What?"

"Nothing. I was just thinking of Partridge's face when I tell him I am leaving to get married."

Jenny knew London well in the early dawn, suspended in milk-white mist, because this was frequently the hour when she returned from night clubs or parties. As on all those other mornings she was tired and drowsy, but not even the least bit drunk, and she was tired with love, not with dancing and laughter and if the truth were told, frequent boredom.

She stole a sidelong look at Riebeck, seeing under the lights and shadows a face that disclosed nothing, scarred fingers on the steering wheel. It was again that absorption in doing something, one thing, that had annoyed her on the way to his flat. Damn him!

He was allowing her her silence, the one man in a thousand who did not ask: "What are you thinking?"

(Months later he told her, remembering: "Your silences often disconcerted me. Women always chatter. But then you put out your hand.")

She held out her hand tentatively, wondering whether he would notice at all. But his fingers closed on hers tightly, until they hurt. Both felt punished without quite knowing why, but beginning to realize that each had the habit of exclusiveness behind which they might many times in the future retreat from one another without wishing it.

She remained silent, knowing from long experience that a too personal remark would never get past his armor of nonsense and barbed politeness. He said nothing either, but keeping one hand on the wheel, put his arm around her drew her to him. Reconciled at once she fell asleep against his shoulder and awoke to see a crane holding two wheels into the sky, a row of trees, very still and dark against the dawn, and neatly ranged jets at the edge of the airfield.

"I don't know where I shall be," Riebeck said. "I'll try and telephone you, and the War Office will send my letters on whenever possible."

"All right. Darling, I've just realized. How disappointing. Why are you in uniform? I always thought you did your work disguised as a dustman or the man that fixes the electric meter."

"Oh, certainly," lied Riebeck, unwilling to shatter her illusions. "But I am stopping off to see General de Gaulle, and while he dislikes me excessively in British uniform he would dislike me even more dressed as a dustman."

An RAF pilot came up and saluted. They bent over a map together and spoke of the weather. Riebeck said good-by to Jenny absently, and the pilot gave a polite little half-salute. Be courteous to women but no more. She was in a world of professionals now and might as well not have existed. Riebeck walked away, his coat slung over his shoulder. He did not look back.

XX

He rang her up the moment he arrived in Paris, waking her from sleep only to ask, "My darling, *comment va tu?*"

Jenny said she felt like Madame Récamier.

"Why?"

"Because she was faithful to a rather dull husband for years and years and found it so worth while when she met Chateaubriand."

"I never liked Chateaubriand. A dreadful show-off."

"He was rather awful."

"I must go. Good-by, my dearest."

That Jenny had not come home all night did not disturb Sir Jonathan. The hours she kept were not the kind a surgeon could share and they were accustomed to spending their evenings apart. But when in the morning he had his kiss refused with a murmur about spoiled make-up, he guessed instantly that Jenny was in love.

He did not mind this, but he hoped with all his heart that it would not upset his life. He did not love her himself, but she was beautiful, charming, and rich; all that man could want in a wife. She traveled a little more than he liked and her clothes were too sophisticated to his English eye, but no woman is perfect and Sir Jonathan was prepared to make allowances.

Whether this pleasant marriage would continue while Jenny discreetly had an affair of which he need take no notice, or whether everything would shatter into divorce, Sunday papers, and chambermaids from Brighton hotels would depend, he knew, not on Jenny but on the lover. Someone like Jeremy would upset their lives without regard because no relationship that did not involve either passion or hatred meant anything to him. Not for a moment did Sir Jonathan suspect Jeremy himself. He had known both Jenny and Jeremy for a long time. They liked each other without illusion, championing their faults as virtues to a gullible world. Nothing could be less like love.

Someone like Colonel Riebeck would be more interested—the French being, Sir Jonathan thought, a practical people—in maintaining an established order. He did not really suspect Riebeck either. Love does not take that long to make itself known. That two people might for fifteen years build a protective wall of duties and pleasures only to kick it down one day after lunch as a child kicks over a castle of sand, Sir Jonathan could not believe. He never quite believed in people who did not fit into patterns. He merely, one by one, at dinner parties and in night clubs, put Jenny's friends in the role of Jenny's lovers. Many of them were in love with her, but it was plain that they had no success. For a while he suspected Larry Leigh, who was handsome and romantic if a little dull. But Larry Leigh went to Paris to make a film and Jenny remained in London, quite content.

Still puzzled, Sir Jonathan congratulated himself on his wisdom in having kept silence. No talk of divorce sullied his house. For three months Jenny expressed no desire for travel. His marriage had never been more pleasant. And still there was no lover.

Jenny's mail was not revealing. She and Jeremy had always exchanged endless letters. Long letters from Colonel Riebeck were nothing new either. Sir Jonathan had never objected to them for he did not think Jenny could read them. He forgot that she had a French father and was used to French handwriting. Occasionally there was a letter scrawled in the childish hand of Larry Leigh. His letters were of the "I take pen in hand" variety. Sir Jonathan could not believe that Jenny, who liked writing and receiving long amusing letters, could passionately love a man who had never developed a decent prose style. At least he hoped not. Americans had such a horrible passion for divorce.

Then Jenny decided that she must go to Paris because she hadn't a thing left to wear. That she decided this on a day when a letter postmarked Paris had come from Larry Leigh was a blow to Sir Jonathan. He looked at her bursting closets and said "But Jenny—"

"You don't want me to walk around in rags, darling."

Sir Jonathan said the danger did not seem to him imminent.

Jenny picked up her huge white poodle and appealed to him.

"We simply must go to Paris, mustn't we, Panache?"

Panache, who like most poodles was very bright and knew exactly which side his bread was buttered on, barked affirmatively.

"There Jonathan, you see."

"One day you will be looking for that damned hound in vain and there will be sausages for dinner—"

"Poor Panache. I bet he'd taste delicious. So, Paris tomorrow."

This was Jenny's way. She could be perfectly content for months going about her London pleasures, then she would suddenly decide that she simply had to be elsewhere. One moment she said Paris or St. Tropez, the next she was at Victoria Station, waving to friends.

Sir Jonathan, who had over the years grown accustomed to her abrupt departures, now forgot all about them and could only think that Larry Leigh had begged her to come.

He said, "I have some people to see in Paris, so I could come with you, or better, follow you in a day or two. There isn't anything here that can't wait at the moment."

"Darling, how lovely. I'll wait for you and we can go together."

"No, you go on ahead," said Sir Jonathan, who knew his limitations and did not want Jenny, who enjoyed the boat train, to see him in the humiliating condition to which sea voyages, no matter how minor, always reduced him.

"All right, darling," said Jenny, knowing that her husband was ashamed of being sick on boats, and left by herself the next morning with no other motive but clothes. She had not heard from Colonel Riebeck for weeks and did not know where he was. She spent much time in the rue Montaigne and went for long walks along the rue de Rivoli and rue de la Paix, this being the essential Paris to her. She dined one night with Larry Leigh at a rather grubby place full of film actors and the next at the American Embassy, which bored her even more than the film stars. Still, once Sir Jonathan arrived it would be dinner with surgeons, and that was the worst of all.

She lunched once with the Duchess de St. Leger, who mentioned all names save one. From the moment she had arrived in Paris her telephone had rung incessantly with invitations and she was glad when her husband arrived. Sir Jonathan was a decorative escort, who had managed to grow into his knighthood. His hair had since that honor turned silver at the temples, his face had become more lined and more distinguished, until he was the very picture of what Hollywood expects an English knight to be. That he was a fraud he admitted only to Jenny, who enjoyed his performance.

"I am so glad to see you, darling," said Jenny when he came to the hotel, "though you do look rather like the inside of an artichoke at the moment. I'm lunching with Larry. Will you come too? I'm sure he'd adore it."

Sir Jonathan, resenting the reference to artichoke hearts, though he knew it to be no exaggeration, said, "Good God, Jenny, don't mention food to me. I shall lie down and drink a large glass of neat whisky."

Jenny poured him a whisky from his traveling flask into a tooth glass and left him with an affectionate kiss.

It was a good half hour before Sir Jonathan began to feel well enough to worry about something besides the fate of his breakfast kippers.

Lunch with Larry Leigh. Damn the man and his handsome actor's face. Damn Jenny too. She was old enough to ask more of a lover than that, to want a person, not a picture. Women! Idiots!

Leigh was probably telling her at this very moment that they could not continue like this, that she must divorce her husband and marry, while their passion lasted, him.

Jenny's admission that she was lunching with Leigh meant nothing. About things that mattered she was a chronic truth-teller. People like that are much rarer, fortunately, than chronic liars. To them the truth is not a virtue to be used with discretion. It is merely the simplest way. They are too lazy and too indifferent to invent the soothing lie. If Larry Leigh was her lover, Sir Jonathan had only to ask her and she would say: "Yes, darling," with no effort.

Sir Jonathan got up, combed his hair, and went downstairs. Jenny and Larry had unimaginatively lunched at the Crillon and had only a moment before finished and decided to go for a walk. Sir Jonathan, aware that he was not behaving like a gentleman and bogus enough to be bothered by it, followed them.

They walked aimlessly, talking, it seemed to Sir Jonathan, with great affection. He was not close enough to hear that in most unloverlike fashion each talked without listening to the other; Larry about the Cahiers de Cinéma and Jenny about Dior.

Colonel Riebeck, after a grueling job and a miserable journey, had arrived in Paris the day before, had fallen into bed and had slept for twelve hours. He had eaten lunch with Albertine and gone to see Latour, who had patted him on the shoulder and arranged for him to fly back to London early next morning. Riebeck would gladly have taken a commercial flight at once, but after all the trouble he had had for the last fifteen years getting any kind of service and cooperation from the French air force, he did not think it wise to refuse even so small a favor as a lift. He returned to the Hôtel de Baro, decided that telephoning Jenny would make it ten times worse not to be able to see her at once, and restlessly went out for a walk.

They recognized each other across the bridge with the presbyopia of lovers who need no more than the angle of a shoulder, the movement of a hand for recognition. Colonel Riebeck stopped his aimless strolling and walked quickly toward them. Jenny caught her breath in mid-sentence.

"What's the matter?" asked Larry.

"Nothing. Oh, look, there's Colonel Riebeck. Funny how one always runs into people in Paris."

"Where?"

"There, across the bridge."

"So it is. You have awfully good eyes."

"I'm a little long-sighted. I really ought to be wearing spectacles."

Larry smiled at her thinking how very beautiful she was, wondering why, with a face like hers, she had never thought of going into films. "Jenny, why haven't you ever—Oh, hello, Riebeck."

"Hullo, Leigh. How do you do, Lady Falconer?"

"How do you do, Colonel Riebeck."

"Are you in Paris for long?"

"I don't know. And you?"

"Not long, till tomorrow morning."

"Oh."

Incapable of further speech that was not the language of love, they gazed at each other until with sudden tact Larry Leigh looked at his watch, and throwing himself into the part as if an Academy Award depended on it, exclaimed, "Good grief, Jenny, I was supposed to meet a producer at the Ritz bar half an hour ago. Will you forgive me if I run?"

They forgave him wordlessly, hardly knowing he had gone.

"Jenny."

"My dear."

"I've never kissed anyone in public before."

"Neither have I."

He laid his scarred hands along the sides of her face and smiled at her. "You are going to be kissed in the middle of the Beaux Arts Bridge for all of Paris to see."

"How nice," said Jenny.

Sir Jonathan, with a great sigh of relief, threw his cigarette into the water and whistling an operetta tune, walked off in search of lunch.

"I had no idea you were in Paris," said Riebeck. "Where are you staying?"

"At the Crillon. Jonathan is with me."

"Damn. And in me you have chosen the one Parisian who does not own an apartment for the *petite amie*. I usually stay with my aunt."

"In a way I am glad to hear it. But it makes it awkward just now."

"Yes, doesn't it. My dear, would you mind a Left-Bank hotel very much?"

"You mean one of those—darling, I'd simply adore it. I've never been inside one and I've always wondered what they are like. It's so educational, being in love with you."

Riebeck laughed. "I am glad that under all that veneer you are quite vulgar."

"Jonathan hates it."

"Never mind Jonathan. I don't like Jonathan."

"How can you not like Jonathan?"

"Well, I just don't. I daresay I shall again, presently, when you are married to me and not to him."

"Are you tired?"

"Is this a complaint?"

"No. But you do look tired, you know."

"I was on one of those filthy jobs where one's always cold and hungry and dirty until one can't remember ever having been warm, clean, or in love."

"Were you successful?"

"Yes, insofar as one ever is."

"Were you coming to London to see me?"

"Partly. Mostly work, I'm afraid."

"I've bought some lovely clothes. Wait till you see."

"What else have you been doing?"

"Dinner with Larry, dinner at the embassy, the usual stuff. Lunch with Katalin, who gossiped about everyone but you. You haven't quarreled, have you?"

"No," said Riebeck, a little uncomfortably. "The fact is, we've sworn eternal friendship."

To give up his old, delightful mistress for Jenny had not been Colonel Riebeck's intention. A mistress who has given pleasure for thirty years (of admittedly erratic cohabitation) might be assumed by even so restless a creature as Colonel Riebeck to be a permanent fixture. The others, casual, effortless girls who kept his bed warm in London, Berlin, or Vienna he would willingly sacrifice to love. But Katalin de St. Leger was a different matter altogether.

Not until he was on the plane from London to Paris did it even occur to him to wonder how he felt about Katalin. Then he knew instantly that he had a great deal of affection for her and not the faintest wish ever to sleep with her again. He hoped she would not be temperamental about it.

He took her to dine that evening at the Tour d'Argent, which was her favorite restaurant. She was beautiful still, with her black eyes in a white face, her black hair pulled back, her serenity and silences. She was like Jenny in that she never fidgeted and did not make conversation very often. Two loves have I—no, one love only, from now until he died. Not without derision did he acknowledge that, at the age of forty-eight, he was at last behaving like a romantic schoolboy. But it did not matter. Nothing, not even his own derision, could ever change what he felt for Jenny.

He said, "You are very beautiful, Katalin. I want to tell you something about myself, if you will play confidante for a moment."

"Dear Schani, what?"

"I'm in love, Katalin. Thank you for not laughing."

"My dear." She took his hand across the table. "Are you happy? I can see you are. I am so pleased for you. Who is it?"

"Jenny Falconer."

Too beautiful, too young a rival. "How nice," she said coolly.

He refused to acknowledge her lack of warmth. He hadn't done yet. He said, "I like you very, very much, Kat."

Her eyes widened, surprised and almost amused. "Are you trying to tell me that we've done, you and I. Yes, I can see you are. In a moment you are going to say you want us to be friends."

He knew that if he could make her laugh it would be all right. He said, "Yes Kat. Platonic friends."

Gratifyingly she saw the joke in this and laughed. "That will certainly be a new experience for us. Is it Jenny who wants you to do this?"

"Will you have a brandy?"

"Is it?"

"I wonder why one is always so willing to lie to people that don't matter to spare their feelings, but insists on telling the truth to friends even at the risk of hurting them. Shouldn't it be the other way round?"

"I see your years in the diplomatic service were not entirely wasted. You mean Jenny doesn't care but you do."

"If she did I would never find it out from her."

"And that puts you on the spot as an English gentleman. Schani, is this Monsieur de Nemours all over again?"

"I don't think so. If it is, may I slink back and have you bind up my wounds?"

"I wouldn't be surprised. I am a creature of bad habits. Come home with me and say hello to Jean."

"How is he?"

"Incredible. He had pneumonia last winter and pulled through magnificently. Then he had a heart attack while he was celebrating his ninety-third birthday in some bagnio in Tangiers and they gave him a battery to put in his pocket that makes his heart go on beating. And now he has given up smoking because his doctor says it gives one lung cancer."

"Give me my cigarettes, Jenny. They're in the left-hand pocket."

"Were you asleep?"

"Not really. I was thinking of my godfather." He told her about St. Leger's ninety-third birthday party.

"He sounds horrible. You had a birthday too while you were away. Did you forget?"

"I think I did."

"Well, I didn't. I bought you a present. It's at your flat in London."

"What is it?"

"You'll find out when you get home."

"Don't be so mean."

"Denham's Vermeer."

"Jenny! Oh my darling, how nice of you. I can't tell you how much I've wanted it. It must have been fearfully expensive."

"Not at all. When I play chemin de fer I don't lose."

"You wretched creature. I love you so much I could go right through Sade's list in *Les 120 jours de Sodome*. Six hundred, I think it was."

"Good heavens."

"Some are highly innocuous, like pushing girls in swings. Sade was easily pleased in many ways."

322

"I expect they're grounds for divorce in England."

"I expect they are. 'Your ludship, my husband is funny in bed.'"

A long time later Jenny said, "I've just remembered. Your aunt, Madame de Valterre, has invited Jonathan and me to dinner."

"Good Lord," said Riebeck, truly shocked for once, "don't you ever think about anything but your stomach? As a matter of fact I'm supposed to dine there myself. The two empty chairs will be very compromising. Do you mind, my dearest?"

"No. I love being compromised by you. But all the same I would like to go to the dinner. The Valterres have the most marvelous cook."

Riebeck returned to London the next morning and Jenny flew back with her husband a few days later. Outwardly they changed little. They hardly saw more of each other now than they had before. It was their act of faith to behave as if there were no hurry, knowing that they would have the rest of their lives together. They threw their confidence on the future, putting it upon its honor.

Their days were filled with delightful incident; the unexpected telephone call, the chance meeting, the unpremeditated act of love. Sometimes they walked in the rain, true London lovers at last, amphibians, pushing streaming strands of hair from their eyes and kissing with rain-washed lips. But such meetings were rare.

They did find time for endless talks on the telephone. Knowing how much Riebeck liked to laugh, choosing for his friends always those people who could push him past his own *bon sens* into unreflecting, exhausting schoolboy laughter, and knowing her own sense of humor to be of a quiet and rather literary turn, she ransacked her friends and relations for his amusement. She had a large and eccentric family at her disposal and friends who often fell into comedy by sheer accident. Jeremy was of course marvelous. One afternoon, finding her in tears over Keats' last letters from Italy, he had told her brusquely: "Cheer up, he would have been dead by now anyway."

But now, too, Riebeck found himself on occasion overcome by a vehement and destructive jealousy of, of all people, Sir Jonathan.

By nature a bridge burner, but also well aware of the precarious nature of his existence, he did not dare to burn Jenny's bridges as well.

Jenny frankly preferred Sir Jonathan to having no husband at all. Husbands make useful escorts, and are especially valuable to serve as excuses for not doing what one doesn't want to do. ("I should have loved coming on your committee for half-caste lepers, Lady Alastair, but Jonathan's forbidden me to do any more committees." "We would have adored to spend the week end with you at Discomfort Hall, but Jonathan has to be at the hospital.") Jenny had no intention of burning so useful a bridge until she had a new one. How soon that was going to be was entirely up to Colonel Riebeck.

When Jeremy Tyrell came to London, Riebeck took him off to the Richelieu, where they were given the table under the largest, most vulgar chandelier in town.

"I just know it's going to fall into our soup one day," complained Jeremy.

Riebeck ordered lobster a l'Américaine and Montrachet. Jeremy asked for steak and kidney pie. The head waiter tottered. Even the great Cardinal in his portrait on the wall seemed for a moment to loose his composure and turn pale.

"Have some kidneys in Madeira," suggested Riebeck.

"All right. And lots of beer. I'm thirsty."

"Next time I take you to lunch we'll eat at a British Restaurant," said Riebeck.

"Do you know what happens to those poor lobsters? They are quartered alive, like traitors."

"Yes, it must be terrible to be a lobster," Riebeck agreed, but did not change his order to something more humane.

"So tell me all your news," said Jeremy after they had been served their lunch. The wine waiter, who had a strong sense of what was fitting, had ignored Jeremy's request for beer and had given him a Pommard of a not very good year.

"How do you know there is news?"

"I can smell it," said Jeremy. "Whenever there is a good piece of gossip in the air my nose starts to twitch."

"How interesting. Very well then, here is your gossip. I am going to resign my commission and marry Jenny."

Jeremy, who had begun his lunch with five double martinis, put his head in his plate and howled with laughter. He laughed until every outraged eye in the restaurant had come to rest on him, then he wiped his eyes and sat up again.

"I knew it," he gasped. "I knew it the day I met you at the office. I knew you were going to make a phenomenal ass of yourself."

"I think," said Riebeck, laughing too, "that you are being offensive."

"No, I am delighted. Please consider that this is the first time that I have ever seen you behave like a jackass, and that nothing so delights us ordinary mortals for whom life is one long pratfall as seeing our betters slip on the banana skin now and then. Besides, I don't believe it. You in a haystack with Jenny, certainly. That was plainly ordained since you were a king in Babylon and she a Christian slave—"

"Please curb your tongue."

"But you resigning your commission, never. Not for all the haystacks in the world."

"Why do you have this fixation about haystacks? You sound like a boy scout."

Jeremy was indignant. "I have not been in a haystack with a boy scout since I was twelve, and then it was a scout master."

"You didn't even invent that. You read it in the *News of the World*."

"They get their stories somewhere."

"If it is from you, that explains a good deal about it. Look, skip the haystacks for the moment. I'm forty-eight years old and I've had far more than my fair share of sex. It's fun but in this case it was not my motive. (And yet he had traveled across a continent because of a kiss on a Cornish beach.) Otherwise, why would I bother to get married?"

Jeremy expressed incredulity in such terms that Riebeck, annoyed with him for once, said, "Do stop, Tyrell. I have not told anyone else and at this point I regret very much having told you."

Jeremy was immediately contrite. He apologized handsomely and said, "Please tell me about Jenny and you. I cannot conceive of anything that would make you give up your work."

"Why? It is not my lifetime occupation. I did it as long as it was the thing I wanted most to do, and a few years longer from sheer inertia, I think. I have given the duty side of my life its head far too long. From now I am going to have fun."

Jeremy snorted. "Fun! It hasn't struck me that in the exercise of your duty you have ever neglected to cultivate your garden."

"One does one's best. But it wasn't all that much of a garden."

Jeremy said, "You are determined to be a fool. No one can or should deflect a man from such a noble purpose. *Vale*."

"I have not gone yet."

"No," said Jeremy, "you haven't, have you."

Jenny brushed her hair, fitting perfectly into the setting of a scene already laughably accurate, a scene occurring in every drawing-room comedy she had ever seen, when the husband, suave, witty, preferably in evening clothes, reveals to his wife without rancor that he has for some time been aware that she has a lover. The wife, usually in a gorgeous negligee, brushes her hair, probably for want of good lines, which in this particular situation all go to the husband.

They had not long been home from a white tie dinner party, and Sir Jonathan was properly dressed for the occasion. Jenny hoped she would get through the thing without laughing out loud; Jonathan was indulging so lavishly, and quite unconsciously, in what Jeremy had once described as Noel Cowardly behavior. At the same time she was annoyed with him for bringing up what it was certainly his right to discuss.

She said, almost ruining the scene, "What do you want? A divorce?"

Sir Jonathan gave her his best Noel Coward smile. "If you wish to divorce me, you may do so, of course, but for my part I shall take no steps to end what has always seemed to me a delightful marriage."

"The thing is," thought Jenny, "he really thinks people behave like this." She said, "That's very nice of you, Jonathan. I don't want a divorce at the moment. Later, perhaps."

"Let's talk about it later, then. Possibly I shouldn't have brought it up at all, but I thought it might relieve your mind to know you needn't be hole and corner on my account."

"I thought I had been very hole and corner. Where did I slip up?"

"My darling, you can't kiss people on the Beaux Arts Bridge and not cause talk."

"My gentleman doll," Jenny thought. "You wind it up and it talks like a character in a drawing-room comedy. It used to amuse me. It's rather alarming that it doesn't any more."

She said, "You are behaving very badly, Jonathan."

"I thought I was behaving extremely well."

"People don't act like this. They either don't give a damn, in which case the proper course of action is silence, or else they get angry and shout or beat their wives."

"Oh, Jenny, we're not living in the dark ages. I'm sorry if this disappoints you, but I don't in the least want to beat you. However, I do want to please you, so tell me what you want, and short of branding you with a scarlet letter *A* and divorcing you I shall do my best."

She thought, "You can't get through because there's nothing to get through to. Might as well play it his way and not waste talk." She said, "I've always rather hoped someone would leap off London Bridge for love of me."

He thought this over. "Perhaps," he said, treating it as a serious proposition, as indeed in a way it was. "If I were really afraid of losing you—"

She turned round to face him, finding that talking to a reflection in the mirror was no longer enough. "You don't believe anything about it, do you. You think this is just a silly love affair and some sex between tea and cocktails."

"Oh, my dear, no, I know it is the *grande passion*. I'm not making fun of you, believe me. But knowing Riebeck as well as I do, that doesn't worry me in the least. You will see, I shall keep you by default."

XXI

"Her Ladyship," said Miss Davidson to Colonel Riebeck, "is upstairs playing the piano." She had been Sir Jonathan's housekeeper long before his marriage and liked to give the impression that but for her everyone in the Falconer household would starve to death. She did not consider piano-playing a reasonable occupation.

"Thanks, Davy, I'll show myself up."

"Thank you, I'm sure, sir. My legs aren't what they were."

Riebeck did not know what answer to make to this, though Miss Davidson paused for one. He made a sympathetic noise and hurried upstairs.

Jenny was playing something slow and beautiful—one of the Mozart fantasias, he thought, but could not remember which. He opened the door and said, "No, don't stop. Go on playing. I've come to say good-by once again and I don't want to. Play the slow bit again and then we'll go out and have lunch."

"Where are you going?"

"Vienna for a start and from there I'm not sure. Poland perhaps, but Budapest with luck. The natives are getting restless. I'd very much like to persuade Istvan Halyi to come out of Hungary. I could retire with an easier mind if he were safe."

"He's lasted well."

"Yes. If he were a general instead of a colonel he would have been purged years ago. Truly God looks after fools and children."

"He's neither, surely."

"I sometimes wonder. Jenny, you've been very patient with me. No, go on playing and don't contradict. You've never asked me when I would quit, and goodness knows there's been no reason for me to stay on for months now. It's simply that I never seem to come to a proper point of departure. But when I think how I would once have looked forward to an assignment taking me to Budapest and how much the whole thing bores me now because it involves leaving you, I think this is as good a time as any. Only I must get Istvan out. Perhaps it's greedy to want you both, but I do."

Jenny said nothing. She had stopped playing. She had known

from the start that she had no hold over him but his love and the gift he chose to make of his time. Unless he came to her with no attachment left behind he would not stay. That was why she had never asked him when he would leave the department, had never shown that she minded when he had to leave her or the even harder times when he was in London but too busy to see her.

He said, "Would you like me to promise that this is my last trip, that I will resign my commission the moment I get back?"

Jenny shook her head.

"But I want to. I promise, Jenny. I sound like a drunkard promising for the hundredth time never to touch a drink again. But I never promised before, did I? I do promise now. I want to be my own master finally. And I do not everlastingly want to be victimized by time. In an ordinary affair the clock is a reprieve, but now that I am in love I find time intolerable. We've never been together that one or the other of us didn't have an engagement ahead. What I want for us is unlimited time. I want to throw my watch away and never again care what time it is. Jenny, my dearest, a few more weeks and I'll throw my uniform in the dustbin and we will go to some sordid hotel in Brighton and commit adultery—really, your English divorce laws—and then we will be together for the rest of our lives. What is the matter? Are you crying?"

"I would like it very much if you would kiss me, please," said Jenny.

"Wait a moment while I lock the door."

"I have to leave in another hour or so. Do you want to come to the airfield with me?"

"Yes. You've lipstick on your face."

"Filthy stuff," he said, wiping his mouth with his handkerchief.

"I think when they say it's indelible they mean it won't come off the other person. Here, give me the handkerchief. Isn't it lucky you don't have a jealous wife who goes through your laundry."

"Would you like to think up a few more complications? Get dressed, darling. We have to go."

At the airfield there were always lots of people about; that was

329

why she liked to come. Partings were easier when they had to be formal.

She said, "Enjoy your trip. Shall I write you to the War Office or the Embassy?"

"The War Office. I may be moving about a lot. Jenny, I love you. I'll keep my promise. Here comes Flight Lieutenant Scott, studying the sky in a markedly tactful manner."

"Ah well," said Jenny, "here we go again." She held out her hand. "Good-by, Colonel Riebeck. Have a nice flight."

He bent over her hand. "Good-by, Lady Falconer. I enjoyed the lunch so much. We must do it again one day."

On October 23, 1956, the Hungarian secret police fired into an unarmed crowd of demonstrators in Budapest's Parliament Square, and precipitated Hungary into one of those incredibly brave, bloody, and futile revolutions which seem to be her particular fate. There are Black Books and White Papers about it now, and the records of the United Nations. One reads them with an indignation which suffers considerably from the bald fact that these things were permitted to happen, and that a great act of courage was allowed to become useless because it could not be matched.

Colonel Riebeck was in Vienna on October 23. He was not quite as surprised as everyone else appeared to be.

He rang up General Partridge and suggested that considering his fluent Hungarian he would be a good person to look into the matter.

General Partridge seemed unimpressed with Riebeck's linguistic qualifications, but he knew enough to bow to the inevitable and said Riebeck might go to Budapest if he could get across the border. "As an impartial observer," he said. "In civilian clothes, unarmed. If you disobey me I will have you court-martialed."

"But sir—"

"I don't care if every one of your cousins gets killed," said General Partridge. "You are not to get mixed up in anything. Is that clear?"

"There is only one cousin, sir, and he's a Communist colonel."

"That," said General Partridge, "is nothing to boast of."

"I know."

"I have no doubt it will all be exceedingly unpleasant," said General Partridge with rare understatement. "Good luck, Riebeck, and remember, no rocking the boat."

"What, me, sir? Certainly not."

He went to Bantain's apartment and changed into his working clothes: old grey flannels, a dark woolen shirt, and a disgraceful duffle coat that someone had forgotten in Bantain's jeep in 1947 and was considered the communal property of the Vienna office.

"Go in civilian clothes, unarmed," he quoted to Bantain. "What the devil did he think, that I would go in full regimentals with grenades hung from my belt? I shall need some press passes; better make it the *Times* and the *Daily Worker*. One or the other ought to get me in. Also a hammer and sickle pennant for the car. Hungarian money, frontier passes, driver's license, cigarettes, brandy—"

"And a partridge in a pear tree," Bantain muttered.

Riebeck knew all the illegal ways of getting into Hungary, but for the sake of speed he decided to bribe his way in. American dollars and American cigarettes got him through without much trouble at a frontier post which, according to Bantain, had reeked with corruption for years. He drove without further difficulty as far as the suburbs of Budapest. From there he was stopped every two minutes by young men with tommy guns who wanted to know where he was from. He tried France, England, America, and Austria, found that England was the most popular and from then on stuck to it.

The young men told him many mixed-up stories, from which only one fact emerged without contradiction; Hungarian students had prepared a list of demands and gone to demonstrate in Parliament Square, where they had been joined by women, children, workers, all unarmed, and had been shot at by the machine guns of the secret police.

Some said the tanks had opened the fire, others said not.

"What is the Hungarian army doing?" asked Riebeck.

The army, it appeared, had chosen a hesitant kind of passive resistance. They had not shot into the crowd. Some had gone so far as to hand over their guns to the students, but they had not taken part in the fighting either.

"How very odd," said Riebeck.

"They are under Russian orders, you see. And yet they're Hungarians. They don't want to kill their own people, and they're not equipped to fight the Russians. There isn't a single antitank gun in the entire Hungarian army. They're in an extremely awkward position."

"What about the officers?"

"Them? They won't do anything against the Russkis. Why should they?"

"And what are you going to fight the Russian tanks with?" Riebeck asked. "Tommy guns?"

"Will the English send help? The Americans?"

Riebeck made a great noise with his gears and avoided answering. Buda was quiet, though one could hear the shooting from across the river. Istvan Halyi was not at home, nor had Riebeck expected him to be. Janos, calling on the Virgin and all the saints, told him Istvan was at Kilian Barracks.

Across the river, in Pest, the signs of battle were already well marked; shell-pocked buildings and streets, the smell of cordite, overturned cars and, faintly over it all, but beginning to be noticeable, the smell of unburied corpses.

Riebeck's car was shot at impartially by freedom fighters and Russians, so he left it in a side street and walked to the barracks. He got lost several times because the streets he knew were barricaded and he had to go through narrow back alleys, but he finally arrived at the entrance only to be stopped by a child, armed to the teeth, and plainly longing to shoot him.

Making heavy weather with the little Hungarian he remembered from childhood summers spent at Hommages, Riebeck tried to explain that he wanted Colonel Halyi, but the heavily armed child only took his Hungarian for further proof that Riebeck was a Russian spy.

"Who is in charge of the barracks?" asked Riebeck.

"Colonel Maleter."

Riebeck remembered him vaguely from the underground fighting in '44. "Well, can I see him?"

"Certainly not."

"Oh, hell!" He began all over again, explaining that he was an English officer, that he was a cousin of Colonel Halyi, that, whatever side the armed child was on, it was his as well. "If you won't let me in, will you at least send someone for Colonel Halyi?"

"Certainly not," said the child again, when Riebeck to his relief saw a familiar face across the court and let out a delighted shout. "Palko!"

Palko, a cigarette dangling from his mouth and a gasoline bomb in his hand, had been talking to a tall, nervous civilian, probably a reporter. He turned and looked at Riebeck, narrowed his eyes and burst into a face-splitting grin. "By God," he roared, "Colonel Riebeck." He ran, gasoline bomb and all, toward him, pounded his shoulders, told the deflated child to save his bullets for the Russians, and took Riebeck away.

"What are you doing here, Colonel? What do you think of us? A nice mess we're in, *hein?* Are you still a colonel or are you a civilian now?"

"I am a colonel in disguise."

"Don't let it worry you. Look at me, a lousy major since '45. Me, the bravest soldier in the Hungarian army. You wouldn't happen to have an antitank gun, would you?"

"I haven't even a carbine. You might let me have one, Palko. Where is Istvan?"

"On the roof. He's teaching the kids to make these." He shook the bottle in his hand. "Gasoline bombs. Molotov cocktails. You know who taught us to make them. The Russkis. I'll bet they're sorry now. We haven't a single antitank gun, you know. But these will do. Have you ever used one?"

"Not for years. But I know how."

Kilian Barracks (still Maria Terezia Barracks to Riebeck) was crowded with civilians: shabbily dressed young men and women, bearing a variety of small arms that would not stop even a staff car, much less a Russian tank.

"They all came to help," said Palko happily. "I don't know how they learned we were in trouble, but they all came."

"I prefer to do my fighting with soldiers," said Riebeck.

"So do I, when there are any. Well, there's Istvan and Andy Nemeth and some of the others of the old crowd. And Colonel Maleter. He did give us a surprise, being such a good commie and all."

"My dear Palko, I remember when you considered yourself the bright red hope of the Hungarian Communist Party."

"I still do," said Palko seriously.

Riebeck laughed. He said, "Tell me, Palko, how do they get on, Colonel Maleter and Istvan?"

Palko shrugged. "The way the Esterhazys and the Maleters of this world always get on."

They climbed to the roof, and Riebeck saw the tall, lean figure of Istvan Halyi, still dressed in Russian uniform, holding a cigarette and a gasoline bomb in the same hand.

"The Russians won't have to send tanks," said Riebeck. "The way you people handle these gasoline bombs you'll all set yourselves on fire soon."

Palko, grinning from ear to ear, said, "Istvan, look what I found."

Istvan laughed, his crooked gargoyle laughter of entire delight. "*Servus* Schani. *Comment ça va?*"

"I might well ask you that," said Riebeck severely. "You seem to be in something of a mess."

They shook hands. "You couldn't keep away, could you?"

"Not when it's your mess."

Another officer came up, shouting for Palko. "Oh, there you are. Come on downstairs a minute."

With a quick look along Ulloi Street—a look Riebeck had begun to notice on everyone who came and went on the roof—they left. Ulloi Street was empty in the gray light of early morning. A Russian armored car lay in the middle, still smoking. Istvan came to his cousin's side and looked down too. Then he looked at the Petofi Bridge. "They'll be sending tanks next," he said.

"I'm only here as an observer, Istvan. I'm under orders not to shoot."

"So long as you're here."

"If you have time, tell me what's going on. It seems very quiet."

"Like the center of a storm. Come and sit down. We are waiting for the Russian tanks. Until they come we can talk. We have only had the armored cars so far, I don't know why."

They sat on the parapet and lit cigarettes. Istvan looked tired and very dirty. His uniform and hair were streaked with black grease.

"I've never seen anyone who could get dirty as quickly as you during a revolution," said Riebeck.

"It's from the guns we unpacked. We got them from the depot."

"So tell what happened. Why are you here? What are you doing?"

"I was here when it started, having dinner with Palko and the commandant of the barracks. I'm supposed to be teaching a course at the military college at the moment. Tanks, as a matter of fact. We wanted to discuss the riots of the afternoon and our position to them. You see, the brass hats, we knew, would side with the Russians, and that, we thought, would complicate things for us. Our minds were made up for us before we had a chance to talk very much. The Secret Police tried to take over the barracks. One of the soldiers saw them and raised the alarm. Some of the AVO men were killed, most of them escaped. They sent for me and we talked it over and decided that, since the fat was in the fire anyway, we might as well fight it out. That's about it. Maleter came round later and took charge."

"Surely that can't be the whole story."

"The rest was just twaddle. Give me another of those American cigarettes, Schani. I can never get any in Budapest."

Later Riebeck found out the part of the story Istvan had not told him. He spent the better part of one night talking to Palko and a young corporal who had been there when the AVO men were killed.

They had been killed on impulse; that is, no one had worried about the consequences until it was too late. Then they were very frightened. In a police state one does not kill the secret police with impunity.

They had not enough confidence in any of their officers to ask their help. They swore and they worried and then one of them, who had been in Istvan's regiment in Russia, said, "Colonel Halyi is here. We could tell him."

The younger soldiers were against the idea of bringing any officers into it, but the older ones, who had fought with Istvan in Russia, said he was all right. A sergeant fetched him from his dinner with a trumped-up message, brought him to the corpses of the AVO men, and told what had happened. They were all very frightened, even those who trusted Istvan.

Istvan listened to their story with a scowl, and then they were silent too, waiting for the verdict. Istvan said, "You damned fools, you should have killed them all. The ones who got away will come back with re-enforcements."

And then they all laughed, with nervousness and with relief because he was on their side, and with gratitude, because someone else had accepted the responsibility and had made their crime his own.

Istvan went back to his dinner and told the others what had happened. Most of the officers promptly went on sick leave. Palko and Andy Nemeth decided to stay and lend a hand.

Later the tanks came, and they stood watching them with choked breath. Then Palko, looking through field glasses, said, "My poor Istvan, I think it's Colonel Maleter."

Istvan, though he did not say so out loud, would almost have preferred the Russians. The enmity between him and Maleter was, as Palko and Karl Marx were agreed, a result of the class struggle. It was of long standing and not of Istvan's seeking.

And now Colonel Maleter arrived at the head of his tanks. Istvan went down to meet him, unarmed against the machine guns.

"I was told to put down an insurrection," said Colonel Maleter with the brisk efficiency that good party members can always bring to the necessity of turning machine guns on crowds.

Istvan's jaw came forward. Hopelessly reactionary, Istvan Halyi still thought of insurrections as caused by human beings, could never forget that the bullets of machine guns tore into living flesh and that each insurrectionist killed was a man finally and irrevocably robbed of his life. He forced himself to remain silent. The first answer that had come to him and now stuck in his throat was the kind his Esterhazy grandfather might have given an impertinent servant. He knew he must not make it. For the sake of the soldiers behind him he had to swallow it back. He said instead, "There are no insurrectionists here. Only Hungarian soldiers who have killed several AVOs."

"I was told nothing," said Colonel Maleter.

"Naturally," thought Istvan. No one ever was, and that way no responsibility could be fixed on the man who had given the order, so that the blame had to be taken by the one who executed it. Istvan smiled with sudden understanding, and Colonel Maleter smiled back.

Istvan told him what had happened. On the roof of the barracks behind him stood the soldiers and a handful of officers. Colonel Maleter listened in silence. When Istvan had finished he remained silent a while longer.

Then he said, "May I come inside?"

"You are welcome," said Istvan formally.

It was Colonel Maleter's idea to tear the red star from the Hungarian flag and raise the ragged green, white, and red standard over the barracks.

"They'll have our heads for this," he said cheerfully to Istvan.

"Yes, I know."

"Pity for that fine Esterhazy nose."

Istvan refused to be baited. "I quite agree with you," he said.

"How is it you're not running the show here?" Riebeck asked him.

"Can you see me do it?"

"Yes, very well."

"Schani, in a million years it would not have occurred to me to tear the red star from our flag. Can you really see me standing up and making a speech: 'Magyars, you are not counterrevolutionaries but fighters for freedom and truth—' I ask you."

"You are a terrible snob."

"Yes. With a barracks full of soldiers I could run it for weeks. But civilians have to have something to fight for; a torn flag, a speech with an inspiring sentiment, and I can't give them that. Maleter will do it very well."

Later the Russians had sent a single armored car. The Hungarians had been expecting tanks and they burned it out with gasoline bombs. "I was wonderful for morale," said Istvan. "They sent some more after that, about fifteen, and they managed to do a good deal of damage. They'll send the tanks next. I don't know why they didn't do so in the first place."

"Can you hold out?"

"Against tanks? Don't be an ass, Schani. You ought to go back to Buda. It isn't your fight, after all."

"Chump," said Riebeck amiably.

The tanks did not come until afternoon. Afterwards Riebeck always remembered the total silence. The barracks, the houses across the street, the Corvin cinema, and the cellars were filled with people, young men and women and boys, holding their inadequate weapons. And yet the silence was so complete that it appeared to blot up even outside noises. The first tank moved as if through cotton wool; it was like watching a film with the sound track cut out. In the silence Riebeck heard beside him Istvan's whispered, irresistible exclamation: "JAI!" It was a word he had not heard in a long time. The uncles used to hold their heads and shout "JAI" when the ecstasy of gypsy music became too much for them. Riebeck grinned at his cousin, but Istvan would not smile, would not by smiling belittle the fear all around them.

Tanks for those not familiar with them (and the fighters at the barracks were mainly civilians) are terrifying. They look like monstrous insects and they appear to be totally invulnerable. The silence was one of perfectly controlled fear.

But for Istvan, thought Riebeck, who knew all about tanks, this must be a moment not only of relief but of positive delight. For Istvan knew that tanks could be fought. He had spent the day moving from group to group, showing them how to fill bottles with gasoline and wet the wick, and later how they would light it at the last moment and which parts of a tank were the most vulnerable.

338

To play David to a powerful, oafish Goliath is exhilarating. But Istvan's Jonathan quailed.

The silence filled suddenly into a roar of anger and, looking into the street, Riebeck saw that besides the tank he had been watching coming from the Petofi Bridge there were several more, at all corners of the street. The barracks were surrounded.

This was the worst kind of battle to endure. Having to stand and take the barrage without being able to fight back; to be trapped here among the buckling walls and bleeding people. It was only a small comfort to watch Istvan standing patiently by the parapet with the small bottle of nitroglycerine held in his hand.

Finally their docility and silence drew a tank close enough to become a target, and now that they were able to fight, their fury was terrible and though they were wasting a great deal of ammunition they could not help but do a great deal of damage as well.

When it was over Istvan gave Riebeck a cigarette and grinned. "They'll send more," he said. "Planes too, I imagine. And the barracks seem none too steady."

"What will you do when they fall down?"

"I don't know," said Istvan. "I haven't thought that far ahead yet. I probably shan't be here anyway."

"Had enough already?" mocked Riebeck, who had.

"I've things to do, you ass. We can't just have people fighting here and give the Russians a free hand all over town. We thought as many of us as possible ought to be here until they'd fought back the first lot of tanks. Civilians are likely to panic at tanks, you know. But they've got the hang of it now. We'll go and organize the ones who're doing the street fighting."

"We who?"

"Me and Palko and some others. You, if you'd like."

"I'd like very much," said Riebeck, glad to have an excuse to get out of the barracks. But Palko, whom they met on the stairs, protested.

"Why, Palko?"

"I am sorry, Colonel Riebeck. At any other time we should be grateful for your help. But this is a Hungarian fight and has to remain one. The Russians will no doubt claim it was inspired by

339

capitalist imperialist warmongers, but they must not be allowed to get the proof. And, forgive me, Colonel, that is after all what you are."

Riebeck was staggered by this attack but found that he could not deny the truth of it. He was a capitalist, thanks to Uncle Rosenstil, and having fought in Indochina, no doubt also an imperialist warmonger.

"I'll tell you what," said Istvan, "borrow one of my uniforms and then no one will be the wiser."

It did occur to Colonel Riebeck that running about Budapest in a borrowed Russian uniform, organizing street fighting, would most definitely come under the heading of activities forbidden by General Partridge. But who, after all, was General Partridge? He accepted Istvan's suggestion with enthusiasm.

"You know, Palko," said Istvan consolingly, "when those Russian tanks have done with us not even Serov will be able to tell a rich imperialist warmonger like Schani from a poor comrade like me."

"A cheering thought," said Riebeck.

Before they left they ran across Colonel Maleter, who said "Hello, Riebeck," absent-mindedly, and then, pulling himself up, asked, "What the devil are you doing here?"

"Visiting Istvan," said Riebeck and walked away before Colonel Maleter could observe that this was hardy a suitable time or place.

All around them people were running and calling out: carpenters, doctors, nurses, masons, boys to collect empty bottles for the gasoline bombs, bee-busy with all the sudden paraphernalia of people who have against improvident expectation survived a disaster.

Istvan was saying something to Colonel Maleter about the Russian tanks, and Maleter said grimly: "They'll be back."

And back they came in ever grey executioner's dawn, sending finally their latest model tanks and their most destructive guns against a tumble-down barracks full of ragged people with homemade gasoline bombs as their only defense. But they never made them lower the green, red, and white flag with its ragged hole in the middle and they never forced a surrender.

For the next five days Istvan and Riebeck did whatever jobs suggested themselves: organizing road blocks from streetcars and park benches, transporting nitroglycerine in Riebeck's car through pocked and cratered streets from a laboratory to the barracks, teaching at every street corner the unorthodox methods of stalling tanks to groups of boys and young men. One day Riebeck heard a radio through the shattered window of an apartment. The broadcast came from Radio Budapest, and declared that the counterrevolution was over. Such counterrevolutionaries as had not yet heard the news had until two o'clock to lay down their arms. If they did not obey by then they would be punished.

"What do they mean, counterrevolution?" Riebeck asked Palko.

"How the hell should I know?" said Palko evasively.

Riebeck held his head and burst out laughing. "You chumps forgot to capture the radio station. Dear God, what a revolution."

Peter Halyi, who was fighting with the students and doing liaison between them and the army, came to make his report at the barracks that afternoon. Riebeck and Istvan happened to be there, and Riebeck met Istvan's son at last. Peter looked very much as Istvan had twenty-five years before, with the same long-boned, graceful body and the same high cheekbones and slanted green eyes. But he had somehow missed Istvan's gargoyle ugliness; he was tall and handsome and not very interesting.

Peter Halyi was nineteen, but he looked and acted as if he had traveled far and tasted all the pleasures of the world only to find them dust and ashes on the tongue. ("It's a pose," Istvan explained afterwards. "Or so I try to remember. Peter and his friends all act so sophisticated that they make me feel ten years old, but it's because they haven't done anything. Children in Communist countries lead very circumscribed lives, you know. There isn't much to drink, the theaters are boring, travel almost impossible, and for some reason known only to themselves they don't seem to care much for sex. I'm quite sure they're all still virgins, poor things.")

Riebeck had time to have a good look at Peter while he gave his report. The boy wore a badly made suit, carried a carbine, and had a dirty, blood-stained handkerchief wrapped around one hand.

"Schani," said Istvan, "this is Peter. Peter, your Uncle Jean."

Peter looked at Riebeck with the weary gaze of one who has experienced everything possible in the way of uncles and has found them to be but apples of Sodom.

"I am happy to meet you finally, Peter," said Riebeck, shaking hands. "And I shall be delighted to be your uncle or not, as you prefer."

"I don't really know," said Peter. "If you are not an uncle, what shall I call you?"

"His intimate friends call him Colonel Riebeck," said Istvan.

Peter permitted himself a fraction of a smile. "I think I'll let you be an uncle," he said.

"Good. What is the matter with your hand?"

"Nothing."

"With so much good will on your part, it will be blood poisoning by tomorrow. Do have a clean handkerchief at least."

"Ah," said Peter unkindly, "You are a real uncle after all."

"And a cigarette," said Riebeck.

For a moment Peter's sophistication deserted him; his green eyes blazed with delight. "American!"

It was Riebeck's last pack of cigarettes, but this was Istvan's son. He said, "Keep them."

Peter looked once again like one who has smoked hashish and can have no possible interest in Chesterfields. "No thank you, Uncle Jean. I am not a charity case, after all."

Riebeck put the cigarettes back into his pocket without further talk. Peter sulkily said good-by and went back to his students.

"I'm sorry, Schani," said Istvan. "He's badly brought up. My fault."

"His more likely. I do like him, Istvan. He's very much like you."

"That's one of our troubles. Because he looks like me I am everlastingly expecting him to be like me. But he isn't."

"He's a different generation, after all."

"I often wish he weren't," said Istvan unreasonably, and turned his head at the sound of shooting from the bridge. "I hope he has enough sense to dive into a cellar. He's a terrible show-off, you know."

"I told you he's like you," said Riebeck.

XXII

Istvan's rooms in Buda were bitter cold, and Colonel Riebeck hurried to get into bed. The nights were quiet now.

He had spent the day driving through the countryside outside town. Several times he had been stopped by Russian tanks. They were the latest model, T54s, immense and apparently unbreachable. They had almost finished encircling Budapest.

Palko snored loudly in the next room. He had returned to his own apartment a few days before for the first time since the fighting started, to find it filled with several families cooking smelly things in tins and having nowhere else to go. He had changed into a clean uniform and had come to Buda to beg hospitality from Istvan.

Palko was a colonel now, and longing with all his heart for a general's gold star, so that Istvan and Riebeck would have to salute him first. Oddly, at a time when general's stars flew like confetti during carnival, Istvan Halyi had kept his old rank. He had an office in the Defense Ministry and like everyone else was riding the whirlwind in three languages. Hungarian was his worst.

Rumor had it that Imre Nagy had offered him, amid many compliments, a promotion to general, and that Istvan had refused so charmingly that no one had noticed the insult until after he had left.

"They say," Palko had told Riebeck that evening, "that he did it to annoy Maleter."

"Nonsense. I'm sure they'd die rather than admit it, but I think they've rather begun to like each other."

"Yes, but Istvan wouldn't be above showing him all the same that Halyis do their duty for duty's sake, without thought of reward."

"Rubbish," said Riebeck.

"Not for any of the ridiculous reasons that have been given behind my back, you may be sure," Istvan had told him wrathfully when Riebeck had asked him why he had refused promotion. "It's very simple, really. I don't want anyone to become too interested in me. All this business of Mama having been an Esterhazy and myself a Horthy officer might just as happily remain in the background."

"But Maleter and Kiralyi were Horthy officers."

"Not with an Esterhazy mother."

"I doubt it will make much difference. Moscow is saying either way that it was the Horthy aristocrats. Besides, you're a Communist, aren't you?"

"I joined the party if that's what you mean."

Riebeck grunted.

"You think that's a terrible thing to have done, I know, Schani. But it was all quite different at the time, and having once given my word I couldn't see how to go back on it afterwards."

"You've done so now with a vengeance, haven't you?"

Istvan laughed. "Haven't I just."

Riebeck dug in his pocket for the disgraceful scraps of paper which made up his daily letter to Jenny. Letter was a somewhat grandiose word; some days he had found time for only a quick greeting, at others he had covered pages upon ragged pages which he could then not mail and continued to carry about in his pocket where they got increasingly more ragged and dirty.

He found a pencil about two inches long—his fountain pen having long since gone in barter for food—and on a sheet of paper stolen from the Ministry of Defense, he wrote:

Donath, Istvan, and I went for a drink to the Duna Hotel today. The newspaper men and such Intelligence people as always manage to be fairly comfortable even during the bloodiest revolution, are all holed up there. I'd hoped that owing to the correspondents I might be able to get through to London on the telephone. I very much wanted to talk to you and hear your voice, but in vain. Not that I had anything in particular to tell you. Only how very much I love you, and I would probably have been too priggish to say that on a public telephone.

I wish you could have seen Istvan—the press club's fair-haired boy—at the hotel. Wherever Istvan and one reporter get together these days you have a press conference. They all adore him because he doesn't speak Hungarian frightfully well, and of course neither do they. He had his picture in *Life*, did you know? Full page.

He wears his Russian uniform with the epaulettes and the partisan star, the only Hungarian officer who still does. No, General Maleter does too. They always ask questions about it.

"Colonel Halyi, why are you still wearing Russian uniform?"

"Haven't got any Horthy uniforms left," said Istvan equably.

"Why do you continue to wear the epaulettes and the partisan star?" Hungarian uniforms, as you have no reason whatever to remember, have the rank badges on the collar.

Istvan, jaw now well forward: "They were honorably earned."

Catalepsy among the British, at the ease with which we continentals use shame-making words, such as "honour."

The earnest young American: "Colonel Halyi, are you a Communist?"

Guffaws from the more sophisticated nationalities. Istvan, determinedly courteous: "I am a member of the party, yes."

"Would you elucidate that?" Really, these Americans.

"Gladly. One could not be an officer in the Hungarian army without being a member of the Communist party. I am, and always have been, a Hungarian officer."

"*Quod erat demonstrandum,*" said Palko helpfully and everybody had another drink.

Things are coming to an end here, tomorrow or the day after, and there is nothing anyone in Hungary can do about it. Still, they work as if there were no tomorrow, work heart-breakingly hard though they must know there will be no future when the results of that work will be needed. And you know, they still hope for help from us. Never before have I been ashamed of my nationality. Istvan has said nothing yet, but it is bound to come, and what will I tell him?

I am going to bully Istvan and Peter into coming to England with me. There can be no future but the firing squad for Istvan, and very little for Peter, who has fought with the students. So we shall be home soon and I shall see you again, which is really all I ever think about. Jenny, my dearest, Budapest really was a last fling. When one cannot keep one's mind on one's work at a time like this, it is a good moment to quit working. Let Partridge worry how he will replace me. I really know that no one is irreplaceable, but I can never work up any conviction about when it comes to me. *Au revoir, mon amour,* very soon I hope, J.

PS. Istvan is delighted about us and I do hope you will like him and Peter who is very young and disapproving, but whom I love simply because he is Istvan's son. Good night, my dearest love.

As he put the pieces of paper in a manila envelope from the Defense Ministry, Riebeck thought with annoyance that in his PS he had not stuck very closely to the truth. Istvan was indeed delighted that his cousin should marry someone so beautiful and rich as Jenny, but if this marriage entailed the end of his work, Istvan, like Jeremy, disapproved. Both seemed to feel that while they could put in a brief stint here and there, during the war or for a week of street fighting, or merely, like Tyrell, to occupy his time, he, Riebeck, had signed up for life, and nothing short of death would be accepted as an excuse for pulling out. While this was entirely irrational, he shared the feeling to a certain extent, which was the reason for his annoyance.

He was sleepy, but decided to stay awake, for Istvan, when he came back from work, liked a cup of tea (courtesy of a London *Times* reporter who had covered every major battle since Mafeking carrying his own blend, and very good it was). If Istvan found his friends asleep he slammed doors, switched light switches on and off without result, as their part of Buda was still without electricity, and undressed with sufficient noise to wake a hibernating bear.

Riebeck picked up the copy of *Life* that had Istvan's picture in it, and looked through it. He paused, smiling, at Istvan's photograph. It was captioned: *Hungarian Freedom Fighter*, and later in the year it was to win several first prizes.

Istvan was forty-nine years old, a professional soldier, a member of the Communist Party, a former Horthy officer and half an Esterhazy. Nothing could have been less like the average freedom fighter. But he was romantic, with his ugly, violent face and easy air of command. The photographer had caught him as he had come into the room and flung his carbine on a table. His hair was streaked with dust, his eyes were full of laughter, his fine strong hands clasped the back of a chair as if he were about to lift it and bring it down on somebody's head. He looked as if at any moment he might wreck the room, get drunk, make love, or with murderous accuracy fling a bottle of nitroglycerine at a Russian tank.

One could not fear for one so violently come into his inheritance, so unafraid for himself, but Riebeck, thinking of the Russian tanks around Budapest, and the Russian method of dealing with the leaders of revolutions, felt cold with apprehension and determined to drag Istvan to England by the hair if necessary.

Fully intending to stay awake, he fell asleep and wasted their last candle but one.

He was awakened by the backfire of Istvan's jeep and listened with increasing irritation to the noise with which Istvan slammed into the apartment, tried the lights and threw his belt and revolver on he floor. A boot crashed into a corner, and another.

"I am glad you are not a centipede," said Riebeck.

"Ah, *servus* Schani. I didn't know you were awake."

"One could hardly help it."

"Let's wake Palko and have a pot of tea. I'm frozen."

"Let Palko sleep. I want to talk to you."

"Oh, Schani, I know. They got your call at the Defense Ministry. I suppose it was bound to happen." Istvan lit the last candle and the primus stove under the tea kettle. "Christ, I'm hungry."

"Have a cigarette."

The tea was rather thin—they were down to the dust—but it was hot, and Istvan, hollow with hunger and overwork and worry, was calmed by it. "We ought to give some to Palko," he said.

"We'll save some in the thermos. He can have it for breakfast."

It was never easy to talk to Istvan about things he had no wish to discuss. He would give a graceful verbal wriggle like an eel and be out of your hands and off somewhere else. But now he said wearily, "It's no use, Schani. We all know it means the end and it won't be improved by talking about it. We're making all the arrangements we can, but they are ridiculous. This time we are really and truly lost." For just a moment he lost his temper. "Oh, but why would the West not help us, Schani. They've always made us believe they would."

"What, and rock the boat?"

"You rocked it fast enough in Suez."

"Suez was oil."

"Oh, of course. Careless of us not to have any. Damn, I didn't

347

mean to attack you about that, Schani. I'm sorry. Perhaps there is still some hope. The Russians are still negotiating, you know."

"Yes. How's it going?"

"Fine, Maleter says. They've gone back to Tokol tonight for dinner and to draw up the final details."

"They'll need a long spoon to sup with the Russians. What are the terms?"

"They want till January to clear out and they want the streets lined with cheering crowds when they do."

"I'm sure you could oblige. Hasn't it struck any of you as fishy that they agreed so easily? They were stalling for time, that's all."

"We're not idiots, Schani. We were stalling too. You see, we really did believe you would help us."

"That makes you idiots."

Istvan stood up, finished his tea, and began to unbutton his tunic. "What the devil do they want," he said impatiently. "We've kept the Commies in the government, Nagy and Kadar. They're a pretty lousy lot except for Maleter, you know. All we want is a free election. Is that so much to ask?"

"It is no more than your right," said Riebeck tiredly. "And yet, Istvan, I do not think there is a country that has those things and has not had to fight bitterly for them."

"We've fought."

"You've fought magnificently. That's part of your trouble. You don't think the Russians are going to accept such a walloping defeat, do you? It's too humiliating, like a boxing champion being knocked out by a three-year-old."

Istvan came to the door, cursing through a mouthful of toothpaste. He had forgotten once again that water runs on electricity.

"There's some left in the teakettle," said Riebeck.

Istvan went back to the bathroom. "There's still hot water," he said after he had gotten rid of the toothpaste. "Do you want a shave?"

"Had one, thanks. Your Cousin Pista has hot water at the American Legation, and he invited me over for a bath and a shave earlier today."

Istvan laughed. "Social life is getting very peculiar. It used to be strong drink people visited Pista for, and now it's water. These Legation boys really live."

"Blow out the candle if you've finished. It's the last one."

"Christ, this bed is cold."

"So are you. Please keep to your side of it. Istvan, what are you going to do when the Russians come back?"

"Fight."

"You can't win."

"I've been aware of that for some time."

"I want you and Peter to come to England with me."

Istvan lit a cigarette. His face was mulish and embarrassed.

"Thank you for Peter, Schani. But no for me."

"Why not?"

Istvan sighed, as one does at the questions of a dull but persistent child. "We've been all over that. You asked me once before and I said no."

"Give me a cigarette too. I'm not just asking you this time, I'm begging you. Please Istvan, as a favor to me, come home with me."

Istvan instantly lost his temper. "Shut up, damn you. It isn't fair."

Riebeck understood him perfectly and regained some of his composure. "Why not?" he said. "You did it to me once, when you asked me to leave the Nazis."

"I'm sorry about that. I always have been. It was a lousy thing to do and it doesn't excuse you. Anyway you said no then and I say it now."

"*Extra Hungariam non est vita*. Though when you remember that millions of people in this world manage to live outside Hungary quite happily, it makes you sit up and think."

Istvan laughed, crossly.

"Besides," Riebeck went on, "it hasn't been much of a life in Hungary these last years and it will be much less of a one when the Russians come back. None for you at all, that's certain."

Istvan yawned with ostentation. "I'm tired, Schani. Shut up and let me sleep."

"Suppose you stay in Budapest, then what? You'll fight until the ammunition runs out, which won't take more than a day or two, and then?"

"Then," said Istvan cheerfully, "they will line me up against a wall and shoot me. Goodnight Schani. Sleep well."

"They won't. They'll arrest you and torture you and brainwash you and when they've got you where they want you there'll be a big show trial where you, Colonel Halyi, the son of General Halyi of the Honved Hussars and the Princess Kira Esterhazy, will stand up, looking like a drooling imbecile, and confess to the most embarrassing bilge. And then they will hang you."

"Here we strangle people. But not officers. They will shoot me."

"And just how will you be helping Hungary then?"

"Dry up and let me go to sleep."

"As soon as you promise to come to England with me."

"What would I do in England?"

"You could work for me. Or you might buy a farm and raise horses again. You'd like that. Jenny and I could visit you week ends."

"Schani, use your head. I'm not really good at Intelligence and I don't like it. And as for the farm, apart from my pay I have no money at all now."

"I'll buy you a farm."

"Ha, so now I'm a charity case. I'd as soon be shot."

"Don't be so middle-class. I've got much more money than I can spend, and I'd like to spend it on you. I'd most certainly not squabble so vulgarly if the situation were reversed."

"It would serve you right if I took you up on it," said Istvan.

"Do. Please do."

"Schani, I can't."

"You're an obstinate bastard. I wonder whether they'll succeed in brainwashing you."

"I imagine they will. They usually do."

Riebeck tried another tack. "There is another consideration. When this is over there will probably be a government in exile. Certainly something will be done through the UN. Either way you would be able to do a lot more alive in England than dead in Budapest."

"Politics," said Istvan. "Gas. I won't accomplish a blessed thing, you'll see." He lit another cigarette from the end of his old one. "I can't leave, Schani," he said, and Riebeck knew that this was final, past argument. "One can't, when things are as fucked up as this. You wouldn't. You know you wouldn't."

"Of course I would. When things are impossible getting out is the only decent thing to do. Martyrs are the most useless people on earth."

"Is there going to be a sermon? Should I sit up?"

"No sermon. Only, staying in Budapest, waiting for the Russians to hang you, it's senseless. Istvan."

"And running away is cowardly."

"Very well, let's compromise. We won't run away. We'll stay as long as you can fight back. But when all is lost, when there isn't a chance on earth left, we'll leave. Peter and you and I. It'll be tricky getting out by then, I imagine, but if I can't get us across a mined border at my time of life my name is mud. Will you agree to that?"

"I suppose I'll never get any sleep otherwise."

"Do you promise then that when you have finished fighting you will come to England with me?"

"We'll walk hand in hand into the gathering sunset. I promise. With Peter and Janos trailing behind. I must have Janos," said Istvan, who had not yet learned, after living for eleven years in a People's Democracy, that one can live without a servant.

"By all means bring Janos. And Palko if he will come. I could use Palko."

"How lucky. What would have become of him, I wonder, if he had not been useful? And what of useless me?"

"You are my one luxury," said Riebeck and added firmly, "Good night, Istvan."

"Luxury," snorted Istvan. "Good night, Schani."

They fell asleep quickly because they were soldiers and had taught themselves to sleep under any circumstances. In the dark the Russian tanks closed their circle around Budapest.

At four in the morning—having arrested the negotiators and without challenge surrounded Budapest—the Russians opened fire.

Istvan was out of bed and into his trousers almost in the same movement. He grabbed the telephone and talked first with someone at the Ministry of Defense and with the Prime Minister while he dressed. Neither conversation, Riebeck gathered, was satisfactory. There was no water for coffee. He gave Istvan a cigarette and lit one for himself. It tasted horrible. The telephone began to ring.

The Russians had taken Gellert Hill and Istvan's apartment was directly in their line of fire. Istvan, accustomed to being understood and obeyed without shouting, never raised his voice. "Palko," he said to Riebeck. "He says he couldn't sleep so he went down to the barracks about an hour ago. Psychic, no doubt. Yes Palko, go ahead. I'll try and get there later. I have to go to the Defense Ministry and the PM wants to talk to me. How the hell should I know where Maleter is, I'm not his nurse. T 54s. Yes, I know. *Servus.*"

The phone rang again the moment Istvan put it back. This time he was much less amiable. "I don't know, I'm not his nurse, after all. Keep your pants on, I'm coming. Yes, I know they're shelling us. If you would stop talking to me I could ring off and come down. Good-by."

He put on his cap and gloves. "All those frightened pen pushers in the Ministry of Defense are yammering for me. Would you wake Peter, please, Schani? I don't know how he can sleep through all this din. Our delegation never came back from Tokol. It's not funny, damn you."

"I know. It's only that I suddenly realized why the pen pushers are so frightened. They're without a minister of defense and army chief of staff, not to mention a minister of state. They'll make you minister of defense, my barefoot boy with cheek of tan."

Istvan looked down at his feet. "*Jessas,* I must be going crazy. I forgot my shoes."

Riebeck went to Peter's room and shook the boy. "The Russians are back," he said and added, "Good morning, Peter." Peter glared at him but got up.

"We've had it this time all right," said Istvan looking down the hill from his ravaged doorstep.

The Russians, taking no chances of a second defeat at the hands of unarmed civilians and children, had entered Budapest with two hundred thousand soldiers equipped with submachine guns and orders to shoot at sight. Migs, Russian bombers, rockets, and two thousand T54s, antitank guns and bazookas were turned against the few captured Russian tanks and homemade gasoline bombs. And to keep the unarmed civilians who had taken refuge in their cellars in line, groups of Russian soldiers with flame throwers went through the streets and roasted people alive.

Against this, Hungarian boys had erected barricades of old street cars and park benches.

Istvan stopped his jeep often and gave what advice he could. They all knew him well, the tall colonel with his gargoyle smile and Russian uniform, and they trusted him to do the impossible.

"Guns, Colonel Halyi. Can't you get us some antitank guns?"

Istvan said, "A tank cannot roll uphill if you grease or soap the road. Here in Buda you have the steep hill on your side. You can immobilize a tank by sticking a lead pipe or a crowbar between the treads. I'll try and send you grenades. You string them across the street, in front of the tank. It's terribly wasteful but it's the only way to do it."

They all knew that T 54s have revolving guns that can hit anything in sight.

"You're telling those children to kill themselves, Istvan," said Riebeck.

"They will be killed anyway. They might as well take a Russian or two along."

Indignation with what he thought was Istvan's indifference made Riebeck suddenly remember Miklos' cache of arms.

"Submachine guns, BARs, that sort of thing," he told Istvan.

"Drop me at the Defense Ministry and then you and Peter can go and get the stuff. I'll be at the barracks later."

Istvan jumped from the jeep before Riebeck could stop. He streaked through the Ministry of Defense like a highly efficient tornado, got people onto jobs they could do, and gave orders that could even now be carried out. He accepted the job of Acting Ministry of Defense with the *caveat* that only politicians could be minister of something that did not exist. Had anyone any suggestion as to what he was supposed to defend Budapest with?

As Minister of Defense, he was told, that was his problem.

The radio was on, playing the national anthem over and over. At five to six there was an announcement: "Premier Imre Nagy calls Minister of Home Defense Pal Maleter, the Chief of General Staff Istvan Kovacs, and the other members of the military delegation who went yesterday at 22:00 hours to the headquarters of the Soviet Supreme Command and who have not returned until now—"

"Poor things," said Istvan, "I don't suppose they will now," and had a talk on the telephone with the Prime Minister, in the course of which he became rude, abusive, and insulting, all because the Prime Minister had told him that the Russian Ambassador had promised to explain everything. Colonel Halyi was not to shoot unless he was attacked.

"I am attacked, damn you. What do you think all this noise is, ping-pong balls? I know it's no way to talk to a Prime Minister. If you live through this, and if I do, you can punish me afterwards. Just now either let me do my job or fire me."

He was not fired.

"It's like a miracle," said Peter, looking down at the guns in Miklos' apartment. His eyes shone.

"A very small miracle. I really wonder if at this point a few guns are better than nothing at all. Well, at least I suppose they will give you the illusion that you are fighting."

Peter was not listening. "A machine gun, Uncle Jean. Could I have it for my students?"

"No. It all goes back to the barracks. Istvan can decide where it will do the most good."

They loaded the jeep and drove to Kilian barracks. Istvan was just back from the Defense Ministry, boilingly angry and not overly pleased about the guns. "Not exactly an *embarras de richesse*, Schani."

But everyone else's enthusiastic admiration of the machine gun soon brought him out of the temper the Prime Minister had put him in.

"Schani, they want you at the Ministry of Defense."

"What, me?"

"You. 'Colonel Riebeck, is there in your opinion any help we can

expect from the West? Radio Free Europe said on July 19, 1953
that—.' I don't envy you."

"Istvan, if you put them up to this—"

"I swear I didn't."

"At least can I have your jeep?"

"No. I need it myself. Take Palko's, why don't you. I'll be keeping him busy here."

"What about you? Where will I meet you?"

"Here. I have to move around, but I'll be back. If we lose each other there's always Cousin Pista. They won't want to shell the American Legation, will they?"

"I daresay they'll want to, but they won't dare. Istvan, try not to get killed. I'd hate it."

"Me too. *Servus*, Schani."

"*Servus*."

In the street Riebeck turned back to look at the barracks. Istvan stood, gaunt and poised at the parapet, the still center in an exploding sky.

XXIII

The armored car drew up in front of Kilian Barracks. A dirty handkerchief served as a flag of truce.

"Whoever it is," said Istvan to Palko, "he has courage."

"Or it's a new sort of trick."

"We'll soon find out." Istvan put down his carbine and took out his revolver.

"You're not going unarmed, Istvan."

"Yes, certainly. A carbine would do me little good against an armored car in any case, and they are flying that filthy handkerchief."

"All right," said Palko, "but I'm coming with you." He carried Istvan's carbine and revolver as well as his own, and on the way down gave orders to young men with gasoline bombs.

But all these precautions were unnecessary. The visitor who emerged from the armored car, resplendent in a long leather coat

355

and shining boots, was their old friend General Altosov. And a General Altosov from whose geniality one might almost conclude that the last ten days had never happened. As was his habit he threw wide his arms, exclaiming delightedly: "Ivan Pavlovich." He took a step toward Istvan to embrace him.

Istvan did not step back, yet something about his eyes checked the exuberant general. They shook hands. Palko saluted.

General Altosov took down the flag of truce, blew his nose in it and put it in his pocket. He asked Istvan to lunch with him in order to discuss a truce. Had Colonel Riebeck been there he might have instanced enough examples of Russian luncheon invitations which had ended in prison or on the gallows to serve as a warning. Even without this Istvan was wary. He asked what had become of the delegation with whom the Russians had so far been negotiating. General Altosov said he did not know. He had arrived in Budapest only in the early hours of the morning at the head of a convoy of tanks. The very latest, most efficient model, the T54s.

Istvan smiled. "So you have come to liberate us once again, Comrade General. From what this time, I wonder?"

"From your own folly," said General Altosov and so obviously believed it that Istvan stopped baiting him.

"What sort of truce had you in mind?" he asked. He meant, "What kind of truce can there be between us now?"

"We will speak of it at lunch," said General Altosov. "I cannot concentrate properly while your desperadoes are only waiting for a word from you to hurl their molotov cocktails into the street."

"It would be a waste of time to discuss anything now," said Istvan, "and we haven't much time left."

"Time is the only thing you have left. What else can you possibly do but discuss a truce?"

"Fight until we drop."

There was no answer to this but agreement, so General Altosov changed the subject. He pointed at Istvan's bloodstained tunic and exclaimed dramatically: "My friend, you are wounded."

"No, Comrade General. The blood is from a boy who died early this morning, shot down by one of the very latest model T54s. An old-fashioned tank would have done as well. They were only chil-

356

dren, and for barricades they had park benches. When this boy realized that he was going to die he said 'Thank God.' I don't suppose he was more than sixteen, but he was glad to die. You see, you have us now in a trap where dying is the only way out."

General Altosov was not impressed. "Let us not be sentimental, Ivan Pavlovich. To fight till one drops is perfectly appropriate for old soldiers like you and me. But what of all your civilians, your women and old people and children? I do not speak of the boy who died in your arms this morning. I do not care whether he was ten or sixteen or twenty. He was not a child. A child with a gun or a gasoline bomb is a grown-up for all practical purposes, including dying. But the others, the people who are too old or ill to fight. How long will they be able to stand a siege? How much food is there in Budapest? How are your medical supplies? Will you really stand by and see Budapest destroyed once more? We will do it if necessary. But could you not give up a few hours of your time to see if we can find a better way out?"

"Who sent you to me, Comrade General?"

"I am not at liberty to tell you that, but I am empowered to guarantee you safe-conduct."

"Our delegation to Tokol had safe-conduct too."

"I tell you again that I know nothing about that. Do you doubt my word?"

"I probably should, but no, I don't. Where shall I meet you, and when?"

"Come to Headquarters at noon, and we'll have lunch and a talk."

Istvan nodded, saluted, and remained in the street until the General's armored car had driven off. Then he went back to the barracks.

Palko, following him up the stairs, said, "You're not really going, Istvan."

"I don't see how I can *not* go."

"Ten to one they'll arrest you."

"Thousand to one, more likely. But I have to take the chance. I mean it's possible they really want to negotiate."

"Then why didn't they negotiate with Maleter?"

Istvan, with a flash of laughter, said, "I don't think it's possible to negotiate with Maleter. Of all the stubborn—"

"And where is he now? Why hasn't he come back here? He had safe-conduct too."

"I know, Palko. Don't go on about it. I'm frightened enough."

"Are you? You're looking quite cocky to me."

"Good. Cheer up, old horse, I'm not dead yet."

Palko pointed at Istvan's bloody tunic. "Listen, you can't go to lunch like that. You'll make everybody sick."

"I'll go home and change. You take over here. For good, if necessary."

"All right," said Palko, and added, not very hopefully, "Good luck, Istvan."

Dear Schani,

I must after all break my promise to you. Having presumably arrested everyone else, the Russians now want to negotiate with me. I don't have to go. No MVD man is standing over me with a loaded pistol. So you see that I am breaking my promise to you of my own will, because the knowledge that I neglected a chance, however small or improbable, to help Budapest, would be worse than anything the MVD can do to me. At least I hope so.

Forgive me then for not keeping my word, and for not waiting to say good-by to you. I was afraid you might try to talk me out of it, and that you might succeed.

I don't know why I am being so dramatic. In another year I should be fifty, and that is certainly not too young for a soldier to die. I've had a good run. I had you for a friend and Eva for a wife. I've fought in some damned good battles.

I know I need not ask you to take care of Peter and Janos. Have a mass read for my poor soul, I expect it needs it badly. And do not be too ashamed of me when you hear that I have confessed to untold crimes—I will be quite ashamed enough of it myself.

Adieu Schani. I can't say *au revoir*. I wish I could.

Istvan.

Dear Peter,

This is to say good-by in case I don't come back from my lunch with Altosov. Please go to England with Schani. I want you out of Hungary.

I should perhaps have told you this long ago, but things like these do not improve by being spoken about. Still, I want you to know that I have always loved you with all my heart, and that I am sorry about what happened when you were a small boy. I know I was wrong, but I am still not able to see how it could have been done differently. I hope you will some day forgive me.

Good-by, Peter.

Your father,
Istvan Halyi.

Istvan folded the letters and left them on his desk.

"Janos, have I a clean tunic?"

"Yes, Monsieur Istvan."

"Take the epaulettes off."

"Yes, Monsieur Istvan. About time."

Istvan grinned at him. He threw his medal ribbons, his partisan star, and the colonel's epaulettes on the desk. He emptied his pockets. Cigarettes, some money, a pencil with the tip broken off, and the medallion of St. Stephen, tarnished and stained with dry blood. He put everything except the medallion in the pocket of his clean tunic. He went into the bathroom to wash. And though he had many times before faced death, it was not till this moment, as he glanced at himself in the glass, that with a sickening dive he knew that this, his body, was mortal, that Istvan Halyi would cease, leaving only flesh that would rot off his bones, down to the hollow-eyed, grinning skull. Not through all the Ash Wednesdays of his childhood, with the ashen cross marked on his forehead—*memento mori!*—not on the battlefields of Russia and Budapest, seeing friends and strangers lie unburied, not until now, though with every breath he drew he smelled the stench of corpses, had he truly believed that he too would die.

It is easy to accept as scientific fact that man is condemned to death on the day of his birth. It was horrible to know it in your belly and heart and head. Istvan stood looking at himself, his hand over his mouth, trying not to retch. His throat ached with the effort. He needed water. He turned on the tap, remembered that the electricity was cut off, and with a shaking hand slammed it shut. And suddenly his exasperation overcame his terror, he stopped shaking and was able to call himself a fool and to laugh at himself in the glass. He combed his hair, went back to his room and put on his clean tunic and his tank corps leather cap, laughing again when he remembered Schani's horrified comment: "It looks like sausages."

And to that laughing face the voice of a younger Istvan Halyi said as clearly as if he heard it aloud: "I never knew that one could feel about a city as one does about a person. I found it intolerable that Budapest should be hurt. If I could have somehow taken the beating intended for the city, I would have been truly happy." "It doesn't work," Riebeck's voice echoed. "It shouldn't stop one from trying."

Schani would understand then and not call it treason. But would he understand the one thing that would make it bearable, that an action undertaken as an intolerable duty had turned to show its other side—the love and joy behind it—before it was too late?

He returned to his desk and standing added a postscript to his letter for Riebeck.

He said good-by to Janos and ran down the stairs. Janos watched him from the window, smiling because Istvan's good moods were infectious. Istvan paused to light a cigarette and put on his gloves, turned back to wave to Janos and with a final gargoyle grin let in the clutch and tore down the street.

General Serov and General Altosov had an argument that would have been acrimonious had not General Serov been the head of the secret police, thus forcing Altosov to practice restraint.

"I don't know what you're upset about," Serov said with the customary mildness so justly feared by his friends and enemies.

"Colonel Halyi was my friend."

(They had just sat down to caviar and vodka when General Serov had entered the room without knocking. He wore a plain uniform with no badges or medal ribbons. Istvan too had worn the plain tunic, with a high collar and no epaulettes. They needed no identification. Colonel Halyi knew General Serov and General Serov knew Colonel Halyi. Istvan had raised a hand in protest and, the motion half completed, had let it drop. It was the gesture of a man who has taken a thousand-to-one gamble and has lost.)

"Colonel Halyi," said General Serov, "is a traitor."

"True, but you have put me in a position where I have had to break my word and my safe-conduct, both given in good faith. I don't like it. It reflects on me."

"These things are necessary," said Serov indifferently.

"It also reflects on the Red Army," said General Altosov.

Serov appeared to be able to bear this with resignation. "You are making an unnecessary fuss, Altosov, and that might reflect on you. I speak as a friend. Be careful."

Altosov was always cautious until he was threatened. Now he laughed and Serov did not like it.

"What are you laughing about?"

"I am laughing," said Altosov, "because you reminded me of the last person who threatened me."

"Who was that?"

"Our late comrade, Lavrenti Pavlovich Beria."

Colonel Riebeck was willing to see anyone: people Peter and Pista thought might help, former friends of Istvan's still in good standing with the Party, and people he himself knew. He used all and any means, bribery, promises, and unashamed reminders of favors and help rendered and debts owed. For years he had known enough about a great number of people in a position of power to ruin them. He had never used his knowledge from sheer lack of interest. But now, in order to save Istvan Halyi, he blackmailed as much as he could and found to his dismay that it was too late; the fear of the enemy had stifled all smaller fears.

"At worst he'll go to jail," said Pista Halyi after they had unsuccessfully tried to bribe, bully, and blackmail a high government official. "If he tries to do anything for Istvan he'll certainly go to jail and probably end with a bullet in his neck. So he gambles on the fact that you're a gentleman and that they most certainly aren't."

Riebeck did not think he could have got through those weeks without the help of Istvan's cousin. He had never known Pista Halyi at all well, for Pista's family had emigrated to America in

1919, and Pista had made his way back to Budapest by way of Georgetown University, the OSS, and the American Legation.

"I wish I knew what to do next," said Riebeck, tired to death and without hope.

"We've gone about it wrong," said Pista. "It's no use at all dealing with Hungarians. The ones who wouldn't be afraid to help us are most likely in prison along with Istvan. And your Russian army friends aren't any use either. We have to deal directly with the MVD."

"Serov?"

Pista was amused. "Not quite. Bogory, who runs the show here for Serov, might be the appropriate person."

"Tell me about him."

Pista found a crumpled pack of cigarettes and held it out to Riebeck, who shook his head. Pista lit two and gave him one.

"When you're too tired to light a cigarette for yourself you're in pretty bad shape, Schani."

"I know. Don't fuss."

"I won't. I remember a time in the OSS when I couldn't sleep without Demerol and couldn't wake up without Benzedrine, and whenever anybody told me I looked like death I had hysterics. Do you need some of either?"

"*American Legation Front for Dope Ring*, says *Pravda*."

"Well, how about a drink?"

Riebeck shook his head. "Tell me about Bogory."

Pista sighed. "Bogory is pleasant, efficient, well-mannered, and intelligent. He's Serov's protégé. I imagine he is going to handle the big publicity people, if you know what I mean. Maleter, Istvan, Nagy, that lot."

"What's he like?"

"I told you, nice."

"That doesn't help very much."

"I can't tell you any more. These new people are all so incorruptible. It makes them very difficult to deal with. From what I have been able to learn, Borgory has no vices at all. He smokes, it is true, but he doesn't drink, and as far as anyone knows he doesn't kiss girls."

"It would be more helpful if he kissed boys. We could blackmail him then."

Pista laughed and said, "That you will have to find out for yourself."

"Lord, don't tell me I have to send for one of my Lionels."

"What are Lionels?"

Riebeck told him and for a moment they managed to relax and laugh. Then Pista, serious again, said, "It isn't funny, that's the trouble."

"I don't need reminding, Pista. Will he see me, do you think?"

"If you are willing to accept a risk. He won't see Mr. Jones from the American Legation, but I think he'll see Colonel Riebeck, don't you?"

Comrade Bogory had reason to be pleased with himself. General Serov had not arrested Colonel Halyi to bait the trap for Colonel Riebeck. At the time Serov had not even known that Riebeck was in Budapest. Istvan Halyi was one of the few officers left at large who had the experience and inclination to lead a successful resistance fight and was as such a danger to the Russians. That Colonel Riebeck should now be willing, apparently, to go to any length to rescue Colonel Halyi was the kind of plum that all too rarely falls to even the best and most hard-working secret police officer.

Bogory had at once gotten into touch with Moscow and to his pleasure his orders were the confirmation of his own brilliant suggestion.

He moved a pad of paper to lie exactly parallel with the edge of his uncluttered desk, lit a cigarette, and told an underling that Colonel Riebeck was to be shown up to him the moment he arrived.

Riebeck was punctual. Bogory guessed from the moment he saw him that his plan would be a failure. And yet he could not help his pleasure at meeting a man who looked as he expected him to, in whom actions and face and mind were all of a piece.

Istvan Halyi was like that too, Bogory now remembered, and suddenly realized that all the men with whom he had been dealing these last weeks had this look in common and that he had never met it before. Not people who were torn between heart and mind, duty and inclination, but people who did what must be done, heedless of the consequences. They had made Atlantis of their prison.

Riebeck too was pleased by his first glance at Bogory. Here at last was someone who was empowered to make a deal, to accept or reject what he had to offer, uninfluenced by the fear of what would follow. This was the end then, one way or the other. Here, whatever else might happen later, would take place Istvan Halyi's trial and judgment, here in this plain office before a man with a young, indifferent face and a uniform recognizable as MVD by the absence of any markings.

"Please sit down, Colonel Riebeck. I—we all—have wanted to meet you, even before you managed to make away with our Major Dyelik. You did make away with him, did you not?"

"He never had a chance," said Riebeck blandly.

"Please sit down. I know of course why you are here, so we need not discuss that. We've watched your progress, or lack of it, for some time with considerable amusement. Forgive my saying it, but you have been very foolish."

"I know. It doesn't matter."

"It wasted time. Have you really never learned that while fear does not keep you personally from doing what is right, most people are entirely motivated by fear? Fear of hunger, loss of property, pain, imprisonment, fear of death. That is fortunate. It makes people obedient. Without fear there would be anarchy."

Riebeck was not prepared to listen to Bogory's juvenile philosophy. "About Colonel Halyi," he said, "what do you want to allow him to leave the country?"

"What makes you think we would consider it at all?"

Once again he was confronted with the Russian unwillingness to get to the point. While they philosophized and talked about anything but what they were here to discuss Istvan was in prison, being tortured, perhaps, starved, made to go without sleep or water. Forcing himself to patience, Riebeck said, "You knew what I wanted before you agreed to see me."

Bogory laughed. "Do not be so modest, Colonel. We have long wished to meet *you*."

"Here I am. What do you want?"

"Make me an offer."

Pista and Riebeck had discussed this problem for a long time and decided on bribery. Pista said it was remarkable how often even Communists in good standing are happy to escape to the West when the opportunity offers. A large sum of money plus help in escaping from Hungary might possibly tempt Comrade Bogory. "Though I must remind you, Schani, that there is still the little matter of yourself getting out, not too mention Peter and Janos."

Riebeck said, "One million dollars."

Pista had thought this sum excessive, but Riebeck felt that it was the sort of round figure that might have some meaning for someone unacquainted with money. And indeed Bogory looked impressed.

"Do you really have that much money, Colonel Riebeck?"

"More. At least I have never yet been able to spend the income from it and I imagine it gets reinvested." If Bogory wanted a million and a half or two million, let him have it. But it was not greed that had prompted Bogory's last question; it was indignation.

"You can't spend your income and all over the world people are starving."

"Yes, certainly," said Riebeck indifferently.

"What would I do with a million dollars?"

"Whatever you liked. You could live where you want, eat marvelous meals, travel, buy paintings, hire a string quartet, buy a yacht or an island—" Riebeck could have gone on, but stopped, aware suddenly of the great flaw in his argument. Bogory could not do anything with the money because the poor, unless they are greedy and rejoice in the mere possession of wealth, do not know how to enjoy its results. That is why the *nouveaux riches* are always such a pathetic spectacle. To be truly rich requires a background in loving the things money buys. One had only to visualize Bogory with his own string quartet or sailing his own yacht to see that it was not possible.

"And have you always done what you liked, Colonel Riebeck?"

"Yes, always."

"Did you really think you could tempt me with money?"

"Only until I saw you and tried to picture you as rich."

"Thank you."

"It wasn't a compliment. Now, suppose you make me an offer."

Bogory gave Riebeck a cigarette and lit one for himself. He looked suddenly less assured.

"What is it you want?" Riebeck asked.

Bogory said, "A very simple bargain, Colonel Riebeck. You for Colonel Halyi. Colonel Halyi will be released from prison and allowed to leave for the West if he so desires, if you will come to Moscow with me."

It astonished him that the impulse to treason was so strong. He had always classed it under the crimes for which there could be no acceptable motive, until this moment when he stood facing the Russian, his mouth dry with the shock of the temptation's intensity and his throat aching with the effort not to say yes.

He was left without the strength for an outright rejection. He said, "I will come gladly as your prisoner, but never as your collaborator."

Bogory sighed. "We underestimated you, I see."

"I don't underestimate myself, if that is what you mean." Any kind of talk was a momentary reprieve from failure. "To me an enemy is someone who is trying to force his way of thinking on me. To you an enemy is someone who is of no use to you. I'm only your enemy as long as I oppose you. I could be damned useful to you."

"To save your friend from a cruel death, will you?"

"No."

"You would come as a prisoner but not as a welcome guest?"

"That's right."

"I don't understand it."

"That's unimportant. If you have any acceptable suggestions I am willing to listen."

"I have no more suggestions. But I would very much like to understand your reasoning."

"I've told you, our definitions of enemy are different. There could conceivably be a change in your relations to me, there can be none in mine to you. People who force agreement with the help of a gun are my permanent enemies. I can't live like that. And since this does not interest you, and is probably not even very clear to you, I will give you a practical reason. If I came to Moscow to work for you I would make a mockery of everything Colonel Halyi has done. He would not want his liberty at the price of an advantage to you and it would be inconsiderate of me to burden him with an unacceptable sacrifice."

"You do not think we will make it appear acceptable?"

"I've no doubt that you will try."

"And succeed."

"No," said Colonel Riebeck. "You won't succeed."

"Really? You seem very sure. You think that if you could survive Buchenwald Colonel Halyi can survive us. My dear Riebeck, Buchenwald was a kindergarten compared to what we are able to do."

"I believe you. But it doesn't matter."

"The Nazis were playing children's games. We know how to impose obedience."

"Obedience? Perhaps, though Budapest was not exactly a proof of that. But obedience is nothing. Any oaf behind a gun can exact a certain amount of obedience. Can you deal with discipline?"

"Discipline and obedience are the same thing."

"No. Obedience is enforced from the outside. In one way or another disobedience is made too costly. It's not a foolproof system, as you have seen here, but by and large it works, for a time. Discipline is imposed from the inside. The people whom you are now trying to convict of treason committed a disobedience because they were disciplined. You can kill them. You probably will. But I will wager you anything you care to name that when they die they will say: 'Not guilty!' "

Much of what Riebeck said had already occurred to Bogory, though his training and background supplied him with neither precedent nor philosophy. He did not relish having it put into words and he said stubbornly, stupidly, "We will succeed. You know, I was sure you would be prepared to make a great—er— who were those two famous friends of antiquity?"

"Max and Moritz?"

Bogory's mouth tightened. "Damon and Pythias. I was sure you would come here ready to make a great Damon and Pythias sacrifice for your beloved Colonel Halyi. Your willingness to let us kill you instead of him is nothing. I have never understood why the sacrifice of a life is held of so much account since every man must in any case die. The true sacrifice, Colonel Riebeck, the sacrifice that is worth something, is that of the mind."

"As long as you consider a mind something that can be sacrificed we'll never have a common point to talk from. We're wasting each other's time. Good-by, and thank you for seeing me."

"Can you think of a reason why I should not simply take you prisoner now that you are here?"

"Yes," said Riebeck, "I can. Don't be ridiculous."

Apparently Bogory could too. Obviously a man as experienced as Colonel Riebeck would not come for an interview with the MVD without the means of blowing up the place as a last resort. Bogory's guards had lackadaisically patted Riebeck's pockets and smugly confiscated the revolver he had brought for that very purpose. And even the MVD could not very well pounce on an American Legation car, if they allowed Riebeck to leave the building.

"Very well, you are free to leave, Colonel Riebeck. Or would you first like some news of Colonel Halyi? I see him often."

Riebeck said nothing.

"He is still alive," said Bogory pleasantly. "Would you care to give me a message for him? I will deliver it faithfully."

Riebeck stood silent and shivering, with the taste of blood in his mouth. Bogory watched him patiently and without derision. It took him a long time before he could speak calmly enough to answer. He dug into his pocket and brought out an almost full pack of Pista's Chesterfields. He threw them on Bogory's desk.

"Give him those, please. And my love."

"I promise," said Bogory. "Good-by, Colonel Riebeck." It is possible that we may meet again."

"Good," said Riebeck, and left.

XXIV

Jeremy Tyrell returned from Vienna, had a hasty shower and change of clothes, and rushed off to bring the bad news to Jenny before anyone else could. He found her dressed in a tweed suit; her mink coat and a small overnight bag were on her bed.

"Darling," she said, kissing his cheek. "How nice."

"You're going away?"

"On down to the country for one night. Cousin Niall's got himself engaged to one of the Penniman girls. She's charming and rich, and we're all delighted. Aunt Melissa is giving him a slap-up engagement dinner party tonight." She pulled off her gloves and threw them on the bed. "There's no hurry. I had meant to be there for lunch but tea will do quite as well. Are you hungry? Where have you been?"

"I'm starved. I've just come back from Vienna with Riebeck. He was in Budapest, I suppose you know."

"Beasts," said Jenny. "The Russians I mean."

"Never mind the Russians. I'm hungry."

"Oh, I'm sorry." She rang the bell and Jeremy, who could never get servants, or if he got them, could not make them heed any summons, was as always entranced with the jack-in-the-box promptness with which Bessie answered the bell.

"Oh, Bessie," said Jenny, "Major Tyrell's come all the way from Vienna without breakfast. Could you find him something?"

"Oh yes, my lady," said Bessie and scrambled out as if Jeremy might vanish in front of her eyes if not promptly fed.

Jeremy, extending himself full length on the sofa and lighting a very dirty pipe, said, "I told you, didn't I, Riebeck came back with me."

"Yes, you did. Did Colonel Halyi come with you too?"

"Here is your breakfast, sir," said Bessie, coming in as fast as she dared with a loaded tray.

"You've saved my life, Bessie. Kippers! Oh heaven." He turned to Jenny and over a kipper held in his hand, said, "No, he didn't."

Jenny's face grew wary. Already she hated Istvan Halyi for the disorder he was bringing into her life. "Poor Colonel Halyi. Was he killed in the fighting then?"

"No," said Jeremy, his mouth full of toast and marmalade. "He wasn't."

Jenny came and sat down across from him. "Let me have some of your coffee. And tell me. If it's as bad as that Jean won't feel like talking about it."

Jeremy, much hampered by the kipper, told her all he knew, his affection for her and his sympathy almost submerged under the delight of being first with the news.

"Poor Jean."

"Yes, he's taken it badly. If only Halyi had had the wits to get himself killed in the fighting. But this—it's such a beastly way to die and it's going to take such a long time."

"Yes, I suppose so."

Jenny's telephone began to ring. She made no more toward it. Jeremy, beginning on his second kipper, said, "Telephone."

"Davy'll answer."

Miss Davidson said it was Colonel Riebeck, my lady, and should she say there was no one at home.

"Yes. No. I'll take it up here."

"Jenny? Hullo. Could I see you? I must talk to you."

"Of course, my dear. When?"

"Now."

"All right. Do you want to come here?"

"No. Come to my place."

"Half an hour then."

She turned to Jeremy, who reluctantly gave up on his breakfast and picked up his burberry. "Jean wants me to come and see him now. I suppose he wants to get everything out of the way at once. Thanks for the warning, Jeremy."

"Poor Jenny. There's no denying that you're lots prettier than Colonel Halyi, but I'm afraid it's going to do you no good at all."

"No, I suppose not. Oh damn!"

Jeremy kissed her and left, having a horror of weeping women. But Jenny did not cry. She went to the bedroom and took her raincoat from the closet. She would have liked time to think, to turn over the shattered pieces of her love affair to see what could be salvaged. But what she must do was simple enough. She must accept Riebeck's choice and not make things more difficult for him than at this moment they were. And since even the motives of love are not unmixed, she was in considerable measure consoled by the knowledge that no one can successfully oppose perfect docility.

Duke Street was always singularly depressing in the rain. It would rain, of course, thought Jenny, teem like at a Hollywood funeral. She had been forced to park her car a good distance down the street, and since she despised umbrellas and people who used them, would now be arriving like a drowned rat. Most appropriate.

She hurried up Riebeck's stairs, her shoes squelching with water, not knowing what to expect, and in a hurry to get it over.

Riebeck opened the door to let her in. "Jenny, how nice."

His face dismayed her. Drained of everything but weariness, it had become again the fine-drawn, unrevealing mask he had worn at the hospital. But he smiled at her, a quick, slightly surprised smile, full of mockery at his own extravagance. How easily he had dispensed with Jenny in Budapest, and how impossible he knew it to be now that she stood before him, very wet and beautiful. His arms went round her hard. "Jenny, I'm a fool." The first complication.

He was exhausted. She could feel it in the touch of his hands.

"When did you sleep last?"

"Lord knows. Why?"

"Sleep now."

"No."

Jenny withdrew herself, extending instead that well-remembered, stinging lack of sympathy. "Stop showing off. Sleep."

With a grunt of laughter he collapsed on the bed. "I am tired," he admitted. "Will you stay?"

"Yes."

"And wake me if I have nightmares?"

"It's all included in the price."

She pulled off her sopping scarf and wet raincoat and threw them over a chair.

"But I must talk to you," he remembered, half asleep.

"Later. Sleep now." By the time she had dug out a damp cigarette from her coat pocket, he was asleep. Jenny went into the kitchen, where Alphonse and Janos were talking like waterfalls over steaming cups of coffee.

"Miladi," Alphonse said delightedly. He liked Jenny because unlike most miladies she was never on a diet. Whenever Alphonse heard the word diet he wanted to spit. Now miladi—the words my lady gave him trouble—had a very healthy appetite.

"Hullo, Alphonse. What's for lunch?"

"Miladi may well ask. Whatever it is, the colonel will mess it around on his plate and send it back. He treats me as if I were a British Restaurant."

"He was very tired. He is asleep now. Make something he won't be able to resist, Alphonse."

"I do my best, Miladi, but I am not appreciated here. Will you have a cup of coffee?"

"All right," said Jenny, sitting down by the scrubbed kitchen table. "You're Colonel Halyi's Janos, aren't you? Do sit down."

Janos was gratified. He thought Jenny had remembered him. She hadn't, of course, having seen him only once, almost twenty years ago, and not really having noticed him then. But Jeremy had told her about Peter and Janos, and this old man with the handlebar moustaches was not likely to be Istvan Halyi's son.

"Tell me how you got out of Hungary," said Jenny, holding her cup of coffee between cold fingers.

It was a story on which Janos would live for years, adding bits of drama to the bare bones, until it filled out into a legend; the farewell to a gutted Budapest, the long walk across the border—Jenny frowned, thinking of Riebeck's lame leg—and the mined fields at the border crossing, Janos' terror of the trained dogs of the frontier guards, Austria at last, and an Embassy limousine picking them up as they were, exhausted and dirty as moles, with swamp mud dried on their clothes and faces.

They had been too tired to eat and had bathed and fallen into bed and slept like the dead, except Monsieur Schani, who had met them on waking with clean clothes and was himself once more in uniform.

Peter and Monsieur Schani had breakfasted with the Ambassador —what Ambassador? Janos didn't know—though Monsieur Schani had only messed with his food and had confined himself to coffee and cigarettes. After breakfast Monsieur Schani had taken Peter and Janos for a ride through Vienna, which Janos had not seen since 1938 and Peter never. They had stopped before a grass-fronted apartment house standing where Baranyi Palace had stood, and Janos had wept as by a graveside. Peter, the young barbarian, had liked the apartment house and had said that it was sure to be an improvement over some moldy old palace. Monsieur Schani had said that financially speaking it was a very good thing and he wished he could drop a bomb on it.

They had picked up a Major Tyrell at some shabby office building, and before Janos could take fright he had found himself bundled into an airplane, not a commercial airliner, but a military one, flown by a young pilot who was mostly slewed around in his seat, conversing in an airy and insouciant manner with Colonel Riebeck. Major Tyrell had slept, Peter, may all the saints preserve us, had wheedled the pilot into giving him a flying lesson, Janos had spent his time in prayer. His nerves were not calmed when they had landed and had been driven to London by Monsieur Schani at a terrifying speed. Peter had fallen asleep at the first sight of a bed, but Janos was still too nervous to rest and was not at all certain that he would ever be able to sleep again.

Jenny was from long experience familiar with the mimosa-like sensibility of the servant class and was not impressed.

"That is very interesting, Janos, and I hope you will be happy in London."

Janos, knowing authority when he met it, thanked her. Jenny went off to telephone her aunt in Cornwall and to tell her that she would not be able to come to Niall's dinner.

Back in the bedroom she found a pile of magazines, the sort of thing people buy in airports and railway stations and rarely read. There were also Hungarian papers, *Nepsbadsag, Magyar Fuggetlenseg, Szapad Nep*, and some others. It seemed to Jenny that from the first moment of the uprising the Hungarians had leaped, not for their guns but for their fountain pens. The last date of

373

publication on these papers told a more eloquent story than any in their pages: November 3.

Jenny picked up *Life* and put her fingers between its pages so that Riebeck would not think she had been observing him while he slept, a thing he very much disliked. He was a disposed and neat sleeper, turned on his side with his head on one outstretched arm, but never a very relaxed one. Even in sleep the exhausted lines had not left his face. My darling, my darling, I wish I could help you. Folly! He would not let her, even if she could.

Her fingers automatically turned the pages, and after a while her eyes too followed the pictures, until they came to a sudden stop on the full-page photograph of Istvan Halyi: gargoyle face and strong slender hands, square, stubborn mouth and violent, oblique eyes. She remembered him very vividly, suddenly, as he had sat across a dinner table from her almost twenty years ago, as if his vitality had been transmitted through the paper. The air of capability and of the pleasure he took in living in a world he could match in courage, toughness, and generosity was as vivid on the paper as it had been in Count Tisza's dining room. She had forgotten his voice and his manner of speech, but she suddenly remembered his laughter, as if by looking at his photograph she had caused the sound to travel not only across space but across time; the scowling laughter that conquered him, apparently against his will, and swept along all those who heard it.

A piece of paper fell from the pages and as she picked it up she saw that it was a letter written in French to Riebeck, signed: Istvan. She was about to put it back between the pages when he word *joie* caught her eye. For the first time in her life she read a letter not addressed to her.

. . . And do not be too ashamed of me when you hear that I have confessed to untold crimes. I shall be quite ashamed enough of it myself. *Adieu* Schani, I can't say *au revoir*, I wish I could.

PS. Schani, don't worry about me. Remember what I said about Budapest during the war. I meant it. Now I am perhaps given the chance to do what I wanted to do then. If they will punish me instead of the city I shall be thankful and accept with joy whatever the punishment must be. Extravagant, you are thinking—I can see your annoyance—and pompous. But Schani, in love only the extravagant is enough and more than anything in the world I love Budapest. So please, whatever comes, remember that I went, very, very frightened, but also joyous. Schani, *au revoir*.

Jenny held the paper between trembling fingers, her throat choked with tears. "In love one always wants to make the extravagant exception," Riebeck had once said to her. "In love only the extravagant is enough."

Riebeck stirred restlessly, but did not waken. Jenny looked down at the photograph. What was it Jeremy had once quoted? Something about tragedy and joy. Tragedy must be joy to the one who dies.

Was the joy his reward then, the one who died? Or was it his final act of generosity, the grace to make his death tolerable for those who loved him?

For Jenny did love István Hayll now, with the wholehearted admiration that she could always bring to an act of courage, and above all to courage like this, not the contagion and exuberance of battle, but courage of the mind, two o'clock in the morning courage, of cold blood and a clear knowledge that is aware of the consequences and is not stopped by them.

Jenny smiled and put out a hand to awaken Riebeck. He woke quickly and neatly at her touch. "Good timing," he said. "You caught it at the beginning."

"What sort of nightmare is it?"

"All kinds. Fine beastly ones. Never mind."

"What are your feelings about lunch?"

"All right."

But when Alphonse set down a high-hat soufflé and a crisp salad (where he got his salad greens was a mystery; he made the only alert salads in London) Riebeck pushed the food ungratefully around his plate and lit a cigarette.

"Eat," said Jenny, "or Alphonse will give notice and I shall take him away from you."

"I'm not hungry. I want to talk to you."

"You needn't unless you feel like it," patience fraying invisibly under the skin. "Jeremy told me."

"What can he have told you? He wasn't with us most of the time and he slept all the way back from Vienna."

"You know how Jeremy picks up news, by radar and osmosis. He said I was rather prettier than Colonel Halyi, but that it would do me no good."

Very much against his will Riebeck laughed. "I'm sorry, Jenny. But I can't retire now. And I haven't changed about combining this business and marriage."

"Of course, darling," said Jenny, who hated unnecessary self-sacrifice more than anything in the world.

At any other time Riebeck would have taken the warning, but just now he was too preoccupied. "You do understand, then."

"My dear, of course I do. I can't tell you how strongly everyone here felt about it . . . " This time the warning got through. Riebeck set his teeth. Jenny's most unforgivable insults were always delivered so, with velvet purr and sheathed claw. " . . . and how terribly frustrating it is not to be able to do anything other than sending one's second-best mink coat to Hungarian Relief."

Riebeck said icily, "You should have sent your sables."

"Darling, I know they are your pals and they were splendid and we're all frightfully proud of them, but sables?"

There remain in the most disillusioned and sophisticated lives areas that can never be made bearable and amusing. The problem for lovers is that these areas are not the same for any two people. Riebeck knew she was baiting him deliberately, that she did not believe half of what she said, and that women resent revolutions when they interfere with love affairs. But he could see them behind anger-blinded eyes, the boys with their park bench barricades, the factory workers in their suburbs, knowing all action was suicide and acting nevertheless, fighting on after all hope of help or UN action was gone. "But sables?"

"Jenny," he said furiously, "say another word and I'll slap you."

Jenny, glad to see him angry, said amiably, "Why not? You never know, you might enjoy it. Though I don't think so. You're more of a masochist, not a sadist."

"Oh that asinine jargon. So I'm a masochist now."

"If you aren't, why won't you eat your lunch?"

376

"Because cold soufflé is not my favorite food."

"Because Colonel Halyi isn't getting any. This must do him so much good. Jonathan says—"

"I do not give a damn what Jonathan says. Why don't you get him to do one of his foul operations on my brain, then I won't mind anything any more. I'll be a happy idiot."

Jenny, incensed as she always was when Sir Jonathan was under well-deserved attack, said, "It would be an improvement. You don't need an audience for all these dramatics, Jean. I am certain you can suffer just as well by yourself. I'm going home."

She had her coat on when Riebeck said, "Jenny."

"What?"

"I'm sorry."

"Huh," she said without looking round.

"Jenny, I'm eating my lunch."

She turned and saw him gagging on a mouthful of the soufflé, which had long since collapsed and had the look of wet washing flannel. "It's awful," he said. "I shall probably be sick. It would serve you right." Doggedly he went on eating.

"Oh my darling." Shaken between tears and laughter she took his plate away and held a glass of wine out to him. "Drink quickly. And don't eat any more."

He drank the wine and then said, "Don't leave."

Incapable of speech now, she shook her head.

He put the empty glass down and caught her to him, hurting her. In her kiss he tasted the sweet of blood and the salt of tears.

They regained their equanimity, lying side by side on his bed, smoking and talking. Often he made her and himself laugh, but all the things he said led him to the day when he had said good-by to Istvan Halyi for the last time. Of the weeks that followed he could barely bring himself to speak. Finally he said, "I think Partridge is going to ask for my resignation. There isn't a sin in the Intelligence regulations I neglected to commit. I stayed in Budapest against orders, I used a friendly legation for cover without their consent, I involved one of their personnel. I exposed myself deliberately to arrest by the enemy, I dealt or rather attempted to deal privately with the enemy, or dear Lord, I will be lucky if they don't court-martial me."

"What will you do if they court-martial you?"

"Go home. I have a great respect for military regulations, but at the moment no time for them. I can work on my own for some civilian agencies I know. Don't worry though, I exaggerated. We're given a great deal of leeway. They don't court-martial us except for treason and collaboration, and I did draw the line at that."

"How splendid of you," said Jenny unkindly. "What did you mean—you exposed yourself deliberately to arrest?"

"When I went to talk to Bogory he could have tried to arrest me. It wouldn't have been worth his while and I think he knew it. He didn't try very hard."

"What would you have done?"

"Blown the place to bits. Believe me, I was tempted."

"But you—"

"You see. You'll always worry about my doing things I've done for twenty years. It's no life for you. Still, you shall choose."

"Choose what?"

"Going on like this or stopping entirely. That's all the choice there is."

Jenny, realizing with panic why he had laughed when she had first come in, said, "I don't think you were going to give me a choice before I came. I think you were ready to say 'Get the hell out of my life, you're in my way.'"

"I told you I was a fool. I love you, Jenny. I want you very, very much. But I must go on working and I don't know if I can have both. That is up to you. There's no future in this for either of us, and if I were you I'd slap my face and get myself a more satisfactory lover."

Jenny was aware that time, her enemy, had turned into an ally. Colonel Halyi could not now live long, and once he was dead Riebeck would surely turn to the living again. He was good at letting the dead bury the dead. One had to be, in his profession.

"Go on, then," she said. "On one condition."

"I won't promise until I know what it is."

"That you eat a proper dinner tonight."

He laughed and said, "That I promise," thinking how like her it was to destroy drama and bring it down to eating one's dinner, how much her ways were his, and that he loved her.

The next morning Riebeck put on, perhaps for the last time, his uniform. He said to Janos, "Let Peter sleep as late as he likes and see that he eats a decent breakfast when he gets up. I'll come back later and take him to my tailor. He can't keep wearing that suit and I may be needing civilian things myself."

"You're not leaving the army, Monsieur Schani?"

"It may leave me," said Riebeck and went for his interview with General Partridge. He was sure he would be asked for his resignation. He could work for Latour, he supposed, or General L'Abbé. Though no doubt L'Abbé, being a general, would also look askance at his recent behavior.

General Partridge was in one of his jovial moods and Riebeck braced himself for the worst.

"I am very sorry indeed about your cousin, Riebeck. It's a beastly business."

"Thank you, sir."

"Made a bit of an ass of yourself about it, what?"

"Yes, sir."

There was a long silence, which General Partridge finally broke with his favorite comment. "Oh," he said. "Ah."

Riebeck thought he might as well get it over with. "Will it help any if I resign my commission, sir?"

"Good heavens, man," said General Partridge.

Riebeck did not know what else to suggest. He told Jeremy later that he was at that moment absolutely certain that Partridge would hand him a revolver and offer to leave the room while he— Riebeck—took the only honorable way out. This thought cheered him so much that he nearly missed General Partridge's next words.

"Didn't you know? No, I suppose you didn't. It came through while you were in Budapest."

"What did, sir?"

"Your promotion to brigadier," said General Partridge, biting on the bullet.

"But, sir—"

"No no no, you can't refuse it. St 2 is much too large to be run by a colonel."

"Good God!"

"Why are you so surprised? I thought St 2 was your one ambition."

"Yes sir, but I didn't think anyone else knew it."

"I daresay you've deceived everyone else, but not me. I knew what you were after since the day you kissed General de Gaulle good-by. And when you refused Burkey's section, I was certain. Well, that's all right. There was never any sense in your wasting yourself in a section you could run with your eyes shut. But don't fool yourself, running the Department is a different bag of tricks altogether."

"I am sure it is, sir. When are you retiring?"

"As soon as you learn to behave like a general. That Hungarian business will take a bit of living down, you know. First of the year suit you?"

"Yes, sir."

"Good. That'll be all for now, then, Riebeck," said General Partridge, who never endured Riebeck's society for longer than was necessary.

Brigadier General Riebeck saluted and walked somewhat dazedly to the nearest telephone. His mind was far from St. 2, back on the day he, Vic de Cavignac, and Jacques Latour had graduated from St. Cyr. They had celebrated in the traditional way, with dinner at La Rue's and visits, according to Latour's subsequent calculations, to half the bagnios in Paris. And like thousands of St. Cyriens before them, they had made the traditional promise; the first one to make it to brigadier obliged himself to buy a slap-up dinner and the most expensive whores in Paris for the other two.

Riebeck had said that he for one was agreeable, Riebecks having never made it past colonel excepting, of course, their marshal. The locution "*notre maréchal*" had aroused the active derision of the other two, and they had held him by the ankles over the railings of the Pont de Solferino until he had consented to admit that marshals of France were the property of the Republic, not of any one family.

They had bought each other many slap-up dinners since then, but never the one to redeem that promise.

He dialed Jenny's number. "What do you think, love? Partridge has made me a general and I'm to have his job when he retires."

"Darling, how nice. I always think three pips are so much more distinguished than two. And everyone who's been saying you were rather old to be a colonel will now say how young you are to be a general."

"What are you doing?"

"I am just going to lunch at the Ritz with Jeremy."

"I see. I must go and break the news to Peter. How he will despise me."

"Why should he despise you?"

"Because Istvan could have been a general and refused. And as rude as Peter always was to his father when he lived with him, he has now canonized him in retrospect."

"You couldn't lunch at the Ritz first, could you? Then you could be despised on a full stomach."

"A good idea. *A bientôt*, then."

Jenny appeared at lunch with both Jeremy and Sir Jonathan. Riebeck knew her too well to suspect her of wishing to make him jealous. More likely she had run into her husband on the stairs and had, without much thought, brought him along.

Sir Jonathan seemed mildly pleased to see Riebeck, and burst-ing to air his opinions on the uprising, a subject of which he knew nothing but the newspaper reports.

"I was so very distressed to hear about Colonel Halyi, Riebeck," he said perfunctorily. "The futility of it all must make it doubly sad for you."

Jeremy said that any act of heroism, even if it ended in failure, had its value as a source of inspiration. It was a thought so unlike Jeremy that Riebeck thought he must be joking. But Jeremy looked quite serious. He was engaged in one of his favorite though con-sistently unsuccessful pastimes, known as "getting Jonathan's goat."

381

Sir Jonathan hooted mildly. "These outbursts are not acts of heroism. They are something much more atavistic and subconscious. They are caused by the West's great fear of the East. The Hungarians are at the furthermost limits between East and West. They have fought against the East so often that I think the Budapest uprising was nothing more than a conditioned reflex."

(I know they were your pals, darling, and they were splendid . . .)

Riebeck turned to Jenny. "You are an amateur, Madame. Take lessons from your husband if you want to learn how to do a real hatchet job. A conditioned reflex."

Jenny, who understood him all too well, gave him her prettiest, most mystified smile, and then said to her husband: "Darling Jonathan, did you know that they have finally made Colonel Riebeck a brigadier?"

Between taking over General Partridge's many duties and relinquishing his own to people who would continue to make Simon Cook look like a live wire instead of the industrious, conscientious dullard that he was, General Riebeck had little time for a private life. When he did manage to get home, he noticed happily that the household was run better and the food was more marvelous than ever before.

Alphonse had tearfully embraced both Peter and Janos when they had arrived, although he had never met Peter and had always despised Janos for not being French. Since then the peace of the kitchen was daily rent by fearful quarrels as each determined to show Riebeck that he and he alone was the indispensable one. Alphonse had on his side his superb, imaginative cooking and his status as senior servant, having been rescued from Nazi Austria by the General in person. Janos scored heavily on having been with poor Monsieur Istvan at the very last, not to mention poor Miss Eva and poor General Halyi, whom he had buried personally. Alphonse said nastily that Janos appeared to have buried everyone he could get his hands on, and that he hoped Janos would not make it a habit in England where the police took a dim view of corpses in the herb garden.

Janos thereupon went off to give the apartment a ferocious cleaning and to brush and press General Riebeck's uniforms within an inch of their lives, while Alphonse put his all into a *filet à la sardelaise*.

Though Riebeck had never been inclined to be critical of Istvan, he sometimes found himself wishing Peter had been brought up a little better. Of course it was not Istvan's fault. It was all those pioneers and young Communists, but it was a bore to have Alphonse's dinners mentally converted into so many pounds of rice for the starving Chinese, to have to listen to lectures about the immorality of owning American dollars in large quantities, and to be unable to come to any agreement about money.

Peter insisted that he must instantly get a job and stop living on his uncle's charity. Riebeck thought Peter ought to have spending money and ought to finish his schooling or take up something else if medicine bored him.

"Medicine doesn't bore me, but I can't keep on living on you, Uncle Jean."

"Why not? I don't mind it. Anyway, I've left you half my money in my will, so you might as well spend it while I am alive. Of course with death duties what they are it won't be such an awful lot when you do get it. But perhaps you could marry Lisa. She gets the other half."

"Who is Lisa?"

"My niece."

Peter, who had acquired great cynicism about nieces and nephews, said, "I'll bet."

"I really know very little more about it than you do. However, she is a delightful girl and she may be coming to stay with us for a while. It seems she's got herself involved with a bounder in Paris —*un voyou*, my brother calls him—and he wants to get her away. I don't exactly know what's wrong with the young man except that he appears to be a civilian. Of course I could make the money over to you and live another five years. That would get you out of paying death duties. But it would be just like you to get run over or something. No, on the whole I think it would be best if you married Lisa."

"You don't mind if I have a look at her first, Uncle Jean?"

"I don't know why that should be necessary. I told you she is charming."

Jenny arrived to have tea with them just then. Peter adored Jenny, despite the fact that the price of any one of her hats would have kept the Chinese quiet for months. Being, despite his world-weary air, a most naïve young man, it had taken him quite a while to realize that beautiful women like Lady Falconer and men like his Uncle Jean do not conduct platonic friendships. This, then, was romance, and Peter found it most satisfactory.

"I am going to be rich when Uncle Jean dies," he said to Jenny. "He is leaving me half his money."

"Good for you. He's simply rolling. What happens to the other half?"

"It goes to Lisa," said Riebeck.

Peter said, "He wants me to marry her sight unseen to keep it all together."

"How like him. Peter, Jonathan wants you to dine with him at his club. It's something to do with cutting up corpses and taking all their insides out at the hospital. I must say it sounds perfectly foul."

"Oh, no," said Peter, shocked. "It's fascinating."

After he had left them in a glow of pleasure at the prospect, Riebeck poured sherry for himself and Jenny and said, "How well you arrange things, my dearest."

"One has to. Three days with nothing but talking on the telephone."

"I know. Awful. Shall we sleep first or eat first?"

Unlike silly Gretel in the fairy tale, Jenny said, "Sleep first, I think."

"You do have the nicest ideas."

At dinner Riebeck said, "I must say these young Communists are very corruptible. Here I have been lectured for months about being a millionaire, but there wasn't a squeak about my leaving Peter half of it."

"He'll give it all to the starving Chinese."

"Poor Uncle Rosenstil. I was told he worked hard for it.

First it goes to a French nephew he never saw, and then it ends with the starving Chinese. That is really awful."

"Well, you needn't die at once," said Jenny comfortingly. "Perhaps we can corrupt Peter between us until he learns to enjoy being rich."

"He's very strange, Jenny. He never talks about home, or about his father. He doesn't try to meet any other Hungarians that have come over. In fact I have a feeling that he avoids them. He has settled down as if he had dropped from the sky with no past at all."

"Give him time."

Riebeck, seeing that this was all rather dull for Jenny, said, "We talk too much about Peter and not enough about interesting things, like us."

"Admit you find Peter interesting."

"Yes. But there is no need to bore you with him. One more bit of juvenile news and then I'll stop. Lisa is coming for a long visit. I fear her existence rather shocked Peter."

"Peter of all people should know blankets have two sides."

"I've been wondering, with all these young people about the house, how will we ever get time to go to bed? Shall we rent a house in St. John's Wood and live in guilty splendor?"

"St. John's Wood? I think that went out with Queen Victoria and the Crawford divorce case. I think people now keep their mistresses—if indeed they do keep them and not the other way round—in those fearfully expensive, very small apartments in Park Lane, and they get all their sense of sin and high living from the ghastly rents they pay."

"I don't think that would suit me, somehow. Dearest Jenny, in that case, shall we make hay while the sun shines?"

"Come and see my office while it is still mine," Riebeck said the next morning to Peter, "and then we will go to lunch."

Peter was surprised at the shabbiness of the place. Jeremy was there, saying good-by before leaving for Cyprus.

"Fly out to Nicosia and lunch with me one day," he said.

"With pleasure," said Riebeck, much impressing Peter, who did not yet know that his uncle could call upon jets the way other people whistle for a taxi. "Have fun."

"My devotion to duty won't let me," said Jeremy. He saluted Riebeck, smiled at Peter, and was a moment later caught by an apoplectic General Partridge in the act of sliding down the banisters.

Major Dyelik looked in, wearing a tartan shirt and gray flannels —a refugee among the neat uniforms.

"This is Peter Halyi, Dyelik. Istvan's son. Major Dyelik, Peter."

"I knew your father in Moscow," said Dyelik and shook hands. He and Riebeck discussed with the detachment of professionals Colonel Halyi's chances in a Communist prison. Peter was at first distressed by their calm, but realized quickly that the detachment was a surface one. Riebeck's face was drawn and tired, with long shadows under the cheekbones, and Dyelik, casual though he appeared to be, was not entirely at his ease.

"You're thinking too much in terms of Buchenwald," Dyelik said. "Torture of that kind is as antiquated as the Vis."

"Now that," said Peter angrily, "I know to be an out-and-out lie!"

Major Dyelik looked at him tolerantly and smiled. "I know," he said. "You are going to tell me that a friend of yours had a mother who disappeared one day and when she returned she wouldn't say anything but all her nails were gone. I don't know who started that canard, but ever since the refugees have been coming over I have heard nothing else. One might almost think the police occupied their entire time pulling the nails off people's mothers."

"You know it's not a canard," said Riebeck before Peter could burst with rage, "and that it is not nice to pull the nails off people's mothers."

"My dear fellow, you know very well what we thought of the AVO."

"I know what they thought of it in Hungary. This was the most law-abiding revolution in history; there was very little murdering outside the actual fighting, there was no looting though shop windows were smashed and people were cold and hungry. But I saw those same law-abiding people tie an AVO man upside down to a tree and light a fire under his head, and I can assure you that I was the only one who was sick."

"How did he die?" asked Dyelik, irrelevantly, Peter thought.

Riebeck smiled. "Very well indeed. I don't think I've ever seen better, considering the circumstances. He called out 'Long live the Soviet Union and Communism,' and managed the rest in silence. I didn't believe it could be done. But Dyelik, the fact that a man dies well does not prove that it was in a good cause."

"No, I know. They were a beastly lot, the AVO."

"It was never out of MVD control. If Russian opinion of it was so low, how is it you never did anything about it?"

Dyelik raised helpless hands to heaven. "How could we interfere in a country's internal affairs?"

Riebeck burst out laughing.

Dyelik turned to Peter. "Those unfortunate mothers and anyone else who suffered physical violence were not in the same category as your father. They were people whom we wished to frighten into obedience or from whom we needed information."

"And what do you want from my father?"

"A changed point of view."

"A polite way of saying treason," said General Riebeck.

Dyelik laughed. "Treason? My dear Riebeck, one man's treason is another's faithful allegiance. All moral concepts are relative."

"No. Moral concepts are absolute. They vary according to the person but never in themselves. Treason is the act of turning against the allegiance of one's mind."

"In that case Colonel Halyi should not have any difficulty. He twice lent his name, his person, and his skill to a system against which he later turned. You cannot hang your coat into four winds without arousing the suspicion that the allegiance of your mind is a weather vane."

"A turncoat never hangs his coat against the wind," said Riebeck furiously. "When Istvan turned against Horthy and against you he did so at the risk of his life because he knew that he had made a mistake and was too honest to continue in it."

"Oh come, you're not writing his obituary, you know."

"Speaking of turncoats, Dyelik—"

Major Dyelik breathed deeply, counted to ten and said, "Sorry. I forgot for a moment that no one is ever allowed to say the slightest thing against Colonel Halyi in your presence. But like it or not, he has not led a blameless life."

"It depends what you mean by blameless. How successful do you think you are, Dyelik? We only see the people like poor Cardinal Mindszenty. What are your failures?"

"It's a risky business," admitted Dyelik, "when it is a matter of a public trial rather than simply getting a signed confession. Most people will sign anything including their own death warrant if you keep them awake a week or so. But once they catch up on their sleep they quite often change their minds. Then one has to start all over again. We have our failures."

"And if you fail with Istvan?"

Major Dyelik put the tips of his fingers together. "Then," he said gently, "they will have to use force."

Peter looked at his uncle, but Riebeck did nothing but mildly change the subject to the Hungarian situation in general, a situation which Dyelik was taking very calmly.

"But why, Dyelik," said Riebeck. "I don't mean the brutality, that was to be expected, but the stupidity of committing an unforgivable action."

"For the strong and successful there is no such thing as an unforgivable action."

"You don't seriously think people will forget what you did in Hungary?"

"Of course they won't forget. We don't want them to forget. What is the good of teaching a lesson if it is forgettable? I said it would be forgiven. The more outrageously the strong behave, the more the weak forgive them."

"Double talk."

"Is it? Watch your neutral UN vote."

Riebeck laughed. "I have been worsted in every argument. Time for lunch, Peter."

"Thanks, but I've lost my appetite."

"Oh, if you only eat when things haven't made you lose your appetite," said Dyelik kindly, "you will soon starve to death. Forgive me if the things I have said have hurt you. I'm not as callous as all that, but I am Riebeck's sounding board for the Russian point of view."

"Is he?" asked Peter when they had gone downstairs.

"Yes," said Riebeck. "And it gives him remarkably little trouble."

Peter went to work at the hospital, made friends, ate his food, and seemed to sleep well. He still avoided other Hungarians and never spoke of his father or the past. Then, late one night, Riebeck, who did not sleep well, heard him crying in his room. He went in and sat on the bed, his hand tightly on Peter's shoulder, not saying anything, for a long time. When Peter stopped, Riebeck gave him a cigarette and said, "What's the matter? Are you homesick?"

"It's not that. I was thinking of Istvan."

"I know. Don't do it again."

"You do. I hear you walking up and down all night in your room."

Riebeck smiled. "All right. Tell me about it, then."

"It's foolish really. You see, I was never very nice to Istvan. When he came back from Moscow and took me to live with him I only came so I could hate him at closer quarters. Does that sound silly?"

"No. Only very uncomfortable."

"It didn't last anyway. How long could you hate Istvan? I soon loved him very much. But I kept on being nasty to him, and now it's too late."

"A commonplace complaint," said Riebeck. "I expect Istvan knew. And you became good friends during the fighting."

"Yes, that's true." With a groan Peter pushed his head into the pillow. "Schani, what are they doing to him?"

"Nothing that Istvan did not know they would do," said Riebeck. "It's not much of a consolation, I know, but it is some. Remember, Istvan chose this. He could have come here with us and been safe except for a bad conscience. He knew all about the alternative. If he chose to live with himself on the hardest terms he did so because he knew they were the only possible terms."

"Are you sure? How can you know all this?"

"I am sure."

"Give me another cigarette, please. I'm sorry I made such a fool of myself."

"A fool? Because you cried? I think it's very appropriate that you should cry for your father. Can you go to sleep now?"

"Yes, thanks. Good night."

"Good night, Peter."

At the door the boy's voice stopped him. *"Bacsi?"*

"Hm?"

"I'm not making the same mistake twice. In case you drop dead tomorrow I want you to know I love you almost as much as Istvan."

Riebeck, laughing, went back to the bed and hugged the boy, who was scarlet with embarrassment. "Thank you, Peter." Istvan's smile in this younger, handsomer face wrenched at his heart. "Good night."

" 'Night, Schani."

"I don't," said Riebeck, recovering his equilibrium, "recall having given you permission to call me Schani."

"You must give Lisa a proper reception or she will be jealous of Peter," said Jenny.

"How?"

"You might take the Bentley and the chauffeur and make an Impression," said Jenny, giving it a capital letter. Both Bentley and chauffeur had been Sir Jonathan's idea of what was due a knight. Jenny had resigned herself unwillingly to this ostentation. Perhaps as a consequence she got very sick in the back seat of the big car, and whenever Sir Jonathan was not with her, put the chauffeur there and drove him.

Riebeck, who owned a noisy and energetic two-seater and was fond of it, declined the offer. He was kept late at the office the day of Lisa's arrival, and dashed off without stopping to wash his hands or change, arriving at the airport at the same time as the Paris plane, which was two hours late.

He had not seen Lisa since his visit to Fontaines, but watching the people come down the ramp knew her the moment he saw her. "Poor girl," he thought, "she looks like me."

She was tall and too thin and her face was a Riebeck face, not a Baro one. She wore a leopard coat and too much paint on her face and walked like a stork. Riebeck remembered that Elisabeth had mentioned something in her last letter about Lisa modeling for Balmain, or was it Balenciaga? Very high fashion, in any case. He lit a cigarette and prepared to be amused.

When she had finished with customs he honked his horn and she came to meet him in her stork walk, but for all her air of sophistication flung her arms around him and greeted him with fervor.

"What a blissful car, Uncle Jean. Can I drive it?"

"Certainly not. For one thing you aren't used to driving on the left and for another I don't like being driven. Get in."

Her legs, he reflected, did him credit. Elisabeth's legs had never been her strong point.

She sat so that he could not drive comfortably unless he put an arm around her shoulders. He did so, thinking how little it cost her to be affectionate, and how difficult it was for Peter. "In case you drop dead tomorrow . . ." Istvan's smile in a younger, much handsomer face, Istvan, dead or alive, being starved, tortured, kept from sleep, perhaps now, at this moment, while he sat behind the wheel of his car, enjoying the speed and the colors of the setting sun. How long since Istvan had seen the sky turn from smoky blue to green and Fragonard pink?

Lisa did not talk. After a while she lit a cigarette and put it between his lips. He thought that she must have seen this in some film, the sympathetic heroine solacing a saturnine Jean Gabin with a cigarette.

"Thank you. Next time without the lipstick, please."

"Yes, Uncle Jean. Do you think I shall like London?"

"Probably not if you were at all enamoured of Paris."

"Well," said Lisa handsomely, "I shall like living with you."

"I hope you will like Peter Halyi. I wrote you about him, didn't I?"

"Colonel Halyi's son? What's he like?"

"Very serious. He is studying medicine." Riebeck thought ruefully that any plans of keeping the Rosenstil money together by bringing about an alliance between his daughter and Istvan's son were down the drain. The girls Peter had occasionally brought home were earnest creatures with spectacles, pony tails, and black leotards.

"Are you hungry?"

"Starved."

"Good. We'll dine at the Richelieu and then we can see what we feel like doing. Didn't you get any food on the plane?"

"Oh, loads. I ate all the way from Orly to Croydon. It was delicious."

"Alphonse will love you."

At the Richelieu Lisa consumed three double vodka martinis and ate her way through the menu with method and an excellent appetite. She regaled Riebeck with all the latest Paris gossip, making it sound like *Psychopathia Sexualis* as told to Jean Paul Sartre.

When they had finished dinner, Riebeck said, "Are you tired? What would you like to do now, Lisa?"

"What I'd really like to do is go to the ballet. Could we?"

"If we can get seats, with pleasure."

In the car Lisa said, "I do believe in speaking the truth, don't you?"

"It depends," said Riebeck cautiously. "Generally I think lies make life a lot easier."

"I only mean about you being my uncle. It's too silly."

"It's also quite possible. I didn't know you had doubts on the matter."

"Maman used to hint at it sometimes."

"You surprise me."

"She's secretly very proud of it, I think. I'm what they call in Victorian novels the legacy of your love."

"Do you have to be quite so vulgar?"

"I'm really only very truthful."

"My dear Lisa, how can one be truthful about a mere possibility?"

"I don't call it so mere. Look at us."

"Lots of Riebecks look alike."

"Maman was quite sure."

"Was she? She never told me that."

"Well, she ought to know if anyone does."

"I suppose she ought."

"Do be pleased, my darling Papa."

"I am, really. Very pleased. But I must say I feel like an utter ass as well, becoming a father at my age."

After the ballet they went to a night club and drank a great deal of champagne, while Lisa told the sad story of her exile from Paris. She had fallen in love with a man who was not only a civilian but an artist. A modern artist at that, with a beard and a flat in Montparnasse. He quoted Heidegger to her while she sat for her portrait with nothing on. Elisabeth had been horrified.

"You are not only very truthful but very foolish," said Riebeck. "Surely there was no need to tell her. If he is as modern as all that you looked like a cube with one eye, a carrot sprouting from your head, and half a tram ticket for your ear."

Lisa laughed and said it was a triangle with five eyes and a mushroom cloud.

They came home at three in the morning, were met by Peter who emerged blearily from the pages of a medical tome, cast a disapproving glance at the elegant minx in the leopard coat, and went off to bed. Riebeck showed Lisa to her room, was fervently kissed good night, and went to bed himself.

His telephone rang together with his alarm clock at 6:30. Jenny, of course. "Good morning, my darling." He yawned and apologized. "I was out on the tiles till three. What energy the young have. You must be perished with curiosity to ring up so early. Oh I see, you just got home. That means it was a wild party, I suppose. Lisa is very nice and amusing. I suppose she will get over Sartre and Kierkegaard one of these days."

"Oh dear," said Jenny. "An intellectual."

"Not exactly," said Riebeck.

"How shall I meet her?"

"Would you like a real dinner party? Very formal. Sir Jonathan and Lady Falconer. Then she can draw her own conclusions. Since she is horribly sophisticated she will probably decide I am sleeping with Sir Jonathan."

"Should I be horribly sophisticated too? I have a Dior dress with practically no front."

"Lisa has practically no front either."

"They're very unfashionable just now anyway."

Peter's alarm went off in the next room and like an echo another went down the telephone line. Jenny said, "There's Jonathan getting up." Riebeck could almost feel her lazy stretch and yawn. "How I love coming home and going to sleep just as all you hard-working good people are getting up to go to work. Good night, my dear."

"Good night," said Riebeck sleepily, half hypnotized by his mistress' turn-about life into forgetting that it was indeed high time he got up and went to work.

XXV

General Riebeck's first act as chief of St 2 was to make Jeremy Tyrell a colonel. Or so it seemed to General Partridge. In fact Riebeck had merely suggested for promotion those people who had been long overdue for it. That these should be his friends was not surprising. Under General Partridge, friendship with Riebeck was death to all hopes of military advancement.

Next he moved the picture of General de Gaulle into his new office. General Partridge, who could not keep away for a day, saw it there and nearly had apoplexy. He criticized endlessly everything Riebeck did, resentful of Riebeck's patience with him, resentful of every change, and inside himself secretly wild with pleasure at seeing how justified his choice of Riebeck had been, how smoothly and impeccably his beloved organization was run.

General Riebeck ordered a thorough house-cleaning. General Partridge, being a good age himself, had allowed a great many friends to grow old along with him without noticing what deadwood they were.

"It's rather hard on these old boys," said kind General Cook. "This office is their whole life."

"I'm running an Intelligence Department, not a home for the aged. By the way, Cooky, how old are you?"

Simon laughed. He was the same age as Riebeck and they both

knew it.

"We'll be good for another ten years," said Riebeck. "After that, God knows."

The Berlin and Vienna offices, which Riebeck had run for years without portfolio, were in perfect shape and needed no overhaul. If Riebeck still continued to haunt Vienna it was for another reason.

Bantain, who headed the Vienna office, said, "I am sorry I have no news for you at all. I've tried and tried."

"Never mind. Dyelik couldn't find anything either. I'm not even sure of what I want to find out. Mostly I hope they will kill him quickly and be done. Suppose we did find him and manage to get him out somehow and he should be like so many of them, living with terror every moment for the rest of his life. It's surely better to be dead."

"I don't know. There was a girl once who went into the cellar to fetch beer and saw an axe stuck in a beam. She thought, 'Suppose I have a child and the child comes down here and the axe falls on it . . .'"

"Yes, I know, it is absurd."

"It's possible that he is in Russia, you know. But I don't think it would do you much good if you could find out. Even if you were to walk in with a signed paper saying Serov wanted him they wouldn't give him to you."

"That trick has certainly been worked to death. Some of L'Abbé's boys tried it the other day in Algeria and the prison guards simply roared with laughter. They had all they could do to throw a few grenades around and get out themselves."

"Poor old L'Abbé. And how is your niece?"

"My niece? Oh, Lisa, you mean. At the moment she is engaged to a Chinese officer. Taiwan, not Communist. But her mother tells me she becomes engaged with monotonous regularity, so I'm not paying too much attention. Last month it was an American jazz band leader. The music was terrible."

"I must try my luck. Couldn't you find me a job in London?"

"I could but I won't. You're doing the Vienna office proud, and if you knew the trouble I have finding people who can run a place like this, you'd realize what a heaven-send you are to me."

"Keep buttering me up. I love it. I think I'll visit you in London during my leave, though."

"Do. But I must warn you that I am backing the Chinaman. He is going back to Formosa soon, and of course he would take Lisa with him."

"And Peter Halyi?"

"He seems content enough. Lisa tried to be engaged to him, but he wouldn't hear of it. He works very hard and he never, never speaks of his father."

Of the ten months before Colonel Istvan Halyi was brought to trial, Riebeck could learn nothing at all. Of the trial and the few hours before the execution he knew nearly everything, for Dyelik had friends among the executioners of Andrassy Prison.

The time between arrest and trial is variable, depending on how amenable the prisoner is to persuasion, and of how much importance a public confession would be from him.

The secret police spent a full ten months on Istvan Halyi. The reason for this was his enormous popularity in Budapest. He had been the town's hero in the fighting in '44 and again in '56. It did not matter any longer that once he had fought the Germans and then the Russians. He had been one of the leaders in two battles against overwhelming odds, and twice he had won; for a few days the city had been free. Istvan was to Budapest as much a symbol of its brief victory as the toppled statue of Stalin, General Maleter's battle for Kilian barracks, the corpses of the AVO men in Republic Square, and the disemboweled flag which for five days had flown over the city.

Through years of trial and error the secret police had learned that one may kill the man but not the symbol. A symbol can only be corrupted, and that was why a confession from Istvan Halyi was imperative.

But the public trial was never held, and why they bothered with a secret one it is difficult to say. It was possibly some bureaucrat's mania for doing a thing through proper channels; a judge yawned and mumbled over an endless indictment, found the prisoners guilty, and pronounced sentence. The defendant said not one word from beginning to end except to point out that as an officer he was entitled to a court-martial, at which the judge could not but smile.

When Istvan entered the room where the trial was to be held he saw that he was not alone. At the other side stood Palko Donath. When Istvan looked at him, Palko grinned from ear to ear, though he had no teeth left. Istvan smiled back and his eyes went to the third person in the room and stopped, startled and for a moment unbelieving. The third prisoner was Captain Janos Kovacs, who had joined Istvan's battalion in '55.

Russia had adopted him as a boy, had trained and taught him, and had treated him well. He had never known another system, had never been taught a single cause for doubt or disloyalty. Yet he was here, accused like Colonel Halyi and Colonel Donath, of crimes against the People's Democracy of Hungary.

"I'll be damned," thought Istvan, and thought it almost with sympathy as he realized for the first time in his life what it must be like for the other side to live in a world where they could trust no one, ever.

The judge, having mumbled through the indictment wiped his *pince-nez*. He had a bad cold and his eyes were full of tears; it looked incongruously as if he were weeping over the sad fate of the prisoners. He said that they had been found guilty on all counts and he would now pass sentence on them.

The sentence for Colonel Istvan Halyi, Colonel Pal Donath, and Captain Janos Kovacs was death by strangulation.

They made no protest. Istvan looked at Palko but said nothing.

Death they had all expected. They had accepted it with the first bottle of nitroglycerine tossed at a Russian tank, with the first bullet that killed a Russian soldier. They had never expected the revolution to succeed, they were not given to wishful thinking, and they had been to Russia and knew; knew also what happens to those who take part in unsuccessful revolutions against the Soviets. And yet they had not accepted enough, they were too bound up in their traditions, in the regulations of the army. Now the last support was gone, the schoolboy dream of court-martial and firing squad was ended.

The judge rose and left the room, wiping his *pince-nez* again.

397

The guards took charge of their prisoners. Istvan was nearest to the door, but it was Palko who left first. He seemed to have the guard well under control; twice Palko's size and armed with an automatic rifle, he stood patiently while Palko stopped before Istvan.

"Well, Istvan."

"Hullo, Palko. I'm glad to see you. Not to see you here. Just glad, anyway."

"Glad as hell to see you too. Every day the bastards told me you'd confessed. I said to myself if Istvan—" Here the guard moved his rifle in an ominous way and said, "Come along. That's enough."

"Why don't you shoot me, oaf?" said Palko mildly. Plainly he had long made it clear who was the fork and who the potatoes. He called it establishing moral superiority and had a happy gift for it.

The guard, knowing that he could not shoot him, used his rifle butt instead. Palko winced but otherwise ignored him. "Good-by, Istvan," he said. "*Au revoir*, who the hell knows?"

"*Au revoir*, Palko." They shook hands.

"Come on, stupid, let's go," said Palko to his guard. When they had shaken hands Palko had slipped a piece of paper into Istvan's hand. It was probably a message, Istvan thought; keep your pecker up, screw the bastards, something of that nature.

Janos Kovacs left next. As he passed his colonel he drew himself to attention and saluted. He looked so young, no older than Peter, and scared. Istvan wanted terribly to tell him that he admired him and loved him for his courage, but he realized that Janos Kovacs' dignity would crack under the strain of a kindness. He returned the salute, and never in the Hungarian army had a colonel saluted a young captain with more respect.

He was taken back to his cell. It contained a cot with a filthy blanket and rats of memorable size. The cell was arranged so that it could be made completely dark or lit so brightly that closed eyes were no protection and sleep was impossible. Istvan had been in worse places. There were cells where one could neither stand nor sit nor lie down, and others, pitch dark, with water on the floor and water pouring from the walls. It was difficult in the dark, with body and mind past the limits of exhaustion, to counter panic, knowing that the water was slowly and inevitably rising.

Apparently it was bright-lights day. Istvan lay down and put his arm over his eyes. For once no guard came to tell him to keep his hands by his sides. Suddenly he remembered the piece of rolled paper in his hand. He sat up and unrolled it. It did not contain a message, it was infinitely better than that; in his hand he held a miracle, a cigarette and a match. He looked at it without quite believing it, then he burst out laughing. It was so like Palko to be able to obtain, in a place where wormy bread and filthy water were often hard to come by, a luxury.

He smiled and lay back, his arm over his eyes again and the cigarette between his fingers. He did not light it. For the moment it was pleasure enough to own it.

For a long time Istvan Halyi lay unmoving. He was weary and in pain. It was easiest to keep still.

Death by strangulation. It was one hell of an undignified way to die, he thought, bothered by it. But he had seen enough death to know that it usually was undignified. And lime would quickly burn the flesh from his bones and with it the indignity.

He turned his thoughts away only to find them in another path he had forbidden himself. He had been strict with himself on this subject, had not allowed himself hope, had argued truly and reasonably that Riebeck did not know where he was and would have no way of helping him if he did know. But the habit of being rescued would not die. Always before, when Istvan had needed him, Riebeck had been there, uncalled. He had arrived in Vienna in time to rescue the uncles and again when Istvan had finally had to face Horthy's betrayal. He had come when Eva had died and had stopped him from killing himself, so that he had been able to continue the fight that had led to Moscow and another long betrayal, and he had been there when this betrayal had ended on October 26, in Budapest. But this time he had not come.

Never while the bright lights were on had Istvan allowed himself to think of it. But when it was dark and he was too exhausted to fight the rats or his thoughts, he had imagined the door of his cell opening and Schani's voice: *"Servus, Istvan, comment ça va?"* He would say—he had it all prepared—he would answer as the Parisians do: "*Je me défends.*" It would make Schani laugh and then perhaps he would not notice other things too much.

But the lights were on and the time for help was past. Within hours he would be dead. There was never enough time between verdict and execution to permit the prisoner to gather the worn shreds of pride and courage.

Panic was an animal as rapacious and familiar as the rats. Istvan lay still, letting it fill his mind, the cell and the world. This he had learned in prison, this trick of not fighting pain and fear but going with it willingly like a swimmer letting the river carry him downstream, until the mind went into a place apart and could look with derisive incomprehension upon the anguish of the body.

The sting of sweat in his eyes brought Istvan back to the realization that the fear and death were his own. But the animal had run itself weary. Panic sulked defeated in a corner. Istvan sat up, wiping his face on his sleeve, and lit the condemned prisoner's last cigarette.

He was very conscious suddenly that he was not alone, conscious, as he had not been for ten months, wrapped in his own battle, pain and terror, of noises about him, people filling the vast prison, and outside it his beloved city in ruins. His suffering and dying had not saved a single life, not a single stone of the city he loved. It no longer mattered. He understood now, finally, what Jean Riebeck had meant when he had said, "It doesn't matter whether I win or lose. The thing that does matter is having made one's stand."

The end of the cigarette burned his fingers and he threw it on the floor. When they came for him he had succeeded in putting on a face of indifference. But the green, oblique eyes in the gaunt face had never been his to control and he could not subdue them now. They savagely mocked his captors.

Though he was in great pain he walked as he had as a boy, as if a sword were buckled to his side and a cloak streaming behind him in the wind, walked among his jailers and murderers arrogantly and swiftly to his death.

A week later Jeremy wrote Riebeck from Cyprus:

We are all death's children and no man can choose the inevitable. Soldiers boast that they go halfway to meet death, but the most suicidal are the last to succeed, for the choice is death's own. And yet, sometimes for the bravest he cannot but return a lifelong courtesy.

Death allowed Istvan Halyi to choose him, in a dreadful guise, it is true, but for a purpose and at Istvan's whim.

There is nothing that can be said for those who must live on. There is no help for it, and the worst of it is, in the end one forgets.

I don't know why the breaking of a safe-conduct is so much harder to bear than other forms of betrayal. Is it because a trust was violated or because we resent the offer accepted from those who cannot but break it? I don't know.

A whole type is becoming extinct; the romantic hero. From Leonidas and that German bore Arminius through Bragadino and Marshal Ney they were men who fought with passion for an idea. Their hopes of winning were usually poor and that is why they caught at the imagination in victory as well as in defeat. World War I killed them by the thousands and the second World War nearly finished them off. The circumstances for creating more of them no longer exist. I think that for future historians the battle of Budapest will mark the end of the individual hero as clearly as Crecy marked the end of the knight in armor.

Who do you suppose the hero of the next generation will be? An encapsulated spaceman? A push-button ideal?

Thank God I am old enough to have known the other kind!

Next to this there was a blot of ink and Jeremy's explanation:

Sorry. Somebody just threw a stick of dynamite into the hall and it rather made me jump. It occurs to me that under the circumstances you may not see me again on this earth. In that case, over the Richelieu's Chambertin, will you remember your old friends now sadly reduced to drinking nectar and ambrosia. T.

XXVI

Istvan Halyi was dead and Riebeck could neither regret nor resent this, but his unconscious mind still had to learn it. He continued to wake with the same apprehensions and every morning he had to repeat like a lesson: "It's over, there is nothing they can do to him now," and feel grateful for the final act of grace, the gallantry with which Istvan had cheated his brutal death of its horror and had made it tolerable for his friend also.

And then one morning he awoke happy without a single thought or reminder. Outside the window the sky stretched plum-blue. It was late October, but the day belonged to September, the first nip and tuck of frosty nights and still warm days, summer ending. A day that was an unexpected gift so late in the year, a day to confer once more the illusion of happiness.

We are all death's children, Jeremy had written, and Riebeck, his face turned to the Messina portrait, smiled. Occasionally Tyrell had a felicitous way of stating the obvious.

Istvan was dead and this day could not reach him any more than days of agony and terror. But though Riebeck waited, this day no pain followed the thought and he accepted at last that Istvan was dead, was dying in his mind too as surely as he had died in the cellar of Andrassy Prison.

Istvan had been the anchor in the very heart of love for him. To pull up anchor leaves a wound. An important part of his life was over, and this was the first day when he knew surely that he could manage with what was left. He could even, finally, assess Istvan's last act for what it was; silly, handsome, futile, incredibly brave and generous, and inevitable.

This was final. Riebeck had no wish for a future reunion in a land of milk and honey, or even Tyrell's nectar and ambrosia. Thoughts of immortality and eternity appalled him. The boredom of forever and a day!

What gave life its point was the fact that it had an end. Even then it was difficult enough to keep boredom at bay. How to find enough laughter, peril, and love to fill eternity?

Eternity made a surfeit of the things he wanted most. One more day with Jenny or fifty years; he would accept either with gratitude. But an eternity of love would be a prison too awful to contemplate. Love without end was elephantiasis of the imagination. No wonder Adam and Eve had to achieve mortality and get out of paradise. That was the tree of knowledge.

He thought he would like to be in Paris this day, to savor its perfection against the filigree of the city he loved most. Or to lie on some level of sand, smooth as cream, to feel the heat of the sun and the cut of the late October wind. And he did not want to go to the office.

Tyrell was in London, and this evening there was a meeting he, Riebeck, had called, so that he could not very well get out of it. But until then the day was his to do with as he pleased.

He reached for the telephone. "My darling, good morning."

"It's too early," said Jenny grumpily.

"I am always up early. You ought to be used to that by now. Have you looked out the window?"

"I can't get my eyes open. Oh darling, what a perfect, perfect day. And you sound so happy."

"*Je suis en fête*. Put on something warm and shoes without heels. We're going to the beach."

"What a lovely idea. Shall I bring lunch?"

"All right. But not sandwiches. I still have a bottle of that very good '52 Chablis. I'll bring that. Can you be ready in an hour?"

"Of course," said Jenny. "I can dress as fast as a midwife in an air raid when necessary," leaving Riebeck yelping with laughter at the dead end of the telephone.

It was too cold to drive with the top down, but they did it nevertheless, their faces numb with the wind and touched unexpectedly with warmth when they slowed down. Jenny was quiet, a little uncertain of this new happy lover, after the months of discipline and courtesy that hid an unrelieved misery. She said, "I am so glad, darling," and he understood that she was happy for him and put his arm round her shoulders for a quick hug before he grasped the steering wheel with both hands and tore around a narrow corner on two wheels. Riebeck driving badly was a good sign. When he was unhappy he was careful and law-abiding.

They stopped not on a creamy beach but high on a cliff over the steel-blue Channel—"white horses," Jenny said happily—exposed to the sun and a tearing, inconsistent wind. Grey funnels of gulls turned silver as they circled into the sunlight.

They lunched out of jars with Fortnum and Mason labels, drank the chilly Chablis, and laughed at nothing at all.

"I don't think I've ever eaten so much caviar at one meal," said Riebeck, lighting cigarettes for them both.

"Do you know, even when I was a little girl and didn't think men were much use, I used to be impressed by the fact that men can light cigarettes in a high wind and women can't."

"An obvious sign of our superior intelligence."

Jenny had wound a raspberry-colored silk scarf around her hair. The ends of it touched his face softly as she leaned back against his shoulder.

"Jenny," he said, vaguely and dreamily, "I think we might get married after all." He had not planned this proposal, it was as much a surprise to him as it was to her, and he was delighted with himself. "Things have turned out differently than I thought. I shall always be very busy, I suppose, but I don't have to travel nearly as much as I used to, and we could be together much of the time. That is, if you still want to marry me."

Jenny did not turn to look at him. "Ask when you've decided," she said lightly. "I couldn't bear to be jilted a second time."

For the first time Riebeck asked himself how much *she* had minded. He put his arms around her tightly. "I'm sorry, Jenny. I don't know much about you, really. You're not given to sharing your feelings much and I'm not either. But I should have known more than I did. Unhappiness is terrible, it's like illness, it locks one into oneself until one can't see anything or anyone. Not even the people one loves. I'm sorry, Jenny. Truly sorry."

Jenny moved away to look up at him and to smile. She touched his mouth. "It doesn't matter."

He shook his head in protest.

"No, really it doesn't. I'm not saying it to make you feel better. In love one doesn't really mind pain that comes from the lover any more than one minds the bite in a kiss. I think there is nothing you could do to me that would not be so tied up with my loving you that I would not welcome it."

"Oh, my Jenny." He could only hold her for a long time, in silence, until he heard her sharply caught breath and felt her shoulders shake under his hands. He knew she was laughing, because he felt the silent explosion of laughter in his own blood. They laughed, clinging together, as they had laughed so many times after making love and for the same reason.

She sat up, pushing back her hair, and Riebeck, exhausted, stretched out on the rock, his head in her lap.

"My dearest, how soon can you get rid of Sir Jonathan?"

"I don't know. I'll ask him tonight. What will Peter say, and Lisa?"

"Lisa will be shocked. Getting married is a very bourgeois idea, you know. But she may not be with us much longer. She's been engaged to Bantain for three months, which is two months longer than ever before, and I rather think he's going to put his foot down. Little did I dream that I would end as Pierre Bantain's father-in-law. Do you know she calls him Bunny?"

Jenny, who had called him Bunny since their first meeting, said, "Dreadful girl."

"What would you think of my giving her Alphonse for a wedding present?"

"Very, very little. Besides, he isn't a slave you can give away for a present."

"It wouldn't work anyway. There's a great chill between Lisa and Alphonse since she asked him how much baking powder one uses in souffles."

The enormity of this was lost on Jenny. "And Peter?"

"Peter, I imagine, will be pleased at my finally doing the right thing by you. He needn't live with us unless you like the idea."

"I do like it. Very much."

"You're too good to be true. You must have some dreadful vice I haven't discovered yet."

"I don't think so," said Jenny complacently. "I think I shall find it very entertaining, being a mother to Lisa and Peter."

Riebeck took her hand and held it against his face. "I love them, you know. It's strange, all my life I never really loved anyone except Istvan. And now I have Lisa and Peter and you. I remember when I was a boy Aunt Albertine was always after me to make friends. I used to tell her, what for, I've already got a friend. I said it to annoy her, but it was the truth all the same. I really felt like that."

"Which of us—" said Jenny and stopped. She had been about to say, "Which of us would you rather have, Istvan or Lisa and Peter and me?" The tightening at the corners of his mouth, which she knew for an effort not to laugh, warned her not to go on. He would without a moment's hesitation or regret push her, Lisa, and Peter over this cliff if by so doing he could have Istvan Halyi alive and happy once more.

"But Istvan Halyi is dead," she thought and closed her eyes so that he should not read the exultation in them and know the reason.

"Look," he said when they were ready to leave, and pointed to a sickle moon poised in the perishable edge of the sunset. "A good omen, surely."

They drove home, their hands clasped tightly in the pocket of his burberry. When he pulled up before Sir Jonathan's house in Wimpole Street, he said, "Dine with me tonight, fairly late. No, dine with the poor husband and tell him the news. But afterwards, will you come to me and stay? I want so very much to sleep with you tonight."

"Yes," said Jenny. "I will do that."

"I love you." He kissed her in full view of Wimpole Street and she did not protest.

"I wonder," she said with the pensive, faraway look he had continued to love even after he learned that it usually meant thoughts of dinner.

"What?"

"What sort of hat, do you think, to get divorced in?"

Simon Cook, Jeremy Tyrell, and Lionel Jennings were waiting in Simon's office when Riebeck arrived.

"Punctuality," said Jeremy, "is the quality that distinguishes a brilliant Intelligence officer from a pedestrian one."

Riebeck smiled at him and said, "Drink, anyone?" which was St 2's time-honored way of starting a conference.

They disposed of some routine business. Then Simon Cook pushed a fat file across the desk to Riebeck and said, "I think Dyelik has been given quite enough rope."

"Yes, quite," agreed Riebeck, not touching the file which he knew almost by heart.

"You might have told me Lionel was tailing Dyelik," General Cook said. He had taken Riebeck's elevation rather hard.

"It wasn't important."

"Not important. A Russian traitor in the Department!"

"Wait," implored Jeremy. "I've been off in Cyprus doing the white man's burden bit. What's going on? I thought Dyelik was so true blue."

"True blue red," said Lionel Jennings.

"I will tell you what has been going on, with pleasure," said Simon Cook with dignity. "When Dyelik came here five years ago, having decided to change sides mostly, as far as one can see, because he liked to get drunk with Riebeck, we put him to work decoding things. He was very good at it. My confidence in Russians isn't very highly developed and I was all for sending him back home to his MVD or whatever it was, but Riebeck said not to muzzle the ox that does something or other, I forget what, to the corn."

"Treadeth out," supplied Jeremy.

"Thank you."

"You can't deny that he did," said Riebeck.

"Did what, tread corn?"

"Far be it from me to describe our coded messages as corn," said Riebeck virtuously.

Simon, using his quelling schoolmaster look on this schoolboy wit, said, "May I go on, Riebeck?"

"Pray do."

"As far as I could see," said Simon huffily, "the idea was that our splendid influence as well as living in a country where people are allowed to vote for more than one party and heckle politicians in public and write to the *Times* about things would, by a process of osmosis, make a Tory of Major Dyelik."

"Why Tory?" Jeremy asked indignantly. "I'm surprised you didn't try to make an absolute monarchist of him, Riebeck. And as for Cooky's so-called Liberalism, which is as reactionary and antiquated as Lady Bountiful visiting the poor with baskets—words fail me. Where was I?"

"I believe it was the word Tory that set you off," said Riebeck. "And I must protest once and for all. I am not a monarchist. I believe in licensed anarchy under absolute military rule."

"You would. Tory! A perfectly good Commie like Dyelik. I'm surprised you didn't try to baptise him and turn him into the Archbishop of Canterbury."

Lionel said languidly, "You're talking the most fearful tripe, Jeremy."

Riebeck agreed.

"I assure you, Jeremy," Simon Cook said earnestly, "that none of us tried to influence Dyelik in favor of one political party or another. And in any case it didn't work. So Riebeck put Jennings on Dyelik's tail. What gave him the idea I don't know, but it turned out to be entirely justified."

Riebeck, who had not suspected Dyelik and had told Jennings to keep an eye on him merely to get Lionel out from underfoot, said that it was that sixth sense which distinguished a brilliant Intelligence officer from a pedestrian one.

"It must have been sixth sense," said Lionel, "because for ages after that Dyelik was perfectly well behaved and the whole thing was the most fearful bore. The Embassy tried to get in touch with him a few times, but he was very huffy, though what story he gave them I don't know. I expect he told them not to stick their silly thumbs into the delicate plans of their superiors. It would work, you know. And then, very suddenly, he gave in. I don't know why."

"I expect he was homesick," said Riebeck. "Russians seem to have a tendency that way."

"We do too," said Lionel broadmindedly, "though anything more dreary than dear old England it would be hard to imagine. Now if I were French I should weep for home every day."

"In France," Riebeck said, "only ladies weep."

"I always thought you turned their lives into a bower of bliss."

"They weep with joy. At any rate, Dyelik suddenly started leaving copies of decoded messages lying about in various places for his Russian friends to pick up," Riebeck said. "Jennings discreetly removed them and whenever possible substituted things we hoped they would believe. It was very useful to us while it lasted. That's why we let him go on so long."

"He was an awfully long time catching on," said Jeremy. "He can't be terribly bright in the upper story."

"He's bright enough. Jennings did his work well, and then, Dyelik has been drinking a lot."

"A bad thing to do in this kind of work," Jeremy said solemnly. "What next?"

"Next we drop on him. It's a pity we can't let him go home to Russia and rest on his laurels, but he knows too much. And now I must go to my office and attend to seven hundred pages of single-spaced bumf before dinner. Dine with me at the Richelieu, Tyrell. I have something delightful to tell you. Delightful for me, that is."

"With pleasure. I thought you were looking chirpy."

It revolted Simon Cook's deepest sense of propriety that he, a brigadier for almost a year longer than Riebeck, now had to stand up because Riebeck stood. He bitterly envied Jeremy, who remained in his chair, his feet on the desk, and who by way of farewell waved his hand and said, "Well, ta-ta." But of course Simon had not the nerve to imitate him.

When Riebeck opened the door to his office he was met by Dyelik, a file in one hand and a gun in the other.

"Come in, Riebeck. And please shut the door."

He thought, My poor Jenny, I am going to jilt you again. But the regret was a formality.

"You won't get very far, you know."

"As far as the Russian embassy, I hope. This gun has a silencer, you see."

Lisa was taken care of. Bantain would look after her. Peter? Peter was the one who worried him. A young man in a strange society coming suddenly into a great deal of money and no idea what to do with it.

"Yes, I noticed. I have had occasion to use them, though I don't like them. They spoil one's aim."

But of course Jenny would look after Peter. And Peter would accept the lesson of how to be a happy, rich young man with no particular purpose in life much more willingly from her than he had from his father or from Riebeck.

"Oh well," said Dyelik, "it's a small office, fortunately, and I shan't have to aim very carefully. As for getting away, I'll take my chances. I don't have much to lose, do I?"

Tyrell and Jennings could finish up all the work he would be forced to leave undone. Seven hundred pages of single-spaced bumf for one. His life bundled neatly, with no loose ends, he smiled and said—*noblesse oblige*—"Your chances would be a lot better if I simply let you walk out of here."

"But you won't. I eavesdropped on your conference."

"I would, to keep from getting shot."

"Would you? I wonder." Dyelik grew businesslike. "What guarantee could you give me?"

"None," said Riebeck, "save my word of honor."

Major Dyelik laughed out loud. "How often, I wonder, have you pulled that one and got away with it? In your study of Russian, did you ever come across a little story about a mouse who was drowning in a barrel of vodka?"

"No," said Riebeck. "I would like to hear it."

"So often, in my dealings with you, or watching you make an ass of some trusting soul, have I been reminded of that story."

"It's a pleasant way to go," said Riebeck, "drowning in a barrel of vodka."

"Probably. But the point of the story is that the mouse did not drown."

"Don't shoot, Dyelik. I'm going to sit down. My leg hurts."

In the drawer of his desk was his old German Luger. He never used it, but he kept it cleaned and loaded, as he did all his guns. He did not know whether Dyelik had already been through the desk, or whether he had started on the files and had been interrupted. It was a chance.

"Of course, do sit down. It was thoughtless of me not to think of it. I suppose I had an idea that you preferred to die on your feet."

Riebeck, amused, said, "Aren't you going to tell me a story first? About the mouse and the vodka. You can tell me when you are going to shoot and to satisfy your sense of the ceremonial I shall then stand up. Would you mind if I opened the desk drawer and took out my cigarettes? Condemned men are always allowed a last cigarette, aren't they?"

"By all means. But I must warn you that I took the precaution of unloading the Luger."

Riebeck laughed. "In that case I shall smoke one of the cigarettes in my pocket. Go on about the mouse."

"If you are really interested I will, with pleasure. Are you hoping to gain something by stalling for time?"

He was, of course. He was not expecting anyone in particular, but this was a busy place, with people walking constantly in and out. Almost anyone might come into the office and distract Dyelik's attention long enough to give Riebeck a chance to crack him over the head with a chair. Possibly even Jeremy might come, though he was probably already at the nearest pub and would remain there for an hour or two.

"It's late," he said. "Everyone's gone home, I expect. Still, while there is life there is hope."

Dyelik considered this idiocy gravely. It was obvious that he had not heard it before and was storing it away for future use.

"The mouse," Riebeck reminded him.

"Oh yes, the mouse. Well, there he was, thrashing about in his vodka barrel and just going under for the last time when he saw, perched on the rim of the barrel, a large cat. He cried out: 'Oh please, kind cat, save me!' This was after all no time to be particular. The cat stretched down a large paw and pulled the mouse out. The mouse confounded himself in gratitude. The cat, still holding on to him, said, 'Not at all. And now, mouse, I am going to eat you up.' At this point one could easily see how the poor mouse might despair. But he was like you, Riebeck, he did not give up easily. He said, 'I think that is entirely reasonable. Only please, dear cat, could I go home and make my farewells to the family. I give you my word of honor that I will come back in the morning and you can have me for breakfast.' The cat agreed to this and the mouse went home. The next morning the cat was waiting at the mousehole, his teeth clicking with hunger. No mouse appeared. Finally the cat called down the mousehole: 'Come out, mouse, so I can eat you for breakfast.'

"The mouse, keeping well in the hole said, 'Who, me? Why?' 'Don't you remember? I saved you from drowning in the barrel of vodka and you promised to let me eat you this morning. You gave me your word of honor.'

" 'I gave you my word of honor?'

" 'You gave me your word of honor.'

" 'The mouse thought this over for a moment, and then, retreating rapidly down the hole, explained, 'I must have been drunk.' "

"An amusing story," said Riebeck, who had not listened, but had spent the time trying to think of a way of getting rid of Dyelik. Being unarmed he could think of nothing better than to try to distract his attention and hit him over the head with his chair, a manoeuvre that he did not believe would be successful. How stupid, he thought, after a life as adventurous as mine, to be killed in my own office by a man who is here only by my whim.

"Yes, it is an amusing and appropriate story," said Dyelik, "And now, have you finished your cigarette? I don't like to hurry you, but I am pressed for time."

It was late and Jeremy was thirsty. He proposed to put away a few drinks with Lionel and discuss a new poetry quarterly for which he and some equally impecunious poet friends were trying to find a backer. Then he would come back and get Riebeck. He locked up his papers, put on his coat and gloves, and went out into the hall. And suddenly he stopped. It was all very well for Partridge to tell him every day that Intelligence is run on brains and not on hunches, and for Riebeck to burst into derisive laughter every time he said, "I've a hunch," and laugh even more loudly when that hunch proved true. Jeremy knew his hunches were reliable. He was Irish and had a grandmother who was a witch, after all. And just now, the hair lifting on his head, he knew that Riebeck was in mortal danger.

"It's damnably inconvenient right now," said Riebeck. "I'd just decided to get married." He walked around his chair so that he could get ready to throw it at Dyelik in the hope of deflecting his aim. Considering the size of the office it was a very small hope indeed. For a moment he was tempted overwhelmingly to let it go, to give in to death, to cast off responsibility, knowledge, and memory. To go to earth on that great cliff in Père Lachaise, among the honor roll of Napoleon's marshals. But it is an officer's duty to fight as long as he can, without hope of victory.

His hand tightened on the back of the chair.

"My dear Riebeck," said Dyelik, honestly distressed, "I had no idea. I am dreadfully sorry. Believe me that ever since our first meeting I have felt nothing but admiration and friendship for you. Having to shoot you gives me no pleasure at all."

"That's all right," said Riebeck tolerantly. "Only don't say it's going to hurt you more than it does me."

"But that," cried Dyelik, delighted to have found the *mot juste*, "is exactly what I mean. It does hurt me more than it does you."

At the absurdity of this dentist's phrase, with a revolver pointed at him at a distance of less than two yards and his inability to think of anything intelligent or memorable for his last words—Crito, we owe a cock to Asclepius—General Riebeck laughed out loud.

Jeremy, his hand stretched toward the door, paused a moment and then walked away. Men in peril of their lives, he thought, do not laugh with such wholehearted delight.